SPIRITS UNITED

ALSO BY ALICE DUNCAN

The Mercy Allcutt Mystery Series

SPIRITS UNITED

A DAISY GUMM MAJESTY MYSTERY
BOOK 12

ALICE DUNCAN

April 2019
Paperback ISBN: 978-1-64457-069-2
Hardcover ISBN: 978-1-64457-070-8

ePublishing Works!
644 Shrewsbury Commons Ave
Ste 249
Shrewsbury PA 17361
United States of America

www.epublishingworks.com
Phone: 866-846-5123

For Lynne Welch and Sue Krekeler, my fabulous beta readers. Mega-thanks to my niece, Sara Krafft, who found pictures of the "old" Pasadena Public Library for me. Many thanks, too, to Sten Voght Cantwell, who gave me the idea for this book. Thank you buckets and buckets. I need all the help I can get! Oh, and before I forget to mention it and somebody screams, I know perfectly well that Caltech's Athenaeum didn't open until 1930, but it's such a lovely, charming place, I decided to give Daisy an interesting location to conduct some of her sleuthing.

ONE

In case you haven't been following my adventures, such as they are, let me fill you in a bit. In late May of 1924 my fiancé, Sam Rotondo, detective with the Pasadena Police Department and my late husband Billy's best friend, was shot in the thigh by an evil woman named Eloise Frances Petrie Gaulding. By the time this story starts, spring had bled into summer, and summer into autumn. Sam had darned near bled to death, thanks to that dreadful Petrie person.

Therefore, it was a crisp Wednesday in mid-October of 1924 when I aimed to make a trip to the Pasadena Public Library. Sam, who had only recently been allowed to return to work but was required to remain at his desk, a circumstance he hated, had just driven to our house. My family and I lived in a tidy bungalow on South Marengo Avenue in the lovely city of Pasadena, California. Sam still had to use a cane because his leg, while mostly healed, still hurt. He also hated having to use his cane. He refused to take any pain medication other than aspirin tablets, too. My Billy had died of an overdose of morphine syrup, and Sam wouldn't take the stuff. I was sorry he hurt but extremely glad of his decision regarding morphine.

By the way, Billy had been a casualty of the Great War. It didn't kill him instantly, but the Germans' poisoned gas ruined his lungs, and his legs were full of shrapnel. He probably could have lived with the shrapnel, but the lungs made him unfit for work. That's why he eventually decided to do himself in. I didn't blame him, although his death precipitated a truly awful time in my life. Thank God for our family physician, Dr. Benjamin, who reported his death as "accidental" on the death certificate. I still missed Billy. A whole lot.

Anyway, it was about one in the afternoon when Sam's knock came at the door. Spike, my late husband's brilliant dachshund, and I greeted Sam at the door. I told Spike to sit and stay. Because he'd achieved first-place in his obedience training class at Brookside Park two years earlier, Spike sat and stayed, although he didn't want to. He wanted to jump all over Sam. Therefore, I wasn't being mean to Spike, but only thoughtful to Sam. Spike didn't understand, but he obeyed. Would that human beings would go and do likewise.

"Hey, Sam!" I said, getting up on my tiptoes to kiss him on the cheek. "I didn't know you were coming over this afternoon."

"I didn't either. But I had to go to the doctor, and my boss told me to take the rest of the day off." Leaning heavily on his cane, he limped into the living room, sat on the sofa, and patted it as an invitation for Spike to jump on it and greet Sam properly.

Spike, good dog that he was, waited until I'd released him from durance vile before he allowed himself to leap on the sofa and welcome Sam. His tail wagged deliriously as he licked Sam on the chin. I gazed with fondness at two of the most important men in my life.

"What did the doctor say?" I asked.

Sam shrugged. "Same as ever. It'll take time, but it will stop hurting eventually. Probably."

"I'm glad of that, even if it is taking a long time."

Sam said, "Huh."

"Good afternoon, Sam," said my father, who used to work as a chauffeur for rich folks in Pasadena but couldn't any longer because he had a bad heart. Pa is the third most important man in my life. Maybe along with my best friend, Harold Kincaid.

"Afternoon, Joe," said Sam to my father as he petted Spike for all he was worth. Sam might be an old grump sometimes—often, even—but he knew how to treat man's best friend.

"I was just going to go to the library, Sam," I said. "We need more books."

He eyed the table upon which my family deposited the books they'd already read. When I wasn't working as a spiritualist-medium for wealthy ladies in Pasadena, I was the official family book-gatherer. I relied a good deal on my favorite librarian, Miss Petrie, to select books for all of us. Miss Petrie and I were approximately the same age and shared similar tastes.

Oh, and if you're interested, I don't really believe one can communicate with people who have died, but pretending to do so made for a much better income than if, say, I'd worked as an elevator operator at Nash's Dry Goods and Department Store or stood for hours beside one of the conveyer belts at the Underhill Chemical Company, where items like fertilizer and cosmetics were packaged. Not that fertilizer and cosmetics have much to do with each other, but the company produced and packaged both.

Sam said, "Huh," again. He said that a lot.

"Would you like to come with me?"

He looked at me as if I'd invited him to join me in jumping off the Colorado Street Bridge. "The library?"

"Yes. We're out of books."

Sam, who had been a *horrible* patient, growled, "I just got here, and you want to leave me and go to the library? Anyway, what are those?" He pointed at the book-laden table.

"Those are the books we've already read. I'll just return those and check out more."

"Detective stories, I'll bet," he grumbled.

"Yes," I said firmly. While he was recovering from his injury, I'd read to him. One of the books I'd read—he said I inflicted it on him—was *The Window at the White Cat*, by Mrs. Mary Roberts Rinehart. I'd wanted to show him that I wasn't out of line when I'd suggested he look for a suspect in a dumbwaiter. I got the feeling he wasn't convinced when I finished the book. On the other hand, he was probably being difficult on purpose. As I said, he was a *terrible* patient.

"Well..."

"Come on, Sam. I heard Dr. Benjamin tell you your leg will get better and stop hurting so much if you walk a lot. I know it hurts, but walking is good for you. We can walk around the library, and I'll introduce you to Miss Petrie."

"Good Lord, you mean there's another Petrie in the woodwork?"

There were two branches of the Petrie clan living in Pasadena at that time. Both branches had originated in Tulsa, Oklahoma, but Miss Petrie's side of family was good. The other side was about as rotten as a family of people could get. Poor Miss Petrie had often suffered for her evil cousins' sins, although I doubt many people connected her with the Petries who were always getting into trouble. And I mean bad trouble. Like murder and child-slavery and stuff like that.

"You know very well Miss Petrie is from the good side of her family's tree. She's even helped you a couple of times through me, don't forget."

"Yeah, yeah."

My father chuckled. "Go ahead, Sam. She might get into trouble without an escort."

"Pa!"

"That's true," said Sam, adopting a judicial mien.

"Nerts."

Both my father and Sam had more than once accused me of poking into other people's business, thereby getting myself into pickles of various types. It wasn't true, but neither one of them would admit as much.

"I'll drive us," I said to my cranky beloved.

"I can drive," Sam said, surly to the Nth degree.

"I know you can, but I'm going to drive us. If you don't like it, you can stay here and play gin rummy with Pa."

"Oh, no you don't," said Sam. "I'm going with you. I don't trust you not to stumble over a crime or a body or something if I'm not with you."

Pa laughed.

I didn't.

Nevertheless, I scooped up the books from the already-read table and headed out the side entrance of our house. Sam, limping behind me and grumbling something about his damned cane and how he should be carrying the books for me, followed. I didn't bother answering the old grouch.

The library wasn't far away from our house, sitting as it did on the corner of Raymond Avenue and Walnut Street. I parked in front of the building so Sam wouldn't have far to walk.

"Would you like me to take your arm?" I asked politely.

With a glare that might have annihilated a lesser person, Sam growled, "No! I don't want you take my arm, dammit. I'm not a total cripple."

"Oh, stop being so miserable, Sam Rotondo. If I didn't love my engagement ring so much, I'd be tempted to take it off and throw it in your face."

I didn't mean it. True, the ring Sam had given me was gorgeous, featuring a beautiful emerald set among some golden leaves, but I'd never take it off. It wasn't huge and flashy, but I loved it. What's more, Sam's father had created the design and made it. For months I'd carried it on a gold chain around my neck, next to another, braided, chain that held a Voodoo juju given to me by a lady named Mrs. Jackson, who was an honest-to-goodness Voodoo mambo from New Orleans, Louisiana. When Sam got shot, she gave one to Sam, too.

Sam said, "Huh." Told you he said that a lot.

"Are you wearing your juju?"

"Yes, I'm wearing the stupid juju."

"It's not stupid. Mrs. Jackson said it would bring you luck and healing."

"Yeah. I believe that about as much as I believe you can communicate with dead people."

"Sam Rotondo, you're impossible!"

"I know it." He sounded a little sulky when he added, "Sorry I'm such lousy company. I'm sick of this cane, I'm sick of hurting, and I want to get better now. I don't want to wait for more months to pass."

"Did Doc Benjamin give you any idea how long you'll have to use the cane?"

"No, but the wound got infected a couple of times, and that's slowed down the process. Maybe another month or two."

I knew all about those infections. I'd worried and prayed and worried and prayed, and was nearly overwhelmed when the good doctor finally released Sam from our house, where he'd been recuperating since his discharge from the hospital, and allowed him to go home to his darling little bungalow on South Los Robles Avenue. I missed him when he left, even if he was crotchety most of the time. I guess that means it was true love. Or something.

We climbed the steps to the library, Sam cursing under his breath as he maneuvered his cane on the concrete stairs. Even though I still carried a big pile of books, I opened the door for him. He eyed me evilly and said, "Thanks."

"You're ever so welcome."

As soon as we got inside the library, I breathed in a deep lungful of library-scented air. I loved the library. It was my second-favorite place in the whole wide world, next to our bungalow on Marengo.

"I'll take these to the returns table, and then I'll introduce you to Miss Petrie."

I didn't wait for Sam to grumble anything, but hurried to the returns table and quietly set down my armload of books. Then I rushed back to Sam, who didn't look any the worse for having been left alone for five or six seconds. I grabbed his arm. "All right, you big galoot. You're going to meet Miss Petrie."

"Goody gumdrops."

"Stop it!" I gave his arm a good shake.

He grinned down at me, and I knew he'd been grumpy on purpose. He did that sometimes just to rile me. Terrible man, Sam Rotondo. I have no idea why I loved him so much. I guess because, beneath his tough exterior, he was an old softie. Not very many people knew that, and I think Sam wanted them kept in the dark.

Miss Petrie watched us walk up to her little desk in the reference section and smiled broadly. We were good friends, Miss Petrie and me. I don't know why we weren't on a first-name basis by that point, but I always called her Miss Petrie and she almost always called me Mrs. Majesty. She'd slipped and called me Daisy a time or two, but she always looked embarrassed afterwards.

For the record, I had once thought Miss Petrie to be a lot older than I, but had recently learned she was only twenty-five to my twenty-four. The way she dressed and wore her hair made her look older and more librarianish, I guess. She always wore boring clothes, and always pinned her hair in a knot on the top of her head. It had long been my opinion that she could be a pretty woman if she took a little more care with her appearance. Maybe she thought librarians were supposed to look stuffy. I don't know, but I sometimes itched to get my hands on her.

Another friend of mine, Flossie Buckingham, had asked me to help her re-create herself, only her reincarnation had been directly opposed to the one I wanted to perform on Miss Petrie. Flossie had been a gangster's moll and needed toning down. Miss Petrie, in my opinion, needed toning up.

"Miss Petrie!" whispered I upon arriving at her desk. "Please let me introduce you to my fiancé, Detective Sam Rotondo. He's with the Pasadena Police Department. Oh, I guess you already knew that."

"How wonderful to meet you at last, Detective Rotondo," said Miss Petrie in a thrilled whisper. She held out her hand, and Sam shook it.

"Pleased to meet you," said he, not snarling for once. He actually behaved properly and smiled as he shook her hand. Sort of like a tranquilized rhinoceros, if you know what I mean.

"Oh, Daisy," said Miss Petrie after Sam had let her hand go. "I have so many books for you!"

"Thank you!"

"Hmm," said Sam. "You're the one who feeds her detective-novel reading habit, I've heard."

"You betcha," I said.

"Yes indeed," said Miss Petrie, her smile faltering slightly.

"Don't mind him," I told her. "He acts grouchy on purpose."

"Do not," said Sam grouchily.

"He's a man, Daisy. I know what men are like."

She did? Her words surprised me since, as far as I knew, Miss Petrie was an unmarried young lady and, also as far as I knew, she'd never been engaged or anything. Maybe she grew up with brothers. I did know that she had more than a handful of ghastly male cousins. Maybe they'd colored her opinions.

Naturally, Sam said, "Huh."

7

"So what do you have for us today, Miss Petrie?" I nearly rubbed my hands with glee.

"Two new arrivals from Mrs. Agatha Christie!" she exclaimed. Naturally, she whispered her exclamation. It can be done; believe me. "*Poirot Investigates*, which is a collection of short stories, and *The Secret Adversary*. The last isn't about Hercule Poirot, but introduces two young people at loose ends after the war. They get together in this book. I loved it. It's ever so much better than *Murder on the Links*. The two young people are Mr. Tommy Beresford and Miss Tuppence Cowley. They aren't married in the book, but I expect they will be soon. Rather like you and the detective." Miss Petrie giggled.

"Oooh, thank you!" I hugged the two volumes to my bosom. Not that women were supposed to have bosoms in those days. But I wore my bust-flattener and did my best. Because of my profession as a spiritualist-medium, I always attempted to look fashionable when I went out in public. Nobody wants to hire a sloppy spiritualist.

"And we just got a couple of books by Mr. E. Phillips Oppenheim, too. I think I've told you that it sometimes takes a while for books to get here from England."

"I love his books!"

"Good. Here we have *The Wicked Marquis*. It was published in 1919, but it still holds up today."

As 1919 was only five years prior, I imagined it did. "Thank you."

"And this is *Jacob's Ladder*, also by Mr. Oppenheim. I think you'll enjoy the tale of Mr. Jacob Pratt. He does have his ups and downs." Miss Petrie giggled again. I think the presence of the large, looming figure of Sam Rotondo by my side intimidated her. I'd never heard her giggle twice in one visit before. I didn't fault her for feeling daunted. Sam loomed rather like a gigantic, unhappy granite obelisk when one first met him.

I said, "Thank you," again, feeling positively joyful.

"But the best is yet to come," said Miss Petrie, her eyes sparkling behind her spectacles. As I've already said, it's long been my belief that she could be quite a pretty woman if she did something with her hair and used a little makeup. Not that it was any of my business. "Here we have *The House Without a Key*, by Mr. Earl Derr Biggers. I think you'll love his detective, Charlie Chan."

"Charlie Chan?" said Sam incredulously.

"Yes. He's a Chinese detective in Hawaii. And I do believe I read somewhere that Mr. Biggers is planning a move to Pasadena!"

"Goodness. Thank you!" I said in hope of preventing more comments from Sam.

I needn't have bothered. At that very second, an earsplitting shriek pierced the silence of the library. I dropped my pile of books. Fortunately, they landed on Miss Petrie's desk. Another scream followed the first one, and then we heard loud sobs coming from the biography section of the library stacks.

Miss Petrie leaped to her feet, and she and I ran toward where the commotion had emanated.

Sam bellowed, "Wait!"

Naturally, we didn't. I heard him thumping after us, and I could tell he was angry by the loudness his cane made when it hit the floor. His feet weren't terribly quiet, either. Sam was a big man.

"Whatever happened?" Miss Petrie whispered.

"I don't know."

We reached the biography section, and we both stopped in our tracks. There, before us on the formerly pristine library floor, lay the body of a woman, face-down in a pool of blood. Another woman with her hands pressed to her cheeks stood, trembling, beside the body. I presumed she was the shrieker.

"Good heavens, what could have happened?" Miss Petrie said in a hushed voice.

"I don't know," said I, likewise quietly. "She couldn't have been croaked with a gat, or we'd have heard the shot."

From behind me I heard a disgusted, "'Croaked with a gat?' Is that what all your reading has taught you?" Sam. Angry, unless I missed my guess.

And then I saw an old school fellow of mine, Mr. Robert Browning —not the poet—swing around the end of the biography stack, a bloody knife in his hand. He stopped dead when he saw the body on the floor, and his mouth fell open.

"Robert!" I cried, appalled. The last person in the entire universe I could imagine killing anyone was Robert Browning. Well, except me and a couple of other folks I knew.

"Wh-what happened?" he asked, sounding and looking dumb-founded. "Good God, is that a dead woman?"

"We don't know yet," growled Sam, pushing Miss Petrie and me aside so he could get to the body. He knelt beside her, even though I knew doing so would hurt his leg. He pressed a finger to where the pulse in her neck would be if she were alive. Then he picked up a hand and felt for a pulse there. Turning to Miss Petrie and me, he snarled, "Call the cops and an ambulance. Now." He got painfully to his feet. "And you," he said to Robert. "What the hell are you doing with that knife?"

"I-I found it on the other side of this row of books. It looked...out of place. I don't know why I picked it up, but when I heard the screams, I ran over here." He looked from Sam to me and back again. "I didn't do anything! I just found the knife."

"And picked it up." Turning to Miss Petrie and me again, Sam said, "Well, get going!"

So we got going.

TWO

After Miss Petrie and I had fulfilled our duty as citizens and called for the police and an ambulance, we both hurried back to the scene of the crime. It had to be a crime, didn't it? People didn't just fall down dead in the biography section of a library in a conveniently handy pool of blood, did they? Then there was that bloody knife Robert Browning had held.

I suppose we should have expected that everyone in the library that day would gather around the dead woman. Poor Sam had his hands full shooing folks away.

"Step back, all of you!" he hollered. Spotting Miss Petrie and me, he said, "Can the two of you stand at each end of this aisle and keep people out? And hold that man there." He pointed to Robert.

"I-I didn't do anything," stammered Robert.

"I don't care. I have to talk to you," growled Sam. He could be a formidable man, could Sam Rotondo.

Carefully, Robert set the knife on a library shelf and stood there, looking helpless. I shooed Miss Petrie to his end of the stacks, and I took my place at the other end. Folks tried to push past me to see, but I ordered them to stay still. Oddly enough, they obeyed me. I suspect the imposing form of Sam had something to do with their compliance.

Not long after we'd called them, three uniformed policemen showed up. I remembered one of them from other occasions. His last name was Doan. Don't know what his first name was.

"What happened here?" demanded an officer who wasn't Doan.

"Somebody stabbed this woman," came Sam's gruff voice. Using a shelf as a lever, he heaved himself to his feet with an audible grunt of pain.

I noticed his cane a few feet in front of him and grabbed Officer Doan's uniform sleeve. I nodded at the cane and Doan, clever devil that he was, picked up the cane and handed it to Sam, who grabbed it most ungraciously. Doan didn't seem to mind. I guess once you knew Sam, you knew how he reacted to things like being forced to use a cane and limp and so forth.

"No one leaves this library until I say so," commanded Sam.

Mumbles from the sparse crowd burbled up. Good thing it wasn't a weekend when all the school children in Pasadena would be in the library studying for various tests, researching for reports and writing essays.

"Take everyone's names and addresses," said Sam.

Another officer who wasn't Doan had already begun to do so, leading me to believe these fellows knew their jobs.

Sam glared at me. "Do you know who this woman is?" He gestured for me to move a bit closer. The officer recording names and addresses took my place at my end of the stack.

"I-I can't see her face," I said, feeling the least little bit sick.

"Well, dammit, *look*, will you?"

"You don't need to swear at me, Sam Rotondo."

Naturally, Sam rolled his eyes. In spite of him, I moved closer to the body and knelt beside the fallen woman, steering clear of the blood puddle.

I gasped loudly. "Oh, my heavens, it's Miss Carleton!"

Miss Petrie uttered her own gasp. "No!" cried she.

"Who's Miss Carleton?" asked Sam.

"I don't know her first name. She was a librarian here. Maybe she still is." I glanced up at Miss Petrie. "Does she still work here?"

"No," said Miss Petrie, her hands plastered to her pallid cheeks.

"She left when she was accepted for a library position at Throop Institute. I mean the California Institute of Technology."

She staggered a step, and Robert Browning laid a hand on her shoulder. She looked up at him, and I couldn't tell if she was grateful for his support or appalled that he might have murdered a former colleague of hers. Why in the world had he been holding that bloody knife?

Glaring at the bunch of people at Doan's end of the stack, Sam said, "Did anyone see a person hurrying out of the library?"

Various shakes of heads and murmurs of "No" came from the crowd.

"And you people?" He said, addressing Miss Petrie's end of the aisle. "Did you see anyone leaving the library? Whoever it was might not have been hurrying."

More shakes of more heads and more murmurs of "No" came from that end, too.

"Do any of you know this Miss Carleton?"

One man said haltingly, "I-I knew her from when she worked here. She helped me find a book about automobile mechanics. But that was a few years ago. I haven't seen her since."

"What about you?" Sam asked me.

"Well, I knew her slightly when she worked here, but I haven't seen her since she left."

"And you?" he demanded of Miss Petrie.

"We worked together for about a year. Then she left, and we haven't kept up our acquaintanceship."

"Why was that?"

"Why? I-I don't know. We were never particularly close or anything. We only worked together. Not that we didn't like each other. It's just..." Her voice trailed off.

"Huh." Sam turned to his copper friends. "Lock the library doors and don't let anyone in or out. Then continue collecting everyone's particulars. We'll have to question them all individually. Why are they here? When did they arrive? You know what to do."

All three officers nodded and herded their personal small groups of people off to be interviewed.

More library staff had showed up at the periphery of the two groups of patrons. I pointed them out to Sam. "Some of those people work here."

"Huh. Everyone who works here stay right where you are. I'll interview you individually."

A couple of librarians (or maybe they were library clerks) uttered unintelligible syllables expressing dismay. One of them asked, "Who is that on the floor?"

No one answered her.

"And you," Sam said, pointing at Robert Browning. "Don't go anywhere. I need to talk to you."

"You can't think Robert did this!" I cried. I know I was in the library, but that point who cared?

"I don't think anything at the moment," growled Sam. "Come here, Browning." He turned to Doan. "Pick up that knife with a paper or something and take it to the department to get any prints from it."

"Yes, sir," said Doan, saluting. Golly, I didn't know folks actually saluted Sam. I was impressed. Robert stepped hesitantly closer to Sam, pointedly ignoring the body on the floor.

"Good. Miss Petrie, you and Daisy, please go to your desk. Browning, you can go with them for now, but don't leave the library."

"Yes, sir," said Robert. His face was kind of ashen. I'd read about this phenomenon in books, but had never seen it for myself until then.

"Come along with me, Robert. I'll introduce you to Miss Petrie, and you can tell us why you're in the library today."

"It wasn't to kill anybody," said Robert, grumbling slightly.

"I know that."

"My goodness, I can't believe someone was murdered in the library," whispered Miss Petrie. There was no need for her to whisper by that time, but I guess she was used to it. "And Miss Carleton! I just can't believe it."

When we got to Miss Petrie's desk, Robert pulled up a couple of those heavy library chairs, and he waited until Miss Petrie and I were seated before he sat, too. A true gentleman, Robert Browning.

"Miss Petrie, please allow me to introduce you to Mr. Robert Browning. Robert, Miss Petrie."

"Pleased to meet you, Miss Petrie, even under these unfortunate circumstances."

"It's nice to meet you, too," said Miss Petrie, holding out her hand for him to shake, which he did. I noticed her cheeks were a little pinkish. The blush became her, and again I thought she could be quite pretty if she took more care with her clothing and makeup. Not that it was any of my business. However, if you believed Sam and my father, that's never stopped me yet.

"Robert works at the Underhill Chemical Company, Miss Petrie."

"Oh. Are you a scientist, Mr. Browning?" she asked.

"Yes, actually, I am, although I'm now co-managing the company under the company's founder's son, Mr. Barrett Underhill."

"I see."

"I didn't know you were a scientist, Robert!" I said, surprised. "I thought you always worked in the offices there."

He smiled at me. "Well, I do work in the offices, but I earned my graduate degree in chemistry at the University of California at Los Angeles. Formerly known as the Los Angeles Normal School."

"I read about the change of name and location, Mr. Browning," said Miss Petrie.

"Chemistry!" I gaped at Robert. "My world, I could barely get through algebra. When I tried to take chemistry and they started talking to me about valances, all I could think of were kitchen curtains. I don't understand it at all. So I dropped out of chemistry and took Spanish instead. That was much easier."

Robert chuckled. "For you, maybe. I've always had a scientific leaning. Couldn't learn Spanish if you paid me."

"I thought mathematics and language skills often went together," said Miss Petrie.

"Not in me, they didn't," Robert and I said together. Then we grinned at each other.

"I must admit I've always been drawn to literary works," said Miss Petrie as if she were a failure somehow.

"And I, for one, am glad you are," I told her. "I don't know what I'd do without you." I turned to Robert. "Miss Petrie picks out all the best books for my family and me to read. She's a wizard at her job."

"Are you now?" Robert smiled at Miss Petrie, whose blush got a little deeper. Yup. She was prettier when her cheeks were pink.

"Speaking of books, why were you here today, Robert?"

He shrugged. "I had to take a late lunch, and I figured I'd come to the library and pick out a couple of biographies. I enjoy reading biographies."

"Were you looking for a biography of anyone in particular?" asked Miss Petrie, her librarian face back in place.

With another shrug, Robert said, "Not really. I…Well, I just wanted something to read in the evenings after work. It gets kind of lonely at home. Not that I should complain," he added with a small smile.

Oh, dear. Poor Robert. He'd lost the love of his life, Miss Elizabeth Winslow, about two years prior. I guess he still had a difficult time coping. I understood completely.

"I can recommend some good biographies for you," said Miss Petrie in her bright librarian's voice.

"Could you? I'd appreciate that. I never quite know what I'm looking for when it comes to books."

"Miss Petrie does," said I. "She always picks out the very best mysteries and detective stories for my family and me. Well, and western novels for my father."

"And don't forget Tarzan," said Miss Petrie.

"Who could forget Tarzan?" asked Robert, laughing a little. I was pleased to see his sad expression ease.

"Indeed," said I. I glanced at the biography section, where police work was still going on. I noticed someone had fastened a string at the near end of the particular aisle where poor Miss Carleton had met her end, and I suspected the police had tied another string at the other end. Glancing around, I saw policemen interviewing people. "But I guess you can't get any biographies today." I shuddered slightly.

"No. I expect not," said Robert, sad-faced once more.

"Oh, dear," said Miss Petrie. "I can't imagine who would want to kill Miss Carleton."

"Miss Carleton?" said Robert, sounding surprised.

"Yes," said Miss Petrie. "Miss Mary Carleton."

"Good Lord," whispered Robert.

"Did you know her?" I asked him.

"Er, yes. Yes, I did. She was a dear friend of Elizabeth's. I can't imagine why anyone would want to harm her."

"Maybe it had something to do with her job at the Institute," I said musingly.

"Perhaps," said Miss Petrie doubtfully.

"And you won't go snooping around the university, Daisy Gumm Majesty."

I jumped at the sound of Sam's voice. Turning to look up at him, I said, miffed, "I wasn't going to snoop around."

"Huh." He glared at Robert Browning. "All right, Browning, you come with me."

The two men walked off to another corner of the library, where Sam had Robert sit and started questioning him; none too gently, if I were to judge.

"Poor man," said Miss Petrie.

"Indeed. He's a very nice young man, too. I know he had nothing to do with Miss Carleton's death."

"It would be hard to imagine such a thing."

"Say, Miss Petrie, this probably sounds stupid, but I didn't know Cal Tech had a library."

"Oh, my, yes. The Millikan Library, named after Robert Andrews Millikan. He's a physicist."

"Physics sounds almost as deadly as chemistry," I muttered.

Miss Petrie laughed softly. I noticed her gaze had strayed to where Sam Rotondo and Robert Browning sat. "Dr. Millikan won the Nobel Prize in physics in 1923."

"Merciful heavens. He must be brilliant."

"I'm sure he is." She cleared her throat. "Mr. Browning seems like a nice man."

"Oh, he is. He and Billy graduated from high school together, but he must have gone on to college and university."

"An intelligent man."

"Indeed. And a nice one." I figured what the heck and went with the sympathy angle. "The poor fellow lost his fiancée two years ago to influenza. It turned into pneumonia, and the folks at the Castleton couldn't save her. He's had a hard time coming to grips with her loss."

"I'm so sorry."

"I'm sure you could help him if you can find him some good books to read."

Miss Petrie patted her hair, which was, as ever, pinned in a tight little knot on the top of her head. "I can certainly help him find reading material." She sounded a bit melancholy.

"Um…Miss Petrie, do you mind if I ask you a personal question?"

She blinked at me but said, "Not at all. What is it?"

"Do you live alone? Or do you live with your family?"

"I don't have much family left," said she. "My mother and I shared a sweet little bungalow in a row of courts on South El Molino Avenue. She died two years ago, and I live there alone now. And no, I don't have cats," she added bitterly. "I swear, Mrs. Majesty, it seems as if the whole world thinks all spinster ladies have cats."

"Do you like being a spinster?" Good heavens. "I'm sorry. That was rude of me."

"No, it wasn't. I wouldn't mind finding a good man, but there seem to be precious few of those around these days."

"True. Thanks to the war and 'flu, there are lots fewer men for women to marry than there used to be."

"It's worse in Europe."

"So I understand."

"And, if you came from a family like mine, you might be a trifle more skittish about men than you are, what with your wonderful family. Most of the men in my family, except my father and his brother, are brutes. As you well know."

"Yes. I do know that, and I'm sorry. But there are a few good men still standing. Just look at Robert Browning."

She didn't need any encouragement from me. When I glanced up from stacking the books I'd dropped when that woman screamed, I saw her gazing soulfully at Robert and Sam.

Naturally, my mind began churning over the possibility of getting

Miss Petrie and Robert Browning together. Both my father and Sam would probably have said that wasn't a good thing. Come to think of it, Billy probably would have said so, too.

Phooey on all of them.

THREE

As we waited to be released from the locked library, Miss Petrie and I chatted about not much of anything for several minutes. I finally, after all these years, asked her what her first name was.

"I think of you as a friend," said I, meaning it sincerely.

"Thank you. I think of you as a friend, too."

"Well, since we're friends, why don't we call each other by our first names? You know mine is Daisy because sometimes you call me Daisy."

She sighed. "I know, and I'm sorry. I shouldn't be so informal with members of the public."

"Good grief, why not? Is it a rule or something?"

"It's not precisely a rule, but I do feel it to be taking a liberty with a library patron to call him or her by his or her first name."

"Nuts to that. It's not a liberty. We've known each other for years and years. You've helped my family and me through terrible times, and I always come to you when I need a lift in my spirits."

She colored again slightly, and this time she wasn't even looking at Robert. "Thank you. That makes me feel quite nice." Her lips pinched. "However, you have decent first name. Mine is ludicrous."

"Ludicrous? Good grief, don't tell me it's Lucrezia Boadicea or anything, is it?"

"It's nearly as bad. Especially since I don't fit it one little bit."

"What is it? You know that when I got into the spiritualism business, I re-christened myself Desdemona. If that's not ludicrous, I don't know what is."

"Well..."

"I won't call you by your first name if you don't want me to, but I'd like to know what it is."

"No, no. Please call me by my first name. You're right. We've known each other for years, and it's silly of me to be embarrassed by my name."

"You don't know what embarrassment is until you've lived most of your life with the last name Gumm."

We both uttered soft chuckles.

Then she said, "Very well. My first name is Regina." She sighed. "My full name is Regina Minerva Petrie. My mother had romantic leanings. She said she nearly named me Rowena, so I guess I got off lucky."

"I think Regina is a lovely name." She was right. It didn't fit her. Prudence, maybe. Or Bertha. Not that there's anything wrong with those names, but Prudence sounds stuffy. On the other hand, Bertha sounds as if its bearer should be fat, and Miss Petrie was definitely not fat.

"Do you really?" she asked, clearly not sure she believed me. "Hmm. I don't think it's lovely. I think it's too dramatic. I'm a librarian, for heaven's sake, not an actress in the flickers."

"I don't think Regina is dramatic at all. Certainly nowhere near as dramatic as Desdemona. Or Ophelia. Aren't you glad your mother didn't name you Ophelia?"

"When you put it that way, I guess I am," she said, grinning at my inanity.

"In that case, may I call you Regina?"

Her lip curled and it was my turn to grin. I guess she meant it about not liking her name. "If you must," said she, but she smiled as she said it.

"Good. Thank you, Regina."

"You're welcome, Daisy."

"Who's Regina?" asked a masculine voice behind me. Both Miss

Petrie and I glanced up to see a shaky-looking Robert Browning. Evidently Sam had set him loose.

I smiled up at him. "Miss Petrie's first name is Regina. I think it's very pretty, but she doesn't."

"I think it's very pretty, too," said Robert with what looked like a genuine smile for Miss Regina Minerva Petrie.

"There. See?" I told Regina.

Very well, I'll admit it was difficult for me to think of the staid librarian with a name like Regina Minerva, but the name wasn't her fault. No more was mine my fault. Who'd want a last name like Gumm? And I'd had to live with it until I married my Billy. On the other hand, the Gumm side of my family consisted entirely of saints, and such couldn't be said of the Petrie clan. But those are last names and not first names, so they don't even correlate; therefore, please forget I even brought up the subject.

"Do you mind if I join you ladies? I guess the detective isn't going to allow anyone to leave the library for quite some time."

"Feel free," I said, gesturing to an empty chair he'd pulled up earlier. "I hope Sam wasn't too hard on you."

"No. He wasn't. I was a fool for picking up that knife. Don't know what possessed me."

"We all do silly things sometimes. I probably would have done the same thing if I hadn't known Sam for so long. He sometimes forgets we aren't all policemen."

"I suppose so." Robert sighed.

"You have nothing to feel bad about, Mr. Browning. We all do things when we're shocked that we wouldn't do otherwise," Regina said, smiling at him.

"I think he suspects me of killing Miss Carleton," muttered Robert.

"He couldn't possibly!" I cried. "He knows you. Well, he's met you before, anyway, and the two of you seemed to get along well."

"Yes. He was quite helpful then." Robert put a slight emphasis on the word "then". He cleared his throat. "I did know Miss Carleton. I think Detective Rotondo is reading more into our acquaintanceship than actually existed."

"I didn't know you knew her," I said, startled by his admission.

"Yes. Er…As I mentioned, she was a dear friend to Elizabeth, and we'd been working together recently."

"Really? I thought she worked at Cal Tech."

"Yes, but I'm working on a project with a couple of other fellows at the university, and Miss Carleton had been helping us." He glanced at Miss Petrie. I mean Regina. "Elizabeth and I were engaged to be married, Miss Petrie. I do believe Miss Carleton—her name is—was—oh, dear." Robert shut his eyes for a moment. "She was Miss Mary Carleton."

"I knew her name was Mary," said Regina. "Did you know her well? We worked together, but we never became well acquainted."

"I…I don't know. We knew each other." Robert shrugged.

Hmm. Why did Robert Browning seem ill at ease whilst discussing the late Miss Mary Carleton, former librarian for the City of Pasadena? I didn't know, but I was still pretty sure he hadn't murdered her. Robert? Heavens, no!

"Daisy told me about your fiancée, Mr. Browning. I'm so sorry," said Regina, her eyes getting teary. I guess she was as emotional as I was. No wonder we liked the same books.

"Thank you. It was…It was a hard loss." Robert gulped. "Still is."

"I'm sure," said Regina, trying to pretend she wasn't wiping her eye when she lifted a finger to same.

"Losing a loved one is…horrible," I said, knowing it to be true, but hoping not to prolong anyone's misery.

"Yes. It is," said Robert.

Out of curiosity, I asked Robert, "So it sounds as if you and Miss Carleton kept in touch after your fiancée passed away"

He hesitated. "Well…sort of. Lately we'd seen more of each other because…because of the project." For some reason he stared at his lap and didn't make eye contact with me.

"I'm certainly sorry about what happened to her," I said, mainly because I couldn't think of anything else to say. I wanted to grill Robert about his knowledge of Miss Carleton, and I *really* wanted to know why he seemed reluctant to talk about it. Had they quarreled? Had they had an affair? I gazed at Robert and didn't think so. I got the feeling he was true-blue to his lost love.

Then again, I'd been wrong before. Quite often.

But no. I couldn't feature Robert Browning as a coldblooded killer. Especially of a woman. Well, of anyone.

"All right," came a deep voice behind me, making me jump slightly in my chair. I looked up to see Sam looming there, frowning.

"All right what?" I asked.

"All right, it's time to go." He turned his frown upon Robert. "I'll need to speak to you again, Mr. Browning. Perhaps you can come to the station tomorrow. About ten o'clock?"

After heaving a sigh, Robert said, "Right. Will do."

"You're leaving?" I asked, surprised. "I mean, we're leaving?"

"Yes." Sam sounded grumpier than usual.

I glanced at Regina. "May I take these books home? I'm not sure how to check them out, what with all the library staff being huddled in that far corner."

"I'll stamp them for you," said she, rising from her chair. "Oh! I forgot to ask you if you've read the Tish books by Mrs. Rinehart."

"Tish? No, I don't think so."

"Wait here for a minute." Regina rushed off to the fiction section of the library. She returned in a minute with three more books tucked under her arm. "I think you'll enjoy these. They aren't precisely mysteries, but the main character, Miss Letitia Carberry, who's known to her friends as Tish, is truly an endearing person. She leads her friends on lots of fun escapades and, in the process, solves some crimes."

Fun sounded good to me just then. "Thank you! I love Mrs. Rinehart's books. Except for *The Amazing Interlude*. But you know that."

"Yes." Regina smiled sadly at me. "But I think you'll enjoy these stories."

Oh, boy. Now, not only did I have all the books she'd selected for me before, but I had *The Amazing Adventures of Letitia Carberry*, *Tish*, and *More Tish*. I was a happy woman. You can never have too many books lying around the house. Heck, I generally carried one in my handbag just in case I got stuck waiting somewhere.

Regina, Sam and I went to the check-out counter, and Regina stamped my books for me. That meant I had two weeks to read seven books. Shouldn't be a problem.

Sam grumbled under his breath as we walked toward the library door, where a uniformed policeman stood, guarding the place so no one could escape, I guess. He saluted Sam. I was impressed all over again.

"Keep me informed," snapped Sam.

"Yes, sir," said the uniform. I couldn't read his badge.

I noticed Sam limping more heavily as we left the library than he'd limped when we'd entered it. "I'm sorry your leg hurts, Sam," I said, trying to sound loving and sympathetic. Which was, as I should have expected it to be, a wasted effort.

"Damn my damned leg," he snarled. "I can't work the case. I have to sit at my damned desk while everyone else works the case, and I don't like it. I was right there when it happened, for Pete's sake."

"I know, but you haven't been released to run around looking for murderers yet." I still attempted to sound loving and sympathetic, although it was kind of a strain.

"Damn it," said Sam.

I gave up. We walked down the library steps and up to the Chevrolet. Sam grunted as he heaved himself into the passenger seat. I placed the books on the back seat.

"Cheer up, Sam," I told him, knowing I was going to rile the rattlesnake. I did it on purpose, what's more, because his attitude irked me. "I can snoop around for you. I know everyone at the library, after all."

I was right. "Damnation, you will *not* snoop around! I won't stand for it."

"Just joking," said I. I don't think I meant it. Darn it, I wanted to know who could have hated Miss Carleton enough to murder her. And in the library, of all unlikely places.

"Not a funny joke," said Sam, snarling like a wounded grizzly bear.

"Huh. I should buy you one of Mary Roberts Rinehart's books to read. It's called *When a Man Marries*."

"Why should I read a book by that woman?" He made "that woman" sound as if he considered Mrs. Rinehart something from the lowest stratum of society. A brothel-keeper or bootlegger or something.

"Because this one is funny. It's adapted from a play she and a man wrote—can't remember his name—called *Seven Days*. All these society swells are at a party when the butler collapses with what they think is smallpox, and they're all quarantined. It starts out, 'Needles and pins, needles and pins; when a man marries his trouble begins'."

"Huh. My marriage to Margaret wasn't troubled."

"Just you wait. When we get married, I'll make your life miserable."

"You do that now."

"It'll get worse. Trust me."

"Why doesn't that surprise me?"

"Stop being such an old grouser, Sam Rotondo! You can't investigate every murder that takes place in the world. Your main job right now is to heal."

"Huh."

"Oh, you're impossible."

We made it back to our house on Marengo with no further conversation, which was probably just as well. I knew Sam's leg was truly hurting when, as he got out of the machine, his leg must have given out, and he darned near crumpled up on the side porch.

"Sam!" I cried.

"Dammit," he said.

Par for the course.

"Let me take your arm."

"No! I don't need your help."

"Oh, for pity's sake, you're being stupid."

"Huh."

I swear. If it weren't for the fact that Spike and my family adored Sam as much as they'd adored Billy, I do think I'd have given up on our engagement then and there.

Opening the door for him to enter, still limping painfully, I told him, "You're impossible."

Naturally he said, "Huh."

After Sam had sat on a dining room chair, I went out to fetch the books I'd left in the car. As I returned, Pa came into the dining room from the hall, smiling. Then he took note of Sam's expression, I guess, because he stopped smiling and said, "What's up? Are you hurting, Sam?"

Naturally, Sam didn't snarl at Pa. Completely ignoring Pa's question, he said, "It didn't work."

"What didn't work?" asked Pa.

"Going with her didn't work."

"What do you mean?"

"She can get into trouble even when she has a police escort."

"That's not true!" I cried, wounded.

"What happened?" asked a clearly bewildered Pa.

"Somebody got murdered in the library while we were there."

"Good Lord." Pa sank into another dining room chair.

"It's not my fault!" I cried, furious.

Both of the most important men in my life stared at me. Come to think of it, Spike stared at me too. I slammed the books on the table.

"Temper, temper," said Pa.

"Nuts! You'd think I attract murders, the way you talk about me. *And* look at me." I scowled at Sam. "I'm going to get you three aspirin tablets and then make you lie down on the sofa with your leg propped up. Maybe that'll make you quit treating me like Typhoid Mary."

"I think you are," said Sam. "Only when it comes to crimes committed in Pasadena."

"Well," said Pa. "I'm sure she doesn't mean to attract crimes."

Naturally, Sam said, "Huh."

I gave him the aspirin tablets anyway. What's more, I then made him lie on the living room sofa and helped him prop his leg on some pillows. Spike napped on his stomach.

I decided Spike wasn't at fault for his lack of taste in human cushions. He was only a dog, after all.

FOUR

S am napped on the sofa for most of what was left of the afternoon. Since I'd just cleaned the house that morning, I sat in the living room to keep him company. Unfortunately for Sam's repose, I began reading *The Amazing Adventures of Letitia Carberry*, and actually laughed out loud at one point.

Sorry for my outburst, I glanced at Sam, hoping he hadn't heard me. Naturally, he had. He had one of his olive-black eyes fixed on me and, also naturally, he was scowling.

"I'm sorry, Sam. I didn't mean to wake you up."

"What's so funny?" he snarled.

"This book." I held it up for him to see.

"Huh."

"Go back to sleep," I told him. "Spike needs more rest."

"Huh."

At that moment the telephone, one of my biggest adversaries as well as the main means of securing my employment as a spiritualist-medium to the wealthy ladies of Pasadena, rang. I muttered, "Bother," and rose to answer the 'phone, which was attached to the wall in the kitchen.

"Gumm-Majesty residence. Mrs. Majesty speaking," said I after lifting the receiver to my ear and speaking softly and soothingly into the speaker. Because I made my living chatting with the dead relations of my clients, I always maintained my spiritualist persona, even over the telephone.

"Daisy, it's Griselda," came a voice I recognized. Griselda Bissel, my second-best client and breeder of dachshunds, one of whom was Spike, didn't sound rattled. I considered this a good sign.

"Good afternoon, Mrs. Bissel. I hope you're well today."

"Quite well, thank you. How is Spike doing?"

"He's very well, thank you. Right now he's napping." I didn't say where.

"I'm awfully glad he found a home with you, Daisy. You and he are wonderful together."

"Thank you. He's a perfect dog for the family and me. Billy loved him so much."

She sighed. "Dachshunds are the best."

"I agree with you." I also wondered if she'd called merely to chat about my dog but didn't ask. I figured she'd get to the point one of these minutes.

She did. "I'd like to set up a séance with you at your earliest convenience, dear. I want to host a dinner party and have a séance afterwards. Will you be able to do that?"

"Happy to," said I, almost meaning it. "Let me check my calendar. Would you like to host this dinner and séance on any particular day of the week?"

"Yes. I think a Tuesday evening would be good. Do you have a free Tuesday evening coming up? My second choice would be for a Thursday, but I think you have choir practice or something on Thursday evenings. Is that correct?"

"Yes, it is, and it's sweet of you to remember." Mrs. Bissel, unlike my *very* best client, Mrs. Pinkerton, actually took other people's convenience into consideration when she set up a séance. On the other hand, she didn't have a felonious daughter who was always getting into trouble. On the *other* other hand, her only son, Dennis, had been arrested for a murder he didn't commit a year earlier. Fortunately for all concerned, that mistake was cleared up speedily, thanks in large part to me.

Murder-magnet, my foot.

Anyway, back to the telephone call. I pretended to look at my calendar—I really didn't have so much work that I had to keep track of it—and told Mrs. Bissel, "I can do a séance next Tuesday, if that would work for you."

"Perfect! I'll serve dinner at seven o'clock. You must come to dinner, too. Then the séance can begin directly thereafter. I promise not to have more than seven people, including you, at the séance."

"You're very kind, Mrs. Bissel. That will work perfectly for me."

What it really meant was that I'd miss one of my Aunt Vi's meals. As Aunt Vi is the best cook in the entire universe, I'd probably eat better at home. But I'd get paid for dining at Mrs. Bissel's house, so I didn't repine. We said our good-byes and each hung up our receivers. By the way, the reason Mrs. Bissel mentioned the number of folks she'd have to dinner is that I don't allow more than eight attendees at any séance I conduct. People are unmanageable at the best of times, and when several of them are supposed to sit still, hold hands, and be silent, the fewer the better. They all ought to go to the Pasanita Dog Obedience Club, in my considered opinion.

I'd no sooner set the receiver on the cradle than the stupid telephone rang again. Frowning at the device, I picked it up and began my usual greeting. I didn't get past the "Gumm-Maj—" part before I was interrupted.

Mrs. Pinkerton.

"Daisy!" cried she, sobbing piteously. "Oh, Daisy, I need you!"

It was nice to be needed. I suppose. "You sound distressed, Mrs. Pinkerton. Whatever is the matter?" I knew, of course, what the matter was. Nevertheless, I also knew how to do my job.

"Oh, I'm just so upset about Stacy. She's going to have to stand *trial!*"

Yeah. As was only right since Stacy, Mrs. Pinkerton's daughter, had abetted if not participated in one or more murders, not to mention the capture and imprisonment of several children. What's more, she'd done this whilst conspiring in the cause of providing perverted men pleasure. The thought made me sick. Truth to tell, Stacy made me sick. I didn't say so.

"I'm so sorry, Mrs. Pinkerton. However, you know she participated in something truly..." I couldn't think of a word that might not get me fired. Detestable was correct but probably wouldn't sound right to Stacy's mother. Ah. I thought of one. "...illegal."

Another hefty sob. "I know. That girl has caused me nothing but grief."

"Yes. I agree with you, and I'm awfully sorry."

"But can you come over, Daisy? Tomorrow? I'd *so* appreciate it."

"Of course I can, Mrs. Pinkerton. Will eleven-thirty be a good time for you?"

"Yes." Sniffle. "Eleven-thirty will be fine." Sniffle. "Thank you so much."

"Of course." I spoke gently. I really did feel sorry for the woman, even if she didn't have two brain cells to rub together.

That was unkind. Please forgive me.

We hung up, and I walked back to the living room where I found Sam and Spike awake and alert, and both sitting up. Sam looked as if he felt a bit less ravaged, too.

"Is your leg feeling better?" I asked him tentatively. In those days, I never knew what would set him off.

"Yes. Thanks for the aspirin and the sofa." He glanced at Spike. "And the dog."

"You're welcome. You do know you're a pain in the neck when you're hurting, don't you?"

He sighed about as heavily as he'd been limping earlier in the day. "Yes, and I'm sorry. I know I shouldn't take my misery out on you."

True. Since I heard what sounded like the purr of an automobile's engine pull up and then stop in front of the house, I opted not to say so. "Wonder if that's Harold bringing Aunt Vi home."

"Don't know. Think I'll stay here while you find out."

Sam didn't care much for Harold Kincaid, Mrs. Pinkerton's son, a peach of a guy and one of my very best friends. There was no legitimate reason for his dislike. Harold was what Sam and my late husband used to call a fairy. What they meant was that Harold was a homosexual. It wasn't Harold's fault, but Sam couldn't be brought to believe it. Men can be so stubborn sometimes.

Hmm. That meant Sam and Spike shared a characteristic. Dachshunds can be stubborn, too. Interesting. I'd have to relay my insight to Sam. He'd be pleased.

I'm joking.

Spike, who had no prejudices about people just because of things over which they had no control, was delighted to go to the door with me. In truth, he got there first, having four legs to my two. After I told Spike to sit and stay, which he did, bless him, I opened the door to see who was out there.

"I was right!" I said for Sam's benefit. "Harold brought Aunt Vi home, and he's carrying what looks like a pretty heavy cardboard box. I'll bet it's full of dinner for the family."

"Huh."

Good old Sam.

"Hey, Harold!" I called. "Good evening, Vi!"

"Hey yourself," said Harold, grinning. "You're going to love what's in this box, Daisy. Your aunt outdid herself today."

"Oh, go along with you, Harold Kincaid," said Aunt Vi.

Harold merely grinned some more, and I opened the door wider. "Oh, goody. I love Aunt Vi's special dinners."

"This isn't really special," said Aunt Vi modestly. "Just a roast of pork."

"I love pork roast," I said, meaning it.

"This is special," said Harold firmly. "It's not your old, every-day pork roast."

"Oh. Good. I guess. I don't think you can ever go wrong with roasted pork, so however you cooked it I'm sure it's delicious, Vi."

"You're a sweetheart, Daisy," said my aunt, which made me happy. I thought about asking her to relay that sentiment to Sam, but didn't.

Harold carried the cardboard box into the dining room and set it on the table, Vi, Spike and me following hard on his heels. Spike seemed especially interested.

Sam had risen from the sofa and limped slowly after us. I don't think either Harold or Vi had noticed him yet.

They did when he said, "Smells good."

"Oh, Sam! How lovely to see you this evening," said Vi. Mind you, Sam dined at our home most evenings, but Vi still enjoyed his company.

"Good evening, Detective Rotondo," said Harold. He gave me a wink and turned to give Sam his hand to shake.

Sam shook it. He didn't allow his prejudices to get in the way of good manners. Usually. "Mr. Kincaid," said he in a gruff voice.

I took the lid off the cardboard box and looked inside, where I saw pretty much nothing but crumpled newspaper. "We're having newspaper for dinner?" I asked.

"Daisy, you're a caution," said Vi. She had a variety of expressions she used often and which made no sense to me, of which "you're a caution" was one.

"Whatever a caution is. May I remove the newspaper?"

"Of course. Then you can take the pot with the roast in it to the kitchen and put it in the warming oven."

So I removed the newspaper. Succulent aromas nearly made me swoon. "Oh, my, this smells good. It smells almost like Thanksgiving, only slightly different." I got a couple of potholders from the kitchen and carefully removed the pot from the box. I didn't uncover it, but did as Vi had told me to do, carried it into the kitchen and put it in the warming oven.

"There's a good reason for that," said Vi.

"How come?" I asked.

"You'll find out," said she, looking mysterious. Very well. That was all right by me.

"You'll love it," said Harold. "Must be off now. Will you be going to see Mother soon, Daisy? She's in a rare state, thanks to Stacy."

Sam huffed. As Stacy had been instrumental in getting him shot, I didn't blame him.

"Yes, she called, and I'll see her tomorrow morning."

"Too bad I won't be there. Gotta work."

"What are you working on now?" I asked him. Harold was a costumer for a motion-picture studio in Los Angeles.

"It's a war epic called *The Big Parade*. I don't think you should see it. It's going to be a really good picture, but it'll make you sad. John Gilbert and Renee Adoree. I love designing clothes for Miss Adoree."

"She's beautiful. You're probably right about the picture, though."

"Yeah," said Sam, surprising me. He generally stayed out of conversations with Harold unless he couldn't avoid them. "Who wants to be reminded of that blasted war?"

"True," said Vi, removing her coat, hat and gloves. She'd lost her only son, Paul, in the war.

"Here, Vi. Let me take those." I grabbed her discards.

"Thank you, Daisy. Just put everything at the foot of the staircase if you will."

Vi lived in the two rooms upstairs in our bungalow. Those two rooms would have been perfect for a married couple, but by the time Billy came home from the war, he couldn't climb stairs. Our house looked kind of like a flat house with another, tiny, house on top of it. Lots of Pasadena bungalows looked like that. Ours wasn't unique.

"It's no trouble to carry them upstairs," said I, proceeding to do same.

"You're a love, Daisy."

"Yes, you are," said Harold.

Sam kept mum this time. He would.

Harold left shortly after that. I saw him out to his snazzy bright-red Stutz Bearcat and bade him a fond farewell. Of all my friends, I think Harold and I have the most in common. Maybe that sounds odd because of his perhaps-peculiar characteristics. Too bad.

Anyhow, after I saw Harold off, I went back inside and set the table for dinner. It was about five-thirty by that time. Pa and Sam were seated in the living room, chatting. Vi was preparing for dinner in the kitchen.

Ma came home just about then. She looked tired and bedraggled.

"Rough day at the Marengo?" I asked her. My mother was the chief bookkeeper at the Hotel Marengo, which was a darned impressive job for a woman to have in those days. Of course, if she'd been a man, she'd have made more money.

"No worse than most," said she with a smile. "It's the fall audit, and things are always busy during the audit. That's why I'm a little later than usual."

I didn't even know what an audit was. Pathetic, I know.

"Would you like some help there?" she asked.

"No. You've worked hard today. All I've done is clean house and go to the library." I omitted the murder.

"Oh, good. I'm sure you picked up some wonderful books for us."

"Indeed, I did. What's more, I learned that Miss Petrie's first name is Regina. Her full name is Regina Minerva Petrie. She doesn't care for it, but I think it's kind of pretty."

"Rather theatrical for a librarian," said Ma, plunking herself down on a dining room chair. She'd rid herself of her coat and hat at the door and stuffed her gloves in the coat pocket.

"Yes. I think that's why she objects to her names. She's not a theatrical person."

"Maybe we should have named you Regina. It would fit your profession better than Daisy does."

"It doesn't matter. Everyone thinks Daisy is short for Desdemona." As mentioned earlier, I'd called myself Desdemona from the very beginning of what became my career, when I first played with the old Ouija Board Aunt Vi had brought home from Mrs. Pinkerton's house. I was ten years old, it was Christmas, and I couldn't believe it when the entire family actually believed I was communicating with the Great Beyond with the Ouija board and a pretend spirit control, whom I called Rolly. At the time of the Carleton murder, I'd long known that both Desdemona and Rolly were silly names, but it was too late by then. I've made my living as a fake spiritualist-medium ever since that Christmas, thanks to Aunt Vi telling Mrs. Pinkerton about my so-called "gift". It's a darned good living, too. It pays better than Ma's job at the Hotel Marengo, which isn't fair. Heck, I didn't even know what an audit was, and I made more money than my mother. I'll never understand life.

Then again, whoever said life was fair? Nobody I know.

FIVE

Harold was absolutely correct when he told me Aunt Vi's meal for that evening wasn't your plain, ordinary roast pork.

"Oh, my!" said I when Vi brought in a platter filled with what looked like a rolled-up bunch of pork chops sitting on their bottoms in a ring with their bony legs in the air and covered with little paper things with frills on them. "I've never seen anything like that before!"

"Me neither," said Pa, looking and sounding intrigued.

"I haven't, either," said Sam, likewise enchanted.

"Nor have I," said Ma unenthusiastically. Ma wasn't big on culinary experiments, although she'd managed to enjoy Mexican, Turkish, and Indian (the kind from India) delicacies, thanks to Vi.

Vi appeared pleased with herself, as well she should have, when she set the platter before her own place at the table. It was then I realized that the fancy pork-chop circle was filled with something.

I sniffed. "Is that turkey dressing?" My mouth had commenced watering the moment I'd put the pot in the warming oven. By that time, I was nearly drooling.

"It's made pretty much the same way. Pork is delicious with dressing. And cranberry sauce. And applesauce. And potatoes."

"I love pork," I said, in awe of my marvelous aunt.

My cooking skills are best not spoken of. Well, truth to tell, I have no cooking skills. I'd been known to burn water—not the water itself, but the pot it boiled in was beyond repair when I finally remembered to turn off the burner under it.

"This is called a crown roast of pork. You can see why," said Vi, gesturing to the circle of pork.

"By George, it does look like a crown," I said.

"Hence, the name," said Vi.

"I love those fancy little paper things on the bones."

"Those, if you'll believe it, are called panties."

"Good heavens." I was kind of shocked, although I don't know why.

"Will you fetch the vegetables from the kitchen, Daisy?" asked Vi. "Then we can all dig in."

So I brought to the dining room table a bowl of green beans *with* almonds (making them what the French called *haricots verts almondine*), a bowl of applesauce, and a bowl of cranberry sauce. I had to make three trips in order to get everything on the table. I'd make a lousy waitress. There were even roasted potatoes and gravy, which I carefully poured into the Gumm-Majesty gravy boat. The gravy, I mean. Not the potatoes.

"Are the Pinkertons celebrating a special occasion or something?" I asked as I carefully placed the gravy boat near Vi at the head of the table. I didn't even spill.

"No. I just feel awfully sorry for Mrs. Pinkerton these days. She's so upset about Stacy. I figured they could use a special meal, even if it isn't a special occasion. And, of course, I always make enough for us."

"Lucky us." I shut my eyes and reveled in the delicious aromas wafting from the various platters and bowls.

"Indeed," said Pa.

"It smells good," said Ma in a tentative sort of voice.

"It smells delicious," said Sam. "I'm a lucky man, to get to dine here."

"Nonsense. You're part of the family now," said Pa.

Sam looked at me. "Not quite yet," said he.

"One of these days," I said. "You're in no condition to marry anyone at the moment."

My mother said, "Daisy!" which she does every time she thinks I'm making an inappropriate comment.

"I'm not being rude. Thanks to his leg, Sam's grumpy as an old bear lately," I told my mother.

"It's not just my leg. You'd be grumpy, too, if your fiancée was always stumbling over dead bodies," said Sam.

"I didn't stumble over anything!"

Pa said, rather loudly, "Let me say grace, and we can dine on this perfect meal." Pa was generally the peacekeeper-in-chief at our house.

So I shut my mouth, bowed my head, and Pa said grace. When I opened my eyes again and looked across the table at Sam, he was grinning at me. Blast the man!

That was one of the most succulent roasts of pork I personally have ever eaten. And Vi was right about it going well with dressing, cranberry sauce and applesauce (not together). It was sooo good, I forgot all about the early part of the day. Therefore, I almost groaned when Ma decided to ask about Sam's comment regarding stumbling over bodies.

I did mutter, "Oh, no."

Bless my father's heart. He said, "When Sam and Daisy went to the library this afternoon, somebody died."

"That's too bad," said Ma.

"Yes," said Vi. "It is. Did you know the person, Daisy?"

This time, I think I heard Sam say, "Oh, no," under his breath. Too bad. It was his fault for bringing up the matter in the first place.

"Yes. I didn't know her well. But she used to be a librarian there. Her name was Miss Mary Carleton."

"Dear me," said Ma. "Was she elderly? Did she have a heart spasm or something?"

Nerts. But what the heck. "No. She was murdered. Stabbed."

Ma laid her fork on her plate and stared at me. "In the *library*?"

Since my mouth was full, I merely nodded.

"Do they know who did it?"

"Not yet," said Sam.

I glanced at him and saw he regretted bringing up the subject. Huh. Served him right.

"Poor Robert Browning—you remember him, don't you? Works at

the Underhill Chemical Factory? He was there, and he picked up the knife. He said it was sitting on a library shelf one stack away from where poor Miss Carleton got stabbed. It was all bloody."

Ma frowned. "That doesn't sound like a wise thing to do."

My mother may lack imagination and an adventurous soul, but she was excellent at knowing what to do and what not to do in any given situation.

"It wasn't," I said. "Sam talked to him for about three hours. I think he thinks Robert killed the poor woman." I sniffed to let everyone know what I thought about that state of affairs.

"It wasn't three hours," mumbled Sam after he'd swallowed a bite of potato. "But he's on the suspect list."

"Oh, dear," said Ma, looking quite unhappy. "I remember Robert from when you were in school, Daisy. He used to get teased about his name."

"I know how that feels," I mumbled, forking up another bite of pork, dressing and cranberry sauce. A notion occurred to me as I chewed happily, and when I swallowed, I said, "I just thought of something! Robert was going to marry a woman named Elizabeth, just like the original Robert Browning! Wouldn't that have been something? Only I don't think his Elizabeth's last name was Barrett."

"I doubt the poet Robert Browning was the first to have that name," said Ma, as literal as ever.

"Probably not," I agreed, stabbing some green beans with my fork.

And the telephone rang.

All heads, which had been bent in rapt concentration of our marvelous meal, lifted, and the entire family plus Sam stared at me.

"Good heavens," said I, rising. 'Phone calls in our home were nearly always for me. "I don't know who that could be. I've already told Mrs. Pinkerton I'll visit her tomorrow."

"That poor woman is in such a dreadful state of nerves," said Vi, her voice oozing sympathy.

Annoyed at having one of the best meals of my life interrupted by the instrument of torture hanging on the kitchen wall, I yet maintained my spiritualist-medium poise when I plucked the receiver from the cradle. "Gumm-Majesty residence. Mrs. Majesty speaking."

"Oh, Daisy, it's Gladys!" came an agitated voice over the wire.

Gladys. Gladys? Who in the world...? Enlightenment came in mere seconds.

"Gladys! How are you?" Gladys, who used to be Gladys Pennywhistle but who had married a scientist named Dr. Homer Fellowes a year or so prior, was expecting their first child soon. As Gladys seldom, if ever, telephoned me, I was surprised by her call.

"I'm fine, thanks. Oh, but Daisy, something dreadful has happened!"

"I'm so sorry to hear it. I hope nothing's wrong with you or the baby or Dr. Fellowes."

"No, no, no." She sounded impatient, which annoyed me. After all, she'd interrupted my dinner. "But oh, Daisy, a woman named Miss Carleton—"

I interrupted her. Rude, I know, but I didn't think Gladys would like our party-line neighbors listening in on this conversation. "Wait a minute, Gladys."

She said, "I beg—?"

"Will our party-line neighbors please hang up your telephones? This call is private, and it's for me."

Gladys said, "Oh."

We both waited. One click. Two clicks. Three clicks. Nothing. In my sternest voice, I said, "Mrs. Barrow, please hang up your receiver. This is a private telephone call."

Another click, this one sounding irked. Too bad.

"Very well, Gladys, please go on."

"A woman named Mary Carleton was murdered today."

"I know. I was in the library when it happened."

"Were you really?"

"Yes. It was awful."

"I can imagine." Gladys hesitated for few moments then said, "The thing is, she worked closely with Homer at the Institute. She was helping him with his research. Her murder has put everyone working on his project in a terrible fix."

"I can imagine everyone who worked with her is shocked and horrified."

"Yes, but there's more."

"Oh?"

"Yes. You see…Oh, this is difficult to explain."

"Give it a try," I suggested, longing to get back to the dinner table.

"Well, you see, other people are working on the same project, and… Well, Homer is afraid there's something shady going on, but he doesn't know where the problem lies."

I squeezed my eyes closed and shook my head. This telephone call didn't make any sense to me. Whatever in the world did Dr. Fellowes, Miss Carleton, and shady goings-on have to do with each other? I mean, murder itself could be considered shady, but…"Um…Perhaps you'd better explain further, Gladys. As I said, I was at the library today when poor Miss Carleton met her end, and I did understand from Miss Petrie that Miss Carleton had gone to work for the California Institute of Technology, but I…Well, what's that got to do with you and your husband and his project?"

"Can you come to our home tomorrow, Daisy? This is terribly important. I can explain it all to you then. It's probably better not to talk about it over the wire, especially since you have a party line."

After thinking about the matter for approximately half a second, I said, "Of course, I can do that. Give me your address. I have another appointment at eleven-thirty, but I can see you earlier than that. Perhaps nine? Will that be all right with you?"

"Nine is fine. Thank you, Daisy." She gave me an address on Santa Rosa Avenue in Altadena. Altadena was where Mrs. Bissel lived, and it was a lovely community just north of Pasadena. Sort of country-ish, if you know what I mean. Gladys and Dr. Fellowes must be doing all right, money-wise, because that section of Altadena was only just being built up with gorgeous homes. Dr. Fellowes was an inventor as well as a professor at Cal Tech, so maybe he'd made some bucks from one or more of his inventions.

"I'll see you then. Try not to worry," I said in my soothing spiritual-ist's voice. Not that Gladys had anything at all to do with spiritualism. A less fanciful person than Gladys Pennywhistle Fellowes I'd never met in my life, unless it was my mother. Why, Gladys even understood *algebra* in high school! What's more, she claimed to enjoy mathematics and science. I suspect my mother did, too, and that's why she worked as a bookkeeper. There's no accounting for tastes.

It was a befuddled Daisy Gumm Majesty who walked back to the family dinner table after she hung up the receiver. What's more, I wasn't sure what to say about Gladys's call. If I told everyone she wanted to talk to me about Miss Carleton, Sam would throw a fit.

Therefore, I decided not to.

"Who was that on the telephone, dear?" asked Ma. She sounded sympathetic, which I appreciated.

"Not Mrs. Pinkerton, I presume, since you don't look riled," said Sam, his sharp eyes trained on me. Suspicious man, Sam Rotondo.

"No. Oddly enough, it was Gladys Fellowes."

"Oh," said Ma, puzzled unless I missed my guess.

"I don't recall a friend of yours named Gladys," said Pa.

"She used to be Gladys Pennywhistle. She was that awful Mrs. Winkworth's secretary back when I was supposed to be spiritual advisor to that insane actress."

"Lola de la Monica?" said Ma. "Good heavens." Lola de la Monica was the aforementioned insane actress.

"Indeed. That was a terrible time." It was as Harold Kincaid and I sat in Mrs. Winkworth's rose garden when Sam came to me with the news that my Billy had taken a lethal overdose of morphine.

"What did she want?" asked Sam. Still suspicious, the rat.

"Just to invite me to her house tomorrow. She's going to have her baby relatively soon, and she said she wanted to show me the nursery."

"She wants you to see her house and nursery? I don't seem to recall her. Were you particularly close or something? I can't remember her at all, and I remember most of your friends," said Ma, remaining puzzled, for which state I couldn't fault her. My lie had been a particularly clumsy one.

"We went to school together, Ma. She was in Lucy's wedding and was worried about her interesting condition showing, but she needn't have. It didn't." Inspiration—or something. You never know about these things until after the fact—struck. "I think she wants to ask me about altering clothes for her or something after the baby gets here."

"Why would she need you?" asked Sam. "Can't she sew?"

"I don't know," I told him, being honest for once. "She was more involved in mathematics and science than home-making classes. Not everyone can sew, you know."

"Huh. Her husband's a professor at Cal—" He stopped speaking suddenly, and I had a sinking sensation inspiration had struck him, too. Crumb. "You're not going to get involved in the case, Daisy. Don't even think about it."

"I can't imagine how Gladys could have anything to do with the case," said I. Which was true, darn it. I *didn't* know.

"Why don't I trust you?" asked Sam after glaring at me for fully five seconds. Five seconds doesn't sound like a long time until you've been stared at by Sam Rotondo for the duration.

"I don't know, and I think it's mean of you to say that," I said. Turning to my mother, I said, "And why don't you tell Sam he's being rude when he says things like that, Ma?"

My mother said, "He's not the one who's always getting into trouble, Daisy."

"Trouble, my foot." I couldn't win. Nevertheless, I struggled on. "Anyhow, I'll be happy to see her new home. It's got to be new, because they're just beginning to break up those huge old estates the millionaires built. The Felloweses lives on Santa Rosa in Altadena. They're building some really fancy homes up there."

"Fancy for a professor," muttered Sam.

"He's not just a professor," I reminded him. "He's the man who invented that thing they used in that flicker, and I'll bet he made a lot of money for it. Kind of like Edison and all his inventions."

Sam had been part of the week from hell, too. He'd hated it. He'd been posted at a motion-picture site as a gesture made by the Pasadena city fathers to show they supported the arts or, more probably, that they appreciated motion-picture money being spent in our fair city. Sam had been miserable the whole time. And *he* didn't have to contend with Lola de la Monica! She was…Difficult, I believe, is the word people use to describe people like her.

"I remember him well. And his wife," said Sam. "I was surprised when they got together. I thought he was keen on that crazy actress."

"He was at first, but he fell out of love with her and tumbled into Gladys's waiting arms."

"Daisy!" said Ma.

"Fiddlesticks, Ma. It's the truth. Gladys and Dr. Fellowes are a perfect match. He's a scientist and a professor, and she liked algebra in high school."

Everyone looked at me.

"It's true," I said.

Sam shook his head. Pa smiled. Vi and Ma both seemed uncertain.

And we all went back to eating. Except for that one brief interlude, dinner was most excellent.

SIX

Thursday morning dawned crisp and foggy. Pa and I had breakfast together, and he handed me a section of the *Pasadena Star News*.

"Does it have anything in it about the murder?" I asked as I took the paper from him.

"Not much. Just a reference on the second page."

So I looked on the second page, and he was correct. A paragraph mentioned that a woman named Mary L. Carleton had been stabbed to death in the Pasadena Public Library. Not pleasant publicity for the library, but there you go.

Another article caught my eye. "Good heavens, somebody's holding a dance marathon in order to break Alma Cummings's record of dancing twenty-seven straight hours. That seems a peculiarly useless occupation to me."

"Me, too," said Pa.

"I mean, why would anyone want to dance for twenty-seven straight hours? Dancing is fun, but why make yourself miserable while you're doing it? I don't understand." I began, in fact, to sympathize with my mother, who thought lots of the things people did were absurd.

"Don't ask me," said Pa.

So I didn't pursue the matter. After we ate breakfast, I tidied up the dishes and walked with Spike and Pa around the neighborhood. Then I got ready for my day. I was looking forward to visiting with Gladys. For one thing, I wanted to see her house. But the main reason was that I wanted to know what she knew, if anything, about Miss Carleton, shady goings-on, and what those goings-on had to do with Miss Carleton's untimely demise. And, of course, Gladys's husband and Cal Tech and whatever project Gladys was talking about on the 'phone.

In other words, both Pa and Sam would say I planned to snoop. And they were absolutely correct. You'd think Sam would be pleased with me, since he was unable to devote himself to the case, wouldn't you? Not Sam. The night before, when Spike and I walked him to his Hudson after dinner, he again told me not to pry into the Carleton case. Nerts.

Out of my over-stuffed closet, I chose to wear that day an ankle-length brown striped day dress. It was a couple of years old, but it was comfy, and I planned to do a lot of running around during the morning hours. Besides, it was becoming to my coloring and went beautifully with my emerald engagement ring. We spiritualists have to dress well. With the dress, I wore a brown felt cloche hat I'd made myself, a string of black beads I'd bought dirt-cheap at Nelson's Five and Dime, black gloves, and black low-heeled shoes with a wide strap across the arch. After I'd donned my dress and accessories and eyed myself in the mirror, I thought I looked pretty good.

For confirmation, I asked, "What do you think, Spike? Do I look like a professional spiritualist-medium?"

Spike wagged at me, and I took that as a sign of his approval. So be it. I grabbed my black handbag, my Ouija board and tarot cards—for which I'd made charming embroidered drawstring coverlets—and headed through the kitchen to the dining room. Because I wasn't sure if Pa was still in the house—he often went visiting—I walked through the dining room to the living room. Sure enough, Pa was there, reading the latest copy of *The National Geographic*. My Billy had adored that periodical, and I'd kept up the subscription after his death because I couldn't bear to part with anything Billy had loved so much.

"Going to visit Gladys, Pa," I called.

He looked up and smiled at me. "As usual, you look like a fashion plate, sweetheart. You really dress well, don't you?"

"I do my best," said I, trying not to feel guilty about my abundance of clothes. In my defense, I made them myself, often from patterns I copied from various fashion magazines I read at the library. And I always bought the material at Maxime's or Nash's when they had fabric sales. Plus, I made clothes for the entire family. The only one who didn't appreciate my enterprise was Spike. "I thought this would go well today, since it's so cold."

"Yes. I nearly froze on our walk."

"I did too, although I was pretty well bundled up."

"You aren't bundled up now," Pa observed, eyeing me critically.

"I'm going to snag my black coat before I go," said I, matching my actions to my words and heading to the coat stand beside the front door. "Oh. Sam left his hat here last night. Maybe I should take it to him."

"Maybe you should," said Pa with another smile.

So after I donned my coat, I snatched Sam's brown fedora and headed back to the dining room and the side door. When I got into the Chevrolet, I carefully placed Sam's hat on top of my Ouija board and headed to Gladys's house on Santa Rosa Avenue.

Santa Rosa Avenue in Altadena is lined with deodar trees. You might have read, as I had, Rudyard Kipling's book, *Under the Deodars*, which contains stories set in India. These Altadena deodars weren't awfully tall yet, but when I read about them in the library, I learned they'd keep growing and generally lived up to a hundred years. They were native to the Himalayas, which I thought interesting as the weather in the Himalayas couldn't be the same as the weather here in Pasadena and Altadena. The trees were planted in the 1880s, and the entire street was supposed to have been the main approach to the John P. Woodbury mansion. The mansion had never been built because of some financial reversals suffered by Mr. Woodbury. Now the estate acreage had been broken up into lots, and people had begun building homes there.

A couple of years prior to the day of my visit to Gladys, Mr. Nash, of Nash's Dry Goods and Department Store, got together with the local Kiwanis Club to hang a number of Santa Rosa's deodar trees with electrical lights at Christmas time and let people drive or walk up the street.

If you were in an automobile, you had to turn off your lights in order to get the full glory of the ride. Folks, including yours truly, loved it. In fact, we loved it so much, the tradition has continued, if you can call a four-year-old event a tradition. Now we call Santa Rosa "Christmas Tree Street," sort of like folks referred to Orange Grove Boulevard as "Millionaire's Row."

Anyhow, I drove up Marengo to Woodbury Drive, turned right, and took a left on Santa Rosa. The deodars were clumsy-looking trees that were considerably prettier at night with Christmas lights blazing on them than in the stark daylight, but I didn't mind. I couldn't help but stare out the window at some of the new homes going up. They looked nice, not to mention expensive. When I got to the address Gladys had given me, I had to make another left and drive across a little bridge over a deep ditch, into the Fellowes's driveway.

It was nine o'clock on the dot when I rang the doorbell to the Fellowes's home. It was a pretty place with a pointy roof (I think you call those pointy things gables) and lots of windows. It looked cheerful and inviting, which surprised me a little, as neither Gladys nor Dr. Fellowes seemed the least bit cheerful upon first meeting. Heck, I'd known Gladys for years, and she still didn't seem cheerful to me, although she wasn't a miserable old grouch like some other people I could mention but won't.

As if she'd read my mind, Gladys appeared anything but cheerful when she answered the door. "Oh, I'm so glad you came, Daisy. I hope you can help solve this thing." She ushered me into the front entryway, which led into the living room. I glanced around, pleased with what I saw.

"This is a nice home, Gladys. It's very pretty." Lame, but true.

"What?" Evidently startled, Gladys peered first at me and then at her surroundings. "Oh, yes. Thank you. We like it. Homer helped design it."

"Did he really? I'm impressed."

"Yes. He's a clever fellow. But that's not why I asked you to come over. Let's sit down in here." She marched to the living room.

Very well. All business, our Gladys. I sat in a comfy wing chair. The Fellowes's living room was painted white, and there was a beautiful Oriental carpet on the floor. The chair upon which I sat was a deep burgundy color, which went well with the carpet. Gladys plunked herself down on a burgundy sofa across from me.

"I really do like this house, Gladys. It's darling."

"Thank you. But I didn't ask you here to talk about our house."

All righty, then.

Suddenly she sat up straight on the sofa. "Oh," said she. "I forgot. I should probably offer you some tea or coffee or something, shouldn't I?"

"I don't need anything," I told her.

"Oh, Daisy, I'm sorry. You know I've always been so…not a gracious hostess, I guess is what I mean, and I forget the social niceties sometimes. I don't mean to be rude."

"You're not being rude," I said, feeling a little sorry for her. She always had been a trifle socially awkward, but I chalked that up to her mathematical brain, which wasn't like the brains of most of us. "And I appreciate the offer, but I truly don't want any coffee or tea right now."

"Thank you. But Daisy, I do hope you can help. I don't know whom else to talk to about this." She glanced around furtively. "I don't want anyone else to hear."

"Is anyone else in the house?"

"No."

I refrained from rolling my eyes. "Then you probably needn't fret about being overheard."

"I suppose not. But Homer is so worried. It's about Mary Carleton, you see. She worked with Homer on a project at Cal Tech. She was helping with the research, being a librarian and all." Gladys squinted at me. For the record, she wore thick spectacles, although I don't think they detracted from her appearance. She'd been a pretty, if sober-sided girl, and she was now a pretty, if sober-sided young woman. Anyhow, Homer Fellowes wore even thicker specs, so they seemed evenly matched in that department. "Did you know she was a librarian?"

"Yes, I did. I met her when she worked for the Pasadena Public Library, although I didn't know her well."

"I see. Well, she was helping Homer and another scientist named Dr. Gregory Malton with some geological studies. Homer said she all of a sudden started acting strange a week or so ago, and then someone went and murdered her, and Homer is desperately afraid Gregory might have done something to her."

"Why would he do anything to her? Did Dr. Fellowes give you a reason or a motive for his having done so?"

"No. He and Dr. Malton divided up the project, and Mary was helping Dr. Malton. Something she said made Homer think there might be something shady about the research they were doing."

"Oh. Hmm." And I was supposed to figure it all out? I didn't even understand what she was talking about, for pity's sake. "I'm not sure what you want me to do, Gladys."

She started wringing her hands. I honestly didn't know people did that except in novels. But her hands, which were sturdy and well-shaped, started wringing each other atop her protruding belly. "I don't know! Oh, I don't know what you should do. But someone has to do something, or the entire project might fail, and it would be a black spot against Cal Tech *and* Homer, and I can't let that happen!"

"If Homer had nothing to do with her death, I don't see how he—"

"Of *course* he had nothing to do with her death!" cried Gladys, offended, unless I missed my guess.

"I didn't think so," I said soothingly. "In fact the police yesterday seemed to be concentrating on another individual entirely."

"Who?" she demanded abruptly.

Not precisely a fount of polite refinement, our Gladys. I answered her anyway. "A gentleman named Robert Browning."

"Oh, no!" Gladys, who had been sitting forward in her armchair, collapsed back into it and looked stricken.

"You know Robert?" I asked her, surprised.

"He's working with Homer and Dr. Malton."

"On a project regarding geology?" What was geology, anyhow? Something to do with rocks, I think.

"Yes. Oh, dear. This is just awful. You mean Robert was in the library when Mary was killed?"

"Yes, as was I. And my fiancé, Detective Rotondo."

"No! We can't have the police involved in this!"

"Detective Rotondo is recovering from a work-related injury and isn't personally working on the case," I said in a repressive tone. What the heck did she mean, the police couldn't be involved? In a murder? Applesauce! "Anyhow, the police pretty much *have* to be involved in the solution to a murder, don't you think?"

With a hand to her brow, Gladys whispered, "Oh, dear. Oh, dear." Dropping her hand, she gazed mournfully at me. "I suppose they do, but the project can't be tainted. It *can't* be, Daisy! It would just kill Homer if anything happened to the project. And a murder of one of his staff might blot his image as a brilliant scientist and inventor."

She spoke as if Homer's precious project were more important than a woman's life. "In that case, I suspect his image might already be blotted. After all, I'm sure the police will find out they were working together."

"Oooooh," said Gladys in something of a moan. "I suppose you're right, but there must be a way to keep Homer's name apart from the killing."

Confused only faintly describes my feelings at that moment. A woman was murdered, she'd worked with Dr. Fellowes, and Gladys didn't want anyone to know about it? "I can't imagine how you can keep Dr. Fellowes's name out of the newspapers, Gladys. I'm sure the police will have to interview him about the work she did for him."

"Oooooh," moaned Gladys again.

"But see here. The police department has every reason not to sully the names of innocent people and institutions. Nobody wants to blacken Cal Tech's good name—or that of Dr. Homer Fellowes, for that matter. Pasadena owes a good deal to the Institute, and the police will make every effort to keep its reputation intact. However, they *do* have to investigate murders. That's what we taxpayers pay them for."

"I know. I know." Gladys resumed wringing her hands. "But...Oh, Daisy! Don't you *see*? Homer simply *can't* be linked to so heinous a crime!"

I heaved an exasperated sigh. "He's already linked to it, if only by association. If Miss Carleton and Dr. Fellowes worked together, there's no way to get away from some sort of link. Anyhow, I'm still not sure what you want me to do about it, Gladys. I'm sure the police will investigate the crime, nab the culprit, and lock him up. I'm also certain Dr.

Fellowes, Dr. Malton, Robert Browning and the other folks who are working on their project will be exonerated."

"But...But, they'll all be linked to a *murder*! A scandal! It might prevent their project from coming to fruition."

Puzzled, I asked, "How?"

"Oh, *I* don't know! They'll be *linked*! Don't you see that?"

"No," I answered frankly. "I don't see that. If the project upon which everyone is working is worthy of...of...of...Well, I don't know what it might be worthy of. I don't know beans about Cal Tech or geological research, but if they discover something useful, I'm sure no one who matters will hold a murder against them."

"You don't think so?"

"I doubt it. What are they working on, anyway? If it's important, the work will go on, and no one will blame them for poor Miss Carleton's murder."

Gladys sat in her chair, pensive, for several seconds. Then she glanced at me with a pleading expression on her face.

"I'm sorry, Daisy. I'm just so worried that all the hard work Homer, Dr. Malton and Mr. Browning are doing will go for naught if there's something like a nasty murder tainting it. Oh, and they're doing a geological study of the local foothills."

"Really?" Why did anyone need to know about the geology of the local foothills? I didn't ask. "At any rate, I'm not a trained investigator, and the police don't like amateurs butting into their work. Besides, I'm still not sure what you want me to do."

"I want you to *snoop*! You're good at it."

Golly. Thanks.

"And you won't allow irrelevancies to get in your way."

"Irrelevancies?"

After hesitating for a moment, Gladys said, "Yes. I mean, you might uncover some things that look bad but that don't relate to the project."

"What sorts of things? And if they don't relate to the project, why would anyone care? Unless, of course, they relate to Miss Carleton's murder."

Gladys stilled her restless hands by clamping them together. With her head thrown back, she stared at the ceiling for a second or two.

Then, again looking squarely at me, she said. "You don't believe that any more than I do."

"I don't?"

"No. You don't. You know very well that if anything the least little bit scandalous shows up in anyone's background, people will hold it against Homer and his fellow researchers." And darned if she didn't turn a glorious crimson color.

Totally befuddled by this time, I said, "I still don't know what you think I can do that the police can't, Gladys. I...Well, if there's any disgrace or shame in anyone's background, I'm sure the police won't advertise it. Not unless it has something to do with the murder."

"It doesn't."

I opened my mouth. Then I closed it. Then I opened it again and said, "*Is* there something scandalous in the lives of anyone involved in the project?"

"I wouldn't call it scandalous."

"You just did."

Gladys's lips pinched into a tight line before she spat out, "Society holds things against women that it wouldn't hold against men, you know."

Whatever that meant in the overall scheme of things. "Yes, I do know that, but if there's a stain on someone's past, I'm sure the police won't advertise it. Unless it's bloody murder or something." Which Miss Carleton's death had been. Thinking about it made me shudder.

"Did you read *The Scarlet Letter* in high school?"

"Yes. I thought poor Hester Prynne was treated shamefully, but I'm not sure what that has to do with anything."

After perusing me with another sharp glare, Gladys said—grudgingly, if were to judge her tone—"Oh, very well. The same thing happened to Mary. Mary Carleton had a baby out of wedlock. There. Is that scandalous enough for you?"

SEVEN

My mouth dropped open for a second. I shut it with a clack of teeth and said, "I had no idea. Poor thing."

"Very few people do. And I don't think it's fair that her shame should follow her to the grave. She wasn't that sort of woman, if you know what I mean."

"I guess I do. I didn't know her well, but she seemed a most unlikely candidate for having a child while unmarried."

"She was, and it wasn't her fault."

"I'm sure of it," said I, not quite knowing what I meant. If she'd had a child out of wedlock, she must have participated in its conception, after all. But I didn't know the circumstances, so I resolved to keep any judgmental opinions to myself. "Did she say who the father of the child was?"

"Um…I'm not sure."

I didn't believe her, but I didn't press the issue.

Gladys went on, "I believed her when she said she was misled into trusting the father of her child. He told her he wanted to marry her."

"But he didn't. Marry her, I mean."

"But he didn't," echoed Gladys.

"Men," I snarled, thinking bitterly about a few other men I'd met (not Sam, who was a gentleman even if he didn't act much like one sometimes). "I'm so sorry to learn of this."

"I'm sure you are, but that's not the point. You know very well that if news of it gets out, her reputation will be smirched forever, and so will Cal Tech's and those of the people working on Homer's project."

"I honestly don't see that," said I. Then I thought about what Gladys had said and what I'd said. "At least, I don't think it will." After all, Fatty Arbuckle's career had been ruined even though he'd been thrice vindicated in the death of a woman who'd attended one of his parties.

"I think it will," said Gladys firmly. "Which is why I want you to pry into the matter. You'll do a much better and more thorough job of it than the police will, and you'll be infinitely more discreet. I know it. As soon as they find out—*if* they find out—Mary was a fallen woman"— she placed a particularly vitriolic emphasis on the last two words— "they'll stop even caring who killed her. They'll just assume she was a wicked creature, the villain was someone at Cal Tech, and the reputations of the school and all of Mary's co-workers will be tarred with the brush of disgrace."

If she said so. Personally, I was a little skeptical. "I still don't know what you expect me to do about it," I told her. "I'm not a detective, you know."

"I know. But you helped find out who was sending those hateful letters to those actors a couple of years ago. I figured you knew how to pry into things without causing alarm."

Not precisely flattering, but true. "Sometimes," I said noncommittally. Something then occurred to me, although it didn't strike me as brilliant. "Um…Could you and Dr. Fellowes host a dinner party or something? You know, a house-warming party or something like that? You might get everyone together that way, and maybe I could look over the suspects."

"A dinner party? Me?" She pointed to her chest.

"Just a thought."

She sat still for a few moments, deep in thought. Then she said, "That's not a bad idea, although I can't cook a lick. Poor Homer and I have to dine out more often than not because I'm so dismal in the kitchen."

"So am I!" said I, thrilled to have found common ground in this one element of our lives.

"Homer wants to hire a cook, but so far we haven't. I do have a woman who comes in to clean the house every morning. She went to the store for some things I asked her to buy for the baby's room, but she'll be back soon."

Must be nice.

"But I don't know about a dinner party."

Another idea occurred to me, and this one didn't sound as hopeless as my last one had. "Perhaps you could host a party at a restaurant. It would be pretty expensive, I guess, but..." My voice trailed off.

"That's a good idea," said Gladys as if she weren't sure of herself or my idea. "We'd have to invent an occasion. Homer's birthday isn't until February, and mine just passed."

"Happy birthday," I said. Conditioning, I guess.

"Thank you. It was two weeks ago. But Daisy, you go to parties all the time. I know you do, because you're always going to rich people's homes and so forth and pretend to talk to ghosts and things like that. There's no way on God's green earth *I* could possibly plan and carry out a party. It's...it's just not one of the things I'm good at."

"I'm not a party-planner, Gladys. All the planning of the parties I attend is done by other people. The homes to which I go are those in which I've been hired to conduct a séance or something of that nature."

Gladys's nose wrinkled. "A séance? Good Lord. I don't think I could host a séance. Everyone would laugh at me."

Thanks again, Gladys. "I'm sorry. But I don't plan parties. I conduct séances and read tarot cards. If you'd like to hire me, I'll be happy to conduct a séance. If you want anything else from me, you're out of luck."

After another several seconds, Gladys sat up straight and beamed at me. It was the first time since I stepped foot in her home that she'd smiled. "Wait a minute! Maybe it would be entertaining to have a séance here. Our friends would laugh, but I think they'd be interested enough to come. That's a wonderful idea! I do like it." Her face fell again. "Oh, but Daisy, I suppose I'd have to feed the people who come to the séance, because otherwise it would seem extremely odd. Perhaps we can make it into a...what do you call it? A fun evening, or something like that. And I can neither cook nor plan parties. Do you think you could help me?"

Fiddlesticks. "I already told you I can't plan parties, Gladys. Or cook."

She sat silent for a few moments, thinking furiously. I could tell.

"But you know people who host parties, don't you?"

"Yes. Lots of them."

"Well, do you think one of them might be able to help me? It's for a worthy cause."

An idea struck me, sort of like the blow from a baseball bat. "Wait a minute. Is there any upcoming occasion you might wish to celebrate? Thanksgiving is coming up, but I don't think you'd have many guests if you hosted Thanksgiving at your house. Besides it's more than a month away."

"Good heavens, no."

"Well, I've already suggested hosting a house-warming party. I think it's a good idea, and it's a valid one. I don't think any of your intellectual friends will scoff at attending a house-warming party."

Pursing her lips, Gladys thought about my suggestion for a bit. "Hmmm. Maybe that's not a bad idea, after all." She glanced around her living room. "Do you think people will even want to see our new home?"

"Of course, they will! It's a lovely new home, and I think everyone will be enchanted with it."

"How do we go from a house-warming party to a séance? Nobody in the world will think I believe in such nonsense." Gladys seemed to recollect with whom she spoke, and pressed a hand to her cheek. "Oh, Daisy, I'm so sorry! I didn't mean to disparage your line of work."

"That's all right, Gladys. If you promise not to tell anyone, I'll let you in on a secret."

"I don't know whom I'd tell, but I'll promise not to tell your secret if you want me to."

"Thank you. I don't believe in spiritualism any more than you do. I have to earn a living, however, and spiritualism a much better-paid job than most of the other ones I might be able to get."

"Really?" Gladys appeared astounded.

"Really. And, you know, your friends needn't think of a séance as a serious business. Pretend you're just holding a party with a friend of yours—Oh! I just thought of something! I've been to many charitable parties in which I set up a tent and read palms and tarot cards and consult the Ouija board and my crystal ball. You could have an amusing party with a pretend-mystical aura to it." Another idea struck me, and this one truly *was* brilliant. I sat up and said, "A *Halloween* party! Host a house-warming Halloween party!"

"Halloween? Good gracious, how did you ever think of that? Oh, Daisy, that might just work."

"I believe it will. And nobody will think anything about me plying my trade at a Halloween party! It'll be all in fun and in the spirit of Halloween."

"You're brilliant, Daisy. You really are!"

"Nonsense. I barely passed algebra in school. You're the one with the brain."

"But I have no imagination," said Gladys, showing a more genuine understanding of herself than I'd heretofore judged her to have.

"Well, I have enough imagination for a regiment of know-it-alls," said I. "No offense meant."

"None taken. I've been called a know-it-all my whole life, even though I never thought I was snooty about it." She sighed, as if regretting her know-it-all-edness.

"No, you never were snooty about it. You were just smart and scored high marks all the time." Truer words were seldom spoken. Gladys never had bragged about being a highbrow.

"But I still don't know how to plan a party. Do you know anyone who can help me?"

I thought for maybe half a second. "Actually, yes, I do. Harold Kincaid is a master at such things." Harold Kincaid was going to love me for this. I'm kidding. Although he truly was a great party-planner and party-thrower. "I'll bet you can host great Halloween party with nothing but canapés and various drinks."

"Drinks?" Gladys appeared shocked. Prohibition was the law, after all.

"Not alcoholic drinks. I'm sure Harold will know what to serve."

"Who is he, anyway?"

"Harold Kincaid. Do you remember him from when they shot that picture at Mrs. Winkworth's estate?"

She shuddered slightly. "That horrible woman." She was speaking of Mrs. Lurline Winkworth, whose secretary she was at the time and she was absolutely correct, but that's not the point. "I vaguely recall him. He was a friend of Mr. Mountjoy's, wasn't he? If he's the one I'm thinking of, he seemed a nice man."

For the record, Monty Mountjoy was about the most handsome man on the face of the earth and a tremendous heart-throb to thousands, if not millions, of picture-going damsels. He was a great guy, too.

"Harold is one of my best friends, and he loves to throw parties."

"Would he mind throwing one at our house?"

"I don't think so, but I'll be glad to ask him. Then you can invite everyone you think might be involved in Miss Carleton's death to the party."

"Sounds grim," said Gladys, frowning slightly.

"Don't make it grim. Have everyone come in costumes of one sort or another."

"Costumes? You mean witches and goblins and so forth?"

"Precisely. My spiritualist act will fit in perfectly."

Gladys sat on the sofa, thinking hard, for quite a long time. I didn't fidget, since I didn't have to be at Mrs. Pinkerton's house for another hour or more.

Finally she said, "All right. I think that might be a good idea. Thank you, Daisy."

"You're more than welcome." And with any luck, Harold wouldn't murder me, keeping the death toll in Pasadena, California, in 1924, lower than it might otherwise be.

"I'll invite Dr. Malton and Robert Browning and a few other people."

"Better wait until I talk to Harold before you extend invitations. I don't think he'd mind arranging your party, but I don't know what his schedule is. When would you like to do this?"

"As soon as possible. We have to get to the bottom of the matter before anything else happens."

"You think other people might be in danger?" I was alarmed.

Pressing a hand to her forehead again, Gladys said, "I don't know! I didn't think anyone was in danger in the first place. I can't believe someone killed Mary. This is just terrible. Oh, Daisy, you *must* help us. And you must keep Homer's name out of it."

Ask for the moon and stars, why don't you, Gladys Pennywhistle Fellowes? I didn't say that. "If it can be done, I shall do my best," I told her.

Huh, as Sam Rotondo might say. On the other hand, it wasn't every day I was actually *asked* to snoop into a vile crime.

Oh, boy!

Sam was going to kill me.

I'd think about that later.

Gladys showed me around her house after I asked her to. I think she was surprised to be asked, but that was just Gladys's way. Anyone else would have been proud to show guests the delights of her new home. I think I've already mentioned Gladys's dearth of social skills. Not that it matters.

Anyhow, I had plenty of time to get from Gladys's adorable gabled home on Santa Rosa Avenue to Mrs. Pinkerton's massive mansion on Orange Grove Boulevard. In fact, I decided to drop by the house and telephone Harold Kincaid. He said he'd be at work today, but I could leave a message with his houseboy for him to call me. Then I could ask about the Fellowes's party, and if he'd be interested in planning it. Of course, I'd tell him why the party was so important. I trusted Harold as I trusted few other people.

I popped by the house, called Harold's number, and his houseboy, Roy Castillo, told me Harold was at work on a picture in San Bernardino and wasn't expected home until the next day. It was what I'd anticipated, but I was still disappointed.

"May I take a message, Mrs. Majesty? Mr. Harold might telephone this evening."

"Thanks, Roy. The next time you speak to him, will you have him ring me?"

"I'll be happy to. Is there anything I can do to assist you in the meantime?" asked the helpful Roy.

"Do you know how to plan parties?" I figured it was as well to ask.

After a slight pause, Roy said, "Well, yes. I do help Mr. Harold and Mr. Del when they host parties here."

"Do you really? Oh, my! Would you be willing to help me plan a party for a friend of mine? It will be sort of a Halloween-house-warming party and a catered affair—Uh, do you know any restaurants in town that cater parties? Just canapés and so forth."

"The Castleton has been obliging to Mr. Harold and Mr. Del. I expect they could cater anyone else's party."

"Great idea." I glanced at the kitchen clock and decided to cut the conversation shortish. "Listen, Roy, I may call upon your expertise in this endeavor later, depending on how Harold feels about it, but right now I have to get to Mrs. Pinkerton's house."

"Ah. Good luck, Mrs. Majesty." Roy must have heard all about Mrs. Pinkerton's travails, since he worked for Mrs. P's son.

For the record, Harold Kincaid and Delray Farrington lived together in a gorgeous mansion in San Marino, and, as already mentioned, they were what Sam and Billy called faggots. Or fairies. *I* called them friends, and I didn't care what they did in their own home. They couldn't help but be what they were, and no matter what any church person or government tells you, there's nothing wrong with them. They were born that way. I won't entertain arguments, so don't even try.

Sorry. Got carried away there for a moment. Back to the telephone conversation.

"Thank you, Roy. Hope I'll be talking to you soon."

As soon as I hung up the receiver, I stooped to bid Spike a fond farewell, which he didn't appreciate. I was then sorry I'd come home before heading to Mrs. Pinkerton's place because I'd got Spike all excited, and now I planned to desert him again. Poor Spike.

"I'll make it up to you this afternoon, Spike. You can sit on my lap while I read a book."

Spike wasn't mollified, but I left anyway. Had to make a living, after all.

EIGHT

As I had expected it to be, my visit with Mrs. Pinkerton was relatively dismal. Mrs. Pinkerton herself had red, swollen eyes and looked as if she'd been crying for days. She probably had been.

But I'm getting ahead of my story.

First of all, after Mr. Jackson, Mrs. Pinkerton's gatekeeper, opened the huge iron gates so my family's almost-new Chevrolet could enter the sacred Pinkerton grounds, and after I'd given Mr. Jackson a cheerful wave and he'd returned it, I parked the automobile in front of the massive Pinkerton porch. After grabbing my bag of tools (Ouija board and tarot cards. I didn't take my crystal ball with me as a rule because it was too darned heavy), I trod up the staircase to the gigantic front porch, patting one of the marble lions on the way, and knocked at the brass knocker on the front door.

As he always did, Featherstone, Mrs. Pinkerton's butler for all the years I'd known her and probably then some, answered my knock. From the looks of him, there was nothing at all wrong with the world or with the Pinkertons. Rather like a statue, was Featherstone. Come to think of it, he wasn't unlike Sam Rotondo in that particular characteristic.

"Good morning, Featherstone."

"Good morning, Mrs. Majesty. Please come this way."

I'm not precisely sure how many words Featherstone knew, but he only used a very few of them whenever I came to pay a call. At any rate, I went that way and ended up, as usual, in the drawing room, where poor Mrs. Pinkerton seemed to be having an unpleasant conversation with a gentleman whom I knew to be her attorney, Mr. Leonard Pearlman. I'd met him before under similar circumstances—that is to say another time when Stacy's lousy behavior had caused her mother grief.

Mrs. P spotted me, clutched her saggy hankie to her bosom, leapt from her seat on the sofa and ran for me, leaving Mr. Pearlman blinking after her. I braced myself against a large piece of furniture to cushion the bump I'd get when she grabbed me. Which she did. She then commenced sobbing onto my shoulder. I was used to it. In fact, I patted her back and said, "There, there."

"Daisy! Oh, Daisy! It's so awful! I don't know what to do, and Mr. Pearlman said he can't help!"

"Oh," said I.

Mr. Pearlman cleared his throat, I presume to catch Mrs. P's wandering attention.

As Mrs. Pinkerton didn't seem inclined to let me go or cease blubbering, I gently pulled her hands away from me, held them in a warm grip, and said in a low, soothing tone, "Mrs. Pinkerton, I believe Mr. Pearlman means to say something to you."

With a loud wail, Mrs. P said, "He's *already* said something to me, and I can't *stand* it."

Over Mrs. P's heaving back, I saw Mr. Pearlman roll his eyes and then remove his spectacles, retrieve a handkerchief from his pocket, and proceed to clean his lenses. His lips were pinched together tightly, and I gathered from that and from Mrs. Pinkerton's precarious state that their meeting hadn't been going well for either one of them.

Taking a deep breath for courage and still holding on to Mrs. P's hands, I said, "Perhaps I can help somehow." Which was one of the more idiotic things I'd said in my career as a spiritualist-medium, but oh, well.

"Oh!" cried Mrs. P. "Oh, yes! I'm sure Daisy can help us, Mr. Pearlman!"

So saying, Mrs. Pinkerton whirled around and charged at the sofa and Mr. Pearlman again. Mr. Pearlman scooted aside so she wouldn't squash him when she landed. I walked slowly to the sofa myself, wondering what I'd got myself in to this time. Well, I didn't really wonder awfully hard. Stacy had participated in a couple of heinous crimes, and Mrs. P wanted her attorney to save her wicked soul. Stacy's, not Mrs. Pinkerton's.

"Perhaps Mr. Pearlman can explain to me about what he can and can't do with regard to Stacy's current problems," I suggested.

Frowning, Mr. Pearlman said, "The conversations between an attorney and his client are privileged and cannot be discussed with other people."

Well.

But Mrs. P, bless her, said, "No! You must tell Daisy everything you told me! I'm sure she can help us straighten this whole thing out."

Oh, boy.

Still frowning, Mr. Pearlman said, "This is quite irregular. I don't know..."

"*I* do!" cried Mrs. P. "Tell Daisy what you told me. I'll sign a—what do you call it? A release or something! Daisy can be *trusted*!"

Mr. Pearlman sat contemplating the state of things for several moments while Mrs. Pinkerton quietly wept next to him. I decided I might as well rest my tootsies, so I drew up one of the exquisite medal-lion-backed chairs decorating the drawing room and sat on it, looking between Mrs. P and Mr. Pearlman the while.

After thinking about the matter for some time, Mr. Pearlman finally said, "I don't suppose anything I shall reveal to Mrs. Majesty"—he already knew my name from earlier meetings—"can be considered privileged."

"Oh, good!" said Mrs. P.

"But the fact of the matter is as I told you, Mrs. Pinkerton, and that is, you will need to retain a criminal attorney to oversee your daughter's case. Cases. Harrumph."

I got the feeling Mr. Pearlman thought about as much of Stacy Kincaid as I did. And what I thought was that she should have been drowned at birth. Better to do away with a no-good waste of space like Stacy than some poor kitten that might do something useful with its life. Catch mice and other vermin and so forth. Naturally, I didn't say so.

Rather, I said, "That sounds reasonable, Mrs. Pinkerton. I understand Mr. Pearlman has been your family's attorney for several years now—"

"Yes!" she wailed.

"But I also understand his specialty is not criminal law."

"Precisely," said the lawyer as if glad *someone* finally understood his problem.

"Oooooooh!" whimpered Mrs. P. It was better than a wail.

"Perhaps," I said in my most reasonable, gentle and encouraging tone of voice, "he might even be able to suggest the names of one or two good criminal attorneys practicing in Pasadena." I smiled hopefully at Mr. Pearlman.

He didn't appear precisely heartened by my words or my smile, but he did say, "Yes. I've already given Mrs. Pinkerton the names of two attorneys whom I know will do their very best for Miss Kincaid. Given the circumstances, which are not encouraging."

"Ooooooh!" Another wail.

I reached over and patted the poor woman's hand. "That sounds reasonable to me, Mrs. Pinkerton. Stacy is going to need a good criminal attorney as her case progresses. I'm sure Mr. Pearlman's suggestions are excellent ones." Not that I knew a hill of beans about criminal attorneys, but I was trying to sound calm and sensible.

Balling her fists and pressing them against her cheeks, hankie trickling wetly, Mrs. P said, "Do you really think so, dear?"

I was the dear in question. Mr. Pearlman rolled his eyes again.

"Yes, I do." I said it firmly, too, what's more.

After sniffling several times, Mrs. P said, "Very well. Daisy, dear, will you kindly write down the information Mr. Pearlman has about criminal attorneys? I fear I'm too upset to do it myself."

No wonder there. Mrs. Pinkerton was unable to do most things by herself. I know that sounds unkind, but it was the melancholy truth. She'd been born rich, reared to be rich, and didn't know how to fix a meal or clean a house or shop for groceries. She could hire all of those things done for her and, therefore, her state of ignorance was probably larger than she was. And she was a large woman. "Of course, Mrs. Pinkerton." And I dutifully pulled my little notebook and pencil out of my handbag. By the way, the notebook was a cunning creation I'd purchased at Nelson's Five and Ten-Cent Store some months prior. It had a spiral binding and a little elastic band to hold a pencil. It came in handy for lots of things.

I smiled at Mr. Pearlman. "Very well, Mr. Pearlman, will you please give me the names of the attorneys you believe will be able to handle Miss Kincaid's case? Cases?"

"Harrumph. Yes. They are Mr. Cecil Grant, who is the criminal attorney operating at my own firm of Pearlman, Cohen and Pickstaff. We're located at 250 East Colorado Street, near Nash's Dry Goods and Department Store."

"Isn't that the building that used to house Mr. Hastings' firm?" I asked. Mr. Hastings, a prominent Pasadena lawyer, and I had had dealings in the past. Not pleasant ones.

Frowning, Mr. Pearlman said, "Yes, it is. However, our firm has nothing to do with Hastings and his cronies."

"I'm glad to know that," said I with the utmost sincerity. I'd darned near died—and not of natural causes—in that building once.

"Harrumph. Yes." Mr. Pearlman cleared his throat. "Another attorney I suggested Mrs. Pinkerton might retain is Mr. Hugh Merriman. His office is across the street from our firm, at 253 East Colorado."

I dutifully wrote down Mr. Merriman's information, then glanced up from my notebook. "Of the two, do you think one is better than the other? Or, if not precisely better, then one with whom Mrs. Pinkerton could…deal with more effectively than the other?"

Mr. Pearlman shut his eyes for about two seconds. "I don't know, but I do believe Mr. Kincaid—the younger Mr. Kincaid, I mean—might well accompany Mrs. Pinkerton when she attempts to deal with whichever man she chooses to retain."

Made sense to me. Harold had common sense and tact, unlike his mother or sister. "Yes, indeed. I'm sure you're correct."

"Dear Harold," said Mrs. Pinkerton as if she wished Harold were there right then. I did, too, come to think of it.

"Will there be anything else, then?" asked Mr. Pearlman, picking up the briefcase on the floor near the sofa. "I don't believe I can be of any more assistance to you, Mrs. Pinkerton, although, of course, our firm is always happy to help you in any way we can."

In other words, they'd be happy to help with non-criminal matters.

After heaving a massive sigh, Mrs. Pinkerton said, "I don't think so. Thank you very much for coming today, Mr. Pearlman. I can't say you've offered me much comfort during these trying times, but I'm sure you did your best."

"Indeed," said Mr. Pearlman, and with another harrumph and a stiff bow, he left the drawing room. What's more, he didn't even run.

Mrs. P and I sat in the drawing room, gazing after him. Mrs. P sniffled another three or four times.

"Thank you so much for helping me with Mr. Pearlman, Daisy."

"I didn't do much except write down the names of two attorneys you might wish to consult," said I with becoming modesty. We spiritualist-mediums try hard to be modest. There's an art to it, believe me. "And I do believe you should get Harold to go with you when you interview potential criminal lawyers to handle Stacy's cases."

"Yes. Dear Harold. He's always such a comfort."

"He truly is. Um...Would you like to consult Rolly on the Ouija board?"

Another sniffle or three. "Yes, please. I don't suppose Rolly will be able to help, but I would like to know what he thinks of these ghastly circumstances."

I knew precisely what Rolly thought about Stacy Kincaid and her antics, because I was Rolly. Nevertheless, I drew up a small table in front of Mrs. Pinkerton, got the board from my bag, and placed it in front of Mrs. P. I made sure the letters and numbers faced her. By this time in my career, I could read upside-down as well as most folks could read upside-up.

Mrs. P shut her eyes for a couple of seconds, as if trying to think of an appropriate question. Then she sighed once more and said, "Rolly, is there anything I can do for Stacy that might help her at this dreadful time?"

That was easy. I had Rolly spell out, "Let her fend for herself."

Mrs. P gasped. "No! She can't fend for herself! You know how easily led-astray, she is, Rolly."

Rolly said, "Yes, we all know that. It's time she learned to behave."

"Oh, dear." Mrs. Pinkerton gazed with me with a woebegone expression on her face. "I don't know what else to ask. Can you think of anything, dear?"

"Not really. I think Rolly is…um…tired of Stacy's behaving badly. She does behave badly, you know."

"Yes. I know. I should have been more strict with her when she was growing up."

"It's no use blaming yourself in this crisis, Mrs. Pinkerton. Stacy might have benefitted from having her behind paddled when she was growing up, but she still knew what she and her gentleman friend were doing was wrong, and she did it anyway. That's nobody's fault but her own."

Mrs. Pinkerton's face crumpled like piece of balled-up paper. "Oooooooh!"

"She did something particularly bad this time, you know," said I, retaining my soothing, gentle voice, but speaking the truth as I knew it. I don't often tell my clients the truth, but I figured Mrs. P needed to understand that murdering people and human trafficking were activities in which no morally upright person would participate. And Stacy had participated in both of those activities. Willingly. "I'm sorry to speak so bluntly, Mrs. Pinkerton."

"No, no. You only told me the truth. Stacy is such a disappointment."

"She probably got her bad qualities from her father," I said in mitigation of Stacy's many faults. Her father was at present residing in San Quentin Prison for embezzling from the bank he ran. A truly bad man.

"That may well be true," said Mrs. P a little, but not much, more brightly.

"I'm sure it is." Boy, was I a staunch friend or what?

Mrs. Pinkerton patted my hand. "Thank you, Daisy. You're always such a comfort. Can you read the cards for me? Maybe they'll tell me what's best for me to do."

Her lawyer, Harold, Rolly and I had already told her what was best for her to do, but Mrs. Pinkerton preferred to believe the tarot cards. I swear...

"I'll be happy to," said, I, reaching into my bag for my pack of shabby tarot cards. I simply *had* to get a new deck, but I wasn't sure where to do that. Probably Harold would know. Or even Sam, although Sam was less likely to impart the information than was Harold. Sam didn't approve of what I did for a living. Nuts to him.

So I shuffled the cards and spread out a Celtic Cross pattern. I was surprised to see not awfully many swords in the layout. Swords are the iffiest cards in the deck, and generally mean trouble. Mind you, the top cards in the spread were the three of swords, which means a time of weeping and deep feelings; and the page of disks (present environment), signifying that Mrs. Pinkerton was soon going to be immersed in a whole bunch of written communications. Heck, I didn't need a tarot card to tell me Mrs. Pinkerton was suffering through a bad time and was facing a mountain or two of paperwork.

The rest of the layout contained a four of cups (distraction), the fool (an element of surprise), the eight of wands (urgency), another couple of pentacles, another couple of cups, the empress, and by gum, it ended on a truly uplifting card. The position of this last card signifies the outcome of any given situation, and this one boded well. The ace of pentacles, which signifies a rosy result after a lot of hard work. I wasn't sure about the hard work—we were talking about Mrs. Pinkerton, after all—but I was more than happy to tell her this card was a promising one.

"Ahhh," she said with a sigh. "I'm so glad."

"So am I. You deserve some good news after everything that's happened lately."

"Um...Well..." Mrs. P paused, then said, "Never mind."

"What," I asked, pretty sure what she was going to say.

I was right.

"You can't tell me what's in store for Stacy, can you?"

"No, I can't. The cards only work for the person whose life they concern. I have a feeling Stacy is going to have to serve her time in jail or the California Women's Penitentiary, but you know, Mrs. Pinkerton, she brought this upon herself."

"You don't think that awful man led her astray?"

"That awful man" was Mr. Percival Petrie, with whom Stacy had run away, and whose aunt had shot Sam in the leg. Petrie had killed himself by tripping over my prone body—prone because Stacy had decked me—and falling down some concrete basement steps, which was a better fate than he deserved. If he'd received the punishment he deserved, he'd have had to suffer a lot more before he died. Not that I'm an old meanie or anything, but that's true. If you don't believe me, just ask Regina Petrie.

"No, I don't," I answered firmly. "Stacy was ripe for mischief, and I have a feeling she'd have found it with or without Mr. Petrie. With any luck, Captain Buckingham will visit with her and help her to straighten herself out." Johnny Buckingham, husband of my dear friend Flossie, worked as a captain in the Salvation Army, and he's never given up on anyone yet that I know about.

"He's a good man," said Mrs. Pinkerton, surprising me. She'd been aghast when Stacy first joined the Salvation Army, but that was only because she was a snob. If Stacy had been saved by Father Frederick, a very kind Episcopal priest of Mrs. P's acquaintance, Mrs. P would have been delighted. As it was, at least she admitted to Johnny's goodness.

"He's a very good man, and I'm sure he hasn't given up on Stacy." Because sometimes I can't help myself, I added, "Even if she doesn't deserve his faith in her."

Ouch. I saw Mrs. Pinkerton wince and was almost, but not quite, sorry I'd voiced such a brutal truth.

She cast her gaze to her hands, which still squeezed her damp hankie. "You're right. She doesn't deserve his help. He did his best."

"He'll try to help her now, too. Johnny doesn't give up on people."

"A fine quality. I'm about ready to wash my hands of Stacy."

Golly! Not that I blamed her.

After handing me a wad of money, Mrs. Pinkerton sent me on my way with many compliments and her very best wishes. And this, in spite of my having spoken my mind about her abysmal daughter. Wonders, as people say, will never cease, I reckon.

NINE

I walked down the hall to the kitchen in order to say hello to my wonderful aunt, who was, as usual, preparing dinner for the Pinkertons (and us). She was up to her elbows in flour and seemed pleased to see me.

"I hope you were of some little help to Mrs. Pinkerton, poor thing. She's been so upset."

"And rightly so," said I, not feeing a whole lot of compassion for Mrs. P or her idiot daughter. I take that back. I did feel sorry for Stacy's mother. Stacy could rot in hell for all I cared, and she probably would one day.

"Yes, I know you're right," said Vi, "but the poor thing really does try, you know."

"I know. I only wish she had more practical sense sometimes. Poor Mr. Pearlman seemed almost beside himself when I arrived. He'd been trying to explain to Mrs. Pinkerton that he couldn't handle Stacy's case, and she didn't want to hear that."

"He can't?"

"No." I plopped myself down on a kitchen chair. "He doesn't handle criminal cases. However, another attorney in his firm does, so Mrs. Pinkerton is planning to take Harold with her to interview him.

I'm sure Harold will do most of the interviewing."

"I'm sure you're right." Vi dumped out her bowl of whatever-it-was onto a floured surface and began rolling out the whatever-it-was.

"Making bread?" I asked, interested. Vi made great bread. Vi made great everything.

"I'm rolling out dough, Daisy. Bread doesn't need to be rolled out. This is crust for a pie," said she. "Peach pie."

"Oh, I love peach pie! I didn't think peaches were in season."

Vi gave me a look. "Why do you think I make you help me preserve so much fruit during the summertime and fall?"

"Oh, yes. I forgot all about preserved peaches."

"That's difficult to imagine," said Vi. "You certainly complain enough when you're helping me." She smiled, though, so I knew she didn't mean it. Anyhow, I really didn't complain when I helped her preserve fruits and vegetables, because I knew we needed them.

"Whatever kinds of peaches they are, the pie sounds delicious."

"I'm making one for us, too," she said, bless her. "Do you want lunch, Daisy?"

Did I? Suddenly I recalled Sam's fedora, at present residing in the front seat of our Chevrolet. "Thanks, Vi, but I'd better not. Sam left his hat at our house last night, and I'm going to take it to him."

She gave me a knowing smile. "Hoping your man will take you out to lunch, Daisy?"

"Not really. The poor guy still has a hard time walking. I just thought I'd pop by with his hat and then go home and have a roasted pork sandwich." The thought of that sandwich made my mouth water.

"That's sweet of you, dear. Tell Sam he'll love dinner tonight. I'm fixing a hearty beef stew with biscuits. And, of course, the pie."

"Yum. Thanks, Vi. You're the best." I rose, kissed her on the cheek, and scrammed out of the house, now hungry for my sandwich. But Sam came first. I probably ought to remember that more often.

I aimed the Chevrolet west on Orange Grove, turned south on Fair Oaks Avenue, and headed to the Pasadena Police Department, which sat behind our city hall on the corner of Fair Oaks and Walnut Street. I parked and walked into the building, twirling Sam's hat on my finger. The officer at the front desk was one I'd seen before, although I'd never formally met him. Evidently, he knew who I was because he grinned impishly and said, "I'll just buzz Detective Rotondo."

"Thank you," I said, striving for dignity. It wasn't easy, what with nearly everyone in the entire Pasadena Police Department knowing Sam and I were engaged.

After hanging up and making a face, at the 'phone, the uniformed officer said, "I'll unlock the door, and you can go right on up. You know where his office is, right?"

"Right."

The officer, named Tilden according to his badge, rose and unlocked the door for me. I took it from there, climbing the stairs to the second floor and marching into Sam's office. To my surprise, I saw a swarthy fellow—actually, he looked quite young; maybe in his teens—seated in the chair beside Sam's. The boy didn't look happy. His appearance was unprepossessing. He'd oiled his hair, which evidently wanted to curl, until it shone and sat on his head like a helmet. He looked, in fact, rather like young men I'd seen in photos of modern-day criminals as they attempted to appear normal. I hope he hadn't been arrested for doing anything stupid. Oddly enough, he resembled Sam to a slight degree.

"Good morning, Detective Rotondo," said I, knowing I should address him thus in his place of work.

"Not so far," he said.

I eyed the young man seated next to him. To my astonishment, Sam gave him a clout upside the head, and the young man said, "Hey!"

"Stand up, Frank," growled Sam. "You're in the presence of a lady."

Frank, whoever he was, glowered at Sam and stood. Looking sulky, he nodded at me. I smiled and nodded back, mainly because I didn't know what else to do.

"Mrs. Majesty"—Sam was being formal, too—"this is Frank. Frank Pagano. Frank, Mrs. Majesty is my fiancée."

Frank seemed startled to hear this news.

"How do you do, Frank?" I asked politely. Because I really did try to act like a lady—most of the time—I held out my hand for Frank to shake. "It's nice to meet you."

After looking at my hand as if he'd never seen one before, Frank shook it. His grip was feeble. "Pleased to meetcha," said he in an extreme back-east accent.

"Frank is my nephew," said Sam as if he didn't want to admit it.

Surprised, I nevertheless rose to the occasion. "Oh! How nice!" I said. "My family and I are quite fond of your uncle. Welcome to Pasadena, Frank."

Frank glanced at his uncle, who was scowling blackly at him, then said, "Thank you, ma'am." He didn't sound as if he meant it. After a sharp gesture from his uncle, Frank sat again.

"Um, Detective Rotondo, you left your hat at our house last night and I brought it to you." I placed said hat on his desk, which was cluttered with papers.

"Thank you." He didn't sound as if he meant it, either.

"Um, will you be bringing your nephew to dinner tonight, Detective Rotondo? My aunt is fixing a hearty beef stew with biscuits. With a peach pie for dessert, made with peaches we preserved earlier in the year." It's odd, but I never forget food, whether it's been eaten or not. Heck, I could probably tell you what I ate on the last Saturday of 1923.

"What's beef stew?" asked Frank in an undertone. "It ain't Italian, is it?"

Another clout and another "Hey" from Frank.

"The word is 'isn't,' not 'ain't.' And it's past time you learned the whole world isn't Italian, Francis Pagano," said Sam in as stern a voice as I'd ever heard him use on anyone other than me. Sam glanced up at me. "I don't know that I can make it tonight. My schedule has been...interrupted." He gave his nephew another ferocious glower.

"Mr. Pagano will be welcome, too. I'm sure we'll all be happy to meet one of your relations."

"I doubt that," muttered Sam.

Frank said, "Jeez."

"Well, think about it. Vi adores feeding people, and she loves meeting new people. New to her, I mean."

"Huh. Not sure anyone is going to enjoy meeting this guy."

"Hey," said Frank.

"Be quiet," Sam ordered. "I'll call you. Is that all right, Mrs. Majesty?"

"Yes. Thank you." I smiled at Frank, who looked at me blankly. "I hope you can make it to dinner, Mr. Pagano."

"Uh...Thanks."

"See you tonight, I hope," I said to Sam and turned to walk to the door.

As I reached the door, I heard Frank whisper, "But Uncle Sammy, she ain't Italian."

I heard another clout and another "Hey," and then I heard Sam say, "It's Detective Rotondo to you, you sorry hoodlum. And again, the whole world isn't Italian. Thank God."

I left on that note, wondering why Frank was there and why Sam seemed so peeved about it. On the other hand, Sam was grouchy most of the time these days, what with his lame leg and all. Frank's sudden presence in Pasadena was interesting, at all odds.

I drove home after that and was greeted by an ecstatic Spike. My father wasn't there, so I figured he was out and about, chatting with one of his thousand or so friends. My father is an extremely sociable individual, and he had friends all over town.

I made myself a roasted-pork sandwich, cut an apple into quarters, and had myself a lovely, lonely lunch. Spike wanted to join me, but I couldn't risk him becoming fat because excess weight is bad for dachshunds. Well, I suppose it's bad for anyone, but it's especially bad for dachshunds because of their long backs and short legs. They truly need another pair of legs in the middles of their torsos, although they would look extremely odd. It would help them carry those long backs, though.

I glanced down at my beloved pooch. "Sorry, Spike. I'll give you a bite after I finish eating."

Pa came home as I was chomping the last of my apple.

We smiled at each other. "Been out gallivanting with your friends, Pa?"

"You betcha. Went down to Hull's Motor Works and talked with Herb and Wilson. We mainly talked politics. Herb likes Coolidge and Wilson is for Davis."

Charmed, I said, "Oh, my! I'll be able to vote this year, won't I? I've never voted in an election before. Which one do you prefer, Pa?"

"I don't like any politicians as a rule. I'll probably vote for Coolidge, because he's a Republican. Republicans used to be reformers, but I don't know if they still are. Harding turned out to be an out-and-out crook. But remember Theodore Roosevelt? He cleaned up New York City some—according to Sam, nobody can ever clean up New York City entirely—and established rules for food processing companies so they can't poison us as easily as they used to be able to do."

Pa wasn't a cynical sort, but he generally knew what was going on in the realm of United States politics. And he was right about Roosevelt who was, so far in my relatively short life, my favorite president. He was also a Republican, although so had been Harding, and he, as Pa just said, had turned out to be as crooked as a dog's hind leg. I'd heard Sam grumble about "Tammany Hall," whatever that was, as running things in New York and knew he disapproved of whatever Tammany Hall was. All I knew was that it was a Democratic institution. The Democratic Party, I mean, not the philosophy of a democratic society. According to Sam, all Tammany Hall cared about was graft and getting rich, which sounded a lot like the rest of the world in its seamier moments.

"Want a sandwich, Pa?" I asked, not caring to discuss politics, which I found a frustrating topic, mostly because people on both sides seemed so stuck in their own opinions, no one could persuade them out of whatever they wanted to believe in. Sort of like religion, if you know what I mean. I don't mean to be sacrilegious, but if you think about it, I believe you'll think so, too. And I was excited about being able to vote for the first time in my life.

"No, thanks. I had some soup and a sandwich at Hull's. Herb's wife brought them."

"Was it as good as one of Vi's pork sandwiches?"

"Nothing is as good as anything your aunt cooks," said Pa.

We all loved and admired Vi. What's more, as I've already mentioned, since neither Ma nor I could cook worth pig slop—if you'll pardon the crudity—we'd probably all have died of ptomaine poisoning by this time if not for her.

"All right. I'm going to take Spike for a walk and then I think I'll read for a bit. Choir practice is tonight, so maybe I'll rest for a while, too. Vi's serving beef stew and biscuits for dinner. With a peach pie for dessert."

"Yum," said Pa.

"Want to go with Spike and me?"

"Sure."

I tossed a little piece of roasted pork to my hound. Spike appreciated it greatly. He appreciated even more when, after washing up my few lunch dishes, I got the leash from the service porch hook and showed it to him.

Pa, Spike and I walked around the neighborhood. Leaves were beginning to fall in places, although we in sunny Pasadena didn't get real fall weather like folks got back east. Both of my parents and Vi came from Massachusetts, where, I understand, the fall leaves are gorgeous. But I didn't mind. I adored my city, and what we lacked in fall colors, we more than made up for on New Year's Day, when we celebrated every new year with a parade featuring lots of floats covered with flowers. Our relations in Massachusetts envied us our weather. Roses in January? Unheard of in other places.

I love Pasadena.

TEN

When we returned home, the stupid telephone was ringing. I sighed, handed Pa Spike's leash, and went into the kitchen to answer the instrument.

"Gumm-Majesty residence. Mrs. Majesty speaking."

"You called?"

"Harold! I thought you weren't coming home until tomorrow. I'm so glad to hear from you."

"That sounds ominous. I was coming home tomorrow, but my mother called, and I get to go with her to interview criminal attorneys to take my idiot sister's case tomorrow, lucky me."

"Yes. I was there when poor Mr. Pearlman was trying to explain to your mother why he couldn't represent Stacy."

Harold sighed. "Mother will never understand how the world works. She doesn't want to. It's deliberate ignorance, if you ask me."

"You may well be right, but I don't really blame her a whole lot. After all, she's never had to do anything for herself."

"No. She's always had other people to take care of things for her."

"She had to put up with your father for quite a few years, don't forget."

"How could I ever forget that skunk?"

Harold and Stacy's father was Mr. Eustace Kincaid who, as I believe I've mentioned earlier, was at present living at the San Quentin Penitentiary. A very bad man, Mr. Kincaid. I'm surprised Harold turned out so well. On the other hand, Stacy more than made up for Harold in the horridness department.

"So what is it you want me to do now? If you expect me to hide another nearly beaten-to-death woman, I won't do it."

"No, it's nothing that drastic. In fact, you'll probably enjoy it."

"Huh," said Harold, sounding rather like Sam only an octave higher.

"All I'm hoping you can do is organize a Halloween house-warming party for Gladys and Homer Fellowes."

"Who are they?"

"Don't you remember Gladys? She was the studious person who used to be secretary to that awful Mrs. Winkworth."

"Oh, yes. The one with the thick cheaters. I thought she was in love with Monty Mountjoy."

"She used to be. She transferred her allegiance to Dr. Homer Fellowes, the man who invented the thing they used on that motion picture."

"Oh, yeah. I remember him. His specs were even thicker than hers. Sounds like a match made in heaven." He was being snide.

"They're both nice people, although neither one of them has a lot of imagination. Or a sense of humor, unless Gladys is hiding hers somewhere."

"And why do I want to organize this party? That is to say, why do you want me to?"

"Because I'm lousy at planning parties."

"And?"

"And Gladys aims to hire me to put on my Gypsy act and read cards and the crystal ball and such for her guests."

A spate of silence ensued. I began to get nervous.

"Very well, Daisy Gumm Majesty. What's the real reason you want me to do this? Don't fib to me. I can always tell, you know."

Harold knew me too darned well.

"Oh, all right." After checking that none of our party-line neighbors were listening in—they weren't—I explained to him about Miss Carleton's murder and how Gladys didn't want her husband's name or that of Cal Tech or that of their precious "project" splattered all over the front pages of the newspapers.

"Hmm. And you expect to spot the crook? I doubt your tame detective will appreciate your snoopery."

"He'll hate it. But I'll make him go with me, and then he can't complain. Heck, I'll just explain to him that all the suspects will be gathered together in one place, and he'll probably love it."

Another spate of silence.

"You don't believe that for a minute, do you?"

I heaved a sigh. "No, I don't. But he really can't accuse me of prying into his case. For all he'll know, the party is truly a house-warming for Gladys and Dr. Fellowes. That's what I'll tell him, at any rate."

Yet another moment of silence. Harold finally said, "He won't believe you."

"You're probably right, but Gladys actually asked me to pry into the case because she fears the police will blacken her husband's name and ruin the precious project he's working on."

"Huh. What project is that?"

"Oh, *I* don't know. Something about a geological survey of the San Gabriel mountains."

"Sounds fascinating."

"Yes, I know. I think so, too."

We were both being sarcastic.

"When does she want to plan this so-called house-warming party?"

"As soon as possible. The sooner, the better."

"Well, Halloween is Friday three weeks from tomorrow. I suppose I could plan the party for that date. Or maybe the week before. A Friday or Saturday would probably work best for folks who have to work."

"Sounds wonderful. I'll ask Gladys which date she'd prefer. And if the police catch the crook before then, you won't have to do a thing."

"And what do you suppose the chances of that are?"

"Slim to none."

"That's what I figured. All right. I'll have to meet your friend. Since I have to visit lawyers with Mother tomorrow, how about we get together on Saturday? Perhaps you can take me to your friend's house, and I can see its layout and decide what to do."

"Sounds perfect to me. Thank you, Harold. You're a true friend."

"Yes. I know." And he hung up.

I got the feeling he wasn't altogether pleased with me. I didn't fault him for that. I'd involved him in a horrible problem a few months prior. But he'd come through like a champ and, acting together, Flossie, Harold, Del and I had actually probably saved a woman's life. Of course, Sam had been shot in the thigh during the denouement of that little episode, but that was only because he'd been sneaky and followed me one day. Then again, if he hadn't followed me, Flossie and I would probably be dead, so I guess it had worked out fairly well except for the bullet hole in Sam's thigh.

Poor Sam.

As soon as I'd hung up after speaking with Harold, the blasted 'phone rang again. I answered with my usual recitation, but was interrupted mid-speech.

"I know who you are," grumbled Sam.

"Oh, hello, Sam! Good to hear from you. How's your nephew?"

"He's a pain in the neck. He ran away from home. My sister was scared to death for him, but I put through a trunk call to her, so at least she knows where the little son of a...gun is."

"It doesn't sound to me as if you're a particularly loving uncle. What's he done wrong? I mean, I know it was wrong of him to run away, but it sounds as if you dislike him for more than that."

"He's a damned little hooligan! He worked for a numbers runner in New York, and he's afraid they're out to get him."

"Good heavens. I didn't know he was in trouble with the law. Why does he think the numbers runner is after him?"

"Because he skimmed off some of the profits, the idiot. Anybody but he would know you don't mess with one of those gangsters. It's one of the more stupid things a person can do in New York City."

"Mercy sakes."

"He's also wanted for questioning by the N.Y.P.D. because the stupid kid got into a fight with some Irish kids. They form gangs, you know. The Irish gang and the Italian gang hate each other."

"I'm so sorry. I didn't realize he was in trouble with the law."

"He's in trouble with the law, all right, in New York City *and* Pasadena, the fool. That would be me in Pasadena, by the way. Anyway, I'd probably better not come to your house with the little thug. He isn't fit to be around decent people."

"Nonsense," I said firmly. "Perhaps if he sees how decent people act, he'll learn the error of his ways."

"Cripes. My parents and my sister and her husband are all good people, and they haven't influenced Frank any. He's a punk."

"You sound as if perhaps you're being a little hard on the boy. Maybe he just needs to learn that the whole world doesn't exist in New York City."

"And that the whole world isn't Italian."

I grinned. "Yes. He seemed a trifle shocked that you should be marrying a non-Italian."

Sam actually laughed a bit. "Yeah. Good thing. It's past time he learned how the world works."

"Oddly enough, Harold and I were discussing the same thing regarding his mother."

"Huh. At least she has money. This kid doesn't even have a brain."

"Well, please bring him along anyway. I'll set an extra place for him, and he'll begin learning how people outside New York behave."

"I doubt it, but if you say so. Keep an eye on him, though. He's apt to steal the silver."

"I don't think we have any silver."

"Won't matter. He'll probably steal something just for the hell of it."

"He can't be all bad. Can he?"

"I don't know. Is Stacy Kincaid all bad?"

"Good Lord, he can't be as bad as Stacy."

"Huh," said Sam, and he hung up the receiver on his end of the wire.

"What's going on?" asked Pa. He'd hung Spike's leash on it hook in the service porch and was looking at me quizzically.

"Sam's bringing his nephew to dinner tonight."

"Oh, I didn't know his nephew was visiting. He didn't say anything about a nephew."

"He didn't know about the visit until the kid showed up. He evidently ran away from home."

Pa's face assumed an expression of surprise. "My goodness."

"Evidently Sam has serious doubts about his nephew's goodness. His name is Frank Pagano, by the way. The nephew, I mean. One of Sam's sisters' children. I think he has three or four sisters."

"Poor guy. No brothers?"

"Nope. Only sisters. He's not awfully fond of this nephew. Says he's a junior hoodlum." I didn't think Pa needed to know that Sam hadn't used the modifier. Let him meet Frank with an open mind. Semi-open, anyway. I guess I'd already spilled a few of the beans in Frank Pagano's regard.

And darned if the telephone didn't ring *again*. I gave it a malevolent glare. "Good Lord, what's going on with the telephone today?"

"I don't know," said Pa with a grin. "But it's undoubtedly for you."

"Undoubtedly." I lifted the receiver, and this time the caller allowed me to render my entire opening speech.

"Daisy? This is Regina," came a soft voice on the other end of the wire.

"Regina! How lovely to hear from you!" To the best of my recollection, Miss Petrie had never telephoned me before.

"Thank you. Oh, but Daisy, I'm hoping you can…Well, I'm hoping you will be able to help me. A bit. A little bit. Just perhaps give me a couple of hints or tips or something."

"Oh." Interesting. "About what?"

"Um…Well, Mr. Browning has asked me to join him for luncheon next Tuesday, and…Oh, Daisy, I don't know what to *do*!"

She sounded desperate. "What do you mean? Just be yourself. He clearly appreciates you."

"But I'm so dowdy, Daisy. And you always look so perfect. I thought perhaps you might help me to…I don't know. Freshen my appearance. Or something."

Oh, boy! Precisely what I'd been longing to do! "I'll be more than happy to assist you, Regina. In fact, I do believe I have a few good suggestions for you." I mentally rubbed my hands together in glee. "In fact, why don't you join us for dinner…tomorrow. Tonight I have to go to choir practice, but if you can come tomorrow evening, we can go to my room and I can give you a few suggestions. I think it will be loads of fun!"

A moment of silence. There was a lot of silent moments going around that day. "Do you really think so?"

"I really do. I'll just tell my family you'll be joining us for dinner tomorrow night, and then we can have a jolly old time."

"Thank you, Daisy. I…I really don't know how to thank you."

"Nonsense. All you need is a little help here and there."

"Do you really think so? I've always been so plain and…dull."

"Nonsense! You're far from plain, and you're definitely not dull. Mr. Browning wouldn't have asked you to dine with him if he didn't admire you."

"Well…Maybe." I could tell she didn't believe me.

"Please trust me about this. I know what I'm talking about. I've known Robert Browning for years. He's a fine man."

Unless, of course, he'd murdered Mary Carleton. But no. Robert couldn't have done such a dastardly thing.

I hoped.

"Are you sure your family won't mind?"

"Of course not! They love having people over for dinner, and I've already told you that my Aunt Vi is the best cook in the known universe."

After a shaky laugh, Regina said, "Yes. I know you've told me that several times."

"Well, then, come to dinner! We dine at six p.m. Not a fashionable hour, I know, but we've never made any claims to being fancy people."

"We always dined at six, too, my mother and me."

"Wonderful. We'll see you then. Of course, you know our address because we're on file at the library."

"Yes. I'll be there a little early."

"I'm really looking forward to this!" I told her honestly. I'm sure my excitement could be heard in my voice.

"Thank you."

"Thank *you*."

"For what?"

"For giving me a chance to perk you up."

"Oh. You mean you don't mind?"

"Mind? Good heavens, Regina, I've wanted to have at you for years now." That didn't sound quite right.

Nevertheless, Regina didn't seem to mind. She even laughed again. "Well, I give you permission to do anything you might have in mind to 'perk' me up, as you term it."

"It will be fun," I told her again, meaning it.

"Very well. See you tomorrow evening." She hesitated. "Um, you haven't heard anything about Miss Carleton's case, have you?"

"Not a thing, unfortunately."

"I didn't think so. Well, thank you, Daisy, and I'll see you tomorrow. Thank you again."

"You're more than welcome." I hung up the receiver grinning, I'm sure, from ear to ear.

"What's up?" asked Pa, looking at me curiously.

"We're not only having a guest tonight, but we'll have one tomorrow evening, too. Miss Petrie, from the library, will be joining us tomorrow for dinner."

"My goodness. I'll be happy to meet her at last. She's been a great source of books for the family for a long time now."

"Indeed she has been. And before dinner I'm going to have at her."

"I beg your pardon?" Pa looked startled.

"Nothing evil, I assure you. But Robert Browning has asked her to take lunch with him on Tuesday. She's terribly worried about the impression she'll make, and I'm going to spiff her up, by gum. So to speak." Honestly, the last name Gumm, while intensely honorable, could be a sore trial sometimes.

"Oh," said Pa. "Does she know about this plan of yours?"

"She's the one who asked me to help her," I told him merrily.

"Well," said Pa.

I couldn't have said it better myself.

ELEVEN

Sam and his nephew showed up at our home at approximately five forty-five that evening. Spike and I met them at the door.

"Good evening, gentlemen," I said, smiling at the two of them. Frank still seemed rather sullen. I had a feeling Sam had a lot to do with his glum mood.

"Good evening," said Sam. "Frank, you've already met Mrs. Majesty." He glanced down at Spike, who was dutifully sitting and staying and sweeping the floor with his tail. Spike loved meeting new people, but he was a brilliantly obedient hound.

"It's nice to see you again, Frank. This is my dog, Spike." I gestured at Spike and released him from his enforced obedience.

Gazing down in astonishment, Frank said, "That thing's a *dog?*"

Sam cuffed his nephew in the accustomed manner and said, "Mind your manners, you lout. That, Frank, is a special, fancy dog. A dachshund. That's German for...What was it again, Daisy?"

"Badger hound," I said. "They were bred to go into badger holes and drag the beasts out. I guess badgers can be pests. They're also tough creatures and quite vicious."

"It's a *German* dog?" Frank sounded as if he disapproved, the U.S. and Germany having not long since been at war with each other.

Truth to tell, I wasn't fond of anything German, either, although I tried not to allow my husband's misery and death from the hands of the foul German gas to color my interactions with anyone. With limited success, I fear.

"No," I said sternly. "Spike was born and bred right here in Pasadena, California. Well, he was born in Altadena, but he's as American as you and I."

"Oh. I've never seen a dog shaped like that before."

"Many people haven't," I told Frank, whom I was beginning to dislike a bit. Perhaps Sam was right about his nephew. "But hang up your coats and hats and come in. I'll introduce you to the rest of the family."

After the two fellows had hung up their hats and coats, Frank looked around uncertainly. Sam clamped a hand on his shoulder and propelled the reluctant adolescent through the living room and in to the dining room. My family stood around, adjusting place settings and so forth. Delicious aromas issued from the kitchen. Vi poked her head out to smile at Sam and Frank.

"Pa, Ma and Aunt Vi, this is Sam Rotondo's nephew from New York City, Frank Pagano."

Pa, who'd never met a stranger, approached the young man, thrust out his hand and said, "Pleasure to meet you, Frank."

"Yeah," said Frank, taking my father's hand as if he weren't accustomed to shaking hands with people. Perhaps he wasn't. He hadn't been sure about shaking my hand, either.

"How nice that you're visiting your uncle," said Ma, also smiling at him and holding out her hand.

Frank, after sending a glance at Sam as if pleading for assistance, said, "Yeah. Thanks." He shook Ma's hand as iffily as he'd shaken Pa's.

"My Aunt Vi is a marvelous cook, Frank. I'm sure you'll love your dinner tonight," I told him.

Frank said, "Uh..."

"Mrs. Majesty is correct, Frank," said Sam. "Mrs. Gumm is a fantastic cook."

"It sure smells different in here," said Frank.

Sam rolled his eyes. He usually only did that to me. "Mind your manners, you dolt. The Gumms and Majestys aren't Italian. It's past time you expanded your horizons."

On a side note, I'd once told my beloved Billy that I wanted to broaden my horizons. He'd glanced significantly at my hips and told me my horizons were broad enough. That was in the good old days, right after we were married, and I was, as I remain, too curvy for modern fashions. But that has nothing to do with the current narrative. By the way, Billy had been joking; he liked my horizons just fine.

"Um…Yeah. I guess so."

Frank earned another clout for his efforts and said, "Hey."

"You're a guest here, Frank. Act like it," ordered Sam.

"Yes, sir," said Frank, sounding as surly as he looked.

Not quite knowing what to do, I decided to take charge. "Everyone, please sit. I'll help Vi get the food on the table. I have to go to choir practice tonight, so I kind of need to hurry."

"You sing in a choir?" asked Frank.

"Yes, indeed. I'm an alto. Your uncle has a beautiful bass voice."

Looking at Sam with perplexity, Frank said, "I didn't know you could sing."

"Not many people do. Sit here." Sam pointed to a chair next to his. Frank sat.

So I carried various viands to the table, and finally Aunt Vi joined us. I introduced her more formally to Frank Pagano, and she nodded, pleased to have a guest at her table. Vi loved to feed people. Frank nodded and looked at her as if expecting another hand to shake. Vi, however, carried a bowl of stew and had no hands to spare.

After all the food had been set on the table, I said, "Pa will say grace," mainly so Frank would know he should bow his head. He appeared a trifle confused for a second, but when he saw Sam's hand reaching for his head, he got the point and bowed said appendage. If a head can be called an appendage.

As soon as Pa said, "Amen," Frank crossed himself and seemed surprised no one else at the table did the same. He eyed his uncle in some befuddlement.

"Not only is the whole world not Italian," Sam said sarcastically, "but it's not all Roman Catholic."

Frank said, "Oh." He seemed a trifle shocked. Sam was right: the kid really needed to widen his experiences and his circle of friends.

The stew was marvelous, as usual, as were Vi's light-as-air biscuits. I ate like a pig. Frank didn't. He carefully examined his first spoonful of stew and then tentatively brought it to his mouth. After chewing for a second or two, his expression lightened, and he ate the rest of his dinner without further doubts.

Deciding to begin a neutral conversation—I didn't want the whole family to know Sam disliked his nephew—I said, "Gladys Fellowes is holding a Halloween house-warming party, Sam. Want to go with me?"

"Who?"

"Gladys! I told you she invited me to her home the other day."

"Oh, yeah. I remember. When is the party?"

Reasonable question, but I didn't know the answer yet. "Not sure. Harold's going to plan the shindig. He and I are meeting on Saturday to arrange the details. I'll take him up to Gladys's house then."

Sam squinted across the table at me. "This doesn't have anything to do with what happened at the library yesterday, does it?"

I gave him my most innocent, wide-eyed stare. "I doubt it, although I'm sure all the suspects will be at the party. In fact, the party will give you a chance to look over the choices and take your pick."

"That's not how it works," growled Sam. "But I'll go with you if I can. I don't dare let you go by yourself."

"How come?" asked Frank. Except for that one initial "Oh," those were the first words he'd spoken since he'd sat at the table.

"I'll tell you later," said Sam. "This is delicious as usual, Vi."

"Thank you, Sam."

"Oh! And I almost forgot to tell you that we'll have another guest for dinner tomorrow night. Miss Petrie from the library will be joining us."

Sam gave me another suspicious squint. "And why, pray tell, is that?"

"I asked her to come. She telephoned me today and asked if I could help her with her makeup and wardrobe." Not precisely, but it would do. "Robert Browning has invited her to go to luncheon with him on Tuesday, and Regina is nervous. I don't think she's had much to do with men. In the romantic sense, I mean."

Yet another squint, this one downright accusative. "You're not getting involved with the Carleton case, Daisy. That *is* clear to you, isn't it?"

If I hadn't been at the dinner table, I'd have thrown my arms up in disgust. "Of course, it's clear to me. I have no intention of involving myself with the case."

"Yet your librarian friend is taking lunch with the chief suspect, and you aim to help her do it."

"Robert didn't kill Miss Carleton, Sam."

"Huh."

"Who got knocked off?" asked Frank, for the first time since he'd arrival at our house showing interest in something.

"The word is 'killed,' Frank, and the dead woman was a librarian."

"Yes," said I. "She used to work at the Pasadena Public Library, but at the time of her death, she worked at the California Institute of Technology."

"Oh," said Frank. I had a feeling he'd have liked to ask more questions, but didn't dare, his uncle's cuffing hand being so close to him and all.

The conversation became general after that. Vi was pleased she'd have another person to feed on the morrow.

When I removed the dinner plates, Vi went to the kitchen and brought out a masterpiece of her bakery art. The pie looked absolutely marvelous, and it tasted like heaven. Vi had artistically spread the top of the peach pie with whipped cream, and sprinkled toasted almond slices on top of that. It was as close to absolute perfection as a pie could get.

When all the plates were empty, I started cleaning everything off the table. Glancing at Frank, I decided to take a chance. "Frank, would you please help me wash and put away the dishes? I have to rush, because I need to get to choir practice."

Giving me a look of what I judged to be total disbelief, Frank pointed at his chest and said, "Me?"

"Oh, Daisy, the young man's a guest," said Ma. "He shouldn't have to wash up the dishes."

"Nonsense," said Sam gruffly. "It's about time he started doing something useful with himself."

"Well..." Ma seemed uncertain.

"Frank, help Mrs. Majesty," commanded Sam. "Now."

So Frank rose from the table, looking as if he'd never had to wash a dish in his life, and stared at me as if I were a monster. *Too bad, you little punk*, I silently told the boy.

Sam helped clear the table.

"You shouldn't be doing that, Sam," I told him. "Your leg isn't up to it."

"Bother my leg," said Sam sourly. "I don't trust this kid to do anything without me overseeing him. He's not used to fending for himself or helping clean stuff."

"Hey," said Frank.

Eyeing Frank curiously, I asked, "Doesn't your mother have you help do chores around the house?"

Before he could answer, Sam said, "Italian women wait on their men, even their worthless sons, like little gods. Frank's never done a worthwhile thing in his life."

"Hey," said Frank.

"Oh," said I.

I got the wash tub from beneath the sink and filled it with warm water and soap. "Why don't you wash, Frank? Sam and I will dry the dishes, and I'll put them away because I know where everything goes."

Looking at his uncle in patent disbelief, Frank said, "Uh, how do I wash them?"

I handed him a dishrag. "With that. Then you rinse them off and put them on the clean counter in front of me." I pointed to the surface of the counter then grabbed one dish towel for Sam and another for me.

"Be careful," warned Sam. "And work fast. I want to go to choir practice with Mrs. Majesty."

"You do?" asked Frank incredulously.

"You do? How wonderful! Thanks, Sam. I hope you'll enjoy it. We're working our way through October and up to All Saints' Day, Armistice Day and then Thanksgiving."

"Great. I'm sure we'll enjoy ourselves. Hurry up, Frank," said Sam.

Frank, after rolling up his shirtsleeves, plucked one dish at a time from the stack beside him and began scrubbing them. He did a fair job, oddly enough. Then again, his uncle was scrutinizing his every move with an eagle eye or two.

After the last dish had been dried and put away, Frank started in on the pots and pans, although not without having been told to do so by his uncle.

"I'll let the two of you finish up here," I said. "I need to get ready for choir practice."

"We'll be happy to," said Sam.

Frank grunted, not at all happy to do so if I were to guess.

Nevertheless, when I returned to the kitchen from my room, which was directly off it, the pots and pans had been scrubbed until shiny, dried, and placed neatly on the top of the stove. "Thanks," I told the two males.

"You're welcome," said Sam.

Frank said nothing until he noticed Sam lift his hand, then he said, "You're welcome," in a hurry.

After bidding Ma, Pa and Spike a fond farewell—Vi had already gone to her rooms upstairs—the men stopped at the coat rack and each donned his hat and coat. Then Sam, Frank and I walked out to Sam's big black Hudson.

"What do you do at home, Frank?" I asked by way of conversation.

"Nothin'," said Frank.

"Do you go to school?"

"Naw. I finished school."

"I see. And do you work anywhere?"

"He's supposed to work in his Uncle Salvatore's restaurant in the Bronx," said Sam, sounding severe.

"I *do* work there," said Frank indignantly.

"Not so far as I can see," muttered Sam.

"What do you do for your uncle at his restaurant?" I asked in an attempt to forestall further unpleasantness. Sam's father owned a jewelry store in New York City somewhere. I glanced lovingly at the engagement he'd designed for Sam and me. Not that I could see much in the dark. An Italian restaurant sounded more like an Italian family's milieu to me than a jewelry store, but I'm sure that's only cultural conditioning and from reading articles in the newspapers and periodicals.

"Waited tables," said Frank, still surly unless I missed my guess.

"Oh!" I said, having just had an idea. I doubted even then that it was a brilliant one, but time would tell. "Perhaps you can help serve at the party your uncle and I will be attending. It will be a combination Halloween and house-warming party being hosted by a couple of my friends."

"Uh..." said Frank.

"He'd be happy to do that," said Sam.

I heard Frank heave an unhappy sigh. Too bad. If the boy was in trouble at home and had been involved in unsavory practices, a little education in how to behave like a proper citizen wouldn't hurt him any.

Since the First Methodist-Episcopal Church we attended was on the corner of Colorado and Marengo, we arrived at our destination before I could question Frank more. Pity, that, but I'd probably see him later. Unless Sam managed to ship him back to New York City any time soon.

TWELVE

T he first person I saw after I'd entered the choir room and gestured for Sam and Frank to sit in the front row of the sanctuary was my friend, Lucille Spinks Zollinger, a young woman approximately my age who had married an older gentleman some months earlier. Lucy and I were assigned to sing duets together quite often by our choir director, Mr. Floy Hostetter. He said he liked the way our voices blended. Lucy, needless to say, was a soprano to my alto. She was also a very nice person. I'd helped her with the gowns for her wedding, and I don't think she's ever stopped thanking me. Heck, I loved to sew, so making dresses for her bridesmaids and altering her mother's old wedding gown to fit Lucy had only been fun for me.

"Daisy, who is that with your fiancée?" Lucy asked me avidly, squinting into the sanctuary. She was supposed to wear eyeglasses, but often didn't, probably because she thought they failed to flatter her. As she was kind of long, skinny and rabbity, I didn't think it mattered. I'm not being mean; she could look nice, but Lucy would never be a beauty. Nor would I be, for that matter. "He looks like a younger version of Detective Rotondo." She giggled. Lucy giggled frequently, probably because she was so happy to be married. Young men were thin on the ground in those days, so many of them having been lost in the Great War and the 'flu pandemic.

"That's his nephew, Francis Pagano."

"Another Italian?" Lucy asked.

"That's a silly question, Lucy Zollinger," I teased her. "Of course, he's an Italian!"

"Oh, of course. That was a silly question. But, oh, Daisy, did you hear about the murder of that poor young woman in the library?"

"Indeed. Not only have I heard about it, but Detective Rotondo and I were there when it happened."

"Good heavens! Do you mean to say a murder took place right in front of the eyes of Detective Rotondo and you?"

"Not really. The detective and I were speaking to Miss Petrie, a librarian friend of mine, when the murder occurred. Sam wasn't there in his official capacity."

"Still. That was bold, killing a woman in front of a policeman," said Lucy, as if she disapproved of people being murdered in the near presence of a police officer. I did, too, but I objected to murder whenever and wherever it happened.

"It didn't happen in front of us. We were speaking to Miss Petrie. The woman was murdered in the biography section, and we couldn't see her from where we sat."

"Oh," said Lucy, as if she'd have to ponder that truth in order to evaluate my culpability in the murder and, of course, that of Sam.

"She was stabbed, Lucy. Nobody heard a single thing until another woman came across the body and screamed."

"Oh." Lucy shuddered delicately. "How awful."

"Yes," I said. "It was." I probably would have shuddered, too, but we were interrupted at that point.

"Mrs. Majesty and Mrs. Zollinger, will you please come here for a moment?"

Lucy and I both jumped a trifle. Mr. Hostetter didn't approve of his choir members chatting together, although choir practice hadn't started yet so if he aimed to berate us, I thought he was being premature.

But that's not what he wanted. He wanted us to sing another duet.

Lucy and I glanced at each other and both smiled broadly. "We'd love to," said I. Lucy nodded enthusiastically.

"Wonderful. The nephew of the Reverend Mr. Smith just graduated from the United States Naval Academy, and I'd like you two to sing 'Eternal Father, Strong to Save,' on November second. He and his mother and father—his father is Mr. Smith's brother—will be visiting that week. The music's not in our hymnal, so I had the church secretary run off a few mimeographed copies. Be careful, ladies, because the blue ink smears easily."

Lucy and I took our mimeographed music sheets, and I pondered the wonders of modern technology for a second. Then I thought of something pertinent.

"What about 'For All the Saints?'" I asked. "That's what we usually sing in celebration of All Saints' Day that Sunday."

"'For All the Saints' will be our anthem that day. 'Eternal Father' will be a special song in honor of the young Mr. Smith's graduation."

"That sounds nice," I said. "Very nice."

"I thought so, too," said Mr. Hostetter, smiling smugly. "I'm sure you two already know the hymn, although we don't sing it often, but you can sing a verse or two with Mrs. Fleming after choir practice is over, if you don't mind giving us about ten minutes extra tonight."

"Fine with me," I said.

Lucy agreed. "Albert won't mind waiting for a little while when he comes to pick me up."

"Excellent." Mr. Hostetter turned from us, clapped his hands to bring the choir to attention and said, "Let us begin, ladies and gentlemen."

So we each took our seats. Even though Lucy sang soprano and I sang alto, we sat together since we so often sang duets. It was kind of hard to refrain from chatting, but we both did our best.

"As you know, this coming Sunday, our anthem will be 'Spirit of God, Descend upon Our Hearts.' We probably should go over that first, and then we can practice next Sunday's anthem. Mrs. Majesty and Mrs. Zollinger will be singing a duet on November second, and they'll go over that with Mrs. Fleming after we finish practice tonight. Some of Mr. Smith's family from out of state will be visiting that day, and the two ladies will sing 'Eternal Father, Strong to Save,' in honor of the younger Mr. Smith's graduation from the naval academy."

"What about 'For All the Saints?'" asked Mr. George Finster, one of our better basses.

"We'll sing that as our anthem. The navy hymn is in honor of Mr. Smith's graduation."

"Oh. That's nice," said Mr. Finster, satisfied.

I glanced out into the sanctuary to see Frank and Sam sitting there, Sam, arms crossed over his chest, subtly smiling; Frank slouching, frowning, oily, and looking as if he felt uncomfortable. I guess he was accustomed to attending his Catholic Church at home and didn't understand us Methodists. Too bad. As for Sam, he wasn't much of a church-goer as a rule, but he'd been attending Methodist services with us since even before he and I announced our engagement. His late wife, Margaret, had defied Italian tradition and attended the West Side Congregational-Unitarian Church on Orange Grove. Sam had attended with her, but I knew—because he'd told me often enough—that he didn't really give a rap about religion. I probably should have found that shocking, but I figured he'd seen enough in his lifetime to decide for himself what he wanted to believe.

"Then we'll practice next Sunday's anthem, which will be"—Mr. Hostetter fumbled through a bunch of papers on his music stand—"Ah, yes. Here it is. 'Forth in Thy Name, O Lord,' by Charles Wesley."

A smattering of applause came from the choir. We all enjoyed the hymns written by Mr. Wesley, the founder (with his brother John, who I believe began the movement) of Methodism. I glanced again into the sanctuary and saw we'd managed to scandalize Frank. Interesting. He attempted to appear as if nothing in the world could touch him, but evidently he wasn't as worldly as he wanted people to think he was. Heh, heh, heh.

We did a good job of 'Spirit of God,' and we did an even better job of 'Forth in Thy Name.' Our choir was large and we sounded excellent, at least from where I sat.

"Very good. Let me read the hymn numbers for the upcoming Sunday's service. You may write them down or put bookmarks in your hymnals."

So he read off the hymn numbers, and I put little ribbons at the sites. I had lots and lots of ribbons, as you can well imagine. Actually, some of them weren't really ribbons, but fabric bookmarks I'd made out of scraps. I'd given Lucy a bunch of them, too, and she also marked her hymnal with them. Every now and then, when I thought about how relatively useless I was on this planet, I recalled some of my good deeds —there had been a few—and managed to pick myself up from the depths.

By that time, the clock on the church wall was inching toward eight thirty-five. Choir practice began at seven sharp, and generally lasted until eight-thirty or thereabouts. Mr. Hostetter ran a tight ship. I noticed Lucy's husband, Albert Zollinger, walk into the church. He and Lucy exchanged fond smiles. Mr. Z sat down next to Sam, who introduced him—almost silently, by the way, because he knew of old that Mr. Hostetter didn't brook any nonsense or extraneous noise at his rehearsals—to his nephew. Mr. Zollinger politely held out a hand for Frank to shake. I guess Frank had become inured to this mode of greeting, because he didn't even stare at Mr. Z's hand before shaking it.

"Ladies," Mr. Hostetter said to Lucy and me, "I know we're a little late this evening, but I hope you can stay a few minutes longer so you can go over the navy hymn with Mrs. Fleming. Perhaps next week, the two of you can arrive a bit early so we won't have to keep you late."

"Just let me tell my fiancé and his nephew," I said.

Lucy said, "And I'll tell Albert. He won't mind at all."

To judge by their mutual smiles, I gathered Lucy was right about her beloved. Sam, too, was perfectly happy to sit still a little longer. Frank, however, appeared slightly aggrieved.

"What? But we've already been here more than an hour," he whined.

"Be still, you," said Sam. And he gave Frank another little whack on the side of his head.

Frank said, "Hey," but settled back into the pew, scowling and re-crossing his arms over his chest. Sam, too, crossed his arms over his chest, but he smiled almost charmingly at me—well, charmingly for Sam, I mean. I swear, I think he was enjoying battering his vagrant nephew. Offhand, I couldn't think of a more perfect target. Frank had already struck me as a fairly pitiful specimen of humanhood. Maybe Sam and I could fix that.

Or maybe we couldn't. Only time would tell.

Mrs. Fleming, the lovely woman who played both the piano and the organ for our church and also played for other occasions as they arose, smiled at Lucy and me as we joined her at the organ.

"I believe I'll play the piano for your duet, girls. It's quieter than the organ, and your voices will blend perfectly with it."

"Sounds great to me," I said.

Lucy nodded.

So we each retrieved our mimeographed pages and stood as tall and straight as possible. Lucy was a good deal taller than I, but I did my best. Mrs. Fleming, still at the organ, played a thrilling introduction to the beautiful old hymn, and Lucy and I started singing. I already knew the alto part, since we'd sung it at appropriate days during the year. You know, Decoration Day, Armistice Day and so forth. Sopranos always got the melody, so Lucy didn't need any practice at all. Next life, if there is one, I want to come back as a soprano because they have it so much easier than we altos. Anyway, we sang the first two verses.

When Mrs. Fleming lifted her fingers from the organ, she practically glowed at the two of us. "You two sound grand together. And you truly do justice to that beautiful hymn."

"Thank you," Lucy and I said, still in a duet.

And darned if Sam and Mr. Zollinger didn't applaud from the front row of the sanctuary. When I turned to grin at Sam, I saw his nephew staring at him, aghast. I guess those Roman Catholics never had fun in church or something because, for a little punk, Frank seemed to be easily taken aback about the carryings-on in our Methodist Church.

Lucy and I retired to the choir room to put away our hymnals and folders and grab our outer wraps. I plopped my hat on my head and took off for the sanctuary. Lucy ran ahead of me, straight into her husband's waiting arms. My goodness. Even I was slightly surprised at the overt affection the two demonstrated in public. Well, in a nearly empty church on a Thursday evening, anyhow.

I didn't run into Sam's arms, but I smiled warmly at him, and he did the same to me. I turned to Frank.

"Did you enjoy the music, Frank?"

"Uh…Yeah, sure."

"Do you have a choir at the church you attend in New York City?"

"Uh…Yeah, I guess so."

"You *guess* so? Don't you know?"

"Well, yeah. There's a choir. I don't know nobody in it, though."

"Anybody," said Sam, looking disgusted.

"No one in your family sings?"

"Not at church," said Frank.

"Oh, well, perhaps you can join us for church on Sunday with your uncle, and you can hear the entire service. It's quite nice, and the music is pretty."

"Uh…"

"He will," said Sam in a firm voice I knew well.

"But…But Uncle Sammy, we're not supposed to go to other churches."

"Don't be stupid, Frank."

"But…"

"Don't 'but' me, Francis Pagano."

"But I don't understand." Frank glanced around as if he were perplexed. Then he pointed to the cross on the wall behind the chancel. "I walked all over the place, trying to find a toilet, and I didn't see a single one of the crosses we use at home. That ain't the kind of cross we have."

"Isn't, you dolt," said Sam. "That's a cross, not a crucifix."

"That's the whole point, Frank," said I, pleased to be giving Sam's idiot nephew a lesson in Methodism. Sort of. "We display an empty cross in our churches, because Christ rose from the grave on the third day. We don't celebrate the suffering He went through, but the miracle of His resurrection." I was rather proud of that simple tutorial.

"Uh…I still don't get it," said Frank. "But we're still not supposed to go to non-Catholic churches."

"Nuts," said Sam "Anyway, from what Renata told me, you haven't graced the local church with your presence for months and months."

"Oh, is Renata your sister, Sam? It's a beautiful name."

"Yeah. Her name is Renata. She's pretty unhappy with young Francis here, too." He frowned menacingly at his nephew.

"Aw, Uncle Sammy."

"Don't Uncle Sammy me, you thug. I'm Detective Rotondo to you, young man, or you may call me 'sir.' You'll have to earn your way back into my good graces if you want to address me as anything else, and don't forget it again."

"Yes, sir," said Frank. Sullenly, I'm sure I need not say. Well, I just did, but...Oh, never mind.

Sam and Frank drove me home. Although I invited them to come into the house for a cup of cocoa or something—the evening was quite chilly—Sam declined civilly. Frank appeared relieved.

By the way, when I mentioned Frank's born-to-be curly hair, I didn't say that Sam, too, had curly hair, but he didn't ever try to oil it into submission. He had it cut relatively short at all times and perhaps used a little hair oil, but not enough to stain his hat or look odd. Sam was, in truth, quite a handsome man. Large. Very large. Rather like a marble sculpture, in fact, but he still looked good, especially when he smiled, which wasn't often. I suspected his smiles would be even less frequent as long as Frank Pagano remained in Pasadena.

Poor Sam.

THIRTEEN

S pike and I slept well Thursday night and when we woke up, Vi still stood in the kitchen at the stove. The time was approximately seven a.m. Ma and Vi got up earlier than I because they both had to go to work. Mind you, I worked too, but I didn't generally plan any Ouija-board sessions until mid-morning at the earliest.

"Good morning, Daisy," said my sweet aunt, flipping something over in a skillet.

"Good morning, Aunt Vi. I'm surprised you're not already on your way to work."

"I'm hoping you can take your mother and me to our workplaces today, dear. It's pouring rain outside."

"It is?" I raced to the window of my bedroom, drew back the curtains, and discovered my aunt was correct. We didn't get a whole lot of rain in Pasadena, but when it rained, it often rained hard.

"Oh, my! Look at that! I'll be happy to take you and Ma to work, Vi."

"Good morning, Daisy," said my mother, coming into the kitchen. She sat at the kitchen table. "Did I hear you say you'll drive us to work?"

"Absolutely. Happy to. You don't need to walk to the bus stop in this nasty weather."

"We need the rain," observed my practical mother.

"Yes, we do," said I.

"Morning, sweetheart," said Pa, joining us in the kitchen.

"Everyone sit down. Breakfast is ready," said Vi "Daisy, will you get plates and so forth? You'll need knives and forks today."

"Yum," said I, having no idea what Vi aimed to feed us but certain it would be delicious.

I suited my actions to my words and had the table set in a trice. Whatever a trice is.

Vi brought a huge platter laden with pancakes and bacon to the table. Vi made the world's best pancakes. Of course, she made the world's best everything.

"Mercy sakes, Vi, this looks so good!" I said, standing again to get the maple syrup our thoughtful relations in Massachusetts sent us for Christmas. I shook it as I headed for the table. "Good thing Christmas is creeping up on us. We're almost out of syrup."

"We can always get more at Jorgensen's," said Vi. Jorgensen's was where all the rich people in Pasadena bought their groceries. I take that back. Jorgensen's was the place all the rich folks in Pasadena sent their servants to purchase food for the rich families. The store carried a lot of foodstuffs most of us couldn't get elsewhere or grow.

We had a vegetable garden in the back yard, of course, and Ma, Vi and I preserved tons of vegetables and seasonal fruits in the fall. Which this was. Which meant we'd soon have to harvest our crops and get 'em into jars and so forth. I didn't enjoy even that much cooking, but I did my best to assist Vi. So did Ma. After all, we ate the fruits of the garden, so to speak, even if neither Ma nor I knew what to do with the individual ingredients growing there.

"I guess, but it's not quite the same as getting it from Massachusetts," I said. "It's sort of nice to get it from near the source. If you know what I mean."

"I know what you mean, sweetheart," said Pa with a chuckle. "I feel the same way."

Ma shrugged. "Maple syrup is maple syrup." Have I mentioned Ma didn't own a sense of adventure or humor? She wasn't awfully senti-mental, either. But I loved her, as I loved all my family members. And she was practical under all circumstances, a trait that came in handy since I sometimes—only rarely, mind you—jumped to conclusions and was fairly quick to take umbrage.

"I'll just say a quick grace, and then we can dig in," said Pa. "Looks as if you, Spike and I won't be taking any w-a-l-k-s this morning."

"Poor Spike." I glanced down at my loyal hound, staring at me with pitiful eyes. If you only looked at Spike's eyes, you'd believe him to be starving to death. If you looked at the rest of him, you'd know his eyes fibbed.

So Pa said grace, and we ate our superb breakfast. We always had a bowl of oranges on the table because we had two orange trees in our yard. This time of year, the navel oranges were going great guns. During the springtime, the Valencia tree bore fruit. We had oranges all year long, in other words, and I was grateful for it, being extremely fond of oranges.

"I'll have to telephone Gladys Fellowes this morning and make arrangements for Harold and me to visit her home tomorrow," said I after eating a couple of bites of my marvelous pancakes. "Harold is going to plan her Halloween party for her."

"That's nice of him," said Ma.

"Harold's a very nice man," I told the table in general.

"He is indeed. I'm quite fond of Harold," said Vi, who knew him well.

And the stupid telephone rang. As I rose to answer it, I glanced at the kitchen clock. It was only seven-twenty, for Pete's sake! It couldn't be Mrs. Pinkerton, who didn't rise until almost ten o'clock most mornings, according to her maid, my old school chum Edie Applewood.

After snatching the receiver from the cradle, I had to restrain myself from growling my usual greeting. "Gumm-Majesty residence. Mrs. Majesty speaking."

"Frank took a silver candlestick either from your house or your church last night. I'll bring it by this evening, if you still want me to come to dinner."

"He did? I didn't know we had any silver candlesticks."

"He might have snitched it from the church."

"Good Lord, you were right about him."

"I know that." Sam sounded grumpy, as usual. "I told you. He's a thug and a thief."

"Oh, dear. Yes, please come to dinner tonight, Sam. And bring Frank. I don't know what to do about him."

"I suggest pressing charges, although the fool will only get a slap on the wrist."

"I don't think we'll do that. Just bring it back. Once we figure out where he got it, we can lecture him."

"I've already lectured him. He said he only took it so he could sell it and get train fare back to New York."

"Has the child ever considered *working* for the money he wants to spend?"

"I asked him the same thing. He only said, 'Gee, Uncle Sammy, I'm sorry.' So I smacked him." I perceived a note of delight in Sam's voice.

"Do you think corporal punishment works, Sam? Really?"

"Can't hurt, and it makes me feel better," said Sam, and he hung up.

So much for that.

"Sam?" said Pa, looking at me as I returned to the table.

"Yes. Evidently his nephew pilfered a silver candlestick from some-place last night. Do we own any silver candlesticks?"

"I don't think so. Good heavens, that boy is a thief?" Ma looked alarmed.

"Evidently," I said. "Sam warned me about him, but he seems to be a slippery little devil."

"Poor Sam," said Ma. "He didn't seem too fond of the boy. Why did he invite him to visit?"

"He didn't. Frank ran away from home and came to Pasadena. Not a very clever idea on his part if he aims to continue his criminous career, since Sam is a police detective and takes his job seriously."

"Well, I doubt he's truly a *criminal*," said Ma, not sounding sure of herself.

I shrugged. "Don't know. The signs pretty much point that way. I mean, he ended up with a silver candlestick that doesn't belong to him."

"He probably snatched it from the church last night during choir practice," said Pa, as practical as Ma, although he did possess a sense of humor.

"Sam will cure him," said Vi as if she believed her words.

"He's attempting to do that," I told her. "Frank might prove to be a tough customer, though. I guess he's been running with a bunch of hoodlums in New York City."

"Oh, dear," said Ma. "I've read about the awful gangs they have back there."

"Yes. So have I," I said.

We finished breakfast in silence. Then I cleared off the table and stacked the dishes on the counter next to the sink. "I'll wash these after I take you two to work."

"I'll take care of the washing-up," said Pa. "You go ahead and get dressed."

"Thanks, Pa." I kissed him on the head as I went back to my room, Spike following disconsolately, having been given only a small bite of bacon for his acting skills that morning. Poor Spike. He was so abused.

Because I didn't plan on doing much in the way of running around that day, I didn't bother gussying myself up, but wore a simple day dress with my sturdy walking shoes and stockings. I'd had my hair shingled and bobbed a couple of years prior, and a brush through my thick red tresses set them to rights. Then I grabbed my hat and coat and the keys and went out to the Chevrolet to warm it up while Ma and Vi got their hats, coats, umbrellas and handbags.

The Hotel Marengo was across the street from our church, on the northwest corner of Marengo Avenue and Colorado Street, so I dropped Ma off first, getting as close to the back entrance as I could with the car. Ma, sitting on the back passenger seat, opened the door, unfurled her umbrella and carefully stepped out of the car. The wind had picked up, and she had to brace herself as she walked to the back door.

"Wow, looks as if we're in for some wild weather," I said to Vi.

"Rain and Santa Ana winds together maybe?"

"Maybe."

Southern California's Santa Ana winds were notorious, at least for those of us who lived in Southern California. They could blow like the dickens and knock down trees, telephone poles, wires and pretty much anything else in their way when they chose to blow. They were one of the extremely few disadvantages to living in our fair city. The other one was perhaps a bit more unpleasant: earthquakes. Frankly, I'll take an earthquake over a tornado or a hurricane any day. Earthquakes could be dangerous, but they didn't pick up houses and toss them around like toys, as did tornadoes. And, while the Santa Ana winds could be bad, they didn't come with huge waves and disastrous floods, as did hurricanes.

Anyway, earthquakes were few and far between, so they weren't much of a problem. When they hit, you'd be scared for a second or two and then pick up, say, the oatmeal box that had fallen off the kitchen counter unless Spike got to it first, which he did once. Blew up like a balloon, too. I was actually a trifle frightened for fear the oatmeal would expand until his little belly exploded. Fortunately for all of us, that didn't happen. He did have a few digestive problems for a day or two, but he was so well-trained that he announced his intentions in time for us to open the door so he could accomplish his task outside.

That's probably more than you wanted to know. I'm sorry.

After Ma made it safely to the insides of the Hotel Marengo, I drove Vi to Orange Grove, waved at Jackson, who guarded the gate, and aimed the Chevrolet to the service entrance of the Pinkerton mansion. My surprise was great when Harold Kincaid, in the flesh, opened the back door and gestured for me to follow my aunt into the house. Since I hadn't packed my own umbrella, I scurried to the passenger's side of the car and squeezed myself under Aunt Vi's umbrella.

"Good morning, Harold. You're up early," I said once Vi and I were in the house and standing on the service porch. Vi shook out her umbrella and left it, open, on the service porch floor to dry out. My hair had become soaked during my short run around the automobile, and my shoes squished. "If I'd known you'd be here, I'd have brought my own umbrella and been prepared to get out of the car."

"Sorry about that. But you know I have to go attorney-shopping with Mother today. I need to know what time you and I will be meeting your friend tomorrow. I have to inspect her home and get an idea how to plan this precious party of yours."

"It's not mine. It's hers," I said, sounding nearly as cranky as Harold, who was not generally unpleasant. "I expect you're not looking forward to today's activities," I ventured, willing to forgive him his churlishness if his sister's crimes were at its roots.

"You've got that in one guess," said Harold, snarling slightly. "And it *had* to rain today, didn't it?"

"I'm sorry, Harold," I said, my voice oozing sympathy. I did feel for the poor guy. Being with his mother all day long would be a trial for anyone. Being with his mother on the errands planned for that particular day with the rain and wind trying to tear everything to bits would be brutal.

"So sorry, dear," said Vi, smiling a bit at Harold, whom she adored almost as much as I did. "But your mother does need you so. Especially during these terrible days."

"Yes," said Harold, trying to sound polite for Vi's sake. I knew that because I knew the symptoms of his false sincerity.

"What your mother really needs is for someone to shoot Stacy through her black heart," I said, knowing as I did so that Vi would object.

She did. "Daisy! What an awful thing to say!"

With an evil grin, Harold said, "She's right, you know." He gave himself a little shake. "But tell me what time to meet you. And should I come to your house?"

"I haven't telephoned Gladys yet. I'll do that as soon as I get home, and…Should I call here? Will you still be here?"

"I expect so," said Harold, gloom writ large on his features and in his voice. "I expect Mother will have a frightful time getting herself ready for the day's visits. She's going to cry all over me, you know. I'll probably be wringing wet by the time I get home, and that's not even counting the rain."

"I know." I gave him a sympathetic hug. "But I'll call you as soon as I get a time from Gladys. You might as well come to our house, and we can drive up to her place together." I bethought me of Harold's adorable, bright red, but alarmingly small Stutz-Bearcat. "Are you going to be driving your mother around in your car?"

"Good God, no. I'm taking her Rolls."

"Jackson's not going to drive you?"

"No. I'm perfectly capable of driving that monster. Poor Jackson still has a little trouble with his leg when it rains or gets cold."

"I'm sorry to hear that."

Jackson, the Pinkertons' gatekeeper (as I've mentioned before) had been shot by a member of the Ku Klux Klan a year or so earlier. It grieved me to know he still suffered from his wound, and I wondered if Sam would be similarly afflicted in years to come when the weather turned cold or rainy. I hoped not.

"Yeah. Jackson's a good soul. He didn't deserve what happened to him."

"He certainly didn't," said my aunt, a staunch defender of the Jacksons of this world. As were we all, including my mother, who might not have any imagination but who held firm principles regarding right and wrong. I believe I've mentioned that before, probably too often. Sorry if I repeat myself.

"Well, you'd better get going before Mother learns you're here. You don't look your usual well-groomed self this morning." Harold eyed me up and down with disfavor.

"When I left home to take Ma and Vi to work, I didn't know I'd be yanked into anybody's house, Harold Kincaid," I told him with equal disfavor.

"Don't get all het up, Daisy. Just joking with you."

To prove it, he gave me a peck on the check.

Vi laughed.

I left, getting even more soaked running to the Chevrolet than I'd become leaving it. It was already a stupid morning, and I sincerely hoped the rest of the day went better.

FOURTEEN

I had intended to telephone Gladys as soon as I got home from my journey to the Hotel Marengo and Mrs. Pinkerton's mansion. However, by the time I brought the Chevrolet to a stop at the foot of the steps to the side door, I was almost frozen solid, turning into an icicle, and shivering to beat the band. Oh, very well, it was probably fifty-five degrees or so, but that's *cold* for Pasadena, dang it. And, of course, I'd neglected to use the Chevrolet's heater. It didn't do much heating, but it helped when I remembered to turn it on.

Therefore, after giving my dog and my father a quivery greeting, I headed straight to the bathroom and drew a bath. Not really. What I did was fill the tub with water and add some sweet-smelling bath salts Harold had given me as a present for something or other. In case you wondered, I've never much cared for the expression "draw a bath." It sounds silly to me. But that's neither here nor there, nor is it relevant to this particular story.

Anyway, once I'd warmed up, washed my hair and brushed it out so that it would dry in its usual stylish bob, I got into another comfy house-dress, donned my soft slippers, and joined Pa in the kitchen. He was playing a game of solitaire, and Spike was watching dolefully from his perch at Pa's feet. Any time anyone sits at the kitchen or the dining-room table, Spike expects them to eat, not play cards. I could sense he was terribly disappointed. Therefore, because I loved my dog and knew he wouldn't get further snacks until dinnertime, I went to the cupboard, took out an arrowroot biscuit and spoke to him in a conversational tone of voice.

"Spike," said I, "what's one plus three?"

Spike, recognizing this question as an indication of food to come, began barking. As if by magic, he stopped when he'd uttered his fourth yap.

"Good boy!" I said, praising him to the skies and tossing him a bite of arrowroot biscuit.

"That's amazing," said Pa. "I didn't see you move a single muscle."

"I twitched my little finger," I admitted. Still, I thought Spike was a most intelligent hound to have caught on to the game as quickly as he had. In the beginning, of course, I'd had to make broad gestures and give him a treat instantly when he'd hit the correct number, but we'd been practicing. "I should show Spike's skill to Sam's nephew. Maybe that would impress the little toad."

"Toad?" Pa laughed. "Sounds as if you don't care for the lad any more than Sam does."

"I don't. He not only stole a silver candlestick from…Well, I'm not sure from where he stole it, but it was probably from our church. And not only that, but he's become involved with some crooks back home in New York City, and he's been driving his mother and father crazy. Oh! And Sam's sister's name is Renata. Isn't that a pretty name?"

"Yes, it is. Italian, I presume."

I shrugged. "I'm sure it is." I gazed down at my dog once more. Spike, alert and wagging, looked happy. "Spike," I said, "What's five minus two?"

Three barks presaged the advent of another tiny arrowroot treat. Then I knelt and petted him, which he enjoyed, although I'm pretty sure he'd have preferred more arrowroot biscuits.

"Sorry, Spike. If I let you get fat, Mrs. Bissel and Mrs. Hanratty will lynch me."

Creaking a bit—I *really* should begin a course of Swedish exercises —I rose to my feet and headed for the telephone on the kitchen wall.

"What's up?" asked Pa. "You don't generally pick up the telephone receiver unless you have to."

I laughed. "I need to call Gladys Fellowes and set up a date for Harold and me to meet with her and tour her home on the morrow. Harold has to visit attorneys with his mother today."

"Poor guy," said Pa, who meant it. He hadn't met Mrs. Pinkerton more than once or twice, but he knew all about her from several sources, and he liked Harold a lot.

So I telephoned the Fellowes's residence. A woman other than Gladys answered, and I assumed she was the "morning help" Gladys had told me about. It would be nice to have someone else clean the house for one, but I cleaned ours because I had the most time of all the women therein. Not that men aren't just as capable as women at... Never mind. I'm not intending to start a revolution or anything.

After Gladys came to the 'phone, I said, "Good morning, Gladys. Harold Kincaid and I would like to stop by your house tomorrow so he can see where to set things up for your party. He'll also be able to assist you in ordering the food from the Castleton. In fact, you can probably leave all the ordering of foodstuffs to him, because he does this sort of thing all the time."

"Thank you, Daisy. I truly appreciate this. Are you're sure you won't mind playing a fortune-teller?"

"I do it all the time."

Gladys chuckled, which sounded rather odd coming from her. "I suppose that's so. This is so kind of you."

"Happy to help," I told her, meaning it. Heck, I had a valid reason to snoop into a murder case, thanks to Gladys! What could be better than that? Well, other than there having been no murder to begin with, but it was too late for that. "Have you drawn up a list of people you want to invite?"

"Um...Yes. I think so. Why don't I wait until you and Mr. Kincaid get here, and you can go over it with me? I don't want to leave anyone out who should be there."

"Good idea."

"Oh, and Daisy, would you be willing to visit Cal Tech with me today? There's a rather nice restaurant there, and I could introduce you to the people who are working with Dr. Fellowes. Just so you'll...well, see them. If you know what I mean. I'm only assuming one of them killed Mary, but..." Her voice trailed off.

"I agree with you."

Gladys sighed. "I can't believe I actually know a murderer."

"It is difficult to comprehend, especially when they're all smart and work at or with the California Institute of Technology. I mean, you don't generally think of people like that as coldblooded murderers."

"Yes, it is." A significant pause ensued. Then Gladys said, "Would you be able to visit with me today?"

She wanted me to...What is it they say? Scope out the suspects? I think that's it. "Um...Sure, Gladys. I'll be happy to do that. Um...It's raining outside, you know."

"I know." She sighed heavily. "But I do so want you to get a head start on...On this thing." I had the feeling Gladys finally recalled we Gumms and the one remaining Majesty were on a party line.

"Yes, I see. Certainly. I'll be happy to join you." Which meant I'd have to get all dressed up and go out in the rain again, but needs must, I reckon.

"Sounds wonderful. Get here whenever you can. We might as well take your machine, since it'll already be warm. That is, if you don't mind. Sorry. I'm not used to being polite. That sounds awful, doesn't it?"

"Only to someone who doesn't know you," I said with a chuckle of my own. "I'll be there as soon as I can. But what time do you want Harold and me to join you tomorrow? I have to telephone Harold and let him know."

"Oh, yes. Hmmm. How about ten-thirty? I believe Homer will be home then, and perhaps you can renew acquaintanceship with each other."

"Perhaps we can," said I, being gracious. From what I recalled of Dr. Homer Fellowes, he'd probably blink several times at Harold and me and wonder what we were doing cluttering up his house. But what the heck. "Very well. I'll be at your house as soon as I can be today, and we can drive to the university."

"Thank you so much, Daisy."

"You're more than welcome."

Drat.

However, rain or no rain, I had to do my duty. I telephoned Mrs. Pinkerton's house. Harold and his mother had already gone on their search for an attorney to represent Stacy Kincaid in her cases—there was no defense for her, as far as I was concerned. She'd willingly participated in ghastly crimes, and the fact she was an idiot was no excuse.

Pardon me. I get rather "het up," as Aunt Vi occasionally says, when I think about the utterly worthless waste of space and oxygen Stacy Kincaid constitutes.

I asked Featherstone, who had answered the telephone in his customary formal, butlerish manner, to have Harold telephone me sometime that afternoon. He took the message. I thanked him, he thanked me for some reason beyond my comprehension, and we both hung up our receivers. I turned around.

Pa stood there, holding the newspaper, and gazing at me with concern. "Going out into the weather again?"

I told him about Gladys's plans for my day. Well, I didn't tell him I'd be prying into a murder case, but I did tell him she wanted to take me to lunch for helping her with her party. That almost wasn't even much of a fib.

"She might have chosen a more pleasant day," muttered Pa.

"You don't know Gladys. She doesn't think about things like weather and so forth. She's a brain."

"Brains don't understand weather?"

"Yes, but…Oh, never mind. It's too complicated. Just know that Gladys was a whiz at algebra and even went on to take geometry and calculus and trigonometry and adored them, and you can kind of get a picture of her. She probably even understood chemistry."

"Good Lord," said Pa.

"I couldn't have said it better myself."

So Spike and I paid another visit to my bedroom, where I flung open the overstuffed closet and gazed at the bounty contained therein. After pondering for a few minutes and recalling the hideously chilly weather, I decided to don one of my more recent creations: a sage-green wool velour long-sleeved suit with a low belt of the same fabric and some charming embroidery on the thigh-length coat. I'd done the embroidery myself, of course. The skirt was ankle-length, and the whole thing was lined with satin de chine, which actually cost more than the wool velour, because it wasn't on sale at the same time the wool was. But when I wear wool, I really need to line it or I'll itch like crazy. I'd make a lousy sheep. The entire ensemble went beautifully with my golden engagement ring with the emerald set into it.

I decided to wear my black cloche hat and black low-heeled shoes with a cross strap. The shoes were elderly, so if they got ruined in one or several puddles, they wouldn't be that great a loss. Anyway, if the shoes died, they'd have gone to a valiant death, helping in the search for a vicious murderer.

Of course, I could have worn my galoshes, but that would have spoiled the effect of my attempt at spiritualistic allure. I always had to keep my job in mind when I went out in public. If you could call the California Institute of Technology public. If all the employees thereof were as uninterested in human interactions as Dr. Homer Fellowes, I could probably arrive in my nightie and bathrobe and no one would notice. On the other hand, that's a gross generalization based upon my knowledge of one professor and his wife. Neither Gladys nor her husband were social butterflies, as I've said often enough already.

But enough of that. By the time I got myself all "dolled up," as Pa said, the rain had slackened. I was happy about that. Even if my shoes didn't get ruined in puddles, I wasn't keen on getting drenched again. By the time I drove up to the Fellowes's residence on Santa Rosa Avenue, the interior of the car was lukewarm instead of icy.

Gladys was waiting for me, and she unfurled her umbrella and scampered as quickly as an extremely pregnant woman can scamper. It was more like a quick waddle really.

Opening the passenger's door, she sort of galumphed into the Chevrolet, shook out her umbrella, furled it, and set it gingerly upright on the floor next to her. "Glad it's not pouring like it was earlier this morning," said she.

"Me, too," I agreed. "I had to go out in the weather this morning and got soaked and frozen. I forgot to turn on the heater in the car."

"Is it on now?"

"Yes. It's not awfully efficient, but it's better than nothing."

"Yes. Homer says automobile manufacturers are making great strides when it comes to comfort and conveniences in machines. He follows all of that stuff."

"That's nice to know. Do you share his interest in automobile mechanics?"

"Good Lord, no. I prefer to study music."

"Really? I like to sing in our church choir, and I play the piano. Do you play an instrument?"

"Yes. I took piano lessons when I was a girl, and now I'm learning to play the harp."

"The harp! Mercy, the harp has always struck me as an instrument that would be difficult to play."

"No more than any other, although I expect that if my hands become rheumatic like those of my mother's, I probably won't be able to play it into my old age."

"That's a melancholy thought," said I. Naturally, I instantly began thinking about my own fingers and if they'd be able to span out and hit the piano keys when I was elderly.

Gladys shrugged. "Getting old is a fact of life, if you're lucky." She shot me a quick glance. "I'm sorry, Daisy. Was that a callous comment? I forgot for a moment about your late husband."

"It's all right," I said with a sigh. "Billy's been gone for a couple of years now. I still miss him, but life for the rest of us goes on, even though…Well, sometimes right after his demise, I wished it wouldn't. But now I'm about as happy as anyone else on this sorry planet, I imagine."

"Yes. One does adjust, doesn't one?" She smiled, an unusual expression for her. "Getting back to my mother's rheumatic fingers, she keeps telling me she's 'losing her grip.'"

"That's funny!" I said and actually laughed. Gladys wasn't known for cracking jokes.

"Mother enjoys a good sense of humor." She frowned. "I didn't seem to inherit that characteristic from her, although both she and Father are excellent mathematicians. They say music and mathematic abilities go together."

"I've heard that before. Not in me, they didn't. I love music, but I definitely wasn't a whiz at math."

"No, but you have lots of other skills many of us lack." She sounded mournful, and I shot her a quick glance out of the corner of my eye.

"What on earth kinds of skills do I possess that you don't?" I demanded. I mean, I knew she was socially awkward, but I couldn't think of any other skill I might have that would mean anything to Gladys.

With a sigh, Gladys said, "Oh, you're so friendly and meet and talk to people so easily. I get nervous and clam up around strangers. And you dress so beautifully, and your hair is so nice, and…I don't know. I just wish I were more like you, I guess."

Good heavens. That was a surprise to me, and a rather welcome one. "Thank you, I guess. I can't imagine anyone wanting to be like me, but I'm flattered."

"It's not empty flattery," said Gladys, being her usual literal self. "I mean it sincerely."

"I know. That makes it all the nicer. Um…I know we're going to the university, but is there an entrance somewhere I should look for?" We were at that moment driving south on Lake Avenue. Tracks for the red cars, our trolley system, ran up and down Lake, and the tires on my vehicle slid a bit on them. Stupid rain. Not really. We needed it. But I'd have appreciated the rain in my nice warm house more than I did in my lukewarm Chevrolet on a slippery street.

"Yes. When you get to California Street, turn left. There's a parking lot off of Allen Avenue just north of California. You'll have to make another left turn into the lot. I hope it isn't all muddy."

So did I, but I didn't say so. "Cal Tech is in a lovely neighborhood," I said, only telling the truth. There were glorious homes around the university, and the Castleton estate wasn't far away from it.

"Yes. Homer and I thought about buying a home closer to his place of work, but I decided if we did that, I'd see him even less than I do now. He's *such* an inquisitive fellow. He adores working on projects like the one he, Mr. Browning and Dr. Malton are pursuing. I think Mr. Browning spends most of his time away from the chemical factory doing research for the project these days. I fear he's not a happy man." She heaved a sigh. "The loss of his fiancé hurt him dreadfully."

"I know. Detective Rotondo and I spoke to him about that a few months ago. We both know what he's going through, because Sam's wife died from tuberculosis about a year or so before my Billy died. It's very difficult to lose a person one loves."

"Life can be hard," said Gladys.

I couldn't argue with her on that one.

FIFTEEN

After I'd parked the Chevrolet in a paved parking lot—thank God for paving, or we'd have been slopping through a muddy mire—Gladys led me into what looked as if it were the main building of the university. It was a pretty place, Cal Tech, and quite an improvement over the school's last headquarters when it called itself the Throop Institute and sat in the middle of Pasadena.

Gladys led the way, since I had no idea where we were going. "Dr. Fellowes's office is up these stairs and down the hall a way." She began climbing said stairs, hanging on to the banister and puffing a good deal. I admit to having puffed a bit myself by the time we got to the head of the staircase, and I didn't have Gladys's excuse. I was carrying no one but myself. I'd take Spike on longer walks I decided on the spot. He'd love them, and they'd help get me toned up. Maybe. Bother.

Panting slightly, Gladys said, "Here's Homer's office. Let me—Oh! Mr. Davidson! I was looking for Dr. Fellowes."

A young man who had been glancing through papers on a very messy desk swung around. After looking guilty for so short a time that I might have mistaken his expression, he smiled and said, "Good morning, Mrs. Fellowes. The doctor sent me up to fetch a couple of his reports. He's in the geology library with Dr. Malton, Mr. Browning and Mr. Jeffreys. We're all quite excited about the project."

"Mrs. Majesty," said Gladys formally, "please allow me to introduce you to Mr. Bartholomew Davidson. Mr. Davidson is assisting Dr. Fellowes, Dr. Malton and Mr. Browning on that project I told you about. He's a student here at the university."

I walked a bit toward Mr. Davidson, holding out my hand. "It's good to meet you, Mr. Davidson." Then, taking a chance, I said, "It must be difficult to carry on after such a tragedy."

Instantly his face fell. Aaaand, there I went again, spouting another silly expression. His face didn't fall. It remained firmly glued to his skull; however, his expression lost its cheery aspect. "Yes. The loss of Miss Carleton is keenly felt by all of us. She was of great service to us and the project."

"Will you be getting another librarian to…er…replace her?" That didn't sound right, but I didn't stop to think long enough to come up with a more sensitive way of expressing the question.

"I'm not sure. That, of course, will be up to Doctors Fellowes and Malton and Mr. Browning. They're in charge of the project."

"I see. I was terribly sorry to learn of her death," I said. "She used to work at the Pasadena Public Library, and I met her there."

"Yes. I understand she did. She was a big help to us all on the project."

There it was again: that stupid project.

"I suppose we'd better go down to the library, then," said Gladys, ignoring the subject of Miss Carleton's untimely demise. "I want Mrs. Majesty to take lunch with us at the Athenaeum. She's assisting me with the planning of what I hope will be a jolly Halloween party." She gave Mr. Davidson a smile that might have looked friendly on anyone other than Gladys. On her, it just looked out of place. Poor thing.

"How nice. I didn't know you were planning a party, Mrs. Fellowes. That sounds charming."

I had to admit that Bartholomew Davidson went a long way toward reminding me that not all intelligent people were stuffy and unsocial. He was a tall fellow with wavy brown hair, lovely brown eyes with long, curling eyelashes, and a downright charming smile. He didn't seem socially awkward at all. I was almost sorry I hadn't frequented Cal Tech more often, although how I could have managed doing it, I didn't know.

"Will you come with us to the Athenaeum, Mr. Davidson? If I don't haul Dr. Fellowes and Mr. Browning away from their research, they're liable to skip luncheon altogether, and that's not good for either one of them."

"Thank you for the invitation, Mrs. Fellowes. I'd be delighted to join you if it's all right with the others."

It was all right by me if he wanted to dine with us, but I didn't think it was my place to say so.

"Then let's go down to the library and see if we can drag the men away from their research for an hour or so," said Gladys, turning and heading for the door. Right before she got there, she looked back, a puzzled expression on her face. "I thought Homer kept his office locked when he isn't in it." She squinted a bit at Mr. Davidson as if she suspected him of doing something dastardly.

He chuckled. "Indeed he does, but he gave me the key so I could fetch the folders he needed. If you'll wait for me downstairs, I'll join you right after I've found them. I...uh, fear Dr. Fellowes isn't the most organized of individuals sometimes."

"Is that so?" said Gladys. I got the impression she didn't believe the ingenuous student. Or was he ingenuous? Perhaps he was a scoundrel.

Bother. I didn't know what he was except an extremely good-looking young man, and I was glad he aimed to join us for luncheon.

We descended the staircase we'd recently climbed, neither of us puffing as much as we'd puffed on the way up, and Gladys led the way down a hallway and into another room filled with books and maps and globes and all sorts of other things I didn't know what to do with. Well, I can read books, but I doubt those particular tomes would be of interest to me, or that I could understand their contents if I attempted the effort. I suspect my impression was correct.

But there they were: Robert Browning; Homer Fellowes; an older man whom I presumed to be Dr. Malton; and a young man whom I presumed to be another student. They were poring over some documents laid out at a big table in more or less the middle of the room. A fussy-looking woman sat behind a desk eyeing the men as if she didn't trust them not to wrinkle the university's property. I supposed her to be the librarian. She sure looked more like a librarian than any of the other librarians I'd met to date. Well, except for Regina Petrie, but I was going to take care of her that evening.

"Good day, Mr. Browning, Homer, and Mr. Jeffreys."

Aha. The younger man *was* a student. Mr. Jeffreys, in fact. I had a feeling I was going to lose track of the names if I didn't concentrate.

Robert Browning jumped a foot and swirled around to face the door Gladys and I had just entered. "Daisy!" he cried when he spotted me. "What are you doing here? Oh, good morning, Mrs. Fellowes."

He didn't look well. In fact, he looked as if he hadn't slept a wink since he'd picked up that bloody knife in the library. I'm using bloody here in the literal sense, and I mean no disrespect to any British persons who might read this. Haggard. He appeared haggard.

"Gladys invited me to take luncheon at the university today, Robert." I smiled gently at him. "You don't look well. Have you been under the weather?" And yet again we have a common and silly expression. Is anyone ever *over* the weather?

Oh, don't mind me.

He gave me a shaky smile. "Not under the weather so much as under intense police scrutiny. Your detective friend can be…rather intrusive and intimidating when he's on a case, can't he?"

"I don't know. He's never investigated me."

Actually, that was a fib, but I didn't think Robert needed to know that. I walked over to him and laid a hand on his arm. He'd tensed his muscles, and his arm felt sort of like an iron rod.

"But why is he concentrating so hard on you? Do you know? I'm really sorry you're being put to so much trouble."

He relaxed a tiny bit. "It's because I knew Miss Carleton quite well and picked up that…horrible knife. She was a dear friend of Elizabeth's, and…and…Well, I knew things about her that I don't believe the police need to know, quite frankly. Elizabeth and I helped her through… a difficult time in her life."

Ha. I'd bet I knew what that time was, too.

"But here. Please allow me to introduce you to my colleagues, Mrs. Majesty. I believe you know Dr. Fellowes."

I smiled sweetly at Homer Fellowes, who blinked at me and looked as if he'd never seen me in his life. I'd anticipated that. I shook his hand, which he hadn't held out, and not, if I were to judge, because he was being impolite, but because he was as confused about social niceties as was his wife. "It's good to see you again, Dr. Fellowes. I don't believe we've met since you and Gladys married a year and a half ago."

"Oh. Uh. Yes, I'm sure," he said, shaking my hand uncertainly. He had *no* idea who I was.

"Mrs. Majesty is helping me plan our Halloween party, Homer. She's going to play the part of a fortune-teller."

"How fascinating," came a voice from behind us. Aha. Mr. Davidson had rejoined us.

I turned and said, "Did you find the folders you needed?"

"Indeed I did, Mrs. Majesty. Here you go, old chap." He handed two brown folders tied with twine to Dr. Fellowes.

"I see you've met Bartholomew," said Robert. He turned to the man I presumed to be Dr. Malton. That was only because he looked older than the other fellow, who was probably Mr. Jeffreys. "Mrs. Majesty, please let me introduce you to Dr. Malton. Along with Dr. Fellowes and me, he's heading up our geological study."

Dr. Malton was a nice-looking man. Perhaps forty, he had vivid blue eyes that twinkled almost alarmingly. Another blow to my preconceived notion of what a genius should look like.

Without hesitation, he took the hand I held out to him, put his other hand on top of it, and shook warmly. "How delightful to meet so charming a lady," said he.

And how, I wanted to ask, do you know I'm charming? "Thank you," I said stiffly. I had to tug to get my hand out of his grip. Hmmm. Could a Cal Tech professor be a ladies' man? That didn't fit my notion at all.

"And this is Philip Jeffreys. Mr. Jeffreys is a student, like Mr. David-son. They're both very helpful individuals who have been of great service to us and our project," said Robert.

"How do you do, Mrs. Majesty?" Mr. Jeffreys, unlike Dr. Malton and Mr. Davidson, appeared rather shy. He even blushed when he asked his question and shook my hand.

"I'm very well, thank you. It's good to meet you." I glanced at the other men. "All of you. Gladys has told me you're extremely excited about the project upon which you're working."

"Indeed, we are," said Dr. Malton.

"Let's go to luncheon," said Gladys, interrupting the proceedings in her customary abrupt manner. "I'm sure you gentlemen can't take too much time away from your precious project, but I wanted to show Mrs. Majesty the Athenaeum. It's such a beautiful place, and the food is so good."

"Ah, yes," said Robert. "I suppose it is about lunchtime." He glanced at the wristwatch on his left hand and said, "My goodness, it's already one o'clock. If you hadn't interrupted us, we'd probably not have had any lunch at all."

"That's what I figured," said Gladys wryly.

She took her husband by the arm and seemed almost to drag him away from his papers. He glanced at the fussy-looking woman behind the desk and said, "Please don't allow anyone to touch our work, Mrs. Langton."

"Of course," said the lady in a nasal voice that sounded snippy. "I know my duties, Dr. Fellowes." She sniffed significantly.

"Of course," said Mr. Davidson, giving the woman a sunny smile. It didn't seem to melt her appreciably.

"Please, Mrs. Majesty," said Dr. Malton, "allow me to help you to the Athenaeum. I'm sure you'll enjoy it. It just opened, you know." He didn't wait for my permission, but took my hand and placed it on his arm.

"Oh. Thank you," I said uneasily.

"It's not often we get to take luncheon with two such charming ladies," he said then.

I heard the two students and Robert following behind us. I glanced over my shoulder, and Robert gave me a significant look. I'm not sure what it signified, but he meant something by it. I'd have to get him alone and ask him later.

"Is Mrs. Langton taking over Miss Carleton's duties?" I asked no one in particular.

Robert Browning heaved a largish sigh. "No. No one can replace

Mary. Mrs. Langton isn't awfully pleasant to work with, and she begrudges everything she's asked to do."

"That's the truth," said Dr. Malton, squeezing my hand on his arm.

"I'm sorry to hear that," I said, repressing an impulse to yank my hand away from Dr. Malton, who seemed to be taking inappropriate advantage of it.

"As are we all," said Robert.

The Athenaeum wasn't too far away from the building where we'd met Dr. Fellowes and the gang—if gang is an appropriate word for a clutch of scientific individuals—and the rain hadn't recommenced, so the walk wasn't difficult. Dr. Malton continued to hold my hand rather tightly on his arm and walked quite close to me. I wasn't accustomed to pushy men, and I didn't find his overtures welcome. Especially since I'm pretty sure someone—Robert or Gladys?—had told me he was a married man.

Gladys turned out to be correct about the Athenaeum. It was gorgeous. Old polished wood, formal place settings, fine china, polished silver and, I'd bet, if I ever were to do anything so foolish as to bet, wildly expensive. Glad I wasn't paying.

Now I love to eat. I adore food. Most foods. I wasn't particularly fond of black-eyed peas, but everyone has his or her limits. Anyhow, we didn't have to endure black-eyed peas in Pasadena as a rule. However, I recalled we were having not two, but three, guests for dinner that night at home—I counted Frank Pagano as a guest even though he was more of a nuisance than anything else—and I tried to pace myself. Gladys ordered for all of us, bless her, and we had soup, a fish course, a chicken course, a salad, and then a waiter who looked like a student in a waiter costume—which, I learned later, he was—brought around a dessert cart. I didn't order dessert, although it was torture to see a slice of fabulous-looking chocolate cake pass us by without grabbing it. I did attempt not to eat too much. I hadn't a clue what Vi aimed to serve us for dinner that night, but I was sure it would be lavish because she adored having guests to dine and, while Frank Pagano wasn't what I'd call prime guest material, Regina Petrie certainly was.

After saying our farewells to the men—Dr. Malton again held my hand a trifle too long for my comfort—Gladys and I headed back out to the Chevrolet. The sky had recommenced dripping, but the rain was spotty.

"So," said Gladys as we pulled out of the parking area, "what do you think?"

"About what?" I asked, looking both ways before inching out onto Allen Avenue.

"About the suspects, of course! I absolutely do *not* believe Robert Browning had anything to do with Miss Carleton's death, but Dr. Malton has always struck me as sort of a slippery fellow, and students are notoriously unsteady of character."

"They are? I didn't know that."

"Mercy, yes. Especially in a university like Cal Tech, the competition among students is sometimes nearly rabid. It's difficult for me to believe either Mr. Davidson or Mr. Jeffreys had anything to do with Miss Carleton's murder, but I can't be sure. You're a better judge of people than I am, Daisy. What do you think?"

Good heavens. "Um...I really don't think anything yet, Gladys. I've only just met the people involved. I must say I was taken aback about by Dr. Malton's instant familiarity. Does he often...attach himself to women that way?"

After heaving a sigh, Gladys said tightly, "Yes. He does. He's a notorious...What do you call men like that? A rake? A roué? He's both of those things. And he's a married man! Shameful."

"Hmm. I feel sorry for his wife."

"I understand she's as bad as he is," said Gladys, sounding irritated. It was the first time since I'd met her—and that was in elementary school—I'd ever heard Gladys utter anything even vaguely resembling gossip. "I try to keep Homer away from her at faculty dinners and so forth."

Hmm. I couldn't quite see the bespectacled, sober-sided, generally abstracted and serious Dr. Homer Fellowes being swept off his feet by a designing woman, especially the wife of a colleague. Granted, he'd been blinded by the beauty of a cinema star, Lola de la Monica, a couple of years earlier, but that was almost understandable. Once he learned her true character, which was deplorable, he abandoned that forlorn hope for the much more compatible—for him—Gladys.

"My goodness. For some reason, I don't think of Cal Tech professors as being...rakes."

"No one does," said Gladys bitterly. "But you'd be surprised. Some of them are terrible cads."

"Dear me. I'm sorry to hear it."

"You'll probably get to watch some of their goings-on at the Halloween party."

"Speaking of that, are all the gentlemen we saw today going to be invited to the party?"

"Yes, and I'll invite a few others, too. I don't want anyone to suspect you're really looking for a murderer."

"Um..." Good Lord. Looking for a murderer? "Please don't give me too much credit, Gladys. I'm not a detective. I'm just a phony spiritualist-medium."

"I know that, but you're very good at assisting people with their problems. You, after all, were the one who discovered it was that beastly woman who was writing those poison-pen letters."

"Harold and I did," I said, giving credit where it was due. "And that was almost by accident."

"Propitious accidents are the way most great discoveries are...discovered."

"Really?"

"Really."

If she said so. Personally, I had my doubts.

SIXTEEN

Because I figured I should, I went to Mrs. Pinkerton's house before I returned home. I mainly wanted to see if Vi wanted a ride home, but I also felt slightly guilty about having been away from the telephone most of the day and unavailable should Mrs. Pinkerton have had a nervous collapse or something. She had those sometimes.

When I knocked at the back door—I didn't necessarily want to announce my arrival to Featherstone, because if Mrs. P were home, she'd surely have cornered me and, unless she was in true distress, I didn't want to deal with her—I was surprised when Harold opened the door.

"Harold!" I cried. "What are you doing, opening the door to the servants' entrance?"

"Daisy!" said Aunt Vi disapprovingly, loading up a cardboard with, I presumed, our dinner. I was still full from lunch, but whatever was in that box smelled awfully good.

"Very funny," said Harold, sounding almost as cantankerous as Sam.

"Rough day?" I asked him, trying to sound sympathetic. Well, I *was* sympathetic. Having spent the entire day with his emotional wreck of a mother couldn't have been any fun.

"You have no idea," said he. "Picture Mother at her most hysterical and having to travel from attorney to attorney all over the city of Pasadena with me riding shotgun and talking to each gent in turn, and you might get an idea. A *vague* idea of what my day's been like. I think poor Jackson was more upset by her antics today than he was when those Klan goons shot him."

"Poor Jackson? I thought you were going to drive and leave him here."

Harold's glower was at least as good as any one of Sam's. "I'd planned to do the driving, but Mother said she needed me to hold her hand. So Jackson got to drive, poor man."

"Oh, dear."

"Yeah. He and I endured more tears and cries of woe than any two men should endure in a lifetime. And Mother's rich. Poor Jackson is just a good fellow trying to help his employer. He didn't deserve to be wept upon. Well, neither did I, but at least I'm her son and have a certain responsibility. Jackson's duties should end at the gate, or at least the front seat of the Rolls."

I took a deep, sustaining breath and then asked cautiously, "Um... Does she need me?" I silently prayed hard she wouldn't.

"I'm sure she wants you," said Harold. "But I gave her some Veronal and told her to lie down and rest until dinnertime. Then I escaped into the sanity of the kitchen."

Vi chuckled. "Harold Kincaid, you're a caution."

I wasn't sure what "a caution" was, but Aunt Vi used the word to describe me from time to time, too.

"It's true," said Harold. "I swear, Daisy, your aunt and Featherstone are the only two sane people in this entire house. At least Jackson gets to stay in the gatehouse. Algie isn't too bad, but Mother's got him wrapped around her little finger."

Mr. Algernon Pinkerton, a round, rosy man with a charming disposition and a huge bank account, was Mrs. Pinkerton's husband. Everyone who knew him well called him Algie, although I wasn't fond of the name myself, since it reminds me of pond scum and other icky, slimy things.

"Your stepfather is a good man, Harold."

"He's a saint," said Harold, plopping himself into a kitchen chair with a huff of exhaustion.

"Did you find a lawyer for your ghastly sister?"

"Yes. We're using the man in Mr. Pearlman's office. Cecil Grant. The one we interviewed first. I was all for hiring him on the spot, but Mother wanted to shop." Harold heaved a heartfelt sigh. "God."

"Does he think he can get Stacy off?"

"Good Lord, no. She's in too deep." A smile crept over Harold's face. He was almost as pleased as I that Stacy's evil career had been cut short. At least for a while. "But he's probably the best man to tackle the job. He'll try to get her as light a sentence as possible."

"That's a shame," I said.

"Daisy!" said Aunt Vi again.

"I think it's a shame, too, Mrs. Gumm. My sister is a worthless piece of garbage."

"Goodness," said Aunt Vi, taken aback, although why she should be was a mystery to me. She'd known Stacy longer than I had. And Stacy had never been worth spit. If you'll excuse the disgusting choice of words. Somehow, Stacy and disgusting just sort of go together.

"I know she's been a sore trial to your mother," Vi admitted.

"That's one of the bigger understatements of the year," said Harold. "And the year's almost over."

"It's only October, Harold. Oh! That reminds me. Can you come to my house at ten-ish tomorrow morning? Gladys would like us to visit her home at ten-thirty, if that's agreeable to you."

"Sure. I enjoy planning parties. I'll be able to make catering arrangements with the Castleton as soon as I know how many people will attend the party and how big the house is. We should be all set. The Castleton can provide a serving staff, too, if it's needed."

"I guess it will be, unless Dr. Fellowes and his cohorts want to have students in charge of the serving. That's what they do at that restaurant at the university. Guess they make money waiting on tables in between classes, and it helps pay for their education."

"I doubt the doctor and his missus would enjoy paying for students to serve them, but students will probably come cheaper than the staff of the Castleton."

"Probably."

"We can ask tomorrow," said Harold.

"Excellent," said I. "Need me to help you carry stuff, Vi?"

"No, thank you, dear. Harold has kindly offered his services."

"You're a good man, Harold Kincaid."

"Huh," said Harold.

But he was. In spite of his proclivities.

As we were driving home, I sniffed the air in the Chevrolet apprecia-tively. "Whatever you're giving us for dinner sure smells good, Vi."

"It's not very fancy, although it looks more elaborate than it is. I'm serving Russian cutlets with a brown mushroom sauce and a variety of roasted vegetables."

"What's a Russian cutlet?" I asked, never having heard of one before.

"It's ground chicken molded on a bed of Russian pilaf. And before you ask, Russian pilaf is a rice dish. You had something like it in Turkey, I imagine."

"Oh. I loved the food in Turkey," said I, having fondish memories of that trip, even if I had been sick most of the time and Harold and I had become embroiled with a nest of vicious criminals.

"And the brown mushroom sauce is self-explanatory," said Vi.

It might have been to her. I decided not to ask. Oh, and for the record, I'm not necessarily a big fan of mushrooms, either, but I trusted Vi to make even a mushroom edible.

"And so are the vegetables," I said, grinning.

"Yes. Banana squash, green beans, carrots and cauliflower."

"Colorful."

"Exactly."

"What's for dessert?" I asked, thinking fondly of that bygone slice of chocolate cake.

"Chocolate cake," said my marvelous aunt. "With vanilla ice cream."

"Oh, Vi, you're wonderful!"

"Thank you." She gave me an odd look, but I didn't explain my enthusiasm as we had made it home by that time. I helped carry in the cardboard box, Vi unloaded it, and I took the box back out to the car, thinking it would come in handy another day. Providing I could drive my aunt to work again soon.

The time was approximately four p.m., so I removed my wool velour suit and replaced it with a nice, comfy day dress. Ordinarily when I get home, I'll slap on any old thing, but I wanted to show Regina that she could look nice even at home. If she wanted to. For all I knew, she liked to loaf around in her bathrobe and slippers during her time away from the library, although she didn't strike me as the loafing type of woman. I hoped she'd come extra early, so we could sneak into my bedroom and I could have at her hair and face and give her some clothing tips. So to speak.

I was in luck! At five p.m. on the dot our doorbell—well, it wasn't really a bell, but one of those things a person twists from the outside, and it makes a scratching noise—sounded, and Spike and I raced each other to the front door. Spike won, but that's only because he has four legs. He sat and stayed at my command, marvelous pooch that he is.

And there she was, standing on our front porch, a drab black hat on her drab brown hair, wearing a drab suit of mud brown and low-heeled black shoes. She carried a drab black handbag in both of her black-gloved hands, and I swear she'd have blended in with the porch itself if we didn't have an outside electrical light to help keep our visitors from tripping. Not that there was anything to trip over.

"Regina!" cried I. "It's so good to see you!"

"It's so good of you to invite me over and help me," she said, sounding timid. But then, she almost always did.

"Come in, come in! This is my dog, Spike." I gestured to Spike and said, "Good boy, Spike. All right." For the record, "all right" was the signal between Spike and me that he could cease being still and welcome our visitor. He was *such* a well-behaved dog. Maybe Sam should take his nephew to the Pasanita Dog Obedience Club. Naw. They'd probably kick him out as a hopeless case.

That wasn't very nice. I'm sorry.

"Oh! What a lovely dog," said Regina. She didn't look as if she meant it. I don't think she was accustomed to dogs greeting her so enthusiastically. Or maybe she was. I knew nothing about her personal life, except that she had a whole crew of criminal relations.

"If you don't want him to bother you, I can send him into the living room."

"Oh, no! He lives here! I couldn't be rude to a member of your family. I'm...just not used to dogs." She leaned over, released one of her tightly clenched hands from her handbag, and held it out to Spike.

He licked it happily. Regina snatched her hand back. "Oh. I didn't know he'd lick me." She didn't sound as if she'd enjoyed the experience, but he'd only licked her glove, for pity's sake.

"He only kisses people he likes," I told her.

"Oh. How...nice."

I laughed. "I won't let him bother you. But he pretty much owns the house and considers us his personal servants, you know."

"I thought only cats thought of their owners like that."

"Nope. Spike is king of the house."

"Well, he's lovely."

We hadn't just been standing in the doorway as we chatted, but I'd led her into the house. "Thank you. I think so, too. And he's the smartest dog I know."

"Really?"

"Really. I'll show you some of his better tricks later, but right now, let me take your hat and coat, and we can hang them on the coat tree here."

Regina slipped out of her coat and handed it to me. She hung her hat on the rack by herself. Then she removed her gloves and stuffed them into the pocket of her coat. "This is so nice of you, Daisy. I...Well, you probably already know that I'm not accustomed to men paying attention to me, and I'm not quite sure why Mr. Browning is doing so, but I don't want to embarrass him or anything when he takes me to luncheon next week."

"Nonsense. Robert Browning is a prince of a man, and he wouldn't have invited you to take a meal with him if he didn't like you. I hope you get to know each other well in the coming days."

"Is that your guest, sweetheart?"

Pa emerged from the dining room and walked into the living room, smiling broadly. Pa generally liked everyone, and he, like Vi, loved having company.

"Indeed, Pa." I turned to Regina. "Regina Petrie, please meet my father, Joe Gumm. He's an avid reader, and you've supplied him with lots and lots of good books to read during the past couple of years."

Pa came up to us, and Regina tentatively held out her hand. He took it in his and shook heartily. "It's a pleasure to meet you at last, Miss Petrie. Daisy is always bringing us books you've put aside for us, and we appreciate it greatly. I don't get out as much as I used to, and we depend on Daisy and you."

"Mrs. Majesty and I have become good friends over the past few years," Regina said, smiling up a storm. Then she looked guilty. "At least, I feel as though we have."

"We have," I said firmly, meaning every syllable. Well, I guess there were only two of them, but I meant them sincerely. "But we have some business to take care of before we dine on Vi's delicious Russian...Well, I can't remember what they are, but they're Russian."

"Fascinating!" said Regina. "My diet is so dull and unvarying, probably because I live alone and it's no fun to cook for one."

"It's not fun for me to cook at all. For anybody."

Regina appeared rather unnerved by my statement, but Pa said, "She's right, you know. If either Daisy or her mother had to prepare the meals in this house, we'd be in sorry shape."

"We'd probably all have died of ptomaine poisoning by this time," I added.

"Goodness gracious." Regina sounded rattled.

"But never mind that. My aunt is the best cook in the world, and we're lucky to have her."

"Yes, you've told me so. I haven't had much experience with cooking, since, as I said, I've lived alone since my mother passed away."

Well, we'd just see what we might be able to do about that, thought I to myself. If Robert Browning and Regina Petrie got together, it would make me, for one, a happy person. As long as Regina didn't leave the library.

Heavens! I hadn't thought of that dire prospect. I'd have to have a stern talk with Robert Browning about women's rights if he and Regina started to get serious about one another.

Not that their relationship—or lack thereof—was any of my business.

However, as Sam would probably have said, that had never stopped me before.

SEVENTEEN

I shut the door to my bedroom, Spike jumped up on the bed, and Regina looked around. "This is a charming room," she said.

"Thank you," I said, waving her to a pretty little chair for which I'd made a quilted cushion. I'd sewn curtains out of the same fabric I'd quilted for the chair but refrained from padding and quilting it for the curtains. If you understand what I mean. "I like it. Since Billy was so badly injured, we took this room because he didn't have to climb stairs to get to it." I heaved a sigh. "The upstairs has two nice rooms that would be swell for a married couple, but Vi lives in them. And she deserves them. Of course, I also have a sewing room. Actually, the whole family uses it from time to time for various projects, but that's where I keep the sewing machine and all my fabrics and so forth."

"You sew?" asked Regina, eyeing me with interest.

"Oh, goodness, yes! You didn't actually think I could afford to *buy* all the clothes I wear, did you?"

"I...I don't know. I never thought about it. You always look marvelous, and your clothing is beautiful. I guess I just thought you made a lot of money in your rather odd profession."

Opening the closet door, I grinned. "Well, that's true. I make a lot more money chatting with dead people than I could as an elevator operator or a clerk in a store. Or a person who works on the production lines at the Underhill Chemical Factory." I shuddered. "Robert Browning took me on a tour of the plant last year, and I wouldn't want to work there. I don't have the education to be a teacher or a librarian."

"Yes. I did have to go to college and get my degree in order to be hired as a librarian."

"I probably should have gone to college, but I was young and stupid and madly in love with my Billy, so we married right after I graduated from high school. He'd just enlisted, and we didn't want to wait...which turned out to be a good thing, considering what happened."

"I'm so sorry. What a terrible war that was."

"Yes. So many young lives lost to one man's vanity and greed. Makes me angry to think of it, so I try not to."

"I don't blame you. Um, Mr. Browning told me he and Mr. Under-hill—the younger Mr. Underhill, I mean—are attempting to make working conditions more pleasant for their employees."

"Yes, I can believe that. I don't think Mr. Underhill's father cared a snap of his fingers about his employees, and he was quite...unsavory in other ways, too." My thoughts slipped back to Miss Betsy Powell, a stupid woman who'd actually believed Mr. Underhill would divorce his wife and marry her. Humbug. Some men are too awful for words.

"Um...I think you're right. Mr. Browning doesn't speak highly of him, although he's great friends with Mr. Barrett Underhill."

In case you wondered, the older Mr. Underhill, the founder of the chemical company, had been foully murdered a year or so earlier. He'd deserved it, so don't waste any sympathy on him. Aside from seducing silly young women, he also committed many other dastardly deeds, and his son and Robert Browning had worked like slaves to save the company from utter ruin.

"Yes. I liked the younger Mr. Underhill when I met him. I disliked his old man a good deal. And I know you're not supposed to speak ill of the dead, but I didn't speak well of him when he was alive, either, so I don't think it matters. Besides, he was a stinker."

I heard an odd sound, turned my head, and saw to my amazement that Regina was laughing! She was trying to do so silently by pressing a hand over her mouth, but she couldn't quite manage.

"I'm sorry, D-daisy. But you're so funny sometimes."

"I am?" I didn't know that.

"Yes. And you always tell the truth."

If she only knew. But I wasn't about to enlighten her.

"Do you know where Robert plans to take you to lunch on Tuesday?"

"No, I don't. I…didn't feel comfortable asking. I have absolutely *no* experience with men, Daisy. I really don't know how to act around them. Except for my father, all the men in my family are loathsome creatures, and I wasn't one of the popular girls at school or anything, so this is all new to me."

"We all have to begin somewhere. I think we can do something about that. Of course, it helps that Robert Browning is a fine man."

"Um…Is he really? I mean…" Her voice trailed off.

I looked over my shoulder again. "What? He really is a wonderful man. He was in Billy's class at high school, but then he went on to college and so forth. Billy went to war." My voice had taken on the bitter edge it always did when I referred to that nasty war.

"That's good to know. Um…You don't think he had anything to do with Mary Carleton's death, do you? I mean—"

Swirling around, I said, "Good heavens, no! Robert is a peach. A truly good man. And, as you've noticed, good men are hard to find, especially these days, thanks to the wretched Kaiser and his evil poisoned gas."

"Yes." Regina heaved a heartfelt sigh. "I'm so sorry for everything you've gone through, Daisy."

"Lots of people had it worse than I did." And that was true, even though other people's problems can't possibly affect one the way one's own problems do. I turned back to my closet and grabbed the outfit I'd been aiming for. It was a charming suit of blue wool tweed I'd made about a year before. I thought it would go well with Regina's coloring.

Which was totally blah. We had to do something about that. Heck, I didn't even know what color her eyes were.

"Will you come here for a minute?" I asked, holding up the suit on its hanger. I padded all my hangers, in case you wondered. Not for Daisy Gumm Majesty to treat her home-made clothing with disrespect.

My wardrobe was the mainstay of my livelihood and that of my family, after all, so I pampered it.

Regina promptly rose from the chair and walked to me. She glanced at the garment I held and said, "That's very pretty," as if she didn't know what I aimed to do with it.

"I think we're relatively the same size, don't you?"

"I…I…Well, I've never thought about it, but I suppose we are," she said, looking mystified.

"What color are your eyes?" I asked. "It's too dim in here for me to see clearly."

"They're sort of blue-gray."

"Good!"

"Why is that good?"

"Would you like to try this on? It's warm, and I think it will look good on you. It will be perfect for a stint at the library and a luncheon with Robert Browning. The blue of the suit will bring out the color in your eyes"

"I doubt it," she said unhappily. "They're always hidden behind my eyeglasses, so I don't suppose what I wear matters."

"It matters," I told her firmly. "Try on this suit, and if it fits, you'll wear it on Tuesday. Then we'll take a trip to our bathroom and I'll show you what to do with your eyes. Just because you wear eyeglasses is no reason to look dowdy." I considered what I'd so blithely blurted out and was ashamed. "Not that you look dowdy or—"

"Yes, I do," Regina said with a sigh. "And you know it as well as I."

"Very well, we're going to do something about that this very evening."

"Thank you." She sounded entirely too humble.

"Fiddlesticks! Just because you're a librarian doesn't mean you have to wear boring clothes or unbecoming hairstyles. For Pete's sake, you're a very pretty young woman. You only need to do one or two things to play up your looks and downplay your profession, if you know what I mean."

"I thought librarians were supposed to be boring," said she. "Part of the job and all that."

I had to squint hard to make sure she was joking. She was.

"Anyhow, I've never much thought about my appearance. I've never been…well, attractive, you know?"

"Applesauce. Robert Browning must think you're interesting and probably attractive, too, or he'd never have asked you to take luncheon with him. To the best of my knowledge, he hasn't seen any woman at all since his fiancée died, poor man. I think it's wonderful that he's asked you to dine with him."

"He's probably just being nice," said Regina in a resigned-sounding voice.

"Nuts to that! The only reason he asked me to dine with him once was so that he could talk about his late fiancée with a friend. And he didn't even *know* you until a couple of days ago, did he?"

"No."

"Very well, then. There you go."

"Hmm," said Regina.

Thinking of her probable modesty, I said, "I'll just leave the room for a minute. Tap on the door when you've changed. I'll be right on the other side of it."

"Very well." She sounded not at all sure of herself. Or of me, come to think of it.

Ha. I'd show her. And Robert Browning, too!

Regina looked positively charming in my blue suit! She appeared astounded when she gazed in the mirror and turned this way and that to assess the improvement the color made. Probably any color other than her usual grays, tans and blacks would help her look better than she generally did, although I'd never tell her that. Not in those words, anyhow.

"My goodness, Daisy. Are you sure you don't mind if I borrow this? It'll only be for Tuesday, and I'll return it instantly. I promise I won't drip anything on it."

"Don't worry about that. I bought that material on sale at Maxime's Fabrics when they were getting rid of their winter merchandise for lighter, spring- and summer-weight fabrics."

"Do you really make *all* your clothes?"

"I do. I sew for the entire family. Including Spike, who doesn't like it much. But he does look adorable in the red coat I sewed for him last year. For walking during the colder winter months, you know. Not that it ever gets very cold in Pasadena."

"Good heavens. A black dachshund in a red coat. Amazing." She turned and grasped both of my hands. "I can't tell you how much I appreciate this, Daisy. You have *so* many admirable qualities, and you're so clever."

"You really think so?" I asked doubtfully. "Maybe you should tell Sam Rotondo that. I only seem to drive him crazy most of the time."

"He must love you. The two of you are engaged to marry, aren't you?"

"Hmm. You're right. I guess I don't drive him *too* crazy."

"This is so pretty," she said, staring into the mirror once more, gazing at the blue suit and herself, her eyes getting a trifle misty. "Thank you *so* much."

"You're welcome. But get out of that now, and I'll take you to the bathroom where some implements of my magical arts are stored."

Because she appeared startled, I laughed and said, "Don't worry. I'm only going to see if I can help you with your hair. And your face. A little rouge and face powder will enhance your natural good looks, and I'm sure the library big-wigs won't mind."

"Ha," she said.

"I mean it! You're a lovely woman, Regina. You just don't know how to make the most of what you have."

After heaving a huge sigh she said, "I hope you're right."

"I know I'm right. I'll be right outside the door. When you're finished, just tap, and I'll whisk you away to my lair."

She laughed as I shut the door. Vi had taken over the kitchen in order to prepare her Russian whatevers for dinner. She smiled at me. "Sounds like you have company in there and that you're having fun."

"I do, and we are. Miss Petrie, my favorite librarian, is dining with us tonight. I asked you if it was all right, remember?"

"Of course! You know I love cooking for a large crowd. Although this one won't be very large, I guess. But we'll only have two extra guests. I consider Sam a member of the family already." She gave me a mischievous smile, which I opted to ignore.

"Right. I'll set the table as soon as I get Regina fixed up."

"That's right. Her first name is Regina, isn't it?"

"Yes, it is. And I'm remodeling her." I kind of liked that expression of intent.

"Remodeling her? What in the world does that mean, Daisy Majesty?"

I guess Vi didn't appreciate my expression of intent as much as I did. "Oh, I'm only letting her borrow a blue suit and I'm going to help her with her hair and give her a few makeup tips and so forth."

"Hmm. Well, if anyone can do it, I guess it's you. You do more with less than anyone else I've ever met."

I gazed at my aunt for a minute. "I'm not sure what you mean by that, Vi. Do you mean I'm ugly but manage to fix myself up so nobody notices? I know I'm not beautiful, but—"

Vi burst out laughing. "Lord, Daisy! Of course that's not what I meant. I just mean that you always look wonderful. You know how to sew beautiful clothing, and you make yourself up so that you fit your profession better than anyone else I've ever known."

"Oh. Thanks, Vi. That's nice of you. I really do try you know."

"I know it, sweetheart. And you succeed admirably. Why, half the time when you go off to a séance or something, you look ghostlike yourself."

Smiling, I said, "Thanks! I aim for the pale-and-interesting look."

"You achieve it well."

"Thank you. I'll set the table as soon as I fiddle with Regina's hair and face a little."

Vi shook her head. "My stars, Daisy, but you do have odd gifts."

"So do you. Only yours aren't odd. They're delicious."

"We each have our own talents," said Vi.

Thinking of my mother and her accounting skills, Vi with her cooking genius, Gladys Fellowes and her mathematical abilities, Regina Petrie with her scholarly bent, and Robert Browning with his scientific leanings, I said, "Yes. I guess we all do." Mine were probably the least important of those listed, but at least I could use them to make a pretty good living.

Regina tapped on the door, and I opened it. She stepped into the kitchen and I introduced her to Vi. Vi was thrilled to meet the woman who'd been supplying us with such marvelous books for so long and told Regina so. Regina's cheeks turned pink, so I presume she was pleased with Vi's commendation.

"Daisy's told me about what a wonderful cook you are, Mrs. Gumm. It's so nice of you to have me over for dinner."

"Nonsense. I love guests!" said Vi.

She meant it sincerely, I assured Regina as I led her to the bathroom.

EIGHTEEN

A knock came at our door at approximately five forty-five. I expected the knock to have been perpetrated by Sam, because I doubted Frank would dare touch anything at all while in the custody of his uncle. By that time Regina had been almost totally transformed. Almost, because she wasn't sure she could re-create my initial creation.

I'd taken her hair down from its usual bun and swept it back behind her ears. I'd also powdered her face, smoothed on a bit of rouge—only a bit, because neither of us wanted her to appear gaudy—used some eyebrow pencil on her eyebrows and some mascara on her lashes. She truly looked pretty, even with her spectacles. "See?" I said. "I knew you to be a lovely woman. You only need to do a few things to yourself. And it didn't take much time at all, did it?"

"Thank you. No, it didn't take much time." Peering at herself doubtfully, she said, "I only hope I'm able to do the same thing at home."

"Just keep practicing. I'll lend you my extra eyebrow pencil, and I'll pick up some mascara for you at the drug store on Monday. I'll take you to a beauty parlor to get a haircut. You'd look wonderful in one of the shorter hairdos, especially since your hair has a natural wave to it. You don't need to go as far as a short, straight bob, but shorter hair would probably be easier to care for. Then we can go shopping together some-time next week, and we can refurbish your wardrobe. Or, if you can't afford a bunch of new clothes, I can make you some."

"I can't ask you to do that!" said Regina, clearly horrified.

"You didn't ask. I offered. I love to sew. It's about the only thing I'm good at in this life, and I enjoy doing it."

"Nonsense. You have so many talents, I can't even count them."

I'd bet I could, but I didn't offer. Rather, I got to the front door slightly after Spike did, told my well-behaved hound to sit and stay, and opened the door. I was right. There was Sam, smiling almost merrily; and Frank, who wasn't. Smiling, I mean—merrily or otherwise.

"Good evening, Sam! Glad to see you again, Frank." I don't suppose God would get me for that little stretcher.

But really. There he was: shoulders slumped, hands stuffed into his coat pockets, hair slicked back, pouty, and looking as much like a New York hoodlum as any I'd seen depicted in the newspapers or magazines—and newspapers and magazines were always showing photos of New York hoodlums. They and their counterparts in Chicago were getting downright famous, thanks to Prohibition and the bootleggers determined to undermine the Volstead Act by providing illegal liquor to fools like Stacy Kincaid and her ilk. Perhaps infamous would be a better word.

"Lovely to be here," said Sam, ever so much more cheerfully than was customary for him. He glanced significantly at Frank, who looked back at him, then started like a scared rabbit.

Quickly, he said, "Likewise," and shut his mouth.

"Likewise what?" Asked his uncle, smiling a smile I wouldn't have wanted directed at me.

"Likewise, ma'am."

"Good enough. Is there anything we can do to help you and your aunt get dinner ready?" asked Sam. I do believe it was the very first time he'd ever offered to help us. Not that he wouldn't have pitched in if asked, but he was clearly attempting to irritate his uncouth nephew. His tactics seemed to be working, because Frank kept sliding looks at Sam as if he didn't dare put one foot wrong for fear of having his head caved in, or at least permanently bruised.

"Not a thing, thanks. Just come on inside, and I'll introduce Frank to Miss Petrie. Miss Petrie," I explained to Frank, "is my favorite librarian at the Pasadena Public Library."

"Uh," said Frank.

"Good evening, Sam and Mr. Pagano," said Pa, grinning genially. Pa liked everyone until given reason not to. So far, Frank had only pilfered one silver candlestick—at least that's all we knew about—so Pa was giving him the benefit of the doubt.

I'm not as nice as my father.

"Good evening, Joe," said Sam, giving Pa a handshake that looked positively ebullient. I tell you, dealing with his beastly nephew was good for the man! I was pleased about it.

"Oh, Sam!" said Ma, beaming a smile and coming into the living room. "It's so good to see you. And you, too, young man." She didn't smile when she turned her gaze upon Frank. Unlike my father, Ma didn't give folks too many chances. They had to measure up to her standards before she'd like them. I'm more like my mother than my father in that regard.

"Thank you," mumbled Frank. After shooting his uncle a frightened glance, he added, "Ma'am."

"Happy to be here again, Peggy," said Sam, who had only recently begun calling my kin by their first names. "Frank's a lucky boy, to get to dine with you folks. If he relied on me, he'd be eating bologna sandwiches."

"Huh," said Frank. I guess the utterance of that particular word ran in the family.

"What's bologna?" I asked, curious. That's because he pronounced balonya.

"I think you non-Italians call it boloney," said Sam, grinning at me. Then he bent and gave me a smooch on the cheek. I tell you, the man was almost jolly!

"I like the occasional boloney sandwich," said Pa.

"Me, too," I said. "But why do you call it balonya?"

"I suspect because it's originally from Bologna," said Sam. "The town in Italy."

"My goodness. I didn't know that. But I do like a boloney sandwich every now and then."

"Yes, but you wouldn't enjoy eating them all day every day, I suspect," said Sam, smiling up a storm.

"Probably not," Pa agreed.

"And here's Miss Petrie," I said, dropping the topic of boloney. "You remember Miss Petrie, don't you, Sam?"

"Of course, I do." Darned if he didn't execute a perfect little bow! "How do you do this evening, Miss Petrie?"

Looking as if she were about to sink into the basement through the living-room floor, Regina stuttered, "I-I'm fine, thank you. It's good to see you again, Detective Rotondo." She held out her hand, and Sam shook it with gusto.

"Shoot, just call me Sam," said Sam. "You're looking lovely this evening, Miss Petrie."

"Oh," said Regina, blushing. "Thank you. Daisy did it."

Sam gave me an odd look. I only smiled back. He shrugged.

"And this"—said he, giving Frank a pat on the back that darned near sent the boy sailing into the dining room—"is my nephew, Frank Pagano. Say good evening to the lady, Frank."

"Good evening."

"Good evening, what?" asked Sam, the smile for his nephew taking on a deadly cast.

"Good evening, ma'am," said Frank. Then he gulped audibly and looked at his uncle. Sam patted Frank's shoulder several times. They looked like awfully hard pats to me. Poor Frank. If he didn't already regret his rash escape from home, he would soon I had no doubt.

"Good evening, Mr. Pagano," said Regina softly, as if she didn't dare raise her voice. Library training, I suppose.

Again, Frank said, "Good evening"—He gave his uncle a terrified look—"ma'am."

"How's your leg feeling, Sam? I notice you're not using your cane this evening," said Pa, glancing at Sam's empty right hand.

By the expression on Sam's face, the question surprised him. He looked around as if searching for his cane and then said, "It hasn't bothered me much at all these past couple of days. I'll be darned. I haven't even thought about it."

"I'm so glad!" said I, wondering if dealing with his nephew was having a healing effect on Sam's overall wellbeing. "Here. Let me take your hats and coats and hang them on the rack."

"Frank can do that," said Sam, grinning evilly at his nephew. "Can't you, Frank?"

"Yes, sir," said Frank, instantly sliding out of his overcoat and reaching for his uncle's. He helped Sam off with his coat, hung both garments carefully on the rack, and then took Sam's hat and added it to his on the same coat rack. That evening, I do believe that poor rack held more garments than it ever had except on holidays when the whole family gathered at our house.

Rubbing his hands together in anticipation, Sam lifted his voice slightly and said, "Whatever you're cooking smells mighty good, Vi."

"Thank you!" called Vi from the kitchen.

"Why don't you fellows and Regina and Ma have a seat in the living room while I help Vi get dinner on the table," said I.

"You don't need Frank's help?" asked Sam, as if hoping for a positive response.

But I thought Frank would probably be more trouble than he was worth, so I said, "No, thank you. But I appreciate the offer."

"You're welcome," said Sam, eyeing his nephew with disfavor.

"Uh," said Frank.

I watched as Frank slunk into the living room behind my father and his uncle. He made a move to sit in one of the chairs, but Sam grabbed his arm and held him upright until my mother and Regina entered the room and sat themselves on the sofa. Then Sam more or less shoved Frank into the chair he'd been aiming for earlier. The kid was certainly getting lessons in manners. And from Sam Rotondo, of all people!

Vi and I had dinner on the table in a very few minutes, so I went into the living room, where I overheard a rather stilted conversation taking place.

"You don't like to read, Mr. Pagano?" Regina asked, as if in response to a comment from someone.

"Well, uh, I don't read much."

"He's an illiterate lout," said Sam, smiling at Frank.

"I'm not illiterate," said Frank, sounding probably as offended as he dared under the circumstances.

"Perhaps illiterate was too strong a word," Sam admitted. "But I won't withdraw the lout part."

"Cripes," muttered Frank.

Both of my parents were smiling. I think they'd caught on to what Sam was attempting—in a relatively crude way—to teach his nephew.

"Reading is very important," said Ma. "You can get a wider picture of the world if you read than you can just sitting home with your family and friends all the time."

"Or running around with gangsters on the streets," added Sam.

Frank said, "I don't—" and shut his mouth with a clack of teeth.

"Reading," said Regina in her soft voice, "can certainly broaden one's view of the world."

"So true," said Sam, sounding complacent. "I showed Frank the September issue of *National Geographic*. The article we read is called *Crossing the Untraversed Libyan Desert*. It was fascinating, wasn't it, Frank?"

Frank looked at his uncle and said, "Uh-huh." I didn't believe him.

Because I was there and my interest had been piqued, I said, "I didn't know you subscribed to the *National Geographic*, Sam."

"Oh, yes. Billy and I used to talk about the magazine all the time. You know how much he loved it."

"Yes, I remember." I sighed.

"This *Crossing the Desert* article of theirs records a two thousand-mile journey across Libya and the discovery of two previously unknown oases in Egypt." He turned to Frank. "Mrs. Majesty and I were in Egypt a couple of years ago, Frank."

"Oh," said Frank.

Grinning at me, Sam said, "Frank was fascinated by the story of the trip across the desert."

"Yes," said I. "I can tell. But it's dinnertime now, so you all can come in and take your places."

"Thanks," said Sam. He rose from the chair in which he had been sitting, and I noticed him grimace. I guess torturing his nephew hadn't completely healed his leg. Yet. I trusted Sam to prevail.

Because I thought it only proper, I sandwiched Frank between my mother and Regina Petrie across from me. If that didn't make him mind his manners, I didn't know what would. Actually, I did, because I seated myself next to Sam on the other side of the table. Generally I put Sam on the chair opposite mine at meals, but I figured what the heck. We were engaged to be married. Not only that, but if Frank turned sulky or said something hateful, Sam could kick him on the shin.

Pa said grace, as he usually did, and I noticed Frank surreptitiously make the sign of the cross—really quickly. I guess he hoped no one would notice. Not that any of us cared what churches other people attended, and he could believe whatever he wanted to believe as far as I was concerned. I do know that Aunt Vi didn't necessarily approve of the Roman Catholic practice of praying to various saints, and she considered them no better than idolaters because of all the statues and so forth in their churches, although she'd no more say so to anyone outside the family than she would smack Mrs. Pinkerton's face. And she'd *never* do that.

"These look wonderful," said Sam as the platter of Russian cutlets arrived at his place at the table. "And so do the vegetables."

"They're Russian cutlets," I told him, having confirmed the name of the dish with Vi before we brought out the serving plates. "And you pour the brown mushroom sauce over them. That's Russian pilaf under the cutlets."

"Precisely," said Vi, smiling at me. She knew I wouldn't know a Russian cutlet from a French poodle if she hadn't explained everything to me.

"Pilaf?" asked Frank in a small voice. Then he glanced across the table at his uncle, fear writ large on his features.

"That's the rice stuff the cutlets sit on," I told him with a smile, hoping Sam hadn't kicked him. Since Frank didn't howl or frown, I guess Sam had held his foot.

"We had pilaf in Turkey, Sam. Remember?"

"Not really, but I do remember eating a lot of rice over there. And in Egypt."

"I loved the food in Turkey," I said. "I didn't feel very good when Harold and I were in Egypt."

"You weren't feeling well in Turkey, either, as I recall."

"You're right." I piled some of Vi's wonderful roasted vegetables on my plate next to my molded Russian cutlet. I'd gone easy on the mushroom sauce, although after my first bite, I wished I hadn't. As usual, Vi had prepared a gloriously delicious meal.

"Pilaf, Frank, is what French people call risotto."

"Really?" I asked, interested. I loved eating food, even if I couldn't boil water without ruining it.

"More or less," said Sam.

Frank said, "Huh."

Ma and Frank both appeared tentative as they poised their forks above their cutlets. Not Regina. She delicately forked up a bite, chewed, swallowed, and smiled at Aunt Vi. "Daisy was absolutely right about you, Mrs. Gumm. This is delectable."

"Thank you, my dear. It's the least I can do for you after all the marvelous books you've found for us over the years."

"I love the cauliflower and the squash, carrots and beans, too," said Regina. "Just wonderful. I should learn how to be a better cook. Even if I only ever cook for myself, it would be nice to dine on toothsome meals instead of my usual dull fare."

"Couldn't agree with you more, Miss Petrie," said Sam, savoring his Russian cutlet, pilaf, mushroom sauce and all. "Mrs. Gumm is the best cook I've ever met in my life."

"Uh," said Frank, as if he intended to say something about his Italian background. Then he winced, so I think Sam's foot connected with his shin, only not awfully hard. "Uh, yes. This is good," he said, after having swallowed the tiniest bite of Russian cutlet he could possibly fit onto his fork.

"Thank you," said Vi.

"This really *is* good," said Ma, surprised. She shouldn't have been. She knew Vi well enough to know she'd never serve us anything that wasn't up to or exceeding par. Whatever par is. I think it's some kind of sports term.

NINETEEN

Sam and Pa both had seconds of Vi's Russian cutlets and mushroom sauce. As I'd had a big lunch, I didn't, although I managed to clean my plate. So did Ma and Regina. Frank left a little rice on his plate but Sam didn't scold him, for which mercy I was grateful.

"I'll clean up the dinner plates and fetch the dessert plates," I said, rising to do so.

So we ate chocolate cake and ice cream, and I felt quite virtuous for not having indulged in chocolate cake for lunch *and* dinner. After we were all through with dinner, I cleaned off the table and stacked the dishes in the sink. I figured I'd wash them later, after our guests had departed.

When I walked into the living room, I noticed that Frank had somehow got himself seated on the sofa between Vi and Ma. I strongly suspected Sam had something to do with that. Sam and Regina each sat on a chair, as did Pa. I smiled at everyone and walked over to Sam.

"May I speak to you for a moment alone?" I asked him softly.

"Sure. Front porch?"

The front porch was about the only place Sam and I could be private together. The temperature outside, even in mild Pasadena, California, was chilly on that October evening, however, and I didn't think the cold concrete would be good for him.

Therefore, I said, "Why don't we chat in the kitchen? It's too cold outside for your leg, especially if we sit on the porch steps."

"Good idea," said Sam, rising with another little grimace. Guess his poor leg had begun paining him. Not that I've studied psychology or anything, but I'd bet a student thereof would put the blame for that on Pa having mentioned Sam's lack of a cane earlier in the evening.

I led him into the kitchen, sat him on a chair, and left him at the kitchen table with Spike at his feet, hoping in vain for Sam to drop some food on him. Then I went into the bathroom, shook out two aspirin tablets from the bottle stored in the medicine chest—I'd learned the hard way to buy aspirin in bottles and not packets because they're ever so much more convenient to remove from a bottle than from a packet.

Returning to the kitchen, I poured a little water into a glass and handed glass and aspirin tablets to Sam.

He took them and frowned at me. "What's this for?"

"I know your leg is hurting. So just take those aspirin tablets with the water and don't argue with me."

"Hadn't planned on arguing," said Sam. He popped the tablets into his mouth and swallowed them with the water. Handing the glass to me, he said, "Thanks. That was sweet of you to think about my leg."

"I know it pains you. But what *I* want to know is what happened to the silver candlestick. You didn't let Frank keep it, did you?"

"Good Lord, no. I drove him up to your church, marched him to the pastor's office, and made Frank confess and hand over the candlestick." Mr. Merle Negley Smith was our minister at the First Methodist-Episcopal Church.

"Bet Frank didn't enjoy that," I said, smiling.

Sam's grin was probably more wicked than mine, although I don't know for sure. "He hated every minute of it. What made it worse was that Pastor Smith didn't scold him. He looked sad and disappointed, and prayed over the little thug."

I laughed. "I'd love to have seen that!"

"I enjoyed it." Sam smirked malevolently. "That kid's about to drive me 'round the bend."

"You'll fix him. I have faith in you."

"You do, huh?"

"I do."

"Next time you say those words, I expect we'll be married." Sam gave me a big frown.

"Let's wait until your leg is all healed. Anyway, I wanted to tell you Harold and I will be visiting Dr. and Mrs. Homer Fellowes tomorrow, and Harold will plan the Halloween party to which all the suspects in Miss Carleton's murder will be invited."

"Good God." Sam rolled his eyes. He did that a lot around me.

"Sam! It's a great way to get them all in one place so you can question them. Surreptitiously, you know. You won't be in uniform or anything." I had a brilliant idea. "In fact, you'll be in costume! I know just the thing, too."

"I'll be cursed if I'll wear a costume to any damned party," growled Sam, his frown turning ferocious.

"Nonsense. You have to be there, because all the suspects will be there. And Frank can help serve food at the party, so you can keep an eye on him, too. We don't want him running loose on the streets of Pasadena and getting into mischief, do we?"

"I want him to get out of Pasadena altogether," said Sam. "Damned kid's a waste of space."

"Precisely what I was thinking about Stacy Kincaid earlier today. You don't like Frank much, do you?"

"No. I don't know how Renata ended up with a kid like him. She's a caring person who loves her kids and has always done right by them. I'll introduce you two one of these days. You'll love her."

"Is she coming to Pasadena?" I asked. Oh, boy! I'd love to meet some of Sam's relatives. Some of his *other* relatives, I mean. I hoped none of the rest of them was like Frank.

"No. But I figured we could have our honeymoon in New York City. That way you can meet my family—God save you—and I can take you to see the sights. New York's an impressive place."

"When Harold took me to Egypt, we spent a couple of days in New York, but I didn't enjoy it."

"You weren't enjoying anything back then."

I sighed. "True. Won't your parents be coming to the wedding?"

"No. They won't set foot in a church other than a Catholic one. Frank's right about that. Catholics aren't supposed to attend other kinds of churches. My parents are strict Catholics and stuffy that way."

"Oh." Gee, I'd never thought of myself as a particularly undesirable daughter-in-law. The idea that Sam's parents might disapprove of me gave me a sinking sensation in my heart. "I'm sorry."

"I'm not. Consider yourself lucky. Don't get me wrong. I love my mother and father and sisters, but get them all into the same room, and you can't hear yourself think. Why do you think I stayed here after Margaret died?"

"I never thought about it. Your family's loud, eh?"

"All Italian families are loud," said Sam.

"Your father didn't balk at creating this lovely engagement ring," I said, staring fondly at my left hand.

Sam picked up my ring hand and kissed it. "He balked. I told him it was either accept you as a daughter-in-law or lose a son."

"You didn't!" Honestly, I was appalled.

"Did, too. Since I'm their only son, they decided to tolerate you."

"How kind of them," I said, feeling picked-on. And just because I wasn't an Italian or a Roman Catholic. Criminy!

On the other hand, my parents would probably have been dismayed if Sam had remained with his church and not gone with us Methodists to ours, or if I'd converted to Catholicism. In fact, they'd have been horrified if I'd done the latter. Hmm.

Religion causes a lot of problems in the world sometimes, doesn't it?

Sam leaned over and gave me a kiss. I kissed him back, and we might have stayed in each other's arms a lot longer than was proper, but Frank interrupted us. Actually, he appeared at the door to the kitchen, said, "Whoops!" and backed up.

Pulling away from me, Sam said, "Damn that boy."

I just sighed. Kissing Sam felt good. After Billy's demise, I didn't think I'd ever be able to love another man. Just goes to show that life is full of tricks, I reckon. I rose from my chair, and Sam pushed himself up from his, grunting a little.

"The aspirins aren't helping?" I asked, concerned.

"Give 'em time. They take a few minutes to start working. They will help, so thanks for thinking of them."

"You're welcome. Wish you could stay longer."

"Must get the brat home."

Holding hands like a couple of school kids, Sam and I walked out of the kitchen and into the dining room, where Frank stood in a corner, looking frightened.

"How'd you escape from the two Gumm ladies?" Sam asked him gruffly.

"I...I, uh...I just said I needed to go to the...the bathroom." Color rose to Frank's cheeks. As his complexion was what they call an "olive" hue, the blush didn't enhance his appearance any.

"Didn't anyone tell you where the bathroom was?" I asked, genuinely interested.

"Um...Yeah, they did, but—"

"Trying to find something else to pilfer?" his uncle asked mildly.

"No!" Frank turned a sort of puce color. Most unbecoming on him.

"Just want to get out of there, eh?" said Sam.

"Um...Well..."

"It's all right, Frank," I told him kindly. "I know you're not used to us folks here in California."

"You can say that again!" the young man blurted out. I think it was perhaps the first truly honest thing he'd said to me thus far in our acquaintanceship.

"Come along, then, you hooligan. We'll be polite, thank Mrs. Gumm for a delicious meal, get our coats and hats, and I'll take you home."

"Where do you sleep, Frank? I know Sam's bungalow isn't large. Is there more than one bedroom?"

"No. He sleeps on the sofa," said Sam, answering for his nephew. "I'm not about to let him have my bed."

Frank hung his head.

Sam grabbed him by the arm, jerked him around, and the three of us walked into the living room together.

Nudging his nephew, Sam said, "It's about time for us to get going. Thank you again for the wonderful meal, Vi."

"You're more than welcome," said Vi, smothering a yawn. She had to get up early in the morning. "Come again any time, young man."

"Uh...Thanks," said Frank. After peering at his uncle from the corner of his eye, he added, "Ma'am. Thank you for inviting me."

"You're welcome, Mr. Pagano," said Ma, rising and yawning in her turn. "I know it's early for bed, but we're early risers in this household."

"We are indeed," said Pa, standing in his turn.

"As am I," said Regina, likewise getting out of her chair.

"So am I," said Sam. He shoved Frank toward the coat rack.

"One of these days when you both can stay longer, we can have a musical evening," I said, attempting to sound bright and chipper. The odds a chipper mood would prevail were slim, what with Frank sulking and Sam wanting to murder him—I knew the signs—but I figured it was worth a try.

"That would be lovely," said Regina. Her voice actually *did* sound bright and chipper, if soft. "I love music, and I noticed your piano. I wondered who in the family played."

"Daisy," came a quartet of voices from my family and Sam.

"Oh, my, you can do *everything*, can't you, Daisy?" said Regina, gazing at me with something akin to rapture.

"Not really. My accomplishments on this green earth are minimal, to say the least."

"Nonsense. You sing and play the piano beautifully."

I had to look at him to be sure the comment had come from Sam. When I did, I found him gazing fondly at me. Good Lord.

"Thank you, Sam," I said, marveling at having been paid a compliment by Sam Rotondo, of all people. And in front of my family, Regina, and his rotten nephew, too!

He grinned, knowing he'd disconcerted me. He was *such* a tease sometimes. If Frank hadn't been there, I'd have smacked his arm. Since Frank was there, and Sam knew I'd never do anything so unlady-like in front of my family, he was safe from repercussions. For the moment.

I didn't see the two men out to Sam's Hudson as I usually did, but rather turned to speak to Regina, since she'd also declared her intention of leaving. She came up to me and held out her hand.

"I can't tell you how much I appreciate everything you've done for me, Daisy. I'll always be grateful."

"Fiddlesticks. Let's set up a date so we can go shopping next week sometime, all right?"

"Next Wednesday, the fourteenth, I'll be leaving at noon, because I have to work on Saturday. Would that be a good time for you? In the early afternoon?"

"Absolutely! I think the Fellowes's Halloween party will probably be the next Saturday, so we can find a costume for you to wear."

"A costume? For me? But...I haven't been invited to any party, Daisy."

"You will be," I said. I'd make sure of it. I aimed to talk to Robert Browning myself and demand he invite Regina to Gladys's party. Whether he wanted to or not. I *would* make sure all the suspects attended that party, dang it. Besides that, I had great hopes for a union between Robert and Regina.

As Ma and Vi went to bed and Pa sat in the living room reading *The Amazing Adventures of Letitia Carberry*, chuckling from time to time, I trod to the kitchen and began washing up the dinner dishes. As I was drying the very last cooking utensil, the stupid telephone rang.

"Good Lord," I muttered as I went to the telephone and lifted the receiver, hoping the caller wasn't Mrs. Pinkerton in a crisis. I'd barely uttered, "Gumm-Majesty—" when Sam's voice broke in.

"In case you wondered what happened to the little Chinese figurine you used to have in the china cabinet in the dining room, it's here now. I just plucked it from Frank's pocket."

"The little thief!" I cried, truly offended. Shucks, the kid had broken bread with us and then he'd *stolen* from us? He really was a lout. "I bought that in Chinatown a couple of years ago. It's a little statue of Buddha, and I like it!"

"That's why we're bringing it back to you tomorrow."

"Thanks. Be sure to call first, because I'll be spending a lot of the day with Harold and Gladys Fellowes."

"Will do. And Frank will apologize most sincerely. He said it must have fallen into his pocket."

"Right."

159

"I can't wait to get rid of him," said Sam.

I heard a faint, "Hey" in the background, but Frank was firmly in my black books by that time.

"Tell himself to 'hey' himself, and stop taking things that belong to other people. He's a purloining pig. You can tell him that, too, if you want to."

Sam must have turned his head because I heard him say, "You're a purloining pig, Frank Pagano, and don't ever forget it. Mrs. Majesty is the kindest person I know, and if she calls you a pig, you're a pig."

"What's that other word mean?" I heard in the distance from Sam's house.

"A damned thief," his uncle explained.

"Hey," said Frank.

Then I thought of something. "I think psychologists and alienists have a word for people who steal things compulsively, as if they can't help themselves. What's that word? Begins with a K, I think."

"Kleptomaniac," said Sam.

"That's it! Maybe he's a kleptomaniac."

"The hell with that. He's a thieving thug, is what he is."

I heard a faint "hey" from Sam's house.

I couldn't help it; I laughed. "Don't tell him I laughed. Tell him I'm outraged, will you?"

"You bet I will," said Sam. "Good-night."

"Good-night. Love you, Sam."

"You, too," said Sam, who probably didn't want to use the L word in front of Frank.

Boy, Frank was sure a handful. I hoped Sam could rid himself of the lad soon, although I felt sorry for Renata. Sam was right. She didn't deserve a weasel like Frank.

Oh, well. One can't choose one's relatives.

TWENTY

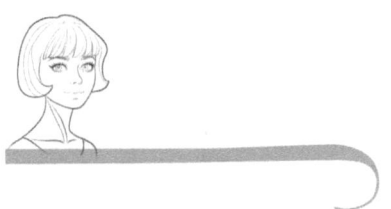

The following day, Saturday, Harold arrived on our doorstep promptly at ten a.m. Pa and I had just taken Spike for a walk around the neighborhood, so I hadn't neglected any particular duties and was feeling quite care-free as Harold and I waltzed out to his gorgeous red Stutz Bearcat.

"I love this car," said I, admiring the Bearcat's shiny surface. It darned near glowed in the October sunshine.

"I do, too. Roy gave it a bath and a wax job this morning before I drove over here."

Have I mentioned that Roy Castillo was Harold's house boy? Well, he was. He did pretty much everything for Harold and Del, from cooking to car-washing. He was a nice young man, too. It was a shame Sam's rotten nephew couldn't be more like Roy.

The drive to Gladys's house was pleasant, although Harold had the top up on his machine because, while the sun shone, the weather remained chilly. "I like Gladys's neighborhood. It's lined with those lovely deodar trees, and it's especially pretty at Christmas, when they hang lights on the trees."

"I have a friend who's building a house on Santa Rosa," said Harold. "Well, you know him too. Fred Greenlaw."

"Dr. Greenlaw! I really liked him. He was so good to tend to Mrs. Bannister on the sly as he did."

"Good thing nobody decided to press charges against us for sheltering a criminal."

Indignant, I said, "She wasn't a criminal! She was a victim of her brute of a husband!"

Harold slipped me a wicked grin. "I know it. I just like to rile you sometimes."

I smacked Harold's arm and he pretended the auto went out of control and zigzagged on the street. Good thing there weren't any other machines on the road. "Stop that!"

"Just funning you," said Harold.

A trifle peeved, I said, "I swear. Sam does the same thing. You two have a lot in common, whether you like it or not."

"Saints preserve us," said Harold in a God-be-with-me voice.

"Nerts."

We arrived at the Fellowes' home. Harold pulled into their driveway. "Nice place," he said.

"I think so, too. Where's Dr. Greenlaw's house going to be?"

"Up the street a little, near Mendocino."

"This is such a pretty neighborhood."

"Yes, yes, but let's get this thing started. I have a lot of planning and ordering to do, depending on when you want to have this party of yours."

"I'm hoping Gladys will want to do it on the eighteenth."

"That's next Saturday, Daisy. I'm good, but I'm not magic."

"Neither am I," I said, grinning.

"My mother thinks you are. She told me to beg you to call her after we're through here today."

"Oh, joy. Your poor mother."

"Anyhow, I suppose the eighteenth will be all right. The Castleton always leaps to obey any requests from Pasadena's elite, you know."

"Yes," I said, not being among Pasadena's elite, but knowing a whole bunch of them, "I know."

We'd reached Gladys's home, so Harold swung his Bearcat over the little bridge—the ditches along some of those streets were really deep—

and we got out. When we reached the front door I rang the bell, which chimed delightfully, just as Harold's did. We Gumms and Majestys, as I've mentioned, didn't have chiming doorbells. No sooner had the chimes begun than Gladys opened the door.

"You're here!" she said. "I'm so glad! This whole thing is becoming a nightmare."

We stepped into the front hall and I asked, "What whole thing?" I'd never seen Gladys perturbed before. Ever since I'd met her in the first grade, she'd seemed the image of brilliant, if distant, serenity. I guess a murder in one's life upsets things. Well, for heaven's sake, I *knew* it did.

"The project is teetering on the edge, Daisy, and Dr. Fellowes is so worried about it! You *have* to find the killer! The police keep interrogating Robert Browning, and I *know* he didn't kill poor Mary."

"Oh, dear. I don't think he did it, either."

"Robert Browning? The name sounds familiar," said Harold.

"This one isn't the poet," I told him. "He's a scientist, and he's one of the top managers at the Underhill Chemical Plant."

"Oh, him," said Harold. He tilted his head to a judicial angle. "He'd never kill anyone. He's a nice fellow."

"*We* know that!" said Gladys, actually going so far as to pull her hair a little. "But the police are too stupid to believe it!" She gave me a guilty look. "Sorry, Daisy."

"That's all right. Sam's not in charge of the case. You can call them all kinds of names if you want to, but don't smirch Detective Rotondo. He's not stupid. At all."

"If you say so."

Gladys didn't sound convinced, which peeved me a little. Granted, neither Sam nor I were mathematical geniuses or anything; still, we each had a few little gray cells. In fact, I hadn't met too many truly stupid policemen. I'm sure there were some—actually, I knew it, because six of them had been suspended from the police department for joining the KKK—but Sam didn't associate with them and, therefore, neither did I. Come to think of it, Sam didn't socialize with very many of his colleagues. Although I'd never much thought about that aspect of Sam Rotondo, just then I wondered why that was. I'd have to ask him.

Harold had been glancing around at his surroundings, seemingly not interested in Gladys's husband's project or much of anything else except the party. "Daisy said you'd like to host this shindig next Saturday night, the eighteenth."

Gladys gasped. "The eighteenth! Oh, no, we can't possibly have it then. That's the date of a faculty dinner, and Homer and I must attend. It's mandatory."

"Oh," I said, a little disappointed. I figured the sooner we held the party, the sooner Sam could arrest someone. Someone other than Robert Browning. "Would the following Saturday be better?"

"Yes," said Gladys. "Or Friday night, the twenty-fourth."

How she kept the days of the particular dates in her head without glancing at a calendar mystified me. Just one more aspect of Gladys's braininess, I suppose.

"Oh, but wait!" said Gladys, clapping a hand to her cheek. "I believe I have those dates confused. Let me look." She took off, I guess to find a calendar, and trotted back almost instantly. Perhaps trotted isn't the correct word. Thumped was more like it. "The eighteenth will be fine. The faculty dinner is on the twenty-fifth."

All right, I take back what I said about Gladys and dates.

"That would be better for me," said Harold. "The sooner, the better. I'll have to do a good deal of planning, although this appears to be a fine place for a party. Spacious. Lots of room for people to dance—"

"Dance?" Gladys cut in. "Do we have to dance?"

"You don't *have* to, but I think folks would appreciate having music and dancing. If you don't want to have dancing, you don't have to."

"I think dancing would be fun," I said, because I loved to dance. Hmm. I'd never asked Sam, but if he liked to dance, too, that would be nice.

"Well..." Gladys let her sentence die out. "I guess people at Cal Tech like to dance as much as anyone else."

"Probably," I said, although I couldn't imagine a bunch of brilliant scientists romping and dancing the foxtrot. Or that new dance, the Charleston, which I thought was delightful.

"I guess we can have dancing then," said Gladys, sounding monumentally unsure.

"You can decide on the dancing later. But having the party next

Saturday will be good for me. I have a lot of work to do for the studio, and my mother has needed me more than usual lately." Harold glanced at Gladys. "You do plan to let the Castleton provide the viands, right?"

With a peek at me, Gladys sounded a little uncertain when she said, "Uh…Yes, I think that's what Daisy and I decided. Isn't it, Daisy?"

"Absolutely. Neither you nor I can cook a lick, and the Castleton has great stuff. Right, Harold?"

"Right. And what the Castleton can't provide, Roy can."

"Who's Roy?" asked Gladys.

"My house boy. He'll help serve, too. He's a very helpful fellow, Roy."

"He studied cookery with my aunt, who's the best cook in the world," I added.

"Oh," said Gladys. "That's nice. Maybe I can get your aunt to teach me to cook."

"I don't know. She tried to teach me, but it didn't work. I still can't cook worth beans."

"Daisy has other talents," said the loyal Harold.

"Yes, I know." Gladys sighed. "But let me take you around to look at the rest of the house. You'll probably need to see the kitchen, right?"

"Right," said Harold.

So Gladys took Harold and me on a tour of her lovely new home. I was favorably impressed all over again, and almost wished I could afford to build my family a pretty new house on Santa Rosa Avenue. On the other hand, it might get a little crowded around Christmas time, what with people driving up and down the street all night.

During our tour of the Fellowes's place, Harold took extensive notes, beginning with the Fellowes's telephone number. We ended our sojourn in the living room. Gladys sighed as she all but collapsed into one of her pretty burgundy-colored armchairs. Harold and I shared the sofa.

"This will be a snap to put together," said Harold. "Between the Castleton and Roy, we can fix your guests up with a fine assortment of canapés and non-alcoholic drinks." He peered closely at Gladys. "You *do* want non-alcoholic drinks, right?"

Gladys appeared shocked by the question. "Of course! Dr. Fellowes and I are not law-breakers, Mr. Kincaid."

"I thought not." Harold appeared a bit downcast, as if he'd hoped he'd at least get a glass of sherry or something for his efforts on Gladys's behalf.

"And…Daisy, did we decide people should come in costumes? I can't remember."

She could solve algebraic equations and probably deal with all sorts of geometric proofs, but she couldn't remember if we'd decided on a costume party. How typically Gladys. I said, "Yes. For Halloween, remember?"

"Oh. Right." She glanced down at her protruding tummy. "I have no idea what I'll dress up as."

Then and there I had another of my brilliant ideas! This time I was pretty sure it actually *was* brilliant. "I know! A globe!"

"A globe?" Harold stared at me.

"A globe?" Gladys, on the other hand, appeared almost pleased. "Oh, that would be perfect! It would go with Halloween and Dr. Fellowes's project." Her face clouded over. There we go again, with another silly expression. But never mind that. "I have no idea how to dress like a globe, but it's a brilliant idea." See? Told you so; even Gladys thought it was brilliant.

"That's all right," said I, the noble seamstress. "I know precisely how to do it. I'll sew up your costume. And Harold, who's a wonderful artist, can draw the pictures of a globe on it."

"I can?" Harold didn't appear precisely honored to be called a wonderful artist.

"Yes. I've seen your work, Harold Kincaid."

After heaving a largish sigh, Harold said, "All right. I guess it's the least I can do for you taking care of my mother."

"Thank you. Anyhow, I have to make a costume for Sam—uh, Detective Rotondo, too."

"What's the detective going to be?" asked Harold, clearly fascinated, as if he couldn't imagine Sam as anything but a policeman.

"A Roman senator!" I said, so pleased with myself I beamed all over. Well, I don't know that actually, since I couldn't see myself, but it sure felt as though I were beaming.

"Great idea! I don't think the detective would approve of looking like a gangster or anything like that."

"No," said I. "He definitely wouldn't."

"You mean he'll wear a toga?" asked Gladys.

"Yes."

"Um…Weren't they rather flimsy garments?"

"Flimsy? What do you mean?"

"Well, didn't they reveal a good deal of…of a gentleman's…body?" Gladys turned red. Red looked better on her than it did on Frank Pagano, although it wasn't her best color.

"Good heavens, no! Whatever gave you that idea?"

Looking puzzled, Gladys said, "I'm not sure, really. I never liked history much. I guess I saw a moving picture with people in togas, and they didn't cover much."

"You're probably thinking of *Cleopatra* or one of those Biblical epics. They always make people wear flimsy costumes in those things," said Harold.

"In Biblical epics?" I asked, shocked. Don't ask me why. I knew enough about the motion-picture industry, thanks to Harold, to understand the industry as a whole will use any excuse to draw people in to see their flickers, and naked skin will do it every time.

"You know better than to ask that, Daisy," said Harold in a don't-kid-me-kiddo voice.

"Yes. I do. I'm sorry I even asked."

Gladys said, "Oh." Then her countenance took on a contemplative cast. "Didn't the ancient Greeks wear costumes that looked kind of like togas?"

"Yes," said Harold and I together. We looked at each other and laughed.

"Harold and I have studied the same history and costume books, I think. We both need information about what people wore when, Harold for his job and I for mine."

"Oh. Well, if the Greeks wore proper kinds of togas that covered the body sufficiently, Dr. Fellowes would probably wear one of those. Do you think you can make two togas, only make them so they'll be different from each other? I'll gladly pay for your services, of course. And yours, too, Mr. Kincaid."

"Fiddlesticks," I said. "I love to sew, and I'll be making a toga for Sam, so I'll just get enough fabric for two togas, and I'll make them look different."

"Perhaps the Roman can wear one of those red sash-things," said Harold. "Lots of them did that. Red or purple. I prefer red."

"True, and red is a good color for Sam. Anyhow, he's Italian, so he really *should* wear a toga."

Both Gladys and Harold looked at me blankly.

In an effort to redeem myself, I said, "But I'll be sure Dr. Fellowes's toga is in the Greek style and all white."

"I didn't know togas came in different styles," said Gladys.

I rose from the sofa. "Learn something new every day, I guess. But I need to get going now. I think I'll probably have to pay a call on Harold's mother, and I know Sam and his nephew will be visiting me today."

"I didn't know Detective Rotondo had a nephew," said Harold, also rising.

"Yes. He has several sisters in New York City, and many nieces and nephews. This one sprang himself upon Sam without warning."

"Goodness. I wouldn't like that," said Gladys. Not one for spontaneity, our Gladys. Well, I wasn't, either, so I didn't blame her for her attitude.

"Nor would I," said Harold. "Fortunately, I have no nieces or nephews."

I thought briefly about his sister and said, "And aren't you glad."

With a shudder, Harold said, "You bet your life, I am."

Gladys appeared puzzled. Then again, when she was communicating with normal people, she generally did.

"I'll give you a telephone call later this week, Gladys. I'll have to figure out how to make you into a globe, but I don't think it will be difficult," I told her

"Thank you. I think," said Gladys.

Harold and I laughed again. Gladys sort of half-smiled.

"I took your telephone number, so I'll give you a ring if I need to clarify anything with you," said Harold.

"Very well," said Gladys as if she hoped really hard he wouldn't need to clarify anything. "Thank you both." That was an afterthought, but I didn't care. Gladys was Gladys, and there was nothing anyone could do about it. Her. Whatever I mean.

When Harold started the Bearcat and headed back to my house, he said wryly, "Well, that was fun."

"Gladys isn't precisely a social butterfly. But she's nice. Really."

"If you say so. I'll get started on the planning at once. It'll take some organizing to get everything done in a week."

Thinking of the three costumes I'd have to stitch up—I already had a Gypsy fortune-teller costume hanging in my overstuffed closet—I said, "Yes. Me, too."

TWENTY-ONE

A s luck—or Mrs. Pinkerton—would have it, the telephone was ringing when Harold and I walked into our tidy bungalow on South Marengo Avenue. I sighed and headed for the kitchen, leaving Harold with my father and Spike.

"*Daisy!*" Shrieked Mrs. P.

I'd had the presence of mind to hold the receiver away from my ear before I picked it up, anticipating who'd be on the other end of the wire. Swallowing my sigh, I said in my most beatific and soothing spiritualist's voice, "Yes, Mrs. Pinkerton. I'm sorry you're in such distress."

"Oh, Daisy! May I see you today? Please? I know it's Saturday, but *please*? I need to consult Rolly. He can tell me if I've selected the right attorney for Stacy's defense."

In my opinion, there was no defense for Stacy. "I'm sure you did, Mrs. Pinkerton. Harold interviewed them all, didn't he?"

"Yes. He was an angel. But...Oh, Daisy, I'd feel *so* much better if the attorney I chose had Rolly's approval."

I swear. Poor Mrs. Pinkerton. She had all the money anyone would ever need in a lifetime or two, one great son, a very nice husband, and she wanted a fake spiritualist's fake spirit control to tell her she'd chosen

170

the right attorney for her villainous daughter. Sometimes—often, in fact —human beings flummox me.

"I'm sure Rolly will approve of your choice," I said. "But I have another commitment today, and I won't be able to visit you with Rolly until after that."

"Oooooooh!" she wailed. She was the best wailer I've ever met in my life. "Very well, if you can't come right now, I understand. Oh, but Daisy, I hope you can visit soon."

"So do I," I lied.

We said our good-byes, and I hung the receiver in the cradle. Instantly the darned instrument rang again. I waited a second or two in order to discern if it was our ring. It was. I picked up the receiver and daringly held it to my ear. I figured Mrs. P couldn't have redialed my number in so short a time, and she was the only wailer I knew.

"Gumm-Majesty residence. Mrs.—"

"Yeah, yeah. I know who you are," said Sam, sounding particularly truculent. Frank seemed to be playing on his nerves like a guitarist. Poor Sam. "Your damned line was busy when I called a minute ago."

"Mrs. Pinkerton," said I.

"Oh. Well, can Frank and I come over? He'll bring the Buddha and apologize for taking it."

"Bet he'll love doing that."

"I don't give a rat's patootie what he wants. The kid's a menace. He's like an albatross around my neck. He's poison. He's stupid, and he's bad."

"Hey!" came, faintly, from Sam's house.

"Yes, he does seem to be all of those things. You may tell him I said so, if you like."

"Good. I will. Be there soon."

And he hung up. Not one for the polite inanities of etiquette, my Sam. Oddly enough, that was one of the things I loved about him.

"Detective Rotondo?" came Harold's voice from behind me.

I turned and saw that he and Pa had entered the kitchen and had each taken a chair at the table. Because we always had a bowl of oranges on the kitchen table, Harold had filched one and was attempting to peel it.

"Yes. He and his nephew are coming over in a few minutes. You might do better with a knife," I suggested to Harold. "The Valencias are more difficult to peel than the navels, but they're sweet and delicious. I think that's the last of the Valencias. The navels are bearing like mad, though."

"Thanks."

"Here," said Pa, handing Harold a knife and a little plate so the juice wouldn't drip all over the kitchen table. Not that it didn't experience drips and spills all the time, but it was a nice thought on his part. My father is a wonderful man. Spike, who didn't much care for oranges, sat at Harold's feet and looked hopeful in spite of things. "So Sam and Frank are going to visit again, are they?"

"Yes," said I. "Frank stole my little Chinese Buddha when they were here last night."

Harold choked on a bite of orange. I whacked him on the back a couple of times. After he caught his breath, he said, "He *stole* something from you?"

"Yes. He's evidently shaping up to be a hard case. But Sam has him well in hand. So far. I think he goes through his pockets every night before he allows Frank to bed down on the sofa."

"Good Lord," said Pa. "First the candlestick and now your Buddha?"

"Yep. He's one of your classic pieces of work, I guess." Whatever a piece of work was.

"A candlestick?" asked Harold, his voice still rather tight.

"He stole it from the church when Sam and he went to choir practice with me."

"He stole it from your *church*?" From everything I'd gathered over the years we'd known each other, Harold didn't respect churches of any variety very much. He called Del's church, St. Andrews Catholic Church on Fair Oaks, "Our Lady of Perpetual Malice," for example. Apparently, though, even Harold had his limits. "Poor Sam."

"You betcha," said I.

We chitted and chatted for a few minutes, and I, being the old softie I am, caved in to Spike's pleading gaze and gave him a little piece of arrowroot biscuit. He was such a good doggie, he deserved a treat.

"I suppose you're going to pamper my mother with your presence after the detective and his criminal nephew leave," said Harold.

"Yes." I heaved a deep and heartfelt sigh.

"Sucker," said Harold.

"Not really. I'm earning a living. She wants Rolly to endorse the selection of attorney you and she made yesterday."

"Good God," said Harold.

Pa guffawed.

"That's what I thought when she told me why she wanted me. I feel sorry for your mother, but I'm not eager to endure her misery."

"She brings it on herself."

"In this case, Stacy brought it on her."

"And whose fault is that?"

"Genetics?"

Pa laughed. Harold grinned. And the doorbell rang. Figuratively speaking. It actually kind of scritched.

"Must be Sam and Frank," I said, getting up and following my faithful hound to the front door. Spike *always* beat me to the door.

"Oh, good," said Harold. "I want to meet this famous nephew of his. Maybe we should get him and Stacy together."

"Bite your tongue, Harold Kincaid," I said, feigning horror. "Anyhow, Stacy's going to be in the clink for a good long time."

"You hope."

"I hope," I acknowledged.

After telling Spike to sit and stay, which he did, I opened the door. Sure enough, there were Sam Rotondo and a morose-looking Frank Pagano standing there, coats buttoned up against the cold. I smiled at them both.

"Come in, gents." I stood back and gave my beloved dog the signal that he could begin welcoming the guests. He did so with gusto. I was sorry to see Sam using his cane again.

Nevertheless, Sam, who knew what good manners were and when they were called for, bent over and gave Spike a friendly greeting. "Good boy," he said to Spike, who loved hearing that he was a good boy. "Want to teach my nephew some manners?"

"Hey," said Frank.

"You could obviously use some lessons," I told the boy. Boy, heck. He was a young man and should know better than pull the shenanigans he'd been pulling. I held out my hand. "Give me back my Buddha."

Pouting, Frank stuck a hand into his overcoat pocket and said, "Here. Sorry."

"Sorry for what?" I asked, looking him square in the eye, which was rather difficult as he was a good deal taller than I. But I have my methods.

"Sorry I ended up with your statue."

"'Ended up' with it? You stole it, is what you did, young man. It's past time you began taking responsibility for your deeds, good or evil. I'm sorry your uncle has to put up with you."

"Jeez," muttered Frank, handing over the little Buddha. It was quite pretty, in a colorful Chinese sort of way. "Sorry."

"Sorry for what?" I refused to relent until he confessed to his evil deed.

"Sorry I took your thing."

"You stole it, is what you did. And it's a statue of Buddha. Well, statuette, I suppose is a more appropriate term."

"Don't waste your time," advised Sam. "He doesn't know the difference between a statue and a horseshoe."

"Hey," said Frank, although his voice was small.

Not that it matters, but I'd looked at several books in the library that dealt with Asian art. The Japanese fold paper in amazing ways to create birds and dragons and so forth. I think the paper art is called Origami. Overall, however, I preferred Chinese art to Japanese art. Not that I'd done a vast study of either. I'd just looked at library books. However, the Chinese pictures I'd seen were bright and vibrant and...well, kind of gaudy. The Japanese art I'd seen was, while lovely, too darned serene for my taste. Give me a lively, active scene any day to one of boring tranquility.

Hmm. I wonder if that signifies something I don't really want to know about my personality. Never mind. I don't care to think about it right now.

"We can't stay long," said Sam. "I have to go to the train station and see when I can get rid of this freeloader."

"Hey," said Frank.

"Oh, be quiet," I told him. "You don't have a say in anything. Take your uncle's coat and hang it and your own on the coat rack. You have to meet a friend of mine."

"I do?" Frank neither sounded nor appeared pleased about the upcoming introduction.

Sam grinned. "Is Kincaid here?"

Odd that he should be pleased Harold was here. He didn't approve of Harold, as I believe I've mentioned before. Harold didn't care about Sam one way or the other, although he'd voiced his appreciation a couple of times. Heck, he'd shot a man in Turkey in order to save Sam's life once! Sam should appreciate Harold and not the other way around, in my humble opinion. Which, needless to say, I didn't voice just then.

"Follow me," I said after Frank had done as I'd ordered.

Pa and Harold had drifted to the dining room. Pa smiled at Sam and said, "Good morning, fellows. Happy to see you, Sam."

"You, too, Joe," said Sam, shaking my father's hand.

"And what do you have to say for yourself, young man?" asked Pa, holding his hand out to Frank.

"Uh...Nothing," said Frank, shaking my father's hand. He dropped it almost instantly.

"Good thing, too," said Sam. Turning to Harold he nodded and said, "Kincaid."

"Good morning, Detective Rotondo," said Harold in a hearty voice, shaking Sam's hand with vigor. "And this is your nephew I've been hearing so much about?"

"Nothing good, I trust," said Sam.

"Not a thing," said Harold.

Frank said, "Hey," only he didn't sound awfully sure of himself.

"That's him, all right," said Sam. "I, for one, am profoundly sorry for it. He belongs in New York City."

"Hey," said Frank again.

"It's good to meet you anyway, young man," said Harold, holding out his hand to Frank.

"Yeah. You, too," said Frank, shaking Harold's hand as briefly as he'd shaken Pa's.

"We'd better be going," said Sam. "We have things to do."

"As do I," I told him. "I have to visit Harold's mother."

"I'm sorry," said Sam.

As his nephew stared at him, Harold laughed. So did Pa.

I didn't, but that's only because I knew what was in store for me. "See you two tonight for dinner, I hope."

"You sure you want to risk it again?" asked Sam, watching his nephew rather as he'd watch a cockroach scuttle across a counter.

"Aw, why not? We'll teach Frank some lessons in good manners one of these days."

"You really think so?"

"Perhaps you'd better handcuff him so he can't steal anything else," I said as I walked the two New Yorkers to the door.

"Not a bad idea," said Sam.

Frank said, "Hey."

TWENTY-TWO

My visit with Mrs. Pinkerton was as fraught as I'd expected it to be. I'd been kind of hoping Harold would go with me to see his mother, but he said he had a party to plan so I forgave him.

Because I figured I should, I took my tarot deck with me along with my Ouija board. Just as I'd foretold—see? I really was good at this spiritualist nonsense—she wanted me to deal out a tarot hand for her. It was as unencouraging as Rolly had been, although Rolly had approved of her attorney.

It had been a busy morning, I'd had no lunch yet, and I was tired and hungry by the time Mrs. P let me go. She wept all over me, as usual, and I decided to take a detour to the kitchen before I left for home. Maybe Vi would feed her poor, starving niece.

She did, bless her.

Setting a plate with a sandwich and some apple salad on the kitchen table, along with a bowl of steaming soup, she said, "Featherstone told me you were here, and when I looked at the time, I guessed you hadn't eaten luncheon yet."

"You guessed correctly. Thank you *so* much, Vi." Then I registered what she'd said. Staring at her hard, I asked, "Featherstone *speaks* to you?"

"Of course, he does," said Vi, sounding and looking surprised. "Why wouldn't he?"

"I don't know." I picked up my spoon, hoping the soup was as good as it smelled. "I just never think of Featherstone as being human. He's always been a butler to me."

Vi laughed. "Daisy Majesty, you're a caution!"

See? Told you she said that to me. I still don't know what it means.

The soup was, as I might have predicted—there goes my spiritualist's wisdom again—delectable. The sandwich, too, which was made with ham and cheese, both of which rested on a bed of rye bread with mustard, lettuce, tomato slices, and very thinly sliced onions, was one of the best sandwiches I'd eaten in my life. I'd have gobbled it down in three seconds had my aunt not been watching.

"That was delicious, Vi. Thank you, thank you, thank you."

"You're more than welcome, sweetie. There's a slice of lemon custard pie with meringue on top for you if you can stuff anything else inside you."

"I can always stuff pie in," said I. "I've never heard of lemon custard pie with meringue before."

"It's a recipe I got from Evelyn McCracken. She calls it 'lemon meringue pie,' so I guess that's what it is."

Glancing up from the slice of delicious-looking pie Vi had set before me, I said, "Didn't she used to cook for the Bannisters?"

"Yes. She still cooks for Mrs. Bannister now that her husband is deceased." Vi sat in another chair at the kitchen table. "Evelyn said Mrs. Bannister is ever so much happier now without him. I don't know whether to be shocked or not."

"Huh," said I, borrowing freely from Sam. "You should be as happy as she. He was a vile person and didn't deserve to be called a human being. He not only beat her to within an inch of her life, but he sold children into slavery to horrible, perverted men."

"Daisy!"

"It's the truth, Vi. You know that. I told you precisely what that evil man did."

After a pause, she said, "Yes, I do know it. I just wish things like that didn't happen."

"So do I." Then I shut up and ate my pie. It was absolutely heavenly. When I'd scraped my plate, seeking the last splotches of lemon curd and meringue, I said, "You ought to make this for the family, Vi. It's wonderful."

"I aim to do just that. Evelyn said you can make any sort of custard pie you want and plop a meringue on top. She said she's even made a custard pie with coconut on it."

"Oh, can you make that for my birthday?" I loved coconut almost as much as I loved Sam.

With a laugh, Vi said, "You won't have to wait that long. I aim to feed the family one tonight."

"You're a saint, Vi."

"Don't be silly."

"It's true," I said firmly. Then I kissed my marvelous aunt good-bye and exited the mansion by the service-porch door. I didn't want Mrs. P to see me and ask me for one more Rolly chat or another tarot-card reading. It would be just like her to think Rolly or the cards might change their minds in the forty-five minutes or so since they'd both told her what they'd told her. Or something like that. Anyhow, some people baffle me. A lot of them do, actually.

By the time I got home, Spike was ready for another walk, and I was bushed. However, knowing where my duty lay, I changed clothes, put the leash on my faithful hound, a coat and hat on me, and walked Spike around the neighborhood. Pa was out visiting someone or other, so it was just Spike and me on that brisk October afternoon. The wind blew, but not hard enough to knock us off the sidewalk, so we enjoyed ourselves.

When we got home, I hied myself to the sewing room, rummaged through my various materials and scraps thereof, and decided I needed to make a visit to Maxime's Fabrics on Colorado Street in order to get enough yards of white fabric for a couple of togas and look around to see if I might find a suitable—meaning cheap—fabric with which to make a globe. I'd also have to figure out a way to make it round. I mean, Gladys was quite round in the front, but a globe is round all over, so I'd have to create something. Perhaps Harold would have an idea. He made clothes for the stars in the flickers, after all. He knew more about how to construct costumes than I did.

I was just about to step out of the house when the dad-blasted telephone rang again. I contemplated not answering it, but my livelihood and that of my family depended on the money I made in my odd profession, and the telephone was a huge part of it, so I took a deep breath for courage and headed to the kitchen.

"Gumm-Majesty residence—"

"Yes, yes, I know all that."

Harold! Thank God!

"I'm *so* glad it's you, Harold! I feared it was your mother again."

"No. Dr. Benjamin paid a call and prescribed a composer for her, so she's napping at the moment. What I want is for you to meet me at Maxime's Fabrics. Can you do that?"

"Now?"

"Now."

"I was just headed there! This is quite fortuitous, Harold Kincaid. You must have read my mind."

"That's your game, not mine. But I figured you'd probably need help rounding out your friend in order to make her look like a globe in the back as well as the front."

"You *did* read my mind! That's precisely why I was going to Maxime's. Well, that and to get enough fabric for two togas."

"And a red sash for the detective's. He'll look quite regal in a white toga with a red sash—or whatever you call it. It will go over one shoulder and tie around his waist with a white cord."

"Wow, you really know your way around a toga, don't you?"

"You bet I do. The Nash Studio is planning a production of *Julius Caesar*, and I've had togas on my mind lately."

"They're doing a Shakespeare play? With no sound? That should be interesting."

"Very. But please join me at Maxime's. I know just what we can do for Mrs. Fellowes to make her look globelike all over."

"Good, because I couldn't think of a way. You're a pal, Harold."

"Damned right I am."

So I met Harold at Maxime's, and he'd already picked out the toga cloth—twelve yards, for crumb's sake! Fortunately for yours truly, the white percale Harold chose wasn't expensive.

"Why make an expensive one? You'll only re-use the fabric to make sheets or something, won't you?"

"Guess I'll have to. I prefer making clothes."

"Well, you can be practical for once and make sheets for your family."

"I'm always practical."

"Right." Harold sounded skeptical. As I've said many times, he knew me well.

The gorgeous crimson percale was heavier and cost a bit more than the white sheeting, but it was worth it. I needed four yards of that, but I could make my nieces beautiful dresses out of it for Christmas after Sam's duty at the Fellowes's Halloween party was over. I'd trim both dresses with white lace, too. I already had the lace, ripped from one of Mrs. Pinkerton's old dressing gowns Edie Applewood had once given me, claiming she didn't know what to do with it but she knew I would. She was right as rain. Good old Edie.

"The detective will appear quite stunning in red and white," said Harold.

"Yes. He will, won't he?" I smiled, picturing a grouchy Sam, whining and complaining as I made him don his toga. But he'd enjoy it. I knew my Sam. Complain as much as he wanted to; he enjoyed acting. Heck, he'd sung the role of Pish-Tush in *The Mikado* a year or so before, the original Pish-Tush having been imprisoned for murder, and he'd done it like a pro. Sam had a spectacular bass voice, which he didn't use often enough in song. He seemed to be using it to good effect on his nephew these days, however, so I didn't repine. I'd get the old grump to sing at Christmas time, providing he'd managed to rid himself of Frank by then.

Because Dr. Fellowes didn't require anything but white for his ancient Greek toga, all I then needed was fabric for Gladys's globe.

Harold had solved that problem, too.

"Here," said he, holding out a bolt of gray-blue muslin.

"What's that?" I squinted at the bolt. The color didn't look awfully jolly to me. Then again, it was going to be turned into a globe, so I guess the color could pass as that of the various oceans.

"Ocean," said Harold, again reading my mind. Or maybe I'd read his. Piffle. It doesn't matter.

"Brilliant. And you can draw the continents and stuff on it?"

"Yes. And then it won't be good for anything else, but maybe you can use it as rags or something."

"I'm not going to rip up a good three or four yards of fabric in order to make rags!" I said, outraged at the thought. "Anyhow, it'll belong to Gladys after the party, and so will Dr. Fellowes's toga material."

"You're too kind. You've already roped me in to planning their party, and you're making the costumes. You ought to get something out of it."

"With any luck, we'll get a murderer out of it."

"Good Lord. The killer of that dead librarian, you mean?"

"Yes. All the suspects will attend the party."

"Good Lord," Harold repeated.

Harold and I marched to the counter and looked around. Generally speaking, there were a couple of women who worked there, eager to consult, advise, offer opinions, and cut fabric for Maxime's customers. Not today. Today Harold called out, "Anybody here?"

Almost instantly, a woman appeared from the back of the store, clearly embarrassed at having been caught not attending to business.

"I'm so sorry," said Mrs. Langlois, a lady I'd know for years from the fabric store. "Oh, Mrs. Majesty, I'm sorry you had to wait."

"It's all right. I was surprised not to see you as soon as we walked in." I gave her a smile to let her know her absence hadn't annoyed me, although it might annoy Maxime—whoever she was—if someone had made off with bolts of material because Mrs. Langlois hadn't been supervising things.

"It's just been a confusing day, is all," said she. "Miss Dabney is ill today, and Mrs. Harris had to leave because her daughter got sick at school and poor Mrs. Harris had to pick her up." She lowered her voice. "I was just devouring my lunch back there." She hooked a thumb over her shoulder to designate the back room. "Hadn't had time to eat since I opened the shop at nine this morning."

"Mercy, that's a long time to go without food. I'm so sorry about Mrs. Harris's daughter. Do you think she'll be all right?"

"I don't know. Mrs. Harris said the school nurse didn't explain the nature of Gretchen's illness."

"I hope she gets well soon."

"As do I," said Mrs. Langlois.

Harold cleared his throat.

"Oh!" exclaimed Mrs. Langlois. "I'm so sorry! You must want to set those heavy bolts down." She cleared off a space on the counter by sliding several pattern books to the side. Harold dumped three bolts of fabric onto the empty space.

"Are these for you, Mrs. Majesty?" asked Mrs. Langlois.

"Yes and no," I told her, smiling. "Please, Mrs. Langlois, allow me to introduce you to one of my very best friends, Harold Kincaid. Harold is a costumer for a motion-picture studio in Los Angeles, and he's going to help me make a friend into a globe for Halloween."

"Pleased to meet you," said Mrs. Langlois, holding out her hand for Harold to shake, which he did. Then she glanced at me and back at Harold as though wondering if we harbored a budding romance. If she only knew.

"Likewise," said Harold. "In order to accomplish the globe costume and ties for the togas, we'll also need some one-inch cord and two packets of bias tape, either this color or white. Doesn't matter what color the cord is. Oh, wait. It does, too, because we'll use it for the togas. So the cord should be white."

"Togas?" said Mrs. Langlois.

"Halloween party," I explained.

She nodded. "Of course. Let's visit the notions section. I'm sure we have the kind of cord you need."

She was right. Harold selected four yards of white cord and two packets of grayish bias tape. Then he stood there, tapping his chin with a finger, thinking. He turned to me. "How much white thread do you have at home?"

"Not enough," I said. "I think we'd better get another large spool of mercerized white thread and one small spool of red. I'd better match the red to the crimson percale you found, Harold. And I'd better get some thread to match the globe costume."

Eager to atone for her earlier absence, I guess, Mrs. Langlois said, "How much do you need of the crimson percale? I'll cut it and bring it over."

"Thank you. Four yards, I believe. Right, Harold?"

"Right."

Eventually we left Maxime's laden with parcels full of fabric and sewing notions.

"Now all we need is cardboard and starch. Do you know where we can purchase cardboard?"

"Nelson's dime store, I expect. They probably have starch, too."

"Good. Because we're going to need both for the globe."

Oh, boy. Gladys was going to love this. I'm fibbing.

But that was all right. She wanted me to find the killer, so she'd just have put up with being a starchy globe instead of merely a starchy professor's starchy wife.

I'm sorry. Sometimes I can't help myself.

TWENTY-THREE

Harold helped me cart all the parcels into our house, said his good-days to Pa and Spike, and then took off to contemplate globe-making.

"Looks like the two of you did some shopping," said Pa, eyeing the packages Harold and I had set on the dining room table.

"We did. I have to make Gladys Fellowes into a globe, and I have to make a Roman toga for Sam and another, Greek, toga for Dr. Fellowes."

"I didn't know there were different kinds of togas."

"Neither did Gladys. But I looked them up in the library once."

Pa shook his head. "You're a wonder to me, Daisy. You know more about things I never even think about than anyone else I've ever known."

I squinted at my father. "I don't know if that's a bad thing or a good one."

He laughed. "It's a good thing."

"You really think so?" After contemplating the packages, I said, "Think I'll take these to the sewing room and open them up. Then everything will be in one place and I won't get confused."

"If you say so, sweetie."

So Spike and I retired to the sewing room, and I opened the parcels of fabric and sewing notions. I'd just put the new spool of white thread into the thread-holder device Pa had made for my multitude of colorful spools—very handy with carpentry, my father—when the stupid telephone began ringing.

I looked at Spike.

Spike looked at me.

Pa called, "Daisy, it's for you!"

So I sighed, said, "Sorry, Spike," and headed to the kitchen.

I'd no sooner taken the receiver from Pa's hand and spoken my ritual speech into the instrument than I heard Robert Browning's voice. Only it hardly sounded like him. In fact, I didn't realize it was he until he told me so.

"Daisy! It's Robert Browning. I'm sorry to bother you, but I've got to talk to somebody about this, and since your fiancé—"

"Wait just a minute, Robert." I know it's impolite to interrupt people, but if you've ever had a party line, you'll understand. Trust me on this.

I cleared my throat. "Will all our party-line neighbors please hang up your receivers? This call is private, and it's for me."

There came through the wire three clicks. I waited for a fourth when: "Well," said our most persistent party-line neighbor, Mrs. Barrow, "you might give other people a chance to use *their* 'phones every now and then, you know! You're always hogging the line."

"Nonsense. I haven't been home all day long, Mrs. Barrow. Now please hang up your telephone."

She did. Slammed it onto the receiver, I think, because it made quite a noise. I'd have thoroughly disliked Mrs. Barrow if she hadn't assisted in the solving of a murder case once. But there was no question that she was an irritating woman. Plus, she had a perfectly hideous back-east accent, much uglier than Sam's—or even Frank's, for that matter, and I hated to think Frank was better at anything than anyone else, even Mrs. Barrow. Did that make any sense?

"I'm sorry," said Robert, sounding as if he were on the verge of a nervous collapse. "I forgot most folks have party lines."

"Yes. We have one. What's the matter, Robert? You sound dreadful."

"You'd sound dreadful, too, if the police believed you to be a murderer!"

"Oh, dear. I'm so sorry, Robert. If only you hadn't picked up that knife."

"That was stupid, I know. But that's not the only thing. I also knew Miss Carleton, and the police think I'm responsible for...for something...well, for something reprehensible that happened to her. And I'm not, Daisy! But I promised both her and Elizabeth I'd never tell a soul what happened."

"Oh. Do you mean about her baby?"

Silence reigned over the telephone wires for several seconds, giving me plenty of time to listen hard and make sure Mrs. Barrow hadn't surreptitiously picked up her own telephone receiver. You can tell when someone does that because you can hear a kind of hollow sound on the line. Hard to describe, but there you go.

At last Robert said in a small voice, "You *know* about her baby?"

"I know she had one. I don't know any more except that she wasn't married at the time." I hurried to explain, "And I'm not blaming her for anything! I'm sure women get into that fix more often than anyone cares to acknowledge, and it's seldom their fault. At least, that's what I think. Men can be so persuasive sometimes."

More silence. Then, "I didn't know anyone else knew."

"Gladys Fellowes told me. I don't know how she knew, unless she and Miss Carleton were friends or something."

Another spate of dead air ensued. After several empty seconds had passed, Robert said, "Daisy, may I see you privately? I don't know when. Maybe...I don't know. When would be good for you? I *have* to talk to somebody about this, and since you and Detective Rotondo are...well, you're good friends—"

"We're engaged to be married, but I won't tell him anything you tell me not to tell him. If that makes sense."

"Yes. Yes, it does. Thank you, Daisy. I really appreciate your willingness to listen. Maybe you can give me some advice. I'd ask...Well, never mind. But thank you. Could we meet somewhere to talk?"

"I can visit your office if you like. I'll probably have to see a client on Monday, but I can go to the Underhill Plant after that."

"Actually, I'll probably be at Cal Tech on Monday. The project is nearing completion, and I have to be there quite often these days."

"Why don't you come to our house for dinner on Monday night? I know you and Regina—I mean, Miss Petrie—are going out to dinner on Tuesday."

"She told you?" He sounded pleased.

"Yes. She told me. She's quite happy about it."

"She is?"

"Yes, she is."

"I'm so glad. She's…Well, I'm not sure exactly how to say this, but she's the first woman I've met since Elizabeth passed away with whom I can converse easily. Except for you, of course, but that's because we've been friends forever."

My insides lit up like fireworks on the Fourth of July. Not because of what Robert had said about us being friends—we were friends, but that's not the point—but because of what he'd said about my very favorite librarian in the whole, wide world. I think Robert Browning and Regina Petrie would make a practically perfect couple. I didn't say so, because I didn't want to spook Robert.

"I think you and she share some common interests," said I, trying to be sly.

"We do. I went back to the library on the Saturday after…Well, after that horrible day, and she guided me to some wonderful biographies."

"I'm so glad. But will you be able to come to dinner with us on Monday?" Then I remembered Sam and Frank. Fiddlesticks. "Nerts. I fear the detective and his nephew will be here, too, but if you could possibly come early—maybe four-thirty or five? That would give us plenty of time to talk alone."

"I'd rather not dine with Detective Rotondo right now. I know that doesn't sound very nice of me, but the man suspects me of a hideous crime, Daisy."

"Does he really? Or is he just treating you like any other suspect, do you think?"

"I don't know how he treats most of the people he suspects of murder, but I wouldn't feel comfortable dining with him. I hope you don't hate me for that."

"Don't be silly. I know you didn't kill poor Miss Carleton. Sam has to treat everyone like suspects until he proves to his satisfaction they aren't."

"I'll be really glad when he clears me."

"Me, too. Would you rather meet at the library or something? There's always an empty table or two for folks to chat at, if we keep our voices down. Nobody uses the periodical room much. We can meet in there, if you like."

"I would like that. I'd get to see Miss Petrie, too. Thanks, Daisy. I really appreciate this."

"Of course, Robert. You can tell me what you have to tell, and I can tell you if you should tell Sam or not."

"Thank you." He sounded uncertain. "Although…Well, I promised Miss Carleton and Elizabeth I'd never tell anyone what she told me."

"Word's already got out in some circles, so I don't think you can keep it a secret much longer, and the longer you delay, the worse you'll look in the eyes of the police. Besides, both of those women are deceased, and they're beyond caring. Unless they're watching from above, and I'm sure they'd rather you clear yourself of a charge of murder than keep a secret that's no longer…I guess relevant is the word I want."

"Oh, God." Pause. "All right. Four o'clock in the periodical room at the library. Thank you, Daisy. You might just be a life-saver."

Dramatic, but I know I'd be frightened if Sam suspected me of murder, too.

"You're welcome. See you then."

We both hung up.

Instantly the telephone rang again. Pooh.

"Gumm-Majesty residence. Mrs. Majesty speaking," said I, as ever.

"Daisy, this is Griselda."

"Good afternoon, Mrs. Bissel!" I always liked hearing from Mrs. Bissel because she wasn't prone to hysterics as was Mrs. Pinkerton.

"Good afternoon. I have a request of you, which I hope you won't mind."

"I'm sure I won't mind," said I, unsure of any such thing. However, Mrs. Bissel was a thinking woman, again unlike Mrs. P, so I didn't anticipate too much trouble from her. Well, there was that time a real, honest-to-goodness ghost showed up at one of my séances held at her house, but the less said about *that*, the better. Scared the bejeebers out of me. I don't even *believe* in ghosts, for Pete's sake.

"A dear friend of mine just lost her daughter, and she's terribly upset."

"I can imagine. The notion of losing a child wrings my heart. It's difficult even to contemplate such a tragedy." Of course, I had no children, but I had nieces...and there was even hope on the horizon, perhaps, of having a family of my own one day.

"It is indeed. I don't know what I'd do if anything happened to Dennis, Genevieve or Joanie." Dennis, Genevieve and Joanie were her children, all three grown up and with families of their own.

"It doesn't bear thinking of," said I, sounding spiritually mournful.

"Indeed. But, Daisy, my dear friend, Ellen Carleton, just lost her daughter. To *murder*. I just can't believe it."

I could believe it, although her words stunned me. Kind of like a boulder to the head, if you know what I mean. "Miss Carleton? The librarian?"

"Yes. Did you know her?"

"Not well, but I met her when she worked at the Pasadena Public Library. I was horrified when she was killed."

"As was I. And I know you've told me before that sometimes it takes a spirit a while to settle into the Other Side"—whatever that was, but my income depended on it—"and that poor Mary might not be available to speak at our séance yet, but would you please give it a try? On this coming Tuesday, if that works for you. It would comfort Ellen to know her daughter is safe in the arms of our Lord."

Whoo boy. It would comfort me to know that, too, but I had no way of knowing it to be true. Or untrue, for that matter. I swear, lying for a living can be downright uncomfortable sometimes. However, it was my duty to forge onward, ever onward, so I did. Undaunted; that's me. Or should that be I? Oh, who cares?

"Certainly I can do that, Mrs. Bissel. I'm glad you already know Rolly might not be able to get in touch with Miss Carleton. If you could explain that to Miss Carleton's mother, I'd appreciate it. I'd hate for her to be horribly disappointed."

"I've already discussed the matter with her, dear. She understands. It would give her great comfort to know her sweet Mary is all right, though."

"Yes. I'm sure it would."

"And is Tuesday all right?"

I took a deep breath and used it to say, "Tuesday will be perfect, and I'll be glad to do that for her, Mrs. Bissel."

"Thank you so much, Daisy. You're such a marvel."

"Thank you. You're too kind."

"Fiddlesticks. How is dear Spike doing?"

I glanced down at my hound, who sat at my feet looking hopeful. We were in the kitchen, after all.

"He's very well. I honestly don't know what I would do without Spike, Mrs. Bissel. When I lost my Billy, Spike was my main source of comfort, even though I have the most wonderful family in the world."

"I understand completely. There's just something…Well, there's something almost magical about the comfort one can get from a dog. And, of course, dachshunds are special."

"They are, indeed."

"When my Francis passed, my children were as upset as I, and the dogs helped us all." Francis was her late husband. I'd never met him, but I'd heard from several sources that he'd been a kind and considerate man. And extremely wealthy, bless him.

"Yes. I'm sure that's so."

"Thank you very much, Daisy. I'll let Ellen know immediately."

"Try not to get her hopes up too much," I warned in my most indulgent spiritualist-medium voice.

"I shall. Thank you, dear."

"You're more than welcome. I look forward to seeing you on Tuesday." So what was one more fib? At least I liked her houseboy, Keiji Saito, who had taught me how to eat with chopsticks, a skill I demonstrated with great joy when my family and Sam and I went to Miyaki's, the Japanese restaurant in town. They were all impressed. So was I, to tell the truth.

TWENTY-FOUR

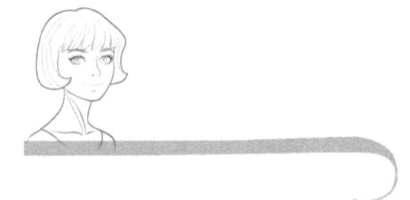

That night, Frank didn't steal anything when he came to our house to take dinner with my family. I think that's because Sam had frightened him into obedience, although I'm not altogether sure. I did notice Frank kept slipping anxious looks at his uncle. Served the little punk right. Anyhow, I know he didn't steal anything because Sam called later in the evening to tell me so.

"I think you're curing him, Sam," I said, laughing. "Did you make him strip down to his underwear and search him?"

"Pretty much. He didn't like it, either." I heard the gleefully evil tone in his voice. I did love my Sam. "May we pick you and your family up tomorrow morning for church?"

"Absolutely!" I said happily. "And stay for dinner afterwards."

"Frank isn't too much to bear for another meal?"

"Heavens, no. We've weathered worse than Frank."

"I doubt it."

I laughed again. He didn't, but he did sigh heavily and hang up his receiver.

The next morning, as promised, Sam came with Frank to pick us up and carry us to church in his big black Hudson. I guess Sam had bought Frank a suit, because he wore one that morning. It didn't fit him very well, so it's possible Sam had rooted through the Salvation Army's charity shop to get it for him. Until Frank got a job and stopped pilfering other people's goods, he really didn't deserve more. Not that the Salvation Army's charity shop didn't offer well-maintained clothing and other merchandise, because they did. My buddies Flossie and Johnny Buckingham made sure of that.

By the way, not that it matters, but did you know that the Salvation Army was born in England? What's more, it separated itself from the Methodist Church, so I guess that's one of the reasons I like it. Not the separation, but because I understand Methodists, being one myself. Besides, they do great work. The only thing about the Salvation Army I don't care for is that they don't approve of people like Harold and his ilk. I think they're dead wrong on that issue, but nobody cares what I think.

However, Pasadena's particular Salvation Army is run by Johnny Buckingham, and I'm almost certain Johnny doesn't care about other people's love lives; his only goal is to help people. Oh, and Sir Arthur Sullivan—of Gilbert and Sullivan fame—wrote the music to "Onward, Christian Soldiers," the Salvation Army's...what would you call it? Their theme song? Pretty darned classy for an organization that takes in anyone from drunkards to drug addicts to the poor and homeless.

But never mind all that. Frank was silent as Sam drove us to our church, which wasn't far from our home. In fact, until Sam was shot, we generally walked to and from church; however, since Sam's leg still hurt, he drove us. I noticed he had brought his cane with him and was sorry to see he still needed it. I guess beating up on Frank wasn't having the curative properties I'd hoped for.

I parted from my family, Sam, and Frank and headed for the choir room as soon as Sam parked his Hudson. The October morning held a distinct chill, so I'd worn a navy blue tricotine suit I'd made a couple of years earlier. It was comfy and warm.

"Daisy!" Lucy cried as soon as she saw me. She rushed up and hugged me. This surprised me a little. I mean, Lucy and I were friends and all, but we didn't normally hug upon meeting each other at church. But I hugged her back. You can never get or give too many hugs, in my opinion.

"Good morning, Lucy. You're looking spiffy today." That day she wore a plain, but pretty, nut-brown tweed suit with a single-breasted, hip-length coat. It looked to me as if had been well tailored by someone and not a store-bought item. Lucy's spouse didn't stint on his wife's spending money, bless him. "I love that suit."

Lucy twirled, grinning broadly. "Albert is so good to me. A woman named Mrs. Wilson made it for me. I'd have asked you if you wanted the job, but I imagine you're too busy with your job and making clothes for your family, except for special occasions."

"You're right about that. I don't know Mrs. Wilson, but she did a super job on that suit."

"Thank you. Albert also bought me a gorgeous coat of brown verona cloth with a raccoon collar."

Poor little raccoons. "Sounds lovely. Did you wear it today? I'd like to see it." As I spoke, I headed to the closet with the intention of hanging up my own black woolen coat. I didn't like the notion of small animals sacrificing their lives so I could wear their fur.

As soon as I opened the closet door, I saw my question had already been answered. There it hung: Lucy's brown verona-cloth coat with its raccoon collar. I petted the collar. "Oh, my, this is so soft, Lucy."

"Thank you. Albert is so good to me."

She'd already said that, but I didn't point it out to her. She loved her Albert, and he seemed to be a loving and generous husband. I approved of him, even if I didn't approve of killing animals so ladies could wear their furs. After all, those animals *needed* their fur. No woman alive, unless she lived in Siberia or somewhere like that—maybe Minnesota, for instance—needed a fur-trimmed coat.

"Good morning, ladies," said Mr. Hostetter, coming into the choir room from the sanctuary. "Mrs. Fleming will begin our organ prelude shortly, so please stop chatting, get your books and folders, and line up." He ran a tight ship, Mr. Hostetter.

We did as he'd bade us and all lined up, sopranos first, altos next. Then came the tenors and basses. Lucy and I sat in the front row. I was the only alto sitting there, but I've already explained why I did so.

The church service went smoothly, as it almost always did—there had been a couple of exceptions earlier in the year when a couple of folks dropped dead during the communion service, but that was extremely unusual—and Pastor Smith gave a rousing sermon that even kept most of our more elderly members of the congregation awake during the entire service. Our anthem went well, and the congregation all stood and sang the designated hymns.

The only reason I mention the attendees standing and singing the hymns is that *Sam* actually sang. He generally didn't sing loudly, but I heard him that day. His gorgeous bass voice rang out during "Now Thank We All Our God." I got the distinct impression Frank was embarrassed by his uncle's enthusiasm, because he kept shooting alarmed looks at him. Fiddle to him. I loved to hear Sam sing. So did the rest of my family; I could tell, because they all smiled during the hymns.

When church was over and we choir members had returned our choir accouterments in their proper places, Lucy and I walked to Fellowship Hall to have a cookie and a cup of tea with our respective families. The Gumms, the remaining Majesty, and Sam Rotondo generally stayed only long enough to partake of one cookie, because Vi had our dinner cooking at home, and we'd all rather eat real food after church than a cookie or two. When we entered the hall, Lucy instantly left me and made a bee-line for her Albert, who stood with her parents.

I, of course, headed toward my family which, of course, included Sam. And Frank. He sat at a table, his hands folded on top thereof, and with a plate holding one cookie in front of him. Sam stood over him, leaning slightly on his cane and looming large and menacing. My parents and Vi sat at the same table, and it looked to me as if they were having trouble not laughing. I'd have to ask about that later.

"Hey, Ma and Pa and Vi and Sam and Frank."

"Good day, dear," said Ma. "Today's anthem sounded beautiful. We're fortunate to have such a fine choir at our church."

"I agree. What about you, Frank?" said Sam, still looming over his nephew. He shoved his shoulder a little bit. Maybe more than a little bit.

Frank nearly fell off his chair, righted himself, and mumbled, "Yeah. Sounded good."

"He loved it," said Sam, grinning.

"Want to sit a bit, Sam? Or do you want to stand there for another several minutes?" I worried about his leg.

"Oh, I'll just stand for a little while," said he. "Have to keep an eye on Frank here. Don't want him taking off with any more candlesticks, do we?"

Frank grunted.

"No, we certainly don't. Eat your cookie, Frank, so we can go home and eat some of Vi's marvelous dinner."

Frank said, "Huh," but ate his cookie. It looked like a molasses cookie to me. I liked molasses cookies all right, but they weren't my favorite, so I eschewed—I always want to say *gesundheit* after I use that word—cookies and sat next to Ma.

We watched Frank devour his cookie. I think we embarrassed him with our stares, because he turned that unbecoming puce color again. Too bad. He deserved it.

As soon as Frank swallowed his last bite, Sam lifted him by his shoulders and stood him on his feet. "All right, then. Let's be off. I'm looking forward to another one of your delicious meals, Vi. So is Frank. Aren't you, Frank?"

"Uh...Yeah. Sure."

"Yeah, sure, what?" asked Sam sweetly.

"Uh...Yeah, sure...sir."

"Good boy. Come along now." He took Frank by the arm and yanked him out to the car. If Frank lived through his stay in Pasadena, he'd probably never run away from home again.

"If Frank lives through his stay in Pasadena, I doubt he'll run away from home again," my father whispered in my ear, thereby confirming my belief that Pa and I were alike in many ways.

I giggled. "I think you're right."

When we trooped into the house, it smelled wonderful. Spike met us at the door, barking joyfully. Naturally we stooped to pet him and tell him what a good boy he was. Even Frank, I do believe at his uncle's command—he shoved him again—petted Spike. Spike wagged his tail at Frank, thereby demonstrating that dogs are more forgiving than most people.

"Daisy, can you set the table and help me get dinner on the table after we put up our wraps?" asked Vi.

"Sure will," said I.

I knew what smelled so good. Before we'd left for church, Vi had put a smoked ham, a bunch of potatoes, carrots, onions and several rutabagas—which are, perhaps, my favorite vegetable—into a huge pot, let it come to a boil, and allowed it to simmer all through church. This was what Vi called a "New England boiled dinner." I guess a lot of New Englanders—my family originally came from Auburn, Massachusetts— ate New England boiled dinners. Of course, we also ate another of New-England's much-loved repasts, baked beans and brown bread. That was my father's favorite meal. I liked the beans, but the brown bread was a little too sweet for me.

Not that anyone cares what I like. Sorry. I got distracted. That happens a lot when I think about food.

I thoroughly enjoyed my dinner, which we ate in the middle of the day on Sundays. I think lots of people do. Then we could loaf for the rest of the day, take naps, read, or whatever and then grab a snack for supper if we wanted one.

Sam and Frank sat in the living room with Ma and Pa while I cleaned up the dishes. Vi went upstairs to take a nap, which she richly deserved. I didn't ask Frank to help, because Sam would have to supervise, and I thought he needed to rest his leg.

Almost as soon as I'd put away the last pot and stored the leftovers in our Frigidaire, the blasted telephone rang. I didn't instantly cross the kitchen to pick up the receiver, but waited until I knew the call was meant for our house. It was.

Grumbling to myself, I walked to the stupid 'phone and held the receiver an inch or two away from my ear, expecting an hysterical Mrs. Pinkerton to be on the other end of the wire. She wasn't. Rather, this telephone call was from the Pasadena Police Department, and the officer calling asked to speak to Sam. I quickly made sure the line was clear of party-line snoopers.

"Good Lord, what's wrong now?" I asked myself as I strode to the living room to deliver the message.

Sam, who'd seated himself next to Frank on the sofa, looked

displeased by my news. Nevertheless, he rose and came toward me, leaning heavily on his cane. "Cripes, what's wrong now?"

"I don't know, but I'll get some aspirin tablets for you to take after you hang up the receiver."

"Thanks," Sam said, lifting the receiver, which I'd carefully placed on top of the wooden telephone box.

I took off for the bathroom. I knew from experience that Sam wouldn't speak into the telephone if I were nearby to "snoop," as he'd call it. That was all right. I'd get the news out of him later.

When I returned to the kitchen to fill a glass with water, Sam was speaking. "All right. I'll be there as soon as I can be. Where did you say it was? On the campus, I mean. I know where Cal Tech is."

I felt my eyes open wide. Cal Tech! Something bad had happened at Cal Tech? As Sam was a homicide detective, I presumed the call signified another murder. Good heavens. As might be expected, my mind began whirling and sorting through possibilities. My money was on Dr. Malton being the perpetrator, but that was only because he was such a slimy character. I hoped like heck Robert Browning hadn't spent the day at Cal Tech, although I suspected he had, because he didn't have much else to do when he wasn't working at the chemical plant.

Oh, dear.

After getting the precise location of whatever he had to investigate from the officer calling him, Sam hung the receiver on the cradle and let out a huge sigh.

"What's the matter?" I asked, handing him three aspirin tablets and the glass I'd just filled.

"I don't think I should tell you," he said, frowning thoughtfully. Then, as he popped the aspirin tablets into his mouth and lifted the glass to drink, the stupid telephone rang *again*. I lifted the receiver and recited my usual greeting, forgetting to hold the receiver away from my ear.

Big mistake. The person on the other end of the wire practically screamed, "*Daisy*! It's happened again! I can't believe this! It's *awful*!"

I blinked at the receiver, perplexed, and said, "Who is this, please?"

"It's *Gladys*! Oh, Daisy! Philip Jeffreys' body was just discovered at

Cal Tech. Oh, Daisy, he was *murdered*! This is terrible! It's *awful*! Oh, my God, what can you do? Please. You have to help!"

"Um…I'm not sure what I can do, Gladys. Detective Rotondo has just been called to the scene of the crime."

"Oh, *no*! Oh, Lord, Daisy, what will this do to the project?"

That stupid project again. It sounded to me as if Gladys thought her husband's project was more important than a human life. Therefore, my voice was much sterner than it usually was when I said, "I have no idea what it will do to the project, Gladys, but I feel awfully sorry for Mr. Jeffreys' family and friends."

I guess Gladys detected my disapproving tone, because I heard her gulp. She'd stopped screeching when she said, "Oh. Oh, of course. Yes, that's true. I didn't mean to sound callous. Really, I don't. But…Well, you know how important this project is to Dr. Fellowes and Dr. Malton."

"Yes, I understand that. Detective Rotondo will find the evil-doer."

"But I want *you* to do it, so there won't be so much publicity!" cried Gladys.

"I fear it may be too late for that, Gladys. Two murders involving people from the Institute will certainly make the newspapers."

"Oh, God," she whispered. Then she said, "Good-bye, Daisy. I'm sorry to have troubled you." And she hung up.

Very well, then.

When I replaced the receiver on its cradle, Sam had finished with his glass of water and aspirin tablets and had begun scowling at me.

"What?" I asked. "It's not my fault Gladys Fellowes telephoned. I'm frightfully sorry about Mr. Jeffreys, though."

"The murder of Philip Jeffreys is none of your beeswax, Daisy Gumm Majesty—soon to become Daisy Gumm Rotondo—so stay out of it, dammit."

"Applesauce. Anyhow, you'll be able to figure out who did the evil deed at the Halloween party next Saturday. All the suspects will be there."

"God."

Sam turned and stomped back to the living room, still relying on his cane, although I hoped the aspirin tablets would take effect soon. I also

wondered what he aimed to do with Frank while he was investigating—
But wait.

"Hey, Sam! Stop for a minute! I thought you were supposed to stay at your desk and not go running around after criminals until after your leg heals completely!" I cried, tearing after him into the living room.

"Too many detectives out sick," Sam said briefly. "Anyhow, I'd rather be working than sitting at my desk." He walked over to his nephew. "Frank, get up and come with me. Say your thanks to the Gumms for putting up with you for another day."

Frank stood instantly, said, "Thank you very much," and bowed! I swear, if Sam didn't cure that bozo, and soon, there was truly no hope for him.

Anyhow, we all bade the two men *adieu*. Well, since we live in Southern California, I suppose I should say we bade them *adios*, but technically we did neither; we just said good-bye. I walked Sam and Frank out to Sam's machine.

"Please be careful, Sam," said I. "Don't be too hard on your poor leg."

Frank, who had been totally intimidated by our dinner that day—I think he was particularly confused by the rutabagas, which he stared at as if they were from Mars—said, "I'll help him, Mrs. Majesty."

"That's nice, Frank," said I, not believing him for a second.

"You will not help me," said Sam. "You'll stay the hell out of my way."

Frank cringed.

I got on my tiptoes and gave Sam a circumspect kiss—we had an audience, after all—and Sam and Frank drove off down Marengo.

Oh, dear. What in the world was so important about Dr. Fellowes's stupid project that people were being murdered for it? At least, I presumed the two deaths had something to do with the project. It would be too much of a coincidence if two people working on the same thing got themselves killed within a week of each other for no reason. Wouldn't it?

Pooh. I had no idea. But I was feeling pretty darned morose when I walked back to the house and explained to my family as much as I knew about what had happened. Which wasn't much, blast it.

TWENTY-FIVE

About five-thirty that afternoon, just when I was beginning to contemplate making myself a ham sandwich, the confounded telephone rang yet again.

You'd never know I muttered curses as I walked from the living room to the kitchen and picked up the receiver. I'd taken a breath to give the caller my standard greeting, when I was interrupted before I started speaking.

"May I come over for a little bit?"

Sam.

"Of course, you may! I'd love for you to come over!" I meant it. I wanted to know what the heck was going on and how poor Mr. Jeffreys had been done in. He'd been so young, too. It seemed especially terrible to me that his life had been cut short almost before it had begun. I felt the same way about Miss Carleton's death, although she'd at least been given a few more years on this green earth than had Mr. Jeffreys.

"I'm not going to discuss the case with you," said he in a gruff voice I knew of old.

"Yes, I know. But come over anyway. I'll make you a ham sandwich."

"Thanks. I'm still full from dinner."

"Well, I'll make you a sandwich anyway. You need to keep up your strength. Will Frank be coming with you?"

"No."

Well, that was definite. "Did you leave him at your bungalow?"

"God, no. I locked him in a cell. I'll pick him up on my way home."

"You locked him in a *cell*?"

"Best place I can think of for him."

"Hmm. You may be right. Will you be coming over right now? I really will make you a sandwich. Even I can't ruin a ham sandwich." As long as I didn't have to cut the bread. I've never yet been able to cut a straight slice of bread, but I knew Pa would be happy to do it for me. Heck, I'd make a sandwich for him, too.

"Thanks. Yes, I'll come over now. I could use another couple of aspirin tablets if you have them to spare."

"Of course, we do. You should get some to keep at home."

"I have some at home. I'm not at home. I'm still at Cal Tech, but we're winding things up here, so it'll only take me a half-hour or so to get to your house."

"See you then, Sam. Love you."

"Yeah. You, too."

He didn't dare declare his emotions in front of his police colleagues. I was laughing when I hung up the 'phone.

"Sam?" asked Pa, stretching and yawning. He'd been dozing on the sofa when the telephone's ring woke him.

"Yes. He's coming over. Maybe if I pester him enough, he'll give us some of the details regarding poor Mr. Jeffreys' death."

Shaking his head, Pa said, "A shame about that young man." He squinted at me. "He *was* young, wasn't he?"

"Very young," I said upon a sigh. "Too young to be foully done to death. I think Dr. Malton did it."

Pa appeared a bit surprised. "Why?"

I shrugged. "I just don't like him much. He's too…familiar, if you know what I mean."

"Not really," said Pa.

"Oh, he was giving me the eye and kept holding my hand and stuff like that when I met him. That day Gladys and I went to lunch at Cal

Tech, remember? I'd only just met him, and he acted as if I were his personal plaything. I didn't like him."

"Good heavens. He sounds like a cad." Pa smiled and headed to the bread box.

"He *was*, darn it. I don't like being pawed by strange men. Or even men who aren't strange."

With a laugh, Pa said, "Want me to cut you some bread? Your mother and I aim to share a ham sandwich."

"Yes, please. I promised Sam a sandwich when he gets here."

"Frank coming, too?"

"No. Sam locked him in a cell at the police department to keep him out of the way for a while."

Pa's eyebrows soared. "That sounds pretty drastic."

I shrugged. "Sounded reasonable to me. I doubt Frank would be much help during a murder investigation. In fact, he'd probably just get in the way. And I expect Sam didn't want him to ransack his house if he left him there while he went investigating."

"That kid is trouble, isn't he?"

"He certainly is. This will give him a taste of jail, too, so maybe he'll hate it so much he'll reform his wicked ways."

With another laugh, Pa glanced in the bread box. "White or rye? I'll take my ham on rye. How about you?"

"Rye, please. And cut enough for three sandwiches, please. Sam and I will each eat one. If I can't finish my second half, I'll give it to Sam. He needs to keep up his strength." I frowned as I headed to the cupboard to grab a jar of mustard. Vi made the mustard we ate in our family, by the way, just as she made our mayonnaise. Vi was a miracle-worker.

"Cut enough for four sandwiches, please, Joe. I'll have one, too." Vi walked into the kitchen through the hall door, looking rested.

"Hey, Vi," said I. "Have a good nap?"

"Very good, thank you. Did I hear someone say Sam is coming over?"

"Yes. He'll be here shortly."

"Good. In that case, I'll make the sandwiches," said Vi. "Here, Joe. Hand me the knife."

"Thanks, Vi," said Pa, doing as she asked and handing her the knife, hilt first.

"I'm so glad," I told her. "I don't think I can ruin a ham sandwich, but it's probably better if you make them."

"Probably," said Vi, smiling.

It's no fun being so bad at doing something that your whole family laughs about it. On the other hand, none of the other people in my family could commune with ghosts. Of course, neither could I, but... Oh, never mind.

When Sam got to our house, his limp was pronounced, and I was sorry to see it. I'd already procured three aspirin tablets and a glass of water for him, so as soon as Spike and I had greeted him, I led him into the dining room, where I'd set out what he needed.

Sitting with a sigh, he said, "Thanks. I wish I'd taken some with me. They help, but they don't last forever."

"I know," said I. "You were at the campus all this time? Since you left our house?"

"Yes."

"My, that was...hours ago."

"I know." Sam took his aspirin tablets like a good boy.

"And it was cold out there, too."

"Yes, it was."

"I'm sorry."

"These will help," Sam said, putting down the water glass he'd drained.

"How was Mr. Jeffreys killed, Sam?" Before he could tell me again it wasn't my business, I said, "It'll be in the papers tomorrow or the next day, so you might as well tell me. Was he stabbed like Miss Carleton?"

After heaving another sigh, Sam said, "Yes. After having a loud argument with someone."

"With whom? Did anyone see with whom he was arguing?"

"No. Your pal Robert Browning was there, and so were Dr. Malton and Dr. Fellowes."

"Oh, dear."

"Yeah. And a bunch of students were there, too. I guess you don't have to be stupid to enjoy a good tragedy. All those brilliant science students were as eager as your average Joe to look at a dead body and find out what had happened."

"That's kind of sad, but it's also human nature. I mean, if a neighbor of ours was stabbed to death, I'd be interested."

"You're always interested in dead bodies."

I decided not to argue. He was right, actually. To a degree.

"A student named Davidson was there, as well. He said he's working on that geological project the two doctors are heading, as was the dead man."

"I know. I met them when Gladys took me to Cal Tech. We ate lunch in the Athenaeum. It's a really nice place."

Glowering at me, Sam said, "I wouldn't know."

Whoops.

"You didn't tell me you'd been dining at Cal Tech with the Fellowes woman."

"I didn't?"

"No. You didn't."

"Oh. Well, it wasn't important. Guess I just didn't think of it."

"Right. As if you *ever* forget anything at all about a murder case."

"I'm sorry, Sam."

"Nuts." He rubbed his chest, then his left leg.

"What's the matter?" Alarm shot through me instantly. I didn't like Sam rubbing his chest like that. "Does your chest hurt?" I stood, ready to run around the table and hold him in his chair should he look likely to fall out of it.

"No." He sounded almost as surly as Frank.

"Why are you rubbing your chest, then?"

"I don't know. It was the damnedest thing." He pulled the juju Mrs. Jackson had given him out of his right trouser pocket. "Every time I talked to those folks working on the project, this stupid thing seemed to get hot." He glared at his juju.

I did, too. Only my look wasn't a glare, but a stare. Could it be? Sam would never believe it. "Um...When did it seem to heat up?"

Sam lifted his head and gaze at me. Not fondly. "I just told you."

"Only when you were with the people working on the project?"

"Yes."

"Sam! Do you know what that means? Or what it might mean, I mean?"

"No. I don't have a single notion what it might mean, and don't you start spouting your spiritualist nonsense at me, either."

Vi appeared from the kitchen with a tray with a plate piled with sandwiches. She'd also sliced up a couple of apples. "Let's just use our napkins so we don't have to dirty any more dishes for Daisy to clean up," she said, smiling happily.

Hmm. Well, I decided later, it was just as well she'd interrupted us, because I doubted Sam would even consider what *I* thought that heated-up juju might mean. Even if I asked him specifically whom he was with when it got hot, he probably wouldn't tell me but would merely scoff.

"Thank you, Vi," said Sam. He sounded unutterably weary.

Poor Sam. I guess I shouldn't pester him. But, boy, I wished I knew more about his juju's antics. Heck, *my* juju never got hot when I was around an evildoer. It didn't seem quite fair that Sam should receive special help from his juju when he didn't even believe in its efficacy.

Well...Truth to tell, I didn't either. Any more than I thought I could talk to dead people. However, there had been one or two times in my career as a spiritualist-medium during which odd things had happened, and I no longer considered anything beyond the realm of possibility. Heck, my crystal ball had once been instrumental in discovering where a missing butler had been held captive. Not Featherstone. This was another butler.

Ma joined us at the table, and Pa didn't bother with saying grace again. I guess he figured one or two blessings per day was sufficient.

Sam noticed his juju lying on the dining-room table and swiftly tucked it back into his trouser pocket. I think I was the only one who noticed.

"Ham on rye," he said, as if to divert attention away from his surreptitious movement. "My favorite."

"Mine, too," said Pa, taking a big bite of his sandwich.

"Where's Frank, Sam? I thought he'd be with you." Ma smiled sweetly at Sam.

"No. I was called to the scene of another murder, this one at Cal

Tech, and I left Frank with some police buddies of mine. I figured they could keep an eye on him."

"Another murder? Terrible! But it's probably a good thing you didn't take Frank to the scene," said Ma, having no idea that Sam had locked him in the clink.

Neither Sam nor Pa nor I enlightened her. Sam smiled.

After we'd consumed our sandwiches, the rest of my family and Sam went to the living room while I cleared off the table and washed the very few implements Vi had used to make our sandwiches. Then I joined everyone in the living room. The time was six-thirty-ish by then.

I sat on a chair near Sam, who shared the sofa with Vi and Ma. "How's your leg, Sam. Have the aspirins helped any yet."

Rubbing his left leg, Sam said, "I think so. It's hard to tell sometimes. It's been a long, cold day, and I don't think the weather or having to stand for hours interviewing people did it any good."

"I'm sorry. I wish I could wave a magic wand or something and make all the pain go away."

"I wish you could, too." Sam didn't smile.

"It's a shame you had to do all that legwork, Sam," said Pa. "I thought you were supposed to sit at a desk for a few weeks or so."

"I was, but there's an epidemic running through the police department, and there are too many detectives out sick for me to be able to sit all day long. Anyway, I'd rather be in the thick of things, even though it's hard on the old leg."

"If I were a policeman, I think I'd rather be interviewing people and visiting crime scenes than sitting at a desk," I said.

"I know you would," said Sam. Not tenderly.

"But listen, Sam," I said, deciding not to pounce on him for his negative attitude, "I need to tell you a couple of things."

"Aw, jeez."

"No. They aren't bad things. Only Mrs. Bissel called me because I'm conducting a séance at her home on Tuesday night, and she asked specifically if I could get in touch with Mary Carleton. If you want to go with me, I'm sure Mrs. Bissel wouldn't mind."

Sam's head flopped back until it rested on the back of the sofa. I got the feeling he wasn't pleased.

"Would you like to go with me?" I asked in a small voice.

Lifting his head, Sam gazed at me with eyes that looked rather like shiny black olives. "I don't even want *you* to go there."

"But I have to."

"Cripes. Will anyone from Cal Tech be there?"

"I don't think so."

"Then what's the use?"

"Um...I don't know. It was just a thought."

"Right." Sam heaved himself to his feet. "But I need to get going now. I have a lot of paperwork to do, and then I'll have to spring Frank and take him home. I hope to God they fed him."

"I'm sure they did," I said, trying to sound loving and supportive.

"Huh."

Typical.

Spike and I walked Sam out to his Hudson. I'd reversed my decision regarding talking to Sam about his juju. Since I didn't want the rest of my family to hear it, mainly because I feared Sam's reaction and I didn't care to sully my relatives' ears with profanity, I waited until we were alone.

We stood in the street beside the driver's side of the machine and I said, "Listen to me, Sam. I know you'll think this is crazy, but you really need to isolate whoever it was that triggered your juju's reaction."

He frowned and opened his mouth to talk, but I help up a hand to stop him. "I know, I know. You think it's insane. But has your juju ever become warm before when you were questioning suspects?"

"No. This was the first time. And it wasn't just warm. It was cursed hot." He reached into his pocket and withdrew the cunning little charm Mrs. Jackson had crafted for him. "Stupid thing."

"It may or may not be stupid," I said. "What I think you should do is interview all the people working on Dr. Fellowes's project and see which one or ones cause the reaction."

Sam stared at me. "You're crazy."

"I'm *not* crazy! Just try it, for Pete's sake. What can it hurt?"

"I have no idea." He started to stuff the juju back in his pocket, but I stopped him.

"Put the string around your neck, Sam Rotondo," I commanded. I can be quite commanding when I put my mind to it.

"Cripes."

"Just do it, Sam."

"Good God." But he put the string carrying the juju around his neck again.

I smiled. "Thanks, Sam." I stood on my tiptoes and gave him a kiss. "I do love you, you know."

"I know. I guess." Then he put his arms around me and hugged me tight. "It's driving me nuts not being able to do more than kiss and cuddle, you know."

"I know. I'm sorry. We can probably figure something out."

"Yeah?" Sam drew slightly away from me and gazed down at me, his brow furrowed.

"Yeah. Why not. We're going to be married."

"Soon."

"I hope so."

"Cripes."

And Sam got in his Hudson, drove into our driveway, backed out again, and headed north on Marengo. I figured he'd turn left on Colorado, then hang a right on Fair Oaks and drive to the police station.

Poor Sam.

TWENTY-SIX

On Monday, I paid another visit to Mrs. Pinkerton. She was as upset as usual, and, also as usual, Rolly and the tarot cards told her life was going to be more than a trifle rocky for a while. Why sugarcoat the truth? She didn't like it, but she had a rotten daughter, Stacy had done a *really* bad thing this time, and Mrs. P would just have to suffer the consequences. I only hoped Stacy would suffer more than her mother, although I doubted she would. Stacy didn't suffer suffering well. If you know what I mean.

After paying Vi a short visit in the kitchen, I went down to Colorado and parked in front of the Rexall Drug Store. After browsing at their cosmetics counter for a bit, I bought some mascara for Regina Petrie. I thought about getting her an eyelash curler, but didn't. Small steps, I reminded myself. She'd probably get scared at the notion of mascara.

And then—I loved this part of my day most of all—I drove to the library. I adored the library. It's my favorite place on earth except home. And I'd get to come back again at four that afternoon to talk with Robert Browning. The day was shaping up well.

I'd brought some books back and laid them on the returns table, and then looked around for Regina. She wasn't at her desk, so I presumed she was helping a library patron find something. Not awfully sure why I did it, I walked to the biography section and gazed at the aisle where Miss Carleton's bleeding body had lain. The floor was clean. I guess the custodian had scrubbed the floor hard, probably with bleach, to get all that blood out. There was no more string up to keep patrons from searching the stacks, either.

Just for the heck of it, I walked down that aisle, peering at biographies on the shelves, thinking a clue might exist there somewhere.

I was wrong. Or, if I was right, I sure didn't spot a clue.

Therefore, I meandered to the fiction stacks and glanced around for something interesting. I noticed what seemed to me to be an odd title: *Abol Tabol: The Nonsense World of Sukumar Ray*, and picked it up. Leafing through it, I saw it was composed of short stories and poetry. I wasn't a big fan of poetry, but I did enjoy nonsense occasionally, so I decided to try it. The fellow who wrote it was, evidently, an Indian. Not one of ours, but one of India's. After moseying around some more, I spotted *Jacob's Room*, by a woman named Virginia Woolf. I'd read something about her, but never having read anything by her, I figured I might give it a try. It didn't sound awfully interesting, but one never knew.

After browsing some more, I left the stacks and glanced at Regina's desk. There she was! I decided to heck with fiction and aimed myself at her. She looked up and smiled a broad smile.

"Daisy! It's so good to see you."

"It's good to see you, too. I have something for you, although, from the looks of you, you don't appear to need much help."

She'd curled her hair somehow, and it fell in flattering waves around her face. Eyeing her critically, I decided she still needed to get her hair cut, but the waves were a marked improvement over that danged knot she generally wore.

"Here," I said, handing over the mascara.

"Thank you! You're so kind to a poor old spinster-lady."

"Fiddle-faddle. A little mascara never hurt anyone."

Regina opened the little box containing the mascara, and stared at it. Then she looked up at me. "What do I do with it?" she asked, as if she should have known and was embarrassed. Nerts to that.

"You see, that black strip is the mascara itself. That little brush is what you put it on with. You wet the brush, rub it on the black strip, and then apply the brush to your eyelashes. That's what I did the other day, remember?"

"Vaguely. It doesn't sound difficult," Regina said doubtfully.

"It isn't. Just be careful at first until you get used to applying it, because sometimes, the brush will touch your nose or forehead or something, and then you'll have to wash off the blot."

"But it's not dangerous?"

"Not at all. It will make your eyes stand out under your eyeglasses."

Regina sighed. "My stupid eyeglasses."

"Fiddlesticks. Lots of folks wear cheaters, and they look just fine."

"If you say so." She leaned over and picked something up. Her handbag. "I'll just put the mascara in here, and tonight I'll practice a bit."

"Good idea. Um…Say, Regina, I was prowling the stacks and found these two books." I showed her my bounty. "But you're better at picking out stuff my family likes to read than I am. Can you suggest something?"

"I can do better than suggest something," she said, sounding almost gleeful. "I held these especially for you."

She plopped *Wanderer of the Wasteland*, by Mr. Zane Grey; *The Eight Strokes of the Clock*, by someone named Maurice Le Blanc; *Mr. Waddington of Wyck*, by someone named May Sinclair; and *The Abbey Court Mystery*, by someone named Annie Haynes. I stared at them.

"Golly, except for Mr. Zane Grey, I've never heard of these other authors. Are they mysteries?"

"They are. Well, most of them are," she said, grinning almost smugly. "Mr. Le Blanc is a Frenchman, and his detective is named Arsene Lupin. Miss Sinclair's book is quite entertaining, and Miss Haynes' book is very good. It's definitely a mystery."

"Thank you! I brought back some of the books I checked out last Friday. I especially loved the *Tish Carberry* stories by Mrs. Rinehart. I just love her books. Well, except for the one about the war."

"I understand. That's why I'm not recommending *A Son at the Front*, by Mrs. Edith Wharton. It's an excellent book, but not for you."

I shuddered. "Thank you." The mere thought of that horrible war made my stomach cramp and my flesh creep.

"However, I've saved the very best until last."

And she leaned over, picked up another tome, and set it on the table in front of her.

"Oh! How wonderful!" And darned if my eyes didn't tear up.

"Daisy! Whatever is the matter? I wouldn't have—"

I picked up *The Discovery of the Tomb of Tutankhamen* by Mr. Howard Carter and hugged it to my chest. "No, no. I wondered when this book would cross the ocean and get to us in the USA." I sniffled and had to dig in my handbag for a handkerchief. Wiping my eyes, I said, "It's just that Billy absolutely *loved* reading stuff like this." Another sniffle, and I had to blow my nose. "I just missed the discovery, you know. Mr. Kincaid and I were in Egypt only a few months before Mr. Carter found that tomb."

"I know. I didn't mean to bring back sad memories."

"That's all right. At least it's not a war book. And Detective Rotondo will probably want to read it, too. He reads a lot."

Smiling sweetly at me, Regina said, "I'm glad to hear that. He didn't...Um...Sound awfully fond of the books I got for you on Friday."

Fortunately, her words dried my tears. In fact, I chuckled a bit. "No. Sam doesn't let on what he likes to do unless he's with people he's known for years. I don't know why that is."

Tilting her head slightly, Regina said, "I believe a lot of men are like that. They aren't as open as we women are."

"I suppose you're right. Thank you very much for this bounty. I'll see you on Wednesday. Maybe we can take lunch together at the Rexall Drug Store or something. Not fancy, but it might be fun."

"It might indeed. It's a good thought. Thank you, Daisy."

"Thank *you*, Regina."

So I checked out my books and headed for home. There I made myself a ham sandwich—yes, the bread was cut crooked, but Pa wasn't there to slice it for me—sat at the kitchen, and ate my sandwich and an orange. Spike sat on the floor and looked at me.

"Aw, jeez," I said as I was about to pop the last of my sandwich into my mouth. I opened it up, tore off a tiny piece of ham, and gave it to my dog. He was grateful.

And then, rather than instantly sit in the living room to read, I petted Spike and told him what a good boy he was, and I took myself off to the sewing room and began making togas. They weren't hard to make. I was more worried about the globe, although Harold would probably do what needed to be done with that. When I'd sewed up the last seam on Sam's toga, I rejected the notion of starting Dr. Fellowes's toga in favor of making the red sash Sam would wear over his shoulder. He was going to look quite dashing if I had anything to do with it.

And then it occurred to me that many Roman gentlemen are depicted as having wreaths made of laurel leaves on their heads. Inspiration struck, I grinned to myself and, for almost the first time in my life, walked to the kitchen with intent. Not that I avoided the kitchen for eating and stuff like that, but I never went there to find an ingredient, mainly because I wouldn't have known what to do with one.

But laurel and bay leaves were the same things, and I knew Vi used bay leaves in some of her recipes. So I rooted around in the spice cabinet and, sure enough, there was a big jar of large, dried bay leaves. I doubted Vi would mind. I'd replace them, after all. Of course, I could have driven up to the foothills and denuded a laurel tree, but the weather was cold and I didn't feel like it.

So I took the jar of bay leaves into the sewing room, cleared off a space at the table against the wall where I did most of my cutting and so forth, and set the jar down. Then I returned to the kitchen and made some paste out of water and flour. Not even I could ruin paste. Probably.

At any rate, I didn't ruin that paste, and I fixed a very nice-looking laurel wreath for Sam's big head. I wished I could paint it gold, but I didn't know where to get gold paint. Maybe Harold would know.

I was disappointed when Sam called and said neither he nor Frank would be coming to dinner that night.

"Why not?"

"Got a murder case to work on."

"Are you going to stick Frank in a cell again?"

"Best place for him."

"I'll miss you, Sam. I won't miss Frank though."

"I wouldn't miss him either. I'd like to try, though."

I wasn't even sure what that meant, but I kind of understood.

"When is he going home?"

"I don't know. Renata's trying to get the money together to buy him a train ticket. I told her to make the kid work for his own money, but she wants him home. Why, I don't know. Anyway, it's probably better this way. If he stayed here very much longer, I'd end up killing him."

"How's the case going?"

Silence greeted my question. Sam didn't like me prying (that's his word) into his cases. However, eventually he said, "Things don't look good for your friend Browning."

"Why? I can't believe Robert would kill that woman or Mr. Jeffreys!"

"According to people who know, Miss Carleton and he were closeted together all the time, and they'd both been acting funny—whatever that means—lately."

"Robert Browning is *not* a cold-blooded murderer, Sam Rotondo."

I could almost hear him shrug over the telephone wires. "Maybe he's a hot-blooded murderer. He's mixed up in this thing somehow, and until he clears up a few things, he's top of the list."

"Nerts."

"Can't help it," said Sam, sounding as if he wished he could.

I decided to let the matter drop. If I probed any more, I'd probably only end up riling Sam, and he had enough on his plate already. "Well, try to find something healthy to eat somewhere, and don't forget to take your aspirin tablets if your leg hurts."

"Yes, ma'am. Are you going to be a nagging wife?"

"Probably."

"Good." And he hung up.

Oh, well. I looked at the clock on the wall. Golly, it was almost four o'clock! I had to scurry if I aimed to meet Robert Browning at the library.

So I scurried. I hadn't changed my clothes when I came home from the morning's errands, so I just wore what I had on, a mid-calf length, sage-green tweed suit. I'd taken the jacket off when I'd come home, so I only had to don it again, grab my brown hat and gloves, slip my feet into my brown shoes with a two-eyelet tie and—thank God—one-inch heels and a relatively rounded toe. I hated having my feet squished.

Then I hared out of the house, taking quick leave of Spike, who didn't approve of me leaving him twice in one day, and hurried the Chevrolet to the library.

Robert awaited my arrival in the periodical room. He rose when he saw me enter the room. He looked exhausted.

"I'm so glad you could come, Daisy. I really need to talk to someone. Now that Mr. Jeffreys has been murdered, the police are doubling up on me. I don't know what to do."

"Let's sit down at that table over there." I pointed to an isolated table on the other side of the room. "So we can be more private."

Running his fingers through his hair—it looked to me as if he'd already done that quite often that day—Robert said, "Good idea," and followed me to the far table.

We sat and bent our heads so that they nearly touched. "Very well, Robert, tell me what it is you can't tell the police."

Robert heaved a huge sigh. "But, Daisy, don't you see? I can't tell you, either! I promised." He propped his elbows on the table and cradled his face in his hands.

I decided it was past time for Robert Browning to behave sensibly. Therefore, my voice was stern when I said, "That's stupid, Robert. Both of the women you promised are dead. And telling the truth now might save your life. Be reasonable."

For several more moments—they felt like extremely long moments to me—Robert just sat there, his head in his hands, not speaking.

Taking matters into my own hands, I said, "Robert Browning, according to the police, both you and Miss Carleton had been closeted together several times, and you were both acting funny lately." Deciding Sam's words had merit, I added, "Whatever funny means."

Several more hours passed, and then Robert heaved a huge sigh, lifted his head, glanced around the periodical room to make sure no one was nearby, and said, "All right. I'll tell you. I guess you'll have to decide whether or not to tell the police."

Hallelujah!

TWENTY-SEVEN

After Robert had told me what he had to tell me, I could only stare at him for several seconds.

"Good Lord," I said.

"Yes. My sentiments precisely."

"He actually promised he would marry her?"

"That's what Mary said. She didn't know he was already married."

"What a slimy character!"

"Yes. It's difficult for me to work with him these days."

"I understand."

"But there's more."

"Oh, dear. Really?"

"Yes. Mary thought the research for our project was being altered. We were both trying to figure out how and why and who was doing it."

That stupid project again. "Altered how?"

"When Mary first came to me about her suspicions, I thought she was crazy. But after I went through the files, I wasn't so sure. And then someone murdered her." Robert gazed at me with tragic eyes. "Daisy, whoever did it *has* to be working on the project. And now Mr. Jeffreys has been murdered, too."

"Have you tried investigating further to see if you can find any...I don't know what you'd call them…discrepancies in what you think the reports should contain versus what they *do* contain?"

"Yes. And I think someone is trying very hard to create another California Gold Rush, only this one right here in the foothills of the San Gabriel Mountains."

"Oh, my. Why?"

"I have no idea. It makes no sense to me."

Robert and I stared at each other for several seconds. I wasn't even sure how to ask what I wanted to ask or even how to phrase it. A geologist, I'm not.

I finally made a stab at it. "Um…Who would benefit from a fake gold rush?"

If his shoulders could shrug any higher, I imagine they would have. "Nobody, as far as I know. We scientists and the students who worked on the project would look like fools if we published a project report that turned out to be incorrect." He shook his head. "I just don't know. It makes no sense to me. We'd all…Well, we'd all look like raving nitwits. Or deliberate liars."

"This sounds very strange to me, Robert, but you *do* need to tell Detective Rotondo everything you just told me. And I mean *everything*."

"Oh, God. I feel as if I've betrayed everyone's trust."

"Don't be ridiculous. If your information can help solve two murders, you'll be doing everybody, including the police department and the folks working on your project, a huge favor. You can't keep it to yourself any longer. Either one of those things."

"You really think so?"

"I know so."

"Cripes. I feel like such a louse. It just"—Robert pressed a hand to his head—"feels like a betrayal. I promised Mary and I promised Elizabeth that I'd never divulge the secret Mary placed in Elizabeth's and my hands. I *promised*, Daisy."

Practicality time. "They're both dead, Robert." I saw him wince and said, "I know. What I said sounds harsh, but two people have been viciously murdered, and you're keeping what might well be pertinent information from the police."

"I suppose you're right."

"I know I'm right. For Pete's sake, Robert, stop being so darned childish about this!"

He stared at me with disappointment writ large on his features. "I don't think of it as being childish, Daisy. I think of it as being true to a promise. If that's a childish attitude, then I guess I'm childish."

"That's all very noble, Robert, but I doubt either Elizabeth or Mary —or Regina Petrie, for that matter—would appreciate it if you were arrested for committing a murder you didn't commit."

Robert lowered his gaze to his hands, now folded on the table in front of him. "You're right, of course." He looked at me. "And I really like Regina Petrie, Daisy. I'm so glad I met her, even if the circumstances were...unfortunate."

"That's one way of putting it," I said drily. "But listen, Robert." I remembered the time. Well, that is to say, I remembered that it might be getting on toward the time I should be home and setting the table for dinner. "There's a telephone booth outside the library, isn't there?"

"I don't know." Robert looked blank.

"Nuts. I think you should scoot down to Detective Rotondo's office right this minute. You shouldn't wait any longer." I stared at him hard. "Don't forget that *you* might be in danger. Whoever killed Miss Carleton and Mr. Jeffreys might do you in next if whoever it is finds you prying into suspicious things about that horrible project."

"It's not horrible. It's going to be quite useful."

"If you say so, Robert. All I know is, it's managed to get two people murdered so far, and if you begin looking into the results as if you believe something to be amiss, you might be next."

"Good Lord, do you really think so?"

I felt like banging my head on the table. "Robert Browning, I've known you for years and years, but I never thought you were naïve before now. *Yes!* I really think so. And I'll bet Sam...er, Detective Rotondo will think so, too. If it's not too late, I'll go with you to the police department."

"Too late? What do you mean?"

"I have duties to perform at home, Robert."

"Oh. Oh, of course." Robert lifted his arm, shook his coat sleeve down and glanced at his wristwatch. "It's four-thirty now."

"Good. Let's go. I *need* to be getting home soon, but I don't think this should wait."

"Well...If you really think so."

"I really think so."

"And you'll go with me? I feel foolish now for not having confessed everything before. But those weren't my secrets. They belonged to other people. People whom I respected and...well, loved, if we're talking about Elizabeth."

I patted him on the arm. "I know, Robert. But you need to tell the detective everything you told me. Trust me about this."

"Very well." Robert rose and stood behind my chair to pull it out for me.

Those library chairs were *very* heavy, and the chair made a terrible scraping sound as he pulled it back. I cringed, expecting an outraged librarian to appear out of the periodical stacks. But we were in luck. No one showed up to scold us, and Robert and I walked outside. Then we faced a dilemma.

"Um...Where is your car, Robert?"

"Right there." He pointed to a Chevrolet parked right in front of mine.

"I should have recognized it," I said. His car was fancier than ours, but I didn't care. I loved our machine. "Perhaps we'd better take both cars," I said. "I'm not sure if Sam will be there, and if he isn't, I'll need to rush home. If he is, I'll still need to rush home, but I'll be there to give you moral support as you tell him your story."

"It's not my story. That's the whole problem."

Aw, crumb. "I know, Robert. Just do it anyway."

"Right."

"So I'll remain with you while you spill the beans to the detective. If it looks like I'll be late, I'll telephone my family from the police station." Providing the people at the police station would cooperate.

So Robert got into his fancy Chevrolet, and I got into our not-so-fancy Chevrolet, and we drove the couple of blocks to the Pasadena Police Department, which sat right behind Pasadena's City Hall.

Together we walked into the station. I didn't recognize the

policeman sitting at the reception desk, but I boldly walked up to him. "We need to see Detective Rotondo," I said firmly.

The policeman gazed up at me. He didn't stand, the rude thing, but oh, well. "Are you Mrs. Majesty?"

Surprised, I confessed that was indeed my name.

"Very good. Hold on one moment, and I'll get the detective for you."

And he did. After what sounded like an unpleasant conversation with Sam—I could only hear one side of it, of course—the man finally rose from his chair. He walked across the room, unlocked a door, and ushered Robert and me in. I led the way to Sam's office, but allowed Robert to open the door for me. He was *such* a gentleman, I feared he might suffer a nervous collapse if I opened the door for myself.

Inwardly, I was still shaking my head in mystification that Robert had concealed so much pertinent information from the police. I didn't roll my eyes, but I wanted to.

"What's going on, Daisy? Mr. Browning?" Sam's rock-solid posture and forbidding countenance didn't invite confidences.

"Robert has some things to tell you. They're important to your investigation, Sam."

Sam's forehead crinkled with his frown. He just *hated* when people came to me with their confessions instead of to the police. Huh. If Sam weren't so formidable, people would confide in him more readily.

Frank Pagano wasn't in the chair next to Sam's desk, so I sat there. Robert pulled up a chair on the other side of Sam's desk and sat.

"All right, what's all this about?" Sam asked gruffly. Papers littered his desk, and it looked to me as if he'd been writing a report or something. He turned it over when he saw me glance at it. I didn't roll my eyes again.

"Go on, Robert. Tell Detective Rotondo what you just told me. Don't leave anything out."

So Robert did and Sam took notes. A couple of times it looked to me as if he wanted to whack Robert Browning upside the head as he so often did to his nephew, but he restrained himself.

As for Robert, he looked and sounded like a little boy who'd been caught doing something naughty. As well he should.

As Robert spoke, I kept a close watch on Sam, wondering if his juju were heating up. He didn't slap a hand to his chest or anything, so I presume it didn't. Ha. I knew Robert wasn't the killer!

When Robert finished talking, Sam sat back in his chair and looked at him. It wasn't a kindly look.

"Why the devil didn't you tell this in the first place? This is important information. If you'd told us what you knew before now, Mr. Jeffreys' life might have been spared. You do know that, don't you?"

"But..." Robert covered his face with his hands. "Oh, God."

"Right," said Sam. He turned to me. "You don't need to play nanny to Mr. Browning any longer, Daisy. Go on home. I'm sure it must be almost time for dinner." He heaved a sigh. "Wish I could be there."

"I wish you could be, too, Sam." Rising from my chair, I contemplated giving him a little kiss on the cheek, but decided not to. It would only embarrass him. This was his place of work, after all. "Hope to see you tomorrow. Even if you have to bring Frank with you."

He smiled, and I left the police station.

By the time I got home, the rest of my family was already there. They all looked at me as if they'd been worried about me. Even Spike, who leapt up on me and gave me doggy kisses. I felt guilty.

"I'm sorry I didn't telephone to say I'd be late," said I. "I had to go with Robert Browning to the police station to talk to Sam." Then I wished I'd kept my mouth shut.

"Why did Robert Browning have to go to the police station?" asked Ma.

"Yes, and why did you have to go with him?" asked Pa.

"Why did Mr. Browning have to talk to Sam?" asked Vi.

See?

Taking off my coat and hanging it on the coat rack, I contemplated my response. Yes, Robert had confided his secrets to me. But I didn't think it was my place to tell his secrets to anyone other than Sam. Therefore, I had to scramble for an answer to three sensible questions.

"Um...Well, he was keeping something from the police. He told me what it was today, and I told him he needed to tell Sam about it."

That was no good. They'd all want to know what Robert had told me.

To forestall further questions, I said, "I can't divulge anything right now. Robert didn't even want to tell me, and I'm sure he'd be annoyed if I told anyone else. Eventually everything will come out, and then everyone will know."

They all looked at me with disapproval on their faces, and I wished I'd lied to begin with. Even Spike seemed irked with me.

I held up my hands. "I'm sorry! It involves the murders of two people, and Sam would kill me if I spilled the beans." They still appeared displeased, so I said lamely, "I'm sorry," again.

A collective sigh went up from my audience.

"Well," said Vi in a tone of voice that let me know she didn't approve of secrets being kept from the family, "Will you please set the table?"

"Yes, ma'am," I said in a small voice, and went to the dining room to do same. I didn't bother changing clothes, although I felt a little crumpled by that time. "Oh, Sam and Frank won't be joining us tonight. Sam has to work. I don't know where Frank is."

"Hmm," said Vi.

Oh, dear. I didn't like having my family mad at me. Believing I'd be better off if I just kept mum and went about my assigned task, I set the table for the family only. I didn't even ask what Vi aimed to give us for dinner.

Fortunately, I didn't have to wait too long to find out, because as soon as the table was set, Vi called me into the kitchen to begin taking viands out for the family to enjoy.

"This smells delectable, Vi," said I, venturing into speech at last.

"Thank you."

Very well. I decided I'd best just keep my mouth shut until the temperature warmed up a trifle. Figuratively speaking. The house itself was warm, even though the weather remained chilly outdoors.

"It's just tomato soup," said Vi, relenting somewhat.

"I love tomato soup, especially if you put milk in it," said I tentatively.

"I did."

"Oh. Good."

I took the tureen to the table and set it beside Aunt Vi's place at the table. Because she hadn't told me earlier that she aimed to serve us soup, I scurried to the china cabinet, took out four bowls, and stacked them at Vi's place, too.

"Will you call your parents in for dinner, Daisy?"

"Yes, indeed."

So I did, and we all sat down. Pa said grace, Vi served soup and passed the bowls around. Her tomato soup was the best, of course. As soon as we finished our soup, which we ate with soda crackers, I picked up the dishes, took them to the kitchen, and brought out a platter and a bowl Vi had warming on the stove.

"I love stuffed cabbage," said Pa, as Vi served up two of the rolled-up cabbage leaves for him, handed me his plate, and I passed it to Pa. I'd already put the bowl of what Vi called Harvard beets on the table, so I passed those to him, too.

Thank the good Lord, by the time the meal was over, everyone seemed to have forgiven me for teasing them. I hadn't meant to tease them, but I still felt guilty. In those days, I felt guilty most of the time, so this was nothing new.

TWENTY-EIGHT

I'd just put the last dish away and was contemplating what to read next when the stupid telephone rang. Sighing, I went to answer it.

"Gumm-Majesty—"

"You don't need to go through the whole speech," said Sam. "Is it all right if I come over? I'd like to talk to you about what we both heard today."

"You would?" This was a whole new attitude on Sam's part. He generally wanted me as far away from his cases as I could get.

"Yes. But don't get your hopes up. I'm not going to allow you to poke and pry."

"I don't poke and pry!"

"Right."

"Anyhow, yes. Please come over. I can heat some dinner for you, in fact. Vi made stuffed cabbage, tomato soup and Harvard beets."

"Really? I haven't had Harvard beets since I left New York City."

"You haven't dined with us enough. Vi makes them fairly often. She's from Massachusetts, you know, home of Harvard."

"I thought your family came from Auburn."

"We do."

"Harvard is in Cambridge."

"I mean the state, Sam, not the precise town. Don't be so picky."

"Oh. All right. Be there soon."

"Good."

But he'd already hung up the receiver on his end of the wire. Good old Sam.

I strode to the living room and told my family Sam aimed to pay us a visit. Instantly, Vi rose to her feet. "I'll fix a plate for him."

"He might have eaten already," I said.

"Nonsense. He's a big man. He can eat again."

"He probably could," I acknowledged, "but I don't necessarily want to marry a fat man."

"Daisy!" said my mother. I should have anticipated as much.

"It was supposed to be a joke, Ma," I explained.

She said, "Oh."

I love my mother.

Not too long after that, Spike raced to the door. I hadn't even heard Sam's Hudson pull up outside. That was probably because the wind was blowing a gale. Have I mentioned Santa Ana Winds? I do believe I have.

I reached the door not long after Spike did, and well before Sam had climbed the porch stairs. He had his cane in one hand and was attempting to keep his hat on his head with the other.

"Come on in, Sam. Vi is heating you a plate of dinner."

"Thanks." He sighed as he stepped into the warm house. "It's nasty out there."

"At least we don't get feet and feet of snow."

"That's true." He hung his hat and coat on the coat tree.

"Where's Frank?"

"All tucked away safe and sound."

"You stuck him in a cell again?"

"Yep."

I couldn't help but laugh. "By the time you get him home, he'll be so terrified of cells, he'll never misbehave again."

"That's what I'm hoping for. He's not happy, but I told him Pasadena cells were heaven compared to New York City cells. Not sure he believes me, but he'll find out if he doesn't change his ways."

"Come on in and say hey to the family, and then you can tell me whatever you want to tell me while you eat your dinner." I thought of Frank again. "Would you like to take something home for Frank to eat?"

Sam eyed me as if I were insane. "Why would I do that? I want the kid to suffer. I'm not about to reward him for being a petty criminal."

"What's he eating?"

Sam shrugged. "Don't know. Whatever they can find, I guess."

"Who's they?"

"The guys at the station. I told them not to be generous."

"You're all heart, Sam."

"I know." His grin was positively wicked.

"Come in here, Sam," came Vi's voice from the dining room. "I have a plate all ready for you, and I'll heat up a bowl of soup for you, too."

"Thanks, Vi," said Sam. He greeted my parents, who greeted him back, and Sam, Spike and I walked to the dining room.

"Here you go," said Vi, beaming.

"I'm a lucky man," said Sam, who gazed greedily at his plate of stuffed cabbage rolls and beets.

"You'll be even luckier when Vi brings in your soup," I told him.

"Tastes great," said he, after swallowing his first bite of stuffed cabbage.

I took over for Vi, managed to heat Sam's soup without burning it or the saucepan, poured the soup into a bowl, and took it out to Sam, who was doing justice to his late dinner.

"Good, huh?" I said.

"Delicious," said Sam.

After he'd slaked the worst of his hunger, I said, "So, what do you want to talk about, Sam? You usually don't want me anywhere near your cases."

"I don't want you near this one, either," said he after swallowing another bite of cabbage roll. "But I want to know more about this precious Halloween party the Felloweses are hosting this coming weekend."

"All the people who are working on Dr. Fellowes's precious project will be there."

"That's what I wanted to know. Good." He relaxed a bit and took a sip of soup. "Great soup."

"And I have your costume just about finished, too," I said.

He looked up sharply. "Costume? I'm supposed to wear a costume?"

"It's a Halloween party, Sam. You're going to attend it as a Roman senator."

"Cripes."

"You'll look great," I assured him. "You'll even have a red sash over your shoulder."

"Good God."

"Will Frank be coming? He can help serve. That should keep him out of trouble."

"Don't bet on it."

"Well, he can't get into *too* much trouble if we keep him busy. I guess."

"He can be crafty and cunning, you know." Sam ate some beets.

"Crafty and cunning? I didn't think he was smart enough to be either of those things."

"He's not, but he thinks he is."

"Oh, well, we'll just have to keep an eye on him."

"I'm going to be watching the suspects."

"And I'm going to be telling fortunes." Before he could tell me fortune-telling was illegal in the City of Pasadena—although the Felloweses lived in Altadena—I held up a hand. "Only for fun, Sam. Nobody will be paying me a red cent."

"Better not be."

The old grouch.

"So, did what Robert Browning tell you help?"

After swallowing again, Sam said, "Don't know yet. I hope so."

"What I can't figure out is who would profit by a phony gold rush."

"Maybe nobody will. Maybe someone only wants the project managers to look like imbeciles."

"Oh. I hadn't considered that."

"I have to consider everything. It's my job."

"I guess so." I leaned my head on my hand, which was propped on the table via my elbow. I'd never dare sit at the table like that during the family dinner hour, but this was different.

After Sam finished eating, I took him to the sewing room and showed him his toga. His lip curled, and he stared at it as if it were a poisonous snake or something equally vile. "I'm supposed to wear that? It's a *dress!*"

"It's not a dress, Sam Rotondo! It's a Roman toga. The big-wigs of the Roman Empire wore them. I don't think the riffraff were allowed to wear togas. Only the governing class. Classes. I don't know much about ancient Rome, actually. But I do know the ancient Roman big-wigs wore laurel wreaths, so I made you one of those, too."

"God."

A trifle peeved, I snapped, "You're Italian, Sam Rotondo. I should think you'd be pleased to wear a Roman senator's toga."

"Right."

"Want to try it on?"

"No."

"But I have to make sure it's long enough for you." I thought of something. "I don't suppose you have any leather sandals, do you?"

"No. I do not have any leather sandals."

"In that case, I'll have to be sure it's long enough to cover your big, copper shoes."

"God."

"Oh, stop being an old grump! Let me get my measuring tape."

So Sam stood still while I measured him from his shoulders to the ground. He was a large man. Six feet tall, by gum, and not precisely slender. Mind you, he wasn't fat, but he was a chunk of a guy. My Billy had been long and lean. Marriage to Sam would bring a whole new perspective to my life, for sure.

"Thank you, Sam. You may relax now. I have your measurements."

I rose to my feet only to be warmly embraced by the man I aimed to marry. I embraced him back, and things might have become quite interesting had not most of my family been sitting in the living room.

Really, Sam and I had to figure out a way to have some privacy one of these days. After all, we'd both been married before. We knew what married folks did with each other. And I also knew ways to avoid pregnancy until we decided to have children.

Is that a shocking thing to write? Oh, who cares? My journal; my thoughts.

Therefore, we broke apart, sighed in unison, and left the sewing room. Spike and I walked Sam to his Hudson and, in spite of the wind, which howled louder than Spike when he got going, we both stood there as he drove down Marengo. One of these days...

TWENTY-NINE

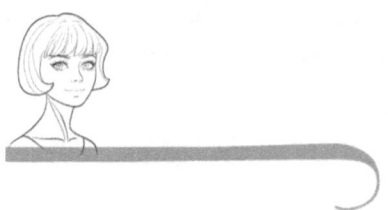

The next day, as I knew she would, Mrs. Pinkerton called me in the morning. Naturally, she was weeping and wailing. Pa and I had just finished taking Spike for his morning walk, so I decided to get the unpleasant part of my day over as quickly as possible.

Therefore, I dressed fashionably, fetched my bag of spiritualist-medium paraphernalia, bade my father and Spike a fond farewell and hied myself to Mrs. P's house. Because I'd been so busy on Monday, I'd have to do the laundry that day, a Tuesday. I don't like doing laundry, but both my aunt and my mother worked away from the house more than I did, so I did the laundry. Because the wind still roared, I aimed to hang it in the basement. Sometimes those blasted Santa Ana Winds would carry an entire line of laundry sailing off down the street. Or up the street, depending on which way they blew.

Neither Rolly nor the tarot cards had any startling revelations for Mrs. Pinkerton, but we both offered her as much comfort as we could. Rolly was such a nice guy.

Before I left the mansion, I went to the kitchen where I found my aunt elbow-deep in flour.

"Making bread?" I asked.

She turned and smiled at me. "Yes. I'm going to make bread and

Parker House Rolls, and the Pinkertons and we will have them for dinner."

"I love Parker House Rolls." Something occurred to me. "Why are they called Parker House Rolls? I mean, did somebody named Parker invent them?"

Vi laughed into her bread dough. "The original recipe came from a hotel in Boston in, I think the 1870s or thereabouts. The hotel was called the Parker House."

"Oh. I guess that makes sense."

"I guess it does. They're really no different from bread or other rolls. They're just folded and then brushed with melted butter."

"Yum."

"Indeed." Vi shaped her dough into a bowl, covered it with a damp dish towel, and set the bowl aside. "But now I have to prepare everything else."

"I'd offer to help——"

"No thank you, dear. I need to get the meals prepared today."

Well, really!

Feeling hurt, although I don't know why—I knew all about the calamities I could inflict in the kitchen—I said, "Very well, then. I'll just go on home and do laundry."

"Don't sulk dear."

Vi'd washed her hands and walked over to me. She kissed me on the top of my head. "Love you, Daisy."

I gave up my sulk, which was undeserved anyway. "Love you, too, Vi." I gave her a quick hug, glanced down to see I'd got flour all over my nice black woolen coat, brushed it off and headed outside. I left by the service-porch door, which meant that by the time I got to the Chevrolet parked in front of the house, my hair had been blown to bits and I had grit in my teeth. I really hated those Santa Ana Winds.

However, that is neither here nor there. I drove home, got out of my working costume, donned a faded blue house dress and the most comfortable pair of shoes I owned and went to the service porch. I sighed heavily when I saw the basket full of laundry awaiting me.

Mind you, I shouldn't complain. A couple of years earlier I'd bought the family an electric Thor washing machine, so washing was ever so much easier than it used to be when we had to scrub the clothes on a washboard. Still, doing laundry was a tedious chore. Maybe one of these days, I could afford to hire someone to come in and do laundry for us.

Probably not.

By the time I'd rinsed the last load, fed everything through the wringer again, and hung it all in the basement to dry, I was pooped. So I went into the living room, grabbed a book, and sat on the sofa. I had to conduct a séance at Mrs. Bissel's that night, so I didn't feel guilty about resting a bit. Not too guilty, anyway.

I'd already read *The Amazing Adventures of Letitia Carberry* and *Tish*, so I started in on *More Tish*. These books were definitely fun, and I enjoyed them. Spike did, too, because he got to sit on my lap as I read. My eyes kept trying to shut, so I finally gave up on *More Tish*, and went to my bedroom to lie down.

When I woke up again, Pa was home, and he was eating a cold cabbage roll at the kitchen table.

"Hey, sleepyhead," said he.

"I'm not being lazy," I said instantly. Guess I did feel guilty. "I did laundry, and I have to conduct a séance tonight, so I rested a bit."

"I'm not accusing you of being lazy," said my father, grinning. "Want a cold cabbage roll?"

"Yes. Thanks."

So, bless Pa's heart, he got me a cold cabbage roll, put it on a plate, brought the plate to me and revisited the Frigidaire. "There are some leftover beets in here, too," said he, peering into the Frigidaire. "Want some of those?"

"Yes, please. You're too nice to me, Pa."

"Nonsense. You work hard, Daisy. All I do is loaf around."

He didn't like doing it, either, but he'd had a heart attack, and Dr. Benjamin had warned him about doing too much. I loved my father and wanted him to stick around for a good long while.

While the rest of my family ate Vi's magnificent dinner—roasted chicken, mashed potatoes and gravy, English peas and Parker House rolls—I got dressed up for Mrs. Bissel's séance. I felt deprived, but I was pretty sure Mrs. Bissel's dinner would be passable. Anyhow, I could have a chicken sandwich for lunch the next day.

Wait a minute! I probably couldn't. Drat! I'd agreed to haul Regina Petrie around to the beauty salon and to some shops. Fiddlesticks. As soon as I realized what my tomorrow would bring, I felt deprived all over again. But never mind that.

As the Chevrolet chugged up Lake Avenue to Foothill Boulevard, I reflected that I didn't really want to meet poor Miss Carleton's mother. She'd almost certainly be devastated about her daughter's death and, while I often told Sam I helped bereaved people by giving them hope and comfort, I still lied for a living. My work didn't sound awfully noble when viewed from that angle. Ah, well. Too late to change my profession now.

Mrs. Bissel's house was large and grand, but it wasn't the castle some of the other rich folks in Altadena and Pasadena owned. Still, it was a nice place. I parked in the circular driveway in back of the house, since if I parked the car on the street in front of the house, I'd have to hike a mile and a half across the two rolling hills on her front lawn, and I was apt to get blown off my feet. The back yard wasn't free from perils, however. A big monkey-puzzle tree sat in the middle of the circular drive, and those stupid monkey-puzzle spikes were perilous. More than once, I'd been attacked by one and had my stockings snagged.

By being extremely careful, I arrived at the back door of Mrs. B's house with my stockings intact. Keiji Saito, Mrs. Bissel's Japanese houseboy, met me at the back door with a smile. "Did you navigate through the blowing leaves successfully?" he asked.

"Yes. It was tough, but I managed. You call those things leaves? They're more like deadly weapons if you ask me."

Keiji and I were good buddies. He'd not only taught me how to use chopsticks, but I steered people to his uncle's Pasadena restaurant as often as I could. I'd never eaten Japanese food before I'd met Keiji. I liked it. Of course, I basically liked food. When Keiji had told me about sushi and sashimi, I cringed, but he said they were both quite tasty. I told him I believed him, but I still didn't want to eat any raw fish.

"Want to go to the powder room and fix your hair?" asked Keiji.

Oh, dear. I patted my hair. "I didn't escape from the wind unscathed? Is that what you're trying to tell me, Keiji?"

He laughed as he took my hat, handbag and coat from me. "You don't look too scathed, but yes. I suspect you'd like to fix your hair. You can use the back stairs and go to the bathroom at the top of them if you'd like."

"Thanks. I shall."

I knew the way, having been coming to this house for almost as long as I'd been visiting Mrs. Pinkerton's. I'd had a frightening experience regarding that particular bathroom once, but the people I'd overheard confessing to and plotting murder were safely tucked away in prison now, so I had no fear that night. I tromped up the back stairs—in other words, the servants' stairs—and entered the pretty tiled bathroom.

Oh, my. Keiji had been right. I plopped my handbag and accouterments on the vanity table, dug my comb out of my handbag, and worked on my hair. Fortunately, I have "good" hair. It was thick and sort of wavy, and it settled down with only a little tweaking. Then I went back down the servants' stairs and walked through the kitchen, breakfast room, sun porch and entered the living room.

As luck—or an ill wind, darn those stupid Santa Anas—would have it, the first person to spot me was Mrs. Pinkerton, who charged at me. Knowing her of old, I braced myself against a wall so we wouldn't both fall over when she hit.

"Oh, Daisy! Oh, my dear, I'm *so* glad you're here! Poor Angela is *so* upset! But you can help her. I know you can!"

Whoever Angela was. I patted Mrs. P on the back. "There, there," said I. "I'll do my best."

Fortunately, Mrs. Bissel had seen our collision and was smiling as she walked over to me. Both Mrs. Bissel and Mrs. Pinkerton were relatively large women, and both had money to burn, so they always dressed in the height of fashion. Sometimes this was unfortunate. That night they both wore evening frocks that didn't flatter them much, being straight up-and-down styles. Neither one of the ladies were straight up-and-down. Mind you, the slim and boyish look didn't necessarily flatter me either, but I didn't have as much flesh to cover as the two matrons. My bust-flattener generally made my clothes look good on me, but I doubted so flimsy a fix would help either of these women. That night, Mrs. B was in purple and Mrs. P was in a rather shockingly pink-colored, floor-length satin gown. Not only did she bulge alarmingly in quite a few places, but the light flashing from the satin made me blink. I wasn't a big purple fan, but at least Mrs. Bissel appeared somber and dignified. Mrs. Pinkerton looked as if she were trying to recapture her girlhood. She didn't succeed.

"Come with me, dear," said Mrs. Bissel, prying Mrs. Pinkerton away from me. "I want you to meet Angela Carleton. It was her daughter, you know, who was so foully done to death last week."

"Yes. I know. Thank you, Mrs. Bissel."

She shook her head, still smiling as we walked. "Madeline can be a bit trying sometimes. I thought I'd better rescue you." Madeline was Mrs. Pinkerton.

"Thank you. I feared I'd smother if she'd held me any longer."

We both laughed.

As soon as Mrs. B led me farther into the room, I spotted that night's victim—I mean main subject. A woman clad in black and almost as pale as I sat on a sofa against the far wall. She had dark circles under her eyes, and she looked sad. Very sad. My heart hurt for her. Mrs. Bissel led me straight to her. The woman glanced up with dull eyes.

"Angela, please meet Mrs. Majesty. I sincerely hope she'll be able to give you some comfort at this terrible time. Desdemona Majesty, please allow me to introduce you to Angela Carleton."

Mrs. Carleton stood with what looked like great effort. I wished she hadn't. Being a total fraud was bad enough; making people stand to meet me didn't seem right at all.

"Mrs. Carleton," said I, "I'm so sorry for your loss. I can't even imagine how terrible it must be to lose a child."

With a quivering lip, Mrs. Carleton said, "Glad to meet you, Mrs. Majesty." She held out her hand, and I took it in both of my own.

"I knew your daughter only slightly, but she was a fine librarian and seemed a lovely person."

A couple of tears trickled down the woman's face. "Thank you. She loved her work. I only wish she'd stayed at the public library and hadn't moved to the Institute. She made more money there, but she wasn't happy."

Hmm. Interesting. "Please, Mrs. Carleton, sit down. May I sit with you for a moment?"

She sat and said, "Yes. Thank you, Mrs. Majesty."

Sitting next to her, I said, "Please just call me Daisy. Most folks do."

"Daisy," she repeated dully.

"I'll leave the two of you to get to know each other," said Mrs. Bissel, who was infinitely more insightful—I guess that's the right word —than Mrs. Pinkerton, who had started making a bee-line for Mrs. Carleton and me. Mrs. Bissel deftly swept the woman off-course and spoke softly in her ear. I suspect she was giving her a tactful lesson in good manners. In other words, she probably reminded her that Mrs. Pinkerton might have a lousy daughter, but Mrs. Carleton had no daughter at all any longer.

"Please accept my sympathy. I have no idea what you're going through, and I'm so very sorry," I said sincerely.

Wiping her eyes with a damp hankie, Mrs. Carleton said, "Thank you."

"Um...You said Miss Carleton wasn't happy at the Institute?"

"No." She shook her head. "She was at first, but...Well, she'd been...I'm not sure what you'd call it. She thought she..." Her voice trailed off.

She thought she what? Dang it! "Did she tell you why she decided to accept the job at Cal Tech?"

Deep, heartfelt sigh. "Yes, but she was wrong."

"I'm sorry." Not enlightened, but sorry. "Um...Why did she move to the Institute? Was it just for the money? Not that there's any *just* about money. We women who have to support ourselves or our families are at other people's mercy sometimes. Most of the time, actually."

"Yes. That's true."

A heavy silence ensued. I didn't break it, having noticed more than once that people got uncomfortable with silence and were apt to chatter if it hung around too long.

Mrs. Carleton finally broke. "She thought she was in love with one of the scientists who worked there," she said in a soft voice. "But the man was already married." Shooting me a quick glance from troubled eyes, she added, "She didn't know that at the time. He…Well, he treated her quite badly."

"Poor Miss Carleton."

"Yes. Poor Mary." She sniffled. "The man was *such* a cad!"

"I'm sorry."

Mrs. Carleton took my hand and peered at me closely. "If I tell you something, will you keep it to yourself?"

"Of course. My entire career depends on confidentiality. I would never tell another person's secrets." Well…Almost never.

"Mary…" She paused, swallowed, and wiped her eyes again. "Mary had a baby two years ago. She…Well, she was naïve, I suppose, but she honestly believed the man would marry her." She gave a rather inelegant snort. "He was already married."

"The cad!" I didn't have to pretend outrage. I'd been outraged ever since I'd learned about poor Mary Carleton's baby. And when I'd learned who the father of her child was, I'd wanted to stab him in the back. Not precisely kind of me, but really. Any man who would lie to a woman in order to secure her favors didn't deserve to call himself a man. I have absolutely no tolerance for some things. "Um…Did poor Miss Carleton have to give up the baby? I mean, did someone adopt the child?"

Shaking her head, Mrs. Carleton said, "No. Mary begged us to keep him. My husband didn't want to, but I insisted. The poor child can't be blamed for the folly of his parents. And Mary wasn't truly foolish. She'd been foully misled."

"I'm so glad you have something of your daughter's to remember her by." Was that a stupid thing to say? Probably. Oh, well.

"Yes. I'm glad we kept him. He's a darling little boy."

"How old is he now? Oh, you said two years."

"Yes." A big sob wracked her. "And now he won't even remember his mother!"

She broke down completely after that, and I put an arm around her and squeezed. She turned in my arms and wept on my shoulder for several minutes. When I glanced around the room, I saw we were being sent lots of sympathetic glances. Well deserved, I believed, although I'm sure some of the woman would be appalled if they knew Mary Carleton had born a child out of wedlock. The world is *so* unfair sometimes. Anyway, I didn't mind my black gown getting its shoulder soaked. It was an old, if lovely, gown, and it had been wept upon before.

We were all called in to dinner then, so I walked with Mrs. Carleton to the table. There were more women than men at dinner, so I sat next to Mrs. Carleton. She didn't eat much. I, however, did justice to Mrs. Cummings' meal. She wasn't *quite* the cook our Vi was, but her roast beef and popovers were quite good, and I didn't feel quite so upset about having missed out on Vi's roast chicken and Parker House Rolls.

THIRTY

"Ach, my love," said Rolly after dinner when we'd gathered in the darkened breakfast room of Mrs. Bissel's home, "Miss Carleton is sorry she had to leave her loved ones"—I didn't mention specific loved ones—"but she's settling in here and is at peace. She prays her mother will not grieve long, for those she left behind need her strength and love."

That wasn't fair to poor Mrs. Carleton, who should be allowed to grieve for her lost daughter as much and as long as she needed to, but such is a woman's lot, I reckon. We get to do all the work and keep the family glued together when a member thereof passes away. Which is another silly expression. Passes away? How does someone pass away?

Oh, never mind.

When the séance was over, we all gathered in the living room again, and Keiji brought in coffee and tea. I didn't take either one, because I feared I wouldn't sleep well. Mrs. Carleton came up to me as I stood near the fireplace, thinking black thoughts about deceitful men and wishing Mary Carleton hadn't met such a grisly fate.

She took my hand. "Thank you very much, Daisy. I didn't know what to expect from this séance, and I honestly didn't think it would do any good, but if Mary is truly at peace now..." She peered closely at me. "She is at peace, isn't she?"

"Yes," I lied nobly. "Rolly knows about the Other Side and those who reside there." You notice I didn't say dead people "lived" on the Other Side, but I figured reside was a good word.

"I'm so glad. I feel more at peace myself now. Especially since he said Mary's killer will be found soon and punished."

Rolly had said that, and I hoped like heck he hadn't fibbed. I held out great hope for the upcoming Saturday's Halloween party.

"Indeed," I said. "I know the detective who's leading the case, and he's extremely thorough and good."

"Is that Detective Rotondo?" asked Mrs. Carleton.

"Yes, it is."

"He was so kind to me when we spoke."

He was? Wow. I was impressed. Sometimes Sam seemed so stolid and blockish, it was difficult for me to imagine him being kind to a grieving mother. And here I thought I knew him. "I'm awfully glad to hear it. He's no stranger to tragedy himself. His wife passed away several years ago. Tuberculosis."

Mrs. Carleton shook her head. "Life is so hard sometimes." She squeezed my hand. "But Griselda told me you suffered your own bereavement not too long ago."

I sighed. "Yes. My Billy died. He'd been shot and gassed in the war, and he never recovered. I suppose I should call it a blessing that he no longer suffers, but I—"

Good Lord! My eyes filled with tears. *Get a hold on your nerves, Daisy Gumm Majesty*, I told myself.

But Mrs. Carleton didn't seem to mind. In fact, she gave me a little hug. "That war," she said. She didn't need to say more.

"Yes," I agreed, digging in my pocket for a hankie.

I didn't stick around for long after that, but made my farewells and again braved the wind. My exit from the house didn't pass as peacefully as my entry had. A big, spiky leaf from the blasted monkey-puzzle tree whacked me on the side of my head just as I reached the Chevrolet. Dang, it hurt. At least my stockings didn't get snagged. Sometimes you have to hold on to the little things, because the big ones hurt too much. I'm not talking about monkey-puzzle leaves here.

When I drove down Marengo Avenue, I was surprised to see both Harold's Stutz Bearcat and Sam's big old Hudson parked in front of our house. Whatever was going on? Only one way to find out. So I parked the machine and walked to the side door. When I opened it, Spike raced to greet me. Sam, Harold, Pa and Frank were seated at the dining-room table.

As soon as the men spotted me, Sam leapt to his feet and rushed over to me. He barely even limped, but put his arms around me and held me close.

"What happened to you? You look like somebody attacked you!"

I returned his hug. "A monkey-puzzle leaf attacked me."

Sam pulled away, his hands on my shoulders, and squinted down at me. "A what?"

"Haven't you ever been to Mrs. Bissel's house?"

"Well, yeah. I was there when those crumbs murdered those people."

Succinct, if not precisely informative. "You didn't notice the huge monkey-puzzle tree in the back yard?"

"No. Do you need help? Iodine? A bandage?"

"Thanks, Sam. I'll take care of it. I was attacked by a sharp, pointy, spiky leaf. I'll just go to the bathroom, clean myself up, and then you can tell me why you're all here. What the heck time is it, anyway?"

"Eleven," said my father.

"Good heavens, that's late for you, isn't it, Pa?"

"Yes. But Sam needed me." He grinned, though, so I suspected him of a slight degree of exaggeration.

I remembered the rest of our guests—if guests they were—and said, "Hey, Harold. Frank."

"Hey yourself," said Harold.

"Good evening, Mrs. Majesty," said Frank.

Golly. The lout seemed to be improving.

"Be right back," I said, and scooted to the bathroom.

When I looked in the mirror, I realized Sam was correct. I had a nasty cut on my forehead, and it had bled freely. That wasn't a surprise.

I've heard more than once that head wounds bleed a lot. So I wetted a washcloth and very tenderly wiped away the blood. Squinting into the mirror, I saw the cut was small, and that none of the blood had landed on my gown. I wiped away the few drops on my coat. I applied some iodine—which hurt like the dickens—and put a little gauze pad over the wound and secured it with tape. I hoped the wound would heal by Saturday. I didn't think Gladys would approve of a bandaged Gypsy fortune-teller at her Halloween party.

When I rejoined the men, Pa had taken himself off to bed. Because my parents' bedroom was right off the hall leading from the dining room, I quietly shut the door so we could chat in private. In fact, I herded everyone to the living room to be extra sure we didn't wake up anyone.

"So what brings the three of you here on this blustery evening?" I asked, sitting myself on the piano bench. Sam and Frank took the sofa, and Harold pulled up a chair.

"Kincaid has the party all planned," said Sam. "And Frank here is going to help serve the canapés and drinks. Just wanted to make sure everything's all right on your end."

"So you really think you'll nab the murderer on Saturday?"

"I hope to," said Sam.

"So do I," said Harold, surprising me. "I don't care for murder or murderers."

"I don't think any of us do," I said. Then I thought of Frank.

Evidently we all thought of Frank at the same time, because we all turned and fixed our gazes on him. He glanced at each of us and threw out his hands. "What? What did I do? I didn't murder nobody."

"Anybody," said his uncle in a cold, cold voice.

"Anybody," said Frank, his own voice small.

"Not yet anyway," said Sam, giving his nephew a ferocious frown.

"Hey," said Frank.

I was tired, and Frank annoyed me. "Oh, be quiet, Frank. You're a thief at the very least, so I don't think you have anything to whine about."

Frank said, "Hey," in a hurt-sounding voice, but he shut up.

I turned to Harold. "Is there anything else you need me to do, Harold?"

"Yes. Sew this into a globe shape, then I'll take it back, starch it to death, and put rounded stays in it. Your friend is a little nervous about her costume for the party." Harold wrinkled his nose. "She's not precisely a fountain of gaiety, is she?"

"No. She never has been. A brain, that's our Gladys." I took the fabric he held out to me and shook it out. "Oh, my! You did a wonderful job with the continents, Harold!"

"I'm good at my job."

"I should say so. Do you want these to go any particular way? I mean do you want the Americas on her tummy and Africa on her back or something?"

"That would be polite," said Harold, smothering a laugh.

Sam smiled, too. "Sounds good to me."

"Have you tried on your toga, Detective?" asked Harold.

"Yes." Sam sobered instantly. "She's making me wear a red sash with it. And a cursed laurel wreath." His nose wrinkled.

Frank said in a tiny voice, "Do I get to wear a costume?"

Before Harold or I could respond, Sam said, "Yes. You're going to be disguised as a brilliant student from Cal Tech in a waiter's uniform."

"Oh, did you find out the students will be serving at the party?"

"Kincaid just told us." Sam said gesturing at Harold.

"Indeed," said Harold. "I spent a good deal of the day dealing with your dear friend Gladys." He made a horrible grimace. "And the rest of the day dealing with my own dear mother. The studio's going to fire me if this keeps up."

"Oh, no! Is your job really in danger?"

Harold grinned. "No. I just wanted you to feel guilty."

"Thanks. I always feel guilty."

"Too bad some folks who *should* feel guilty don't," said Sam, aiming a pointed glare at his nephew. I hoped the kid would be going back to New York City soon. I didn't think Sam could stand much more of Frank Pagano cluttering up his life.

Frank said, "Hey."

Harold heaved himself to his feet. "Well, I just came over to give you the globe material. The detective said you were conducting a séance for the poor Carleton woman at Mrs. Bissel's house today. My mother said she'd be there."

"She was," I said.

"Sorry," said Harold, who knew his mother well. He came to the piano bench, gave me a brotherly kiss on the cheek, and headed for the front door. Spike and I followed him.

"Not your fault," I told him.

"I know it, but I'm sorry anyway."

He left, and I turned upon a deep sigh to glance at the remaining two men strewn about the living room.

Sam got to his feet. "We're leaving, too. Just wanted you to know everything's in place for Saturday. I'll have a couple of men there in plain clothes. They should blend in fairly well as long as nobody talks science to them."

"Does Gladys know they'll be there?"

"Yes. I spoke with her today."

"Good. Then I guess everything's on its way to being solved."

"Who knows? This party idea is a good one, but we don't know what the results are going to be."

"I suppose that's true." I yawned and slapped a hand over my mouth. "Sorry."

"Rough evening?" Sam actually sounded sympathetic.

I peered at him closely, but he didn't seem sarcastic or anything. "Yes. It's difficult, trying to comfort someone who's just lost a daughter so horribly."

"But I'm sure you did your best."

Again I searched his face for sarcasm. Didn't see any.

"Yes. I did my best. By the way, she said you were very kind to her when you spoke to her."

"I try to be kind to grieving parents. That's a rough thing to go through."

"Indeed. I can't even imagine it."

"Nor can I." He glanced at his nephew, who had risen, too, and now stood directly behind Sam. "Although it might be worth a try."

"Sam!" I said, although not awfully vehemently. Frank was a sore burden for him to bear.

Frank said, "Hey."

"Shut up, you," said Sam.

Frank looked huffy as the two men left the house. As soon as they were gone, Spike and I went to my room, where I quickly divested myself of my evening frock and so forth, donned my comfy old night-gown, and climbed into bed. Spike joined me, and we both slept like the dead for a long, long time.

But not quite long enough. It was about seven o'clock when I heard stirrings in the kitchen. With a groan, I opened what felt like grit-filled eyes, flung on my robe, stuffed my feet into my slippers, and left my room. Spike went with me. I let him out the side door so he could do his duty as a dog in the yard. Spike was *such* a good dog.

"Morning, sweetie," said Pa, who stood beside the stove, dishing up something that smelled good. "Your aunt fixed some scrambled eggs and bacon for us. I'll toast some bread for you."

"Thanks, Pa. I'm really sleepy this morning. Not used to late nights, I guess."

"None of us are." He smiled sweetly at me. "Have an orange."

"That sounds like a good idea." I found a little plate, sat at the kitchen table, and began peeling a lovely navel orange that had come straight from our own orange tree. I loved oranges.

"Here you go," said Pa, setting a plate before me. "Very good eggs."

"Of course, they're good eggs," said Vi, walking into the kitchen buttoning up her coat.

"Thanks, Vi. Do you need me to drive you to work this morning?"

"No, thanks, dear. I'll take the bus. The wind isn't blowing as hard this morning as it has been."

"Glad to hear it. I think we were all getting tired of the wind."

"True." Vi peered closely at me. "What happened to your head?"

I'd forgot all about my wound. I touched my bandage and said, "I was attacked by a monkey-puzzle leaf."

"You were what?" said Ma, walking into the kitchen behind Vi. "Somebody attacked you? Good Lord."

Good old Ma. "No, Ma. Mrs. Bissel has a monkey-puzzle tree in her back yard, and the wind blew one of its spiky leaves at my head as I walked to the machine last night. It got me pretty good."

"I'm sorry, dear." Ma came over and gave me a kiss on my bandage. "I don't know precisely what a monkey-puzzle tree is, but if it has leaves sharp enough to wound people, I don't think people should plant them."

Ever practical, my mother. "It's kind of a pretty tree, in its way."

"Why in the world is it called a monkey-puzzle tree?" asked Ma, tying a scarf over her hair.

"Its bark looks like pieces of a jigsaw puzzle," I told her.

"Oh. How odd." And Ma walked with Vi to the front door. "Have a good day, dear."

"Thank, Ma. You too. And you, too, Vi."

"Thank you, Daisy. I expect you'll be visiting Mrs. Pinkerton again today?"

I heaved a sigh. "I guess so. She hasn't telephoned yet, but——" The telephone rang. Dang.

Mrs. Pinkerton wailed on the other end of the wire when I answered the telephone, and I told her I'd be at her house at nine-thirty. That was earlier than usual, but I had a lot of gallivanting to do with Regina Petrie that day, so if Mrs. P didn't like it, she could lump it.

She didn't like it, but she agreed to the early hour. Therefore, I telephoned Regina and told her I could meet her at the library at noon.

"I have to visit a client first, but that should give me plenty of time," said I.

"That's perfectly fine," Regina said in her soft voice. Which, by the way, had an unusually happy lift to it this morning.

"How did your luncheon with Mr. Browning go yesterday?" I asked, not particularly slyly.

I could almost feel her joy winging its way through the telephone wire. "Oh, Daisy, it was delightful! And he asked me to go to the Halloween party with him this coming Saturday evening."

Yay! And I hadn't even had to pressure him to do it. Well done, Robert Browning. "I knew he would," I fibbed. Not sure why. I'd hoped he would, was more the truth. But what the heck.

"So perhaps you can help me with some kind of costume?" She

spoke timidly, as if she didn't want to ask too much of me. Me. A phony spiritualist, but a crackerjack seamstress.

"Absolutely! We'll fix you right up." Wasn't sure how, but I knew I'd think of something. When it came to clothes, I had faith in myself.

"Thank you so much."

"You're welcome. I'll pick you up at noon. We can take lunch together somewhere."

"There's quite a nice little Chinese place on Fair Oaks not far from the library," she said.

"Indeed. The Crown Chop Suey Parlor. I've eaten there quite a few times." With Sam. I didn't add that part.

"Are you tired of it?" asked Regina, sounding as if she were sorry she'd mentioned it.

"Not at all. I love Chinese food!"

"Wonderful. See you then."

"Looking forward to it," said I, pretty much meaning it.

Then and there, I decided to go to the library a little early and see if I could find a picture of a monkey-puzzle tree to show my mother.

THIRTY-ONE

My visit with Mrs. Pinkerton held no surprises. It also held no enjoyment. But Rolly and I did our best. Mrs. P cried all over me again, but I was used to it. After I was through with her, I walked to the kitchen to see if Vi could tell me if I needed to change my clothes before I met Regina at the library.

Vi looked at me critically. "I don't think so. Your shoulder's a little damp, but I'm sure it will dry. That's a lovely suit, dear."

I gazed down at my three-quarter-length brown silk tunic dress with bishop sleeves gathered into long blue-silk cuffs. The collar of the dress matched the cuffs, as did a panel down the front of the dress and its belt that buckled below my waist. It was a comfortable costume, except for the stupid bust-flattener I had to wear under it. I wore my trusty black woolen coat, black hat and shoes. I'd put it on mainly because it was comfy, and I knew I'd be wearing it for a long time that day.

"Thanks, Vi. I've worn it before."

"I don't remember it, but you do have a lot of clothes, you know."

Guilt flooded me. "I know. I'm sorry." I scuffed the toe of my shoe on the floor.

"Why should you be sorry? You have a gift. Might as well use it."

"Hmm. When looked at in that light, I guess you're right."

"Besides, you sew clothes for the whole family."

"True. And you use your gift to feed us all. I think your gift is more valuable than mine."

"Get along with you, Daisy. It's a good thing we're not all experts at the same thing, or we'd be in real trouble."

"I suppose you're right."

"Now, go on. I have to get luncheon for the missus together."

"Thanks, Vi. I'm meeting Regina Petrie at the library, and we're going to get her all dolled up."

Vi shook her head. "You amaze me sometimes, Daisy."

"Why?" I didn't understand.

"Never mind." But she smiled, so I guess my being amazing wasn't a bad thing.

I got to the library at about eleven-thirty, which gave me lots of time to ask Regina about a book in which I might find photographs or drawings of a monkey-puzzle tree. As usual, she came through like a champ, and I checked out a book about horticulture along with several novels she'd saved for my family.

Then we went to the Crown Chop Suey Parlor, where whom did we see when we walked in but Sam Rotondo and his idiot nephew, Frank Pagano. As soon as he saw us, Sam stood and beckoned us to join him. He yanked Frank out of his chair to stand, too. Regina pulled back a little.

I looked at her quizzically.

She said, "I don't want to be in the way."

"Don't be silly. The only one who'll be in the way is that stupid nephew of Sam's." So I tugged on her arm a little, and she followed, as docile as a lamb.

"Good day to you both," I said when we got to their table. I noticed Sam had hung his cane on the back of his chair. I guess the leg hurt. Because I blamed Frank—don't ask me why, because I don't know—I glared at him.

He swallowed hard and said, "Good day, Mrs. Majesty. Miss...Um..."

Sam's hand whacked the side of Frank's head, eliciting a "Hey" from his victim. "That's Miss Petrie, you dolt. You just met her a couple of days ago."

"Miss Petrie," said Frank dutifully. Then he gave his uncle a frown, but Sam scowled hideously back at him, and his face cleared as if wiped by a magic cloth. Sam had him intimidated into some kind of behavior, anyway.

"Sit down, you two," said Sam, sounding as happy as I'd heard him sound since Frank had come to town. "I didn't expect to see you today, Daisy."

The four of us all sat. "Aren't you coming for dinner tonight?" I asked.

"If I can. I'll give you a call."

"Thanks. Miss Petrie and I are going to do some shopping. She's going to be attending the Halloween party with Mr. Browning."

"Ah," said Sam. "I see."

I could tell he still considered Robert Browning a viable suspect even after Robert's admittedly late disclosure, the silly man.

"It's nice to see you two," said Regina in her soft, nearly inaudible voice.

Sam raised his hand to summon one of the Chinese waiters, who promptly came to the table with a menu for Regina and one for me. "Go ahead and order, you two. We just ordered a minute ago, and our food hasn't arrived yet, so maybe we'll all be able to dine together."

"Great. I already know what I want," I said, smiling at the waiter. "A number three, please."

"That sounds good to me, too," said Regina, who also smiled at the waiter.

He bowed, took our menus, and departed to convey our orders to the kitchen.

Fortunately, our food all arrived at the same time, so nobody had to wait on anyone else's order. I love Chinese food. Also, if you ordered one of their pre-planned menus, you got a whole lot of different stuff. I particularly loved the Chinese spareribs.

We talked about not much of anything as we dined. Frank didn't say a word, but he minded his manners beautifully. He almost spoke up when the food arrived, but a look from his uncle shut his mouth before anything emerged therefrom.

For the rest of the afternoon after that, Regina and I made the rounds of stores from Nash's Dry Goods and Mercantile, to Maxime's Fabrics, to Norma Golding's Beauty Parlor and on and on and on.

At one point, we came across the Salvation Army band playing "Onward Christian Soldiers" on a corner. In those days, you couldn't stroll down Colorado without meeting the band. Regina seemed slightly alarmed when I headed straight at the Army, but I just tugged her along with me. When we got to the band, Johnny Buckingham, who played the trumpet, stopped playing and greeted me. I introduced him to Regina, who shook his hand tentatively.

"Where's Flossie?" I asked Johnny.

"Home with Billy," said he. Made sense to me. Billy, named for my late husband, was Flossie and Johnny's baby boy.

Regina and I each contributed something to the tambourine held out to us by a uniformed maiden of the Army, I waved good-bye to Johnny, and as he resumed playing we walked down the street.

"I didn't know you were so close to the folks at the Salvation Army," said Regina. "Not that there's anything wrong with the Salvation Army, of course, but…I'm just a little surprised, is all."

"I've known Johnny for years. He and my late husband were great friends. I met his wife, Flossie, a couple of years ago, and we became dear friends, too."

I didn't bother to relate Flossie's entire story to Regina. She might have been shocked, although she continued to surprise me. However, if I'd told her Flossie and I had met in a speakeasy that was almost instantly raided, she might have looked upon the both of us askance. The fact that I'd only gone there to conduct a séance was, while true, still stupid of me, a fact of which Sam Rotondo never fails to remind me. The fact that Flossie had at the time been a gangster's moll was nobody's business. Anyway, she'd reformed, unlike some former Salvation Army members I'd known. Stacy Kincaid naturally leaps to my mind. I didn't like her doing that and wish she'd keep out of my life entirely, but oh well…

"Oh," said Regina. "How nice."

I guess. Anyhow, we had a good time at Hertel's Department Store, where Regina was persuaded to purchase a very pretty day dress and some fashionable shoes. Both items were on sale, which appealed to my skinflint soul; I don't think Regina cared much.

All in all, we had a good time. I have to admit, however, that by the time we emerged from Norma Golding's Beauty Parlor, I was about to drop dead of fatigue. But boy, did Regina Petrie look like a new woman!

She kept patting her hair, which had been cut and marcelled into a stylish not-quite-bob. "I can't believe it," she whispered time and time again. "I can't believe it."

"You look wonderful," I told her, wishing I were home napping with Spike.

"I'll never be able to thank you enough for this, Daisy."

"I didn't do a thing. You did all the shopping. And I'm so glad you got your hair cut. You look stunning." Perhaps that was a slight exaggeration, but really, she did look like a whole other person. A stylish, very attractive other person. I was proud of myself, even though she'd paid all the money and had all the work done. Still, she'd never have had it done if it weren't for me. Probably.

"I'm so grateful to you, Daisy. I truly am."

We went through that many times: her thanking me, me telling her not to, and her thanking me some more. I was tired.

We'd stuffed all the packages into the Chevrolet, to which we now returned. I drove Regina home, helped her carry all the parcels to her darling little bungalow and took myself and my tired body to our house. I don't think I'd ever been so glad to be home before. Spike was pleased, too. As was Pa.

"Sam called," he said as I stooped to greet my darling hound. "He said he and Frank can come to dinner tonight."

"Oh, good." I stood, creaking a little. "What time is it, anyway?"

Pa took a step back into the kitchen and looked at the clock. "Three-fifteen."

"Is that all? I feel as if I've been on my feet for a hundred years."

"Rough day?" Pa looked concerned.

"Not really. Just tiring. I had to see Mrs. Pinkerton this morning, but the rest of the day I spent with Regina Petrie, getting her all spiffed up. If things go the way I hope they will, she and Robert Browning will be a couple soon."

"If he's not arrested for murder," said Pa dampeningly.

"He won't be. He didn't do it."

"If you say so, sweetie."

"Say, Pa, is it all right with you if I lie down for a little while? Regina and I tromped all over Pasadena this afternoon in order to get her prettied up."

"You needn't ask my permission, Daisy," said Pa, laughing. "You deserve to rest as much as anyone else does. Especially after having done such a good deed."

"Thanks, Pa."

So Spike and I both went to my bedroom, where I slipped out of my comfy dress, my uncomfy bust-flattener, and flopped onto the bed. Spike jumped up and snuggled beside me. We had a nice nap.

When Spike and I awoke, Vi was in the kitchen preparing something that smelled delicious, as was her wont. She greeted me cheerfully, as I did her.

Sam and Frank arrived on the dot of six p.m., and Frank hardly moved during the entire meal. Sam didn't make him wash dishes with me, for which I was glad. The two of them didn't stay long after they ate, because Sam said he had to return to the office to complete some paperwork. I wanted to ask him how the case was progressing, but knew better. He was *such* a grumbler about what he calls my interference with his cases.

The rest of the week passed peacefully enough. Naturally, I had to visit Mrs. Pinkerton every day. Also naturally, Rolly and the tarot cards told her nothing they hadn't told her thousands of times before. Nevertheless, Mrs. P seemed to be more and more reliant on me. I didn't understand then, never have understood, and doubt I ever will understand why she put such faith in a fake spiritualist, but I made a whole lot of money that week, so I'm not complaining.

Harold, Gladys and I consulted several times, and I delivered Dr. Fellowes's toga in plenty of time for him to try it on. When I asked her, Gladys said it needed no alterations. It's kind of hard to make a too-small toga. The only thing I'd wondered about was the length, and since Gladys had told me her husband's height—five feet, ten inches—I'd even made it the correct length.

Gladys's globe costume took a little persuasion on the parts of Harold and me in order for her to accept and agree to wear it.

"I can't wear that!" Gladys cried in horror as she gazed upon the full globe-ish-ness of her Halloween costume. "It's...It's *round*!"

"So are you," I pointed out.

"Well, but not *that* round. Will I be able to sit down in it?"

"Yes. I made sure of that. See? The globe part ends right below your waist, and if you wear a comfortable skirt under it, you'll be able to sit very well."

"But don't lean back too hard against a chair," Harold warned, "or you'll flatten it."

"Good Lord," said Gladys.

"It's only for one evening," I reminded her. "And it's for a good cause. I expect Sam to nab the murderer of Miss Carleton and Mr. Jeffreys on Saturday night."

She looked uncertainly at me. "You really think so?"

"I really think so," I said, sounding more confident than I felt. I sure hoped so, anyway.

"Well..."

"Oh, by the way, Robert Browning told me the name of Miss Carleton's infant's father." I turned to Harold. "Go into the kitchen or something, Harold. This isn't for popular consumption."

"Oh, for God's sake," said he, but he vamoosed, bless his heart.

For some reason, Gladys clutched at her heart. "Who was it?" she whispered as if she wasn't sure she wanted to know. I thought that was odd.

"Dr. Malton."

Gladys practically collapsed on to the ottoman at the foot of a burgundy chair in her living room. "Oh, I'm so glad!" she whispered.

I thought *that* was odd, too. "Why are you glad? I think Dr. Malton is a beast and a reprobate and a miserable human being."

"Oh, yes. Yes, he is. Oh, but Daisy! I *so* feared it might be Homer. That was why I wanted you to investigate Miss Carleton's murder. I was *so* afraid he might have killed her if she tried to get him to divorce me and marry her."

"*Homer!*" I all but shouted. "Why did you fear that? He's madly in love with you, for Pete's sake."

To my horror, tears dripped from Gladys's eyes. "Oh, but I'm so fat and ugly these days, Daisy. You don't know what it's like, being pregnant."

Outspoken young woman. She didn't even use a euphemism for the word "pregnant."

"You weren't pregnant when Miss Carleton got with child." I, on the other hand, used euphemisms all the time and figured now should be no different.

"I can't explain it," said Gladys, seeming to catch her breath. She wiped her eyes. "But I was *so* afraid."

"I don't know why," I said frankly. "He seems totally smitten with you."

"Maybe. But there was that actress."

"True, but that was a momentary...I don't know what to call it. Lapse, I guess. He got over it as soon as he realized what a stupid, ego-mad woman she was."

Gladys pulled a hankie out of her pocket and wiped away the last of her tears. "You're right, of course," she said, standing once more and sounding like the Gladys I'd become more or less accustomed to. I don't think I'd ever be able to relate profoundly to Gladys Fellowes. I mean... Algebra? No, no, no.

"Oh, Daisy," said she. "You've made me a very happy woman. Perhaps being pregnant does something to a woman's...I don't know. Hormones? Don't we have hormones or something?"

"I...guess so. You should know, being more apt to...um, know what goes on in a human body than I."

"I think it's hormones. That's why I've been so crazy since Mary's death. I liked her so well, and if Homer had been intimate with her...Well, I guess I don't have to worry about that. Thank you so much, Daisy."

"You're welcome," I said, thinking she was nuts.

But no. I could understand her trepidation. Sort of. Dr. Homer Fellowes had been infatuated with Lola de la Monica until her true nature was revealed unto him. And the rest of us. She was a ghastly woman. Still is, probably. But once Dr. Fellowes had fixed his attention on Gladys, he didn't look at anyone else. If there was a match made in heaven, theirs was it, by golly.

So after the costume problem was solved to almost everyone's satis-faction, and Gladys's fears had been allayed—I swear to goodness, I still couldn't quite imagine her calling me in to find a murderer because she thought her *husband* might have done it—there remained only choir practice to get through, which I did on Thursday evening. Sam and Frank didn't attend that evening, and I was sorry for it. Not because I missed Frank, but because I missed Sam. It occurred to me to ask him if he'd like to join the choir at our church once we were married.

He probably wouldn't. Still, you never knew.

And then came Saturday.

THIRTY-TWO

Sam and Frank came to our bungalow early on that Saturday evening, although we didn't plan to dine there. Harold had assured me there'd be enough food at the Felloweses' home to feed several armies. They came early so that I could assist Sam with his toga. Not that he needed a lot of assistance. For the record, I'd already donned my Gypsy fortune-teller costume. Frank looked at me as if he thought I'd lost my mind to wear such a thing. I ignored him. Anyway, I assisted Sam with his costume.

"It's a toga, for God's sake. How much fitting does it need?" he asked, sounding cranky. Then again, he nearly always sounded cranky in those days. He had a lot to put up with, what with his sore leg and his despicable nephew.

"Don't be a spoilsport, Sam Rotondo. I want to see how wonderful you look with that red sash over your shoulder and that laurel wreath on your head."

"Lord."

"He gets a red sash?" said Frank, sounding as if he wanted a red sash of his own.

"Yes. He's supposed to be a Roman senator."

"Oh," said Frank, gazing down at his black pants and white coat with disdain. He clearly didn't like having to be a waiter on this occasion. Too bad for him. If he were a decent person and didn't pilfer silver crosses and Buddha statues, I might have made him a costume, too, but he didn't deserve such consideration. Anyway, he was only going to be there to serve food, so he didn't need a costume.

"And don't you dare steal anything from the Felloweses' place!" I told him sternly.

"Hey," he said.

Sam cuffed him for the heck of it, eliciting another "Hey."

"Oh, be quiet," I told him.

He didn't say another word.

Sam and I retired to the sewing room, where Sam donned his toga and plopped the laurel wreath on his head. He looked perfectly splendid with both of them. I told him so. He said, "Huh." Typical.

However, when we exited the sewing room, my family agreed with me.

"Did you make that costume, Daisy?" asked Ma. Why, I don't know. Who else would have made it?

"Yes, I did," I told her modestly.

"It's quite nice," said she. "You look good in it, Sam."

Faint praise. On the other hand, it had come from my mother, who wasn't effusive at the most exciting of times.

"You look wonderful, Sam!" said Vi, eyeing him up and down.

"Yes, you do. You look very senatorial," said Pa, chuckling.

Spike liked the costume, too. Don't ask me how I know. I just do.

"Thanks," said Sam as if it cost him to thank anyone for saying he looked good as a Roman senator. He was *such* a moaner!

We made our way to his Hudson and climbed in. Sam made Frank carry my bag of tricks—that is to say my Ouija board, tarot cards and crystal ball—with the strict admonition that he was not to drop the bag or he would forfeit his life. Frank succeeded in doing that, even if he was useless in all other ways.

I'd arranged with Gladys and Harold to arrive at the Felloweses' home early because I wanted to eat something and organize my fortune-telling table. Or booth. Or tent. Or whatever Harold had arranged for me. Turned out to be a table in a corner, which was fine by me, because

I'd be able to see the party-goers from a table much better than if I'd been stuck in a tent or a booth.

Harold himself looked quite charming in a costume I'd last seen worn by men in Turkey. He wore black trousers, a white shirt with big sleeves, a big red belt around his rather rotund tummy, a colorful vest and black boots. On his head he wore an embroidered tarbush with a black tassel.

"Love your outfit, Harold."

"Thank you. I borrowed it from the set of the next *Sheik* flicker."

"I thought sheiks wore turbans."

"Have you ever tried to wind a turban so it won't unwind when you don't want it to?"

"No."

"Try it, and you'll discover why I chose the tarbush."

"Well, you look quite fetching," I told him.

"Thanks. I like Sam's toga." He smiled at Sam, who actually smiled back at him. Sam did look awfully good in his toga.

Gladys joined us. She hadn't donned her globe costume yet.

"Can you help me get into the thing?" she asked me. She noticed Sam's toga and frowned slightly. "I like Detective Rotondo's toga better than Homer's."

"The detective is a Roman senator. Dr. Fellowes is a Greek philosopher," I said, creating that excuse on the spot.

Gladys said, "Oh."

"Let's go get you dressed," I said.

"Thanks. Come on to my bedroom. Homer is in the kitchen, I think, but he'll join us soon. He and I will have to greet our guests. Harold told me that's proper etiquette for things like this."

She didn't sound as if she wholly approved of "things like this". Poor Gladys.

But boy, she sure looked swell in her globe costume! I was *so* pleased. "Gladys, you are totally charming! And what a perfect costume for a geological project leader's spouse."

Eyeing herself in the cheval-glass mirror in her bedroom, she turned and surveyed her costume all the way around. "You know, I think you're right."

"I know I'm right." Something occurred to me then. I tell you, you never know when brilliant ideas will strike a person, do you? "Say, Gladys, do you want to keep that costume after tonight?"

Still frowning at her image in the mirror, she said, "I can't imagine why I'd want to keep it. Anyway, you bought the fabric and sewed the thing. You should take it back. That way it won't clutter up my closet."

"Wonderful. I just thought of a great way to use those maps."

"Really?" She turned from the mirror and squinted at me.

"Really."

With a shrug, she said, "Then it's yours."

"Thanks, Gladys."

She and I returned to the living room, where Sam, Dr. Fellowes, Dr. Malton, Mr. Davidson, three other Cal Tech students, and Frank were going over everyone's duties for the evening. I noticed Sam frown and brush at his chest, and I felt my eyes open wide. Was the murderer in that bunch of people? And was Sam's juju telling him so?

Hmm. I'd have to think of a way to get Sam alone with each person and see what his juju did when confronted with the suspects individually. Sam would never believe his juju was pinpointing the murderer, of course, but I'd think of some way to make the villain confess. My money was on Dr. Malton, because I disliked him intensely and he was a cad and a bounder.

Sam gestured for me to join him and the crew, so I did.

"Mrs. Majesty, you know Dr. Fellowes, Dr. Malton and Mr. Davidson, I believe," said he in a formal manner.

"Yes." I smiled at the men. "Nice to see you gentlemen." I used the word gentlemen in its broadest sense.

"Lovely to see you again, too," said Dr. Malton, grabbing my hand and kissing it.

I snatched it away from him before Sam could pop him one. I saw him scowling at the bad doctor.

"Behave yourself," said Dr. Fellowes, frowning at his colleague in his turn.

"Tut, tut, fellows. I can't help but admire a beautiful woman."

"No, you sure can't," came the waspish voice of a female outside the circle of people I'd joined. I turned to see a lovely woman in an extremely low-cut costume consisting of a fitted top and billowy—and nearly transparent—trousers. She wore a whole lot of clanking jewelry with her costume and red slippers that curled up at the toes. I couldn't identify the country from which her costume originated, but I'm sure Harold could have told me. I didn't ask.

"Ah," said Dr. Malton, stepping back a pace. "Virginia. Come here, my dear. Allow me to introduce you to Mrs. Majesty, who will be our fortune-teller tonight."

Virginia Malton slithered up to the men and gave me a smile she didn't mean. "How do you do, Mrs. Majesty?" She held out her hand.

I shook it heartily and said, "I'm fine, thank you. Please let me introduce you to my fiancé, Detective Sam Rotondo." I put special emphasis on the fiancé part of that sentence.

"Ah. You're engaged," she whispered suggestively. I swear, she and Dr. Malton deserved each other. "How nice."

She held her hand out for Sam to shake, which he did. Once. Then he let her hand drop as if it were a hot rock.

Merciful heavens, *she* wasn't the murderer, was she? I squinted at Sam's chest, but he only swatted at it once, and I don't think it was because of Virginia Malton.

"And this is Detective Rotondo's nephew, Frank Pagano," I told Virginia.

As Frank's tongue practically hung out of his mouth and he gaped at Mrs. Malton's cleavage, I presumed she'd have better luck with him should she be bent upon seduction this evening.

"Mr. Pagano," she whispered suggestively.

"Yes," said Frank, gawping.

Sam smacked him upside the head and said, "Get to the kitchen and start bringing out the food."

Frank jerked himself out of his Virginia Malton-induced stupor, stood to attention and said, "Yes, sir." And, by golly, he did as Sam had ordered.

"You, too," Sam said to the other students.

They all straightened like soldiers and saluted him. Then they, too, left to perform their duties. I was impressed. Sam was a formidable fellow when he wanted to be. Sam made one last swipe at his chest, but I couldn't determine which man had produced the telling heat.

"Why don't the two of you stick together tonight," Sam suggested to Dr. Malton and his wife. "We don't want any trouble."

"Trouble?" said Dr. Malton as if he were shocked and dismayed.

"Yes. Trouble," said Sam briefly. "Keep away from women who aren't your wife. And you," he said, turning to Virginia, "stay away from men who aren't your husband. This is a party, not an orgy."

"Absolutely correct," said Dr. Fellowes as if he wished he'd thought to issue the order himself.

I noticed Sam's hand stayed at his side.

"Well!" said Virginia Malton.

Gladys, who had joined us, said, "You know it's true. Both of you act like alley cats. This is our home, and I don't want any monkey business tonight."

"Well!" said Virginia Malton again.

My impressedness was aimed at Gladys that time.

"Come along, my dear," said Dr. Malton, his sugary voice a trifle sour. He took his wife's arm, and the two of them moseyed off to a corner where, I'm sure, they told spiteful stories to each other about the awful detective and his fortune-telling fiancée. And probably Gladys and Homer Fellowes, too.

"Well done, you two," said Harold, grinning from ear to ear. "I've never seen two people put in their places quite so well."

"Yes," said Dr. Fellowes, smiling fondly down upon his wife, who blushed up a storm. "You were wonderful, Gladys. Those two really get under my skin."

Gladys clutched his arm and smiled up at him. "I was afraid you'd be annoyed if I spoke up."

"Good God, no. It's past time those two started behaving themselves."

"Right," said Sam in a no-nonsense voice. "I expect people will begin arriving soon, so the two of you will probably want to stay by the door. That kid—what's his name? Johnson? Jackson?—anyway, he'll answer the door, but you need to be there to tell my officer who's who."

The officer, Doan, whom I'd met many times before, had come to the party as—ta-da!—a policeman! I told Sam I thought that was an inspired choice of costume for his man.

"Yeah, well, the people attending this shindig won't know he's not really in costume."

"Precisely." I sighed as I looked around. Canapés had been set out on various tables, and a long table had been placed against the far wall of the living room, where more food was arranged. Harold had outdone himself by the looks of it. It was a sure thing no one would leave the party hungry. "All right. I'm going to my table. I hope you get the person tonight, Sam."

"So do I."

His cane detracted only slightly from the senatorial image he presented. Overall, he looked as if he were in charge of the entire party. I hoped to heck Frank wouldn't steal anything.

People showed up in droves. I was a little surprised, not having previously pegged genius scientists as having the souls of party-goers. Shows how much I knew.

Robert Browning and Regina Petrie arrived looking darling together. He was dressed as a devil, and Regina had dressed as a witch. I squealed, "You both look *adorable!*" Then I felt silly. But I was so excited to see the two of them together and looking as though they truly belonged together.

Naturally, Regina blushed. "Thank you. Robert got both costumes for us."

"I sure did," said Robert, twirling his pointed red tail in his hand. "I found them at a junk shop on Fair Oaks and Walnut. I think it was the Salvation Army. They actually had several costumes. I thought these two went together well. Isn't Reggie lovely?"

Reggie? Better and better. "Absolutely!" I said.

"Thank you, Daisy." Still blushing, Regina walked off arm in arm with Robert. I was pleased. Her pointy witch's hat looked cunning on her newly marcelled hairdo. And her long black dress made her look slim and svelte. Good work. Reggie. I giggled to myself and got to work.

My table was probably the hit of the entire evening. *Everyone*, or so it seemed, wanted me to read my crystal ball, do a tarot reading or fiddle with the Ouija board. By the time two hours had passed, I was dying of thirst and about to throttle everyone in the room. Before that happened, fortunately, Sam rescued me.

"You need a break. Come here and have some punch and some of these things. I don't know what they are, but they're good." He held out a plate upon which rested some little toasted round pieces of bread with something grayish on top, garnished with a couple of little green roundish things each.

Doubtful but hungry, I took one of the little toast rounds and bit into it. "Oh, my, this is good!"

"Told you so," said Sam. "Come on and get some lemonade and some more food. You must be hungry."

"I'm starving. Those two little chicken sandwiches and six grapes I ate wore off an hour or so ago."

Sam led me to the long table against the wall and handed me an empty plate. I proceeded to fill it with more of the toast rounds. Harold came over, and I asked him what the topping was made of.

"Chopped chicken livers and capers."

"Oh. Are the capers those little round green things?"

Rolling his eyes, Harold said, "Yes, Daisy. Hasn't your aunt fed you a caper before now?"

"I don't know," I told him honestly. "But I really like the chopped chicken livers set off with the salty capers."

"I do believe you're developing a palate, Daisy Gumm Majesty," said Harold.

"Cripes," said Sam. "I didn't know those were chopped chicken livers." He made a face.

"You liked them before Harold told you what they were," I said.

"True," said he, and took a few more of them.

I added a couple of tiny sandwiches to my plate, some olives, some carrot sticks, took the lemonade Sam held out to me, and retired to a corner of the living room with him and Harold.

THIRTY-THREE

After I'd had my fill of chicken-liver things, sandwich things, and carrots and had drunk most of my lemonade, I sighed and asked, "So, have you discovered anything yet?"

"Yeah," said Sam. "Most Cal Tech people are as nutty as anybody else."

"That's not helpful. Did you discover whom it was who heated up your juju?"

"Cripes. You're not going to start with that again, are you?"

"Juju?" said Harold, looking intrigued.

"She'll tell you all about it later," said Sam.

"Good," said Harold.

"Don't fib to me, Sam Rotondo. I saw you bat at your juju when you were with those people from Cal Tech before the party started."

He frowned. Then he said, as if he didn't want to, "Yeah. It got hot when I was with those Cal Tech folks."

"Fascinating," said Harold. Then he leaped to his feet. "Better see to it that the waiters keep that long table filled."

"See you later," said I. Then I said to Sam, "You need to talk to them individually and find out which one of them makes it get hot."

He rolled his eyes at me much as Harold had done moments before.

"Even if I find one person who makes the stupid juju heat up, that's not proof the person is a murderer."

"I suppose not." I hated to admit it. "So what are you doing to find the culprit?"

He shrugged. "Watching. Asking questions. Annoying the hell out of people."

"Any people in particular?"

"Malton's wife, for one."

I sat up straight in my chair. "Did she try to seduce you?"

"Not precisely."

"The hussy!"

"I guess. So what does that make him?"

"A male hussy?"

Sam grinned. "I don't think there's a term quite like hussy for a man."

"There should be," I said, irked on behalf of women everywhere. How come we get called names when men don't? I mean roué, cad, and heel don't come close to hussy, strumpet, whore, and "fallen woman". Life just isn't fair, darn it.

"Probably," said Sam. "But I'd better get moving."

"Where's Frank?"

Glancing around as if hoping to spot his miscreant nephew, Sam frowned and said, "I don't know. He'd better be in the kitchen or some-where he's supposed to be or I'll kill him."

"I'll look for him," I said. "I really need to stretch my legs a little."

"Don't get into trouble."

Because the gesture seemed to be going around that night, I rolled my eyes at him. "I won't."

I walked down one of the hallways in the Felloweses' home, glancing into different rooms as I passed. No Frank. I made a special trip to the kitchen. No Frank.

Darn that little twerp anyway! If he was casing the joint for stuff to steal, I'd kill him and save Sam the trouble. I tried not to stomp as I went up the stairs and started down the hallway to the various bedrooms.

Hearing a sort-of-quiet commotion going on in one of them, I paused, tiptoed closer to the door and listened with all my might.

"How dare you!" Virginia Malton.

"Don't be ridiculous, Virginia!" Dr. Malton.

"She's *not* being ridiculous, you monster!" came a voice the owner of which I couldn't identify, although it sounded kind of familiar. "She had your *baby*!"

I heard a loud smack. Then Dr. Malton said, "Ow! Damn it, Virginia!"

"Don't you 'damn it, Virginia' me, you louse! You fathered her *baby*? I want a divorce!"

"That's not the only thing, either," came the familiar but un-place-able voice. "You stole my research, wrote a paper, and took credit for the whole damned thing! You *stole* my research!"

"Don't be stupid, Davidson."

Davidson. Ah. Now I recognized the voice.

"That's the way academia works, young man. You help with the research. I, as the professor in charge, can add your name to the credits if I wish, but it's not required."

"Help with the research, my foot! I worked myself to death for you, and you didn't even mention me in that book you wrote! You're a thief as well as a stinking woman-chaser."

"Yes, he is," said Virginia, who had begun to sob. "He's despicable! A cad! A vile seducer! A villain!"

Dramatic and a trifle old-fashioned, although nothing but the truth, I reckon.

"Well, you can use all the research I've done for your precious project, Malton, and you'll make a total ass of yourself, because you'll only look like a fool when you publish."

"What are you talking about?" demanded Malton.

"You'll see. And just because I hate you, I'll make sure you're the only one who looks like a fool."

"Listen to me, young man, If you—"

"Don't threaten me, you! I'll get you. Just like I got Jeffreys."

"Jeffreys?" came Dr. Malton's voice. "What do you mean?"

"This is what I mean, damn you!"

Virginia Malton screamed.

"Shut up, you. He deserves a knife to his heart. If he has a heart, which I doubt."

Good Lord. Carefully, I peeked around the door into the room and saw a wild-eyed Mr. Davidson with a very long, very serviceable knife in his hand. "And you'll be next, *Virginia*," snarled Davidson. "You're as bad as he is. I saw you with that toga-fellow. You're both evil."

"No!" shrieked Virginia.

Unfortunately for yours truly, nobody else could hear what was going on in that room because someone had begun playing the brand-new Victor Talking Machine Player Gladys had bought especially for this party, and it sounded as if folks had begun dancing. The strains of "The Charleston" blared above the noise in the room, and a whole lot of stomping commenced belowstairs.

In other words, I didn't know what to do. I didn't dare leave my position at the door and shout for Sam. He probably wouldn't hear me, and anyway, things in that room sounded as if they were too far along for any kind of delay.

And then Frank sidled out of a room across the hall from me. He was carrying a pretty little ornamental picture frame of Gladys and Homer at their wedding that I'd noticed in Gladys's bedroom earlier. As soon as he saw me, he stuffed the frame in his jacket pocket and tried to look innocent. Then he heard the noise from the room filled with the Maltons and the murderous Davidson.

"What's going on?" asked he.

Glowering at him for all I was worth, I hissed, "Somebody's getting killed in there." I pointed to the room.

Frank, being the toad he was, whirled around, preparing to run for it. I grabbed his coattails and stopped his forward progress. Then, because I was scared and furious and probably out of my mind, I shoved him into the room holding the Maltons and Davidson.

"Hey!" Frank hollered.

"Hey yourself!" said I, rushing into the room after him, and taking advantage of everyone's astonishment to butt Mr. Davidson in the stomach with my head. The knife flew from his hand, and he doubled up, clutching his stomach.

And then, because I didn't expect Davidson to stay incapacitated for too long, I told Frank, "Hang on to this man. Don't let him go! Punch him if you need to."

He didn't actually need to, but Frank punched Mr. Davidson in the face so hard, he bounced against the wall and fell down.

I pointed to Dr. Malton. "You! Sit on him! I'm getting Sam. Frank, you help him! You," I said, pointing at Virginia, "don't move a step. In fact, don't any of you *dare* to move or I'll have you arrested for abetting a murderer."

Frank said, "Hey!" But he stayed in the room.

To my utter amazement, Dr. Malton took me at my word and sat on Mr. Davidson.

I bellowed, "And don't any of you *touch* that knife, or I'll have you arrested for obstruction!" Whatever obstruction was in police parlance. Then I took off like the proverbial bat out of hell, tearing along the hall, thundering down the staircase, and grabbing Sam's arm. Fortunately, he was standing at the foot of the stairs, glaring around, probably looking for his errant nephew.

Stumbling a little because I yanked on him hard, Sam said, "What the—?"

"Upstairs!" I panted. "It's Davidson!"

"What's Davidson?" He limped as fast as he could after me. I guess his laurel wreath had slipped when I grabbed him, because it sagged over one side of his face. He shoved it back as we both scuttled up the staircase.

"He's the *murderer*, darn you!" It wasn't fair of me to darn Sam, but I was upset.

"Doan! Follow me!" bellowed Sam.

After jumping only slightly, Doan didn't argue. He followed Sam and me up the stairs at a fast clip.

We got to the room just in time to prevent Virginia Malton from battering her husband to death. He still sat on Davidson, and was trying to cover his head with his hands. Frank was attempting to grab her hands, but was having no luck. Davidson was groaning under Dr. Malton's weight.

"Doan," said Sam. "Get that woman out of here."

Doan did so, although Mrs. Malton didn't make it easy on him. When one of her breasts bounced out of her skimpy top, she had to pause and stick herself back into it, however, and Doan managed to handcuff her. She screamed about that, but nobody cared.

"Frank, stand in the corner," ordered Sam of his nephew.

Frank stood in the corner.

"And don't move," I added. "He stole a picture frame from Gladys's room," I told Sam.

"I'll take care of him later. Now tell me what's going on here."

Dr. Malton, considerably ruffled of hair and beginning to show signs of bruises-to-come on his cheeks, stood and sighed.

Gazing down upon the reclining Mr. Davidson, Sam frowned and swatted at his juju.

"He killed Mr. Jeffreys," said Malton. "He admitted as much to me, and he was going to kill Virginia and me."

"Huh. No big loss there," said Sam. He bent, grabbed Davidson by one arm and yanked him to his feet.

"Hey!" said Dr. Malton. And here I'd thought Frank was the only one who used that word.

"Come with me, you," said Sam to Davidson. His laurel wreath fell off when he bent to grab one of Davidson's arms, and he picked it up and thrust it at me. I took it, not even annoyed at my beloved.

"I didn't kill anyone!" said Davidson, still out of breath unless I missed my guess. "And nobody can say I did."

"I heard you confess it to Dr. Malton. Then you threatened to kill Dr. and Mrs. Malton. And that knife has your fingerprints all over it." I pointed to the knife, which I'd kicked into a corner.

"Good job, Daisy," said Sam, nearly shocking me into a faint.

"I told everyone not to touch it," I told him. "I hope they did as I commanded." Irked with the crushed laurel wreath, I tossed it into a nearby waste-paper basket.

Sam scowled at his nephew, and Frank said, "Nobody touched it," as if he hoped that would make up for him having pilfered a pretty picture frame.

Oddly enough, the party didn't break up even after the criminals,

Dr. and Mrs. Malton, Frank, Sam, Officer Doan and I left. I know that because Harold told me so the next day.

Because I'd ridden with Sam and Frank in Sam's Hudson, I got to go to the police station with them. Sam was annoyed about that, but I was positively gleeful. I *really* wanted to hear what Davidson had to say for himself.

What he had to say proved him to be a disgusting, petty, jealous worm. Mind you, I thought it was mean of Dr. Malton not to give him credit for doing research on the book Dr. Malton had written and claimed all the credit for, but according to what Gladys told me later, that sort of thing went on all the time in academic circles.

Hmm. And I'd been under the silly assumption that scientists and professors were above such things. Live and learn.

Eventually, two fingerprints on the knife used to kill Miss Carleton were matched to Davidson's fingers. Robert Browning's prints, of course, were on the knife, too, but Sam now believed him when he said he hadn't killed the librarian.

Because I was there and Sam couldn't very well stop me, I asked Davidson, "How'd you get out of the library so fast after you murdered poor Miss Carleton?"

"I wasn't fast. I just walked out the door. I guess someone found her after I left."

Sam had commenced frowning at me, so I only said one more thing. "You're a terrible man. Murder is much worse than theft."

"Not if you're trying to earn your doctorate at Cal Tech, it isn't," Davidson said.

I just shook my head. I was as quiet as a mouse for the rest of the interview.

Davidson confessed to having killed Mr. Jeffreys after Jeffreys had confronted him about altering the results of Dr. Fellowes's and Dr. Malton's stupid project. And, faced with his fingerprints on the knife used on Miss Carleton, he admitted to killing her, too, because she'd confronted him about his having fudged the project's research records.

In the end, however, it all turned out all right. Well, except that two people were dead for no better reason than scientists are as petty and selfish as anyone else in the world.

A couple of months after the party, Robert Browning and Regina Petrie became an engaged couple and told me they aimed to be united in holy matrimony in June of 1925. That made me happy.

After relieving Frank of Gladys's picture frame and cuffing him a few more times, Sam shipped his stupid nephew back to New York City. I went to the train station with him to make sure Frank got on and stayed on the train until it had left the station in Pasadena.

Sam said, "If he gets off in San Bernardino or somewhere in Arizona, at least he won't be my problem any longer."

What's more, after we saw Frank off, Sam and I retired to his cunning little bungalow on South Los Robles Avenue and did some serious canoodling. Sam's leg hurt, but he said it was worth it. We both felt better afterwards.

And then came Thanksgiving! Not only did Vi outdo herself with the turkey, stuffing, potatoes, gravy, vegetables and pies, but we wiped our various lips on brand-new napkins!

Daphne's daughter Polly—Daphne is my sister—looked at her napkin said, "What's this?"

Squinting across the table at her napkin, I said, "I think that's the southern tip of Africa." Another squint, this time at Polly's sister, and I said, "Peggy has Australia."

Jeanette, Walter's wife—Walter's my brother—looked at her own napkin. "I do believe I got the state of New York!" She grinned at me. "You're so clever, Daisy."

"Thank you." I beamed at her.

Sam and I both got parts of California. We liked it that way.

The End

SPIRITS UNEARTHED

A DAISY GUMM MAJESTY MYSTERY, BOOK 13

On the Monday before Christmas in 1924, the weather was frigid. Well, that is to say, it was darned cold for Pasadena, California, where the weather seldom, if ever, gets truly frigid. It must have been in the low forties. That might account for the reason Sam Rotondo, my fiancé, was in such a foul mood. Or maybe the cold weather made his wounded leg hurt. I don't know. All I know is that he didn't want to do what I wanted him to do.

"This is stupid," said he, as he limped through the Mountain View Cemetery in Altadena, California.

To give him the benefit of the doubt, I must say that walking to my late husband's grave was a struggle for him. He still had to rely heavily on his cane, given to him by Dr. Benjamin after Sam was shot in the thigh by an evil woman. As it had rained recently, the cane kept getting stuck in the moist soil, and Sam kept having to yank it out.

Spike, my late husband's brilliant dachshund, trotted beside Sam and me. I'm still not sure if dogs were allowed in the cemetery, but nobody kicked us out so what the heck.

"It's not stupid," I told Sam. "It'll make me feel better."

"It's stupid whether it makes you feel better or not," Sam grumped.

"Oh, stop it. You just enjoy complaining, don't you?"

"No. I don't enjoy complaining. Ow!"

He had inadvertently stepped into a hole with his left leg, the one that had been shot, and I guess he wrenched it pretty badly.

"Watch where you're going, Sam," I said. Not awfully sympathetic of me, I know.

"Cripes. This is stupid."

"You've said that before."

Spike at least was enjoying himself. He ran this way and that way and generally tore around, as happy as a hound ever was. He had a nice big yard at home to snoop and sniff in, but it was nowhere near as large as the cemetery.

"That's because it is," snarled Sam.

"Pooh."

But we made it to Billy's grave eventually. I stood beside it, looking down, and wishing Billy was still alive. On the other hand, then I'd have two men in my life, and one was almost more than I could handle. Poor Billy had suffered terribly after the Great War. He'd been gassed and shot and had been in constant pain until he'd finally taken matters into his own hands and drunk an overdose of morphine syrup. I understood his reason, but I'd suffered mightily after his death. It's hard to lose a person you've known and loved all your life, even when you knew it's going to happen eventually.

Sam had suffered, too. His late wife, Margaret, was buried not far from Billy. My aim that day was to tell both Billy and Margaret that Sam and I were engaged to be married, and we hoped we had their blessing.

So, technically, Sam was correct. This trip *was* stupid.

Heck, I made my living—a darned good living—as a spiritualist-medium to the wealthy ladies of Pasadena who had more money than sense. If I *actually* could talk to dead people, I'd have asked for Billy's blessing regarding Sam and me a long time ago. I remained relatively undaunted, however, because it seemed somehow important to me to say the words to Billy, even if his soul had long since departed this earth. And I wanted Sam to say the words to Margaret, too. He probably wouldn't, so I'd have to say them for him, Sam not being one to ask for people's blessings on a regular basis. Well, I wasn't either, but this trip to the cemetery just felt right.

Still staring at Billy's beautifully carved headstone—it said "Sacred to the memory of William Anthony Majesty. Beloved husband of Daisy. July 12, 1897-June 10, 1922. Rest now as you could not in life. *The Good Die First*"—I said softly, "Billy, you got your wish. You asked Sam to take care of me after you were gone, and he's going to do just that—"

Sam said, "Huh," interrupting me. I shot him a glare.

"Anyway," I continued. "I hope Sam and I have your blessing for our union. We don't know when the ceremony will take place, because Sam got shot and is still recovering, but we'll get married one of these days."

Spike rushed up to Sam and me, a man's shoe clutched in his teeth, his tail wagging deliriously.

"What the heck?" said Sam, looking down at Spike.

Distracted from my purpose, I too, peered at my dog. "Where in the world did you find that, Spike?"

Because he was a dog, Spike didn't answer. Rather, he dropped the shoe at our feet, smiling up at us. Don't tell me dogs can't smile, because they can. He looked quite pleased with himself.

"Where'd you get hold of a shoe, Spike?" Because I knew Sam's leg hurt, I was the one who bent and picked up the shoe. It was quite heavy for a shoe.

I squealed when I saw the reason for its heaviness. The stupid shoe held a foot! I dropped it and clutched Sam's arm.

"What the—?" said Sam, startled

"Sam! That shoe has a foot in it!"

"What?"

"It's got a foot in it!" Because I figured I should, I bent and picked up the shoe again. It smelled awful. "See?" I said, thrusting the shoe and foot at Sam.

He recoiled. "Where the hell did you find a foot in a shoe, Spike?"

Spike didn't answer for reasons stated above. I noticed dried blood on the ankle part of the foot and grimaced. "Sam, could Spike have dug up a grave? Good Lord, the managers of the cemetery will kill us if he did."

"Don't be ridiculous," said Sam, as gracious as ever. "He couldn't dig up a grave. Even if he could, he'd have found a coffin, not a foot."

"Good Lord. I guess that's true."

"This isn't right," said Sam, master of the obvious.

"We'd better see if we can find the rest of the body, if there is one," I said tentatively. I didn't want to look for loose bodies in the cemetery.

"Oh, there is one," said Sam, sounding even grouchier than he'd sounded before. "You make a habit of stumbling over bodies. I should have figured you'd find one in a graveyard."

"I don't either!" I cried, miffed. "Anyway, the graveyard is full of bodies."

"Not fresh ones."

"It doesn't smell awfully fresh to me," I murmured. The shoe was truly disgusting. It stank, and it was covered in dirt. I stared down at my dog, who still looked up at us, happy as a clam. And how anyone knows clams are happy is beyond me.

"You know what I mean," growled Sam.

"Yes, I do." I gazed at him. "So do we need to search for the rest of the body? Or should we telephone the Altadena Sheriff's office?"

"There is no such thing as an Altadena Sheriff's office. The community of Altadena has a contract with the Pasadena Police Department to investigate crimes committed in Altadena. That's probably because there are so few of them.

"Do you think this was the result of a crime?" I asked, gazing at the icky foot.

"Well, now, I just don't know. Maybe somebody cut off his foot and tossed it into the cemetery. Just for a lark, you know?"

"There's no need to be snide, Sam Rotondo."

"Huh."

"I'm glad we don't have to call in anyone else, because I don't want to have to explain Spike's presence."

With a look that told me he considered me, if not insane, then as close to it as made no matter, Sam said, "We're going to have to tell people how we came to find a fresh foot in the cemetery."

"Oh, dear."
"Right."

**Available in Paperback and eBook from Your Favorite
Bookstore or Online Retailer**

ABOUT THE AUTHOR

Award-winning author Alice Duncan lives with a herd of wild dachshunds (enriched from time to time with fosterees from New Mexico Dachshund Rescue) in Roswell, New Mexico. She's not a UFO enthusiast; she's in Roswell because her mother's family settled there fifty years before the aliens crashed (and living in Roswell, NM, is cheaper than living in Pasadena, CA, unfortunately). Alice would love to hear from you at alice@aliceduncan.net

www.aliceduncan.net

 facebook.com/alice.duncan.925